f3

THE INTERNATIONAL POLITICAL SYSTEM

THE INTERNATIONAL POLITICAL SYSTEM

F. S. Northedge

**Professor of International Relations
in the University of London**

FABER & FABER
3 Queen Square, London

First published in 1976
by Faber and Faber Limited
3 Queen Square London WC1
Printed in Great Britain by
Latimer Trend & Company Ltd Plymouth
All rights reserved

ISBN 0 571 11009 6 (Faber Paperbacks)
ISBN 0 571 11008 8 (hard bound edition)

Contents

PREFACE *page* 9

1. THE SUBJECT IN FOCUS 11

2. ANCESTORS OF THE MODERN SYSTEM 34

3. ORIGINS AND GROWTH OF THE SYSTEM 53

4. THE IMPACT OF CHANGE 66

5. CENTURIES OF WAR AND PEACE 81

6. THE POLITICAL PROCESS 107

7. THE ANATOMY OF STATEHOOD 134

8. A TAXONOMY OF STATES 154

9. THE MOTIVES OF STATE BEHAVIOUR 177

10. THE EXPANSION OF STATES 202

11. THE MUTUAL IMPACT OF STATES 225

12. STATES OF INTERNATIONAL RELATIONS 250

13. WAR IN THE INTERNATIONAL SYSTEM 276

14. CONFLICT AND CONFLICT RESOLUTION 299

15. THE POLITICAL KINGDOM 317

BIBLIOGRAPHY 325

INDEX 328

Preface

THE object of this book is to provide as simple as possible an account of that highly complex thing, the world-wide political system as it exists between the 140 or so sovereign states which now divide the world map between them. There was a time when the study of this subject in universities and other places needed to be defended against its detractors. Today it hardly seems that the intellectual properties of the subject, and certainly not, in the nuclear age, its social relevance, are in need of further argument. The assumptions of this book are, first, that international politics are at least as much a challenge to the intellectual powers of the university student and the casual reader as any other study of the human performance, and, second, that international politics today concern the lives of all of us in a way in which perhaps no other human activity does.

There is one important point to be made about the approach to the subject which is adopted in this book. I have done my best to expound the main features of international politics in as simple and clear a manner as possible. I do not believe that much is added to the understanding of the international system by the sort of obfuscation of its basic features and the tortured jargon which today in so many quarters passes as the 'scientific' approach to the subject. I have tried to be scientific in my understanding of the international system in the sense of being as emotionally detached from it as possible. But that any field of human behaviour can be made the subject-matter of a science in the sense of an aggregate of laws stating that if such-and-such conditions exist, such-and-such results must follow, I strongly beg leave to doubt.

Hence the reader will not find much of what is sometimes called 'contemporary theory' in this book. This is not because I

have not closely followed the development of that form of speculation in the past twenty years, but because I deprecate the arid
and wholly unimaginative style of writing of that school, and,
more importantly, because little work of that school appears to
me to throw much light on the politics of the real world. It is an
intellectual approach which seems to me remote from reality,
which takes the student further away from, rather than nearer
towards, his subject, and which, to my mind, represents a
digression from the high roads of political study into the desert.
But this does not mean that I have not borrowed from time to
time some idea or expression from this school of thought.

Most of this book incorporates material which I have presented
to students at the London School of Economics in lectures over
the years. I apologize to those who attended the lectures for re-
tracing what may seem familiar ground.

F. S. NORTHEDGE
The London School of Economics and Political Science,
July 1975

One

The Subject in Focus

THROUGHOUT its history the human race has been faced by certain problems resulting from its division into more or less self-conscious, and more or less organized, groups. These groups have been and remain racial, religious, economic, social, political and so on, and they have tended to overlap. Race consciousness may and often does cut across national boundaries and economic solidarities of interest or feelings of class unity may transcend loyalties based upon religious belief. Moreover, inter-group relations, from relations between individual families to relations between the nuclear super-Powers of the present day, have almost invariably been characterized by frictions and disputes, and the desire to mitigate or eliminate these has provided one of the strongest motives for the academic study of inter-group relations. Such frictions and disputes have many sources: all groups tend to generate among their members certain common interests, habits of thought, customs and internal loyalties, which may lead to antagonisms with other, similar groups. It has indeed been argued that the very existence of a feeling of group consciousness demands and depends upon a degree of hostility towards the outsider or the out-group.[1] If that is so, it is perhaps open to doubt whether mankind will ever be free from inter-group tension and conflict, no matter how effectively this may be contained within tolerable limits.

One of the dominant forms of inter-group relationship in the twentieth century, and certainly one which in the nuclear age gives rise to continuous and universal concern, is that between the organized state-members of the international system. It is dominant in the obvious sense that the entire world population is now partitioned into these political units, and although the sense of loyalty to state varies from one individual to another and from one state to another, membership of the state is absolute in the sense in which religious or ideological affiliation, for example, is not. It is absolute in that there is no choice for the modern man or woman except to belong to a particular state and to conform to the laws of that state, which have, incidentally, made an ever increasing inroad into the private lives of the inhabitants of the state in the twentieth century. It may be contended that in the United States, for instance, tensions between negroes and whites can on occasion exceed in intensity tensions between Americans as a whole and (let us say) Russians or Chinese as a whole, and that in a country such as Vietnam or Korea ideological divisions are more meaningful for the ordinary person than his relations, as a Vietnamese or Korean, with other people of other nation-states. But these must be counted as exceptions rather than the norm, and if social tensions within the state become so great as to prevent that state acting as a member of the world political system—as is or has been the situation for both Vietnam and Korea—the lives of its people run the risk of being controlled by the actions and policies of other states. For the vast majority of those who possess any political consciousness the dominant group feeling which they experience is that of state membership, their own state being in turn a member of the wider and now global international system.

We have referred to the harnessing of nuclear energy in the mid-twentieth century as a further reason for regarding relations between states as the dominant type, or one of the dominant types, of inter-group relationships of our time. Plainly, on the capability of modern states in a nuclear age to moderate their mutual conflicts depends the survival of mankind, or at least of civilization as we have known it. This is not merely a matter of the control of potential conflict between the two super-Powers, the United States and the Soviet Union. Indeed the recent acceptance by these two giants of the need for restraint in their mutual relations in order to minimize the dangers of a war between them makes even more vital the necessity for stability in the relations between lesser states. Moreover, if the efforts to halt the spread of nuclear weapons should fail—and the outlook for their success is by no means bright at the moment (1975)—the restraints at present operative on the super-Powers may be less effective, for a variety of reasons, on less rich and powerful countries as they acquire these weapons. Hence, the character of relations between newcomers to nuclear status, and between them and states which remain at the non-nuclear state of development, may be decisive for the avoidance of international catastrophe.

On the other hand, nuclear weapons did not need to be invented for the consequences of inter-state conflict for every branch of modern life on this planet to become apparent. Since the First World War it has been brutally clear that the application of science, technology and mass production to the waging of inter-state conflict has been profound in its implications, not merely for peace between the different states, but for the freedom of the individual, the use of resources for the advancement of human happiness and welfare, and indeed for almost every social value esteemed by Western civilization. Furthermore, quite apart from the problem of war in modern society, it is hard to see how other great problems of the present-day world, such as the threat of overpopulation, the fact of famine and other such social disasters, the destruction of the environment, the conservation and equitable distribution of natural resources, can be solved, without improvements in international relationships. Hence, there is hardly need to emphasize that the state of international relations and the forces which govern those relations necessitate the most searching inquiry of which modern man is capable.

The question arises, however, if we are to take the contemporary international system as a focus of inquiry and as the present-day answer to the age-old problem of organizing relations between the dominant social units of the day, whether this subject, by reason of its boundless scope, the complexity and heterogeneity of its subject-matter and its tendency to change, is sufficiently stable and coherent to form the focus of an inquiry with pretensions to be scientific. This question, and others of a similar kind, has often been raised when the introduction of the subject of international relations into British universities has been proposed, and in those universities the study of that subject is still exceptional rather than normal. We will not attempt to answer these questions exhaustively here since the worth of any intellectual enterprise can only ultimately be assessed in terms of the worth of the products which constitute its outcome, of which the present book is a modest example. It is enough to say that we can surely hope to know more about any human activity through inquiry into it, which is as dispassionate and realistic as we can make it, more at least than we knew before. The importance of knowledge of the international system in which we live is sufficiently attested by the fact that the wisdom and skill with which our own country manages its affairs in that system are bound to profit from the widest possible diffusion of that knowledge.

Moreover, it is not essential to the proposition that *some* understanding of the international system is indispensable to contemporary man that such understanding must take the form of a general, comprehensive theory of inter-state relationships in the sense of a set of related propositions of universal validity and possibly of predictive value. The question whether there ever can be such a general theory has been, and still is, fiercely debated among the *cognoscenti* in this field of study. Some of the relevant issues in this debate will be discussed in the following chapters. For the present it is sufficient to insist that any improved understanding of the international system, whether or not this takes the form of verifiable 'laws', must be preferred to ignorance. The sole requirement is that any such improved understanding should derive from an honest attempt to organize intelligently the subject-matter, to adhere to the normal standards of intellectual integrity, and to be ready to revise conclusions in the light of further or contradictory evidence. That the study of human behaviour, individual or collective, can ever become a science, in the sense of the natural sciences, remains for the present controversial; that the approach to that study should be *scientific*, in demanding the same sort of intellectual detachment as that of the natural scientist, is not open to question.

Thus far we have introduced certain terms which must be clarified before proceeding further. They are: nation and state; inter-state and international; and system. This is in fact a convenient place in which to define what we have in mind in speaking of the international political system, although the whole of the rest of this book will serve as a fuller explanation. What do we mean by such words? What objects 'out there' in the external world are we referring to when we use them? And are there other objects which may be thought to have a prior claim on our attention in the general field of world affairs?

It is well-known that the expression 'international' came into use through the famous mistake made by Jeremy Bentham when he coined it to describe the system of law between sovereign states as a translation of the term *ius gentium*, which the Romans used to refer to the corpus of rules, controlled, of course, by Rome itself, between themselves and the tribes of Italy and later the various parts of the Roman Empire.[2] Clearly, 'international law' is in reality law between sovereign states since nations have no *locus standi* in the system we now know as international law. When the United Nations (UN) Charter in Article 1(2) enjoins 'respect for the principle of equal rights and self-determination of *peoples*'—which must mean *nations*—it is plainly referring to a moral or political principle. The legal obligation to respect that principle, if a legal obligation is implied (the language of the Charter is so imprecise), rests upon the state members of the world organization, which are expressly and correctly referred to as such in Articles 3 and 4 of the Charter.[3] Similarly by 'international politics' we in fact mean the politics between sovereign states.

A state, in the sense used in this book, is a territorial association of people recognized for purposes of law and diplomacy as a legally equal member of the system of states. It is in reality a means of organizing people for the purpose of their participation in the international system. A nation, on the other hand, is a numerous group of people united by certain cultural and psychological affinities, and by a will to constitute a state at some time in the future if they do not already do so. As a result of the increasing adoption of the principle of national self-determination since the French Revolution, there is a tendency for state boundaries to be identical with national boundaries, or, to put it another way, for the political map of the world to correspond to the national or ethnical map. But there are obviously many exceptions to this rule, and although the tendency for states in the modern period to be assimilated with nations does have an influence, as we shall see, on the behaviour of states in the international system, it is not indispensable to the study of our subject that every state should consist of one nation and every nation should form one state. Our subject is essentially the system of states, as it may have been affected by the principle of national self-determination, whether or not all those states are nationally homogeneous. The question may be asked, however, why not then speak of an 'inter-state political system', if that is what we mean? The answer is twofold: firstly, that the word 'international' has

become embedded in our language by usage, and it seems pedan-
tic not to go on using it, providing its history is borne in mind;
and secondly, that 'inter-state' is an expression used to refer to
transactions between the states of the American federation,
which are not, of course, sovereign in the sense in which that
word is used in diplomacy. We shall therefore continue to employ
the term 'international' except where the reference to states,
rather than nations, needs especially to be emphasized.

There remains some margin of choice between the terms
'international relations' and 'international politics', as used to
refer to the activities going on within the international system. In
many learned Anglo-Saxon institutions today the two terms are
apt to be used interchangeably, with perhaps a slight preference
for the latter. 'World politics' is preferred by some—and 'world
society' by others—as against 'international system'[4], but is
rejected here as tending to obscure the distinction, which we
believe to be fundamental, between political activities carried on
under a single government and political activities carried on by
governments representing independent and separate states. 'International relations', to refer back to our first two terms, is the older
expression, covering all relations across national frontiers between governments *and* peoples, and including non-governmental
organizations as well as the formally constituted authorities of the
states. From the mid-nineteenth century until the Second World
War, it was a common tenet of European liberalism, that ultimately the non-official type of international relationship was
more important than the inter-governmental one, and that, as
unofficial relations between the peoples of the world developed,
this would have a depoliticizing effect on all international relations and hence remove their propensity to conflict. This belief
weakened in its appeal in the late 1930s, though there has been
some revival of it in the recent schools of functionalism and
'neo-functionalism'.[5] Hence we would prefer the expression
'international politics' as referring to the mutual dealings of
constituted legal authorities acting on behalf of their peoples
within the international system.

There are, however, two difficulties about this formula. The
first is that it may appear to depreciate the role of those important
entities in the world today, international non-governmental
organizations, which have mushroomed with the increasing com-

plexity and specialization of modern life and which have achieved
a recognized consultative status within the United Nations system.[6] They include such international economic and commercial
organizations as the International Chamber of Commerce (ICC),
the International Co-operative Alliance (ICA), the World
Federation of Trade Unions (WFTU) and the International
Confederation of Free Trade Unions (ICFTU); international
religious organizations such as the Catholic Church and the
World Council of Churches; and international political bodies
such as the socialist internationals.[7] We shall have to take account
of these in so far as the policies of official state authorities are
influenced by them. It is, however, postulated here that decisions
taken by governments on behalf of states (which includes decisions *not* to take action) remain the essential heart of our subject
even though they may be powerfully affected on occasion by the
activities of these international non-state entities.

In the second place, we must be careful not to overlook those
other groups and organizations of miscellaneous character which
in the twentieth century have played an increasingly important
role in world affairs. These comprise non-state bodies such as
guerrilla or other revolutionary formations competing for power
with the formal state authorities, as for instance (before 1975) the
Vietcong in South Vietnam and their political arm, the National
Liberation Front, or the IRA; quasi-state organizations which
claim some degree of autonomy within a formally united state,
like the Kurds in Iraq or the Naga people in India; and the para-
military formations which may or may not be under the control
of the central government of a state, such as the SA or SS in
Nazi Germany or the Red Guards in Communist China. Once
again, we would prefer to regard all such bodies in their bearing
on the flow of decisions issuing from the state authorities of that
country in which they operate, rather than as initiators of internationally significant actions. A guerrilla contingent operating
against the government of a state, for example, may prevent it
from acting as efficiently within the international system as it
otherwise might do. It would to that extent be significant in any
study of that state's performance within the system. Or a para-
military formation may be used by the governmental authorities
of a state in order to evade responsibility for their own actions. In
that sense para-military groups may be described as instruments

in a certain international strategy pursued by those authorities. Or all these non-state bodies may be conceived as forming part of the external circumstances in which the modern state lives. They figure among the external facts of life of which the state has to take account. But in all these cases our focus will lie upon the state and its official controlling authorities.

Governments representing sovereign states, however, deal with one another at many levels: the political, economic, commercial, financial, cultural and so on. We are proposing in this book to abstract their mutual dealings at one level only, the political, including therein the political aspects of other levels of their relationships. The question therefore arises as to what we mean by 'political'. What exactly is that complex of relationships between states which we label 'international politics'? Some writers argue that the word 'politics' must refer exclusively to certain relations between individuals and groups under a common sovereign authority, and that a 'political system' can only exist where binding rules are issued by a sovereign to those legally subject to it. This is the contention of Morton Kaplan, despite the title of his book, *System and Process in International Politics*.[8] Kaplan in this book describes the essential requirements of a political system as follows:

> The political system is distinguished by the fact that its rules specify the areas of jurisdiction for other decision-making units and provide methods for settling conflicts of jurisdiction. It is hierarchical in character and territorial in domain. The existence of a government is an unambiguous sign of a political system since governments are hierarchical in organisation and since they arbitrate jurisdictional disputes between other subsystems of the society.[9]

According to such a formulation there can neither be international politics nor an international political system since the characteristic mark of the aggregate of sovereign states is the absence of a single world authority with competence to promulgate laws binding either individual men and women or the states themselves.

We contend, on the contrary, that there are important senses in which the words 'politics' and 'political system' can properly be used to describe a particular level of international relationships, while insisting, as will be argued in some detail later in this book, upon the uniqueness of the political process as it operates internationally.[10] Three reasons may be given for this statement. Firstly, the units whose mutual intercourse is the subject of this study, that is, states, are by every test political associations. They are, even if we limit ourselves to Kaplan's definition of the political system, political in being hierarchical associations, each having a single government and being bound together by certain common political doctrines and co-ordinated by a congeries of binding rules. It is hard therefore to believe that the wider world system of which they form constituent parts is unaffected by the essentially political character of its ingredients. Secondly, the objectives which states appear to set themselves in the international system have much in common, if they are not exactly identical with, those pursued by groups within the political system of the state. H. D. Lasswell's famous trinity of political goals —deference, income, safety—could be used as a first approximation to a characterization of both.[11] And finally, we do habitually use the word 'politics' to refer to many situations outside the context of the state, especially those in which individuals and groups are in a condition of rivalry and competition. We speak, for instance, of 'trade union politics', 'academic politics', 'church politics'. A not dissimilar competition has traditionally characterized the mutual dealings of states.

Hence we define international politics as those mutual dealings of governments representing sovereign states which involve considerations of status, standing, power and prestige of the states *vis-à-vis* each other and which concern the general welfare of peoples as an object of governmental action. An agreement between two governments for the exchange of professors may thus be said to have a political aspect if it involves the considerations referred to. The cultural agreement signed by France and Rumania in 1965 was no doubt regarded by the two governments as helping to counteract the dominant position held in their policies by the United States and the Soviet Union respectively. To that extent the agreement is a matter of interest to students of politics.

We have now introduced that highly controversial term 'power', which sooner or later makes its way into all writing about international relations. Since the meaning and role of political power has been so fiercely debated in the literature on this subject, it is vital to be as clear as we can concerning the use of this term for the purpose of this book. By 'power' we intend simply to mean the general capacity of a state to make its will felt within the decision-making process of another state or any other organization within the international system. A question which all organizations have to face in the act of taking a decision is: whom can we afford to ignore? The more other states find it possible to ignore a particular state in reaching their own decisions on matters of foreign or domestic policy, the less powerful that state may be said to be, and *vice versa*. Plainly, power is sharply to be distinguished from sovereignty. Power exists in the realm of fact; it is a social relationship visible to the eye. Sovereignty exists in the realm of law; it is a thing of the mind. Sovereignty, like other legal attributes, is absolute; a state is or is not sovereign in the sight of its peers. Power varies, not only from state to state, but for the same state from time to time, even perhaps, on some occasions, from hour to hour. Sovereignty provides a state with an entrance ticket to the international club. Power determines how much respect will be paid to its voice when it speaks in the club. Power may clearly be a matter of military force backed by economic strength, both being actual or potential. A state may with definite effect threaten forceful reprisals unless its will is heeded, and that may suffice to ensure that its will is heeded. But power is ordinarily the end-product of a whole range of a state's attributes. Many states have the capacity to affect another state's decisions, not because they are economically or militarily strong, but because they are weak. This explains the power exerted by many small states over United States policy in the last twenty years or so. They have been able to threaten that, unless they have their way, they will collapse and open up the gates to Communism.

Is the acquisition and maintenance of power, so defined, an object of state policy in the international system? It is surely bound to be, since a state with capability to affect another state's decision-making process is in a better position than a state without it, however it may wish to use that capacity and for whatever ends. The possession of power is, and must be, the normal indispensable condition for the attainment of whatever goals a state sets for itself in the international system, and for the defence of

any interests and values it deems to be important. Power in the
international system may accordingly be compared with an
individual's income in a private enterprise economy. The individual, unless he be in that unusual situation in which he has
more money than he knows what to do with, must at all times be
concerned with the balance of his financial resources and for the
same reasons as those for which the state must at all times be
concerned with the extent of its power in the international system.
Money and power, in the individual's and the state's situation
respectively, are the indispensable condition for the defence and
the advancement of values preferred by individual and state. It
is true that the possession of money in itself and for itself may
become *the* preferred value for a certain individual—misers are
by no means unknown—just as the acquisition of power as an
end in itself may become *the* preferred value for the miser-like
state in its international relations. But to insist that concern for
power must be a condition of existence for the state within the
international system does not mean that it is pursued for its own
sake, or that man is instinctively acquisitive or aggressive, any
more than to insist that concern about money is an indispensable
condition for living in a society in which everything is not provided free of charge means that all men are misers. The condition of states, like that of men, may sometimes be pathological,
but normally it is normal.

In a later chapter the differences between the two forms of
politics, the international and the domestic, or intra-national,
will be developed.[12] Without anticipating what will be said there,
it is enough to indicate here the persistent interdependence between the two forms. A branch of international theorizing, known
as 'linkage politics', has been somewhat superfluously created
with this interdependence as its focus.[13] On the one hand, the
international political process makes its daily impact on the intra-
national. For example, international issues provide some of the
themes of debate for the political competitors within the state. In
more specific terms, general elections in parliamentary democracies may be fought, though in practice this is not often the rule,
on issues of foreign policy. International programmes and
policies may be the symbols on the basis of which internal political parties are formed and by which they differentiate themselves
from one another; in 1917 in Russia it was attitudes towards the

war which most crucially distinguished the Bolsheviks from other parties and, at one point, Lenin himself from his party colleagues. Or participation in international politics may affect a state's actual political structure and practices. Thus, it has been plausibly argued that the strengthened position of the President in the United States since 1919, and especially since 1945, has been partly due to that country's more active international role and the resulting need for a stronger executive to speak for the United States in world affairs.

On the other hand, internal politics exert a continuous influence on the state's international performance. In the current jargon, it is one of the 'inputs' in the foreign-policy process. Certain foreign policies may be ruled out, however much they may be in the state's interest, because the necessary internal support for those policies cannot be secured. Commitments to party supporters or promises made to the voters in election campaigns have to be fulfilled in the foreign-policy field, or at least a pretence of fulfilling them has to be made. And at all times a government, even in a totalitarian state, must calculate how far it can pursue a desirable foreign policy without affecting adversely its internal basis of support.

It is not always easy in practice to distinguish between the two sides of this interdependence between internal and external politics, but for our purposes we are more concerned with the effects of intra-national politics on international politics than with those of the latter on the former. Published studies of 'linkage politics' have not always made this point clear. In short, our interest in the internal political process in any state will concentrate only upon the extent to which the formation within a state of a consensus strong enough to support the government in power conditions that government's conduct of the state's external relations.

We may also deal briefly at this stage with the question of why such primary interest should attach to the *political* level of international relations as we have defined it. Why not the whole range of contexts in which states encounter each other?

One answer is that the political level of international relations is in itself an intellectual concern of heroic dimensions. If it can be effectively segregated, in the way we have suggested, from other levels of international life—though naturally all these are bound in their own way to affect the political level—we will have a subject of manageable, though barely manageable, proportions. If the entire social world of sovereign states is included, we run the risk of being defeated by the subject's sheer dimensions. But it may be further argued that the continuance of other levels of international relations has come to depend to a very large extent in modern times upon the state of international political relations. During the Cold War, for example, social, economic, cultural and athletic contacts between peoples of the Communist and non-Communist states were governed by the condition of their political relationships rather than the other way round. This may be less the case with states not so divided by ideological differences. Nevertheless, the mere fact that movement into and out of a state's territory tends to be regulated today by governmental authorities as a political matter ensures that non-political contacts across frontiers are tolerated only so long as they have no adverse effect upon the general political policies of the state. Finally, the primacy of political relationships between states as a focus of study is established by the fact that in the twentieth century it is the condition of political relations, especially between the greatest Powers, which has determined whether there will be peace or war and, in the nuclear age, whether an organized form of life can continue in which it is possible to maintain non-political relationships.

Finally, we must consider the significance of the term *system* of international politics. What is a 'system' and what are the properties of international politics which warrant their being described as a 'system'? Of the two meanings usually ascribed to the word 'system' one is less relevant to our purposes, the other more so. In the less relevant sense emphasis is laid on the *conscious co-ordination* of relations between certain determinate units, as when we speak of a system of manufacture or of teaching. There is a suggestion here of rational direction of relations between the parts by some central authority. Social systems, such as the economic or political system of a national community, especially in the liberal society, may be free from over-all conscious co-ordination, though such co-ordination may be attempted if the absence of it becomes too inconvenient. There is, it is true, some measure of conscious co-ordination in the international political system. Signatories of the UN Charter, for instance, agree, according to Article 1(4), that the Organization shall be a 'centre for harmonizing the actions of nations' in the attainment of certain common ends. But this is more of an aspiration than a description of fact. For the most part, such order as exists in the international system derives less from conscious co-ordination than from the disposition of each separate unit to keep its relations with its peers as orderly as possible.

Hence the second meaning of 'system' is more germane to our purposes, that is, the one which lays emphasis on the existence of an intelligible, regulated and orderly set of relationships between the parts such that they form a coherent, though complex, whole. 'System' is used in this sense, and without the assumption of conscious co-ordination, when we refer to the solar system (provided we take a rationalist view of the universe), or the social system of a country. The four properties of the international system to which we would like to give special emphasis are accordingly: the intelligibility of relations within the system; the presumption of the existence of rules for the regulation of these relations; orderliness; and the existence of a certain coherence and unity in the whole. It will be useful briefly to spell out more fully the nature of these properties.

Firstly, international political relationships are intelligible in that they are capable of rational explanation. If we study the position of a state in the international system we may not be able to forecast what its reaction will be if such or such an event occurs outside its borders. However, we will generally be safe in assuming that its reactions will not be capricious or unconsidered, but will be based upon more or less careful estimations of what it stands to gain or lose by various courses of action. This does not mean that on occasion a government may not 'take leave of its senses', but before we are justified in concluding that it has done so, we will be wise to examine the reasons it may have had for doing what it did. And reasons, often good ones, governments generally do have. Nor does this postulate of rationality which we are making here imply that no government ever acts from passion or prejudice nor (what is more likely to be the situation) is ever compelled to act from its constituents' passions and prejudices. However, these emotional forces themselves will generally be found to be understandable in the light, among other things, of the state's past experience of the international system. One must bear in mind, too, that the system as a whole may be irrational while the behaviour of its component parts remains entirely reasonable. Looked at from another planet, the world's lavishing of resources on armaments may seem insane, and no doubt would be insane if practised by a single person or group. But, given the existence of a state of international competition in armaments, and given the absence of any superior force to defend the state when it is threatened by another's armaments, the decision of a state to participate in the arms race may be considered unavoidable and indeed rationally prudent. If we were unable to postulate rationality in state behaviour, diplomatic criticism, like the criticism of any human performance, would not be possible. We cannot say that, if we ourselves were in government, we would have acted thus and thus unless we assume that there would follow from other states a set of rational reactions to our proposals, which are more or less capable of being forecast. If all state action were capricious, a matter of 'hunch', the rule to recommend would be 'back your hunches'. This, however, is not a recommendation which critics of a government's international policy generally make.

Secondly, international politics are 'systematic' in that they are for the most part regulated by distinctive rules. The rules, as in other social situations, are of two kinds: the technical and the normative. The technical rule tells you what you should do if you want to achieve a certain objective. Of the Ten Commandments only one is technical, the fifth, which states that we should honour our mothers and fathers *in order that* our days may be long in the land which the Lord gives us. Over the centuries diplomatic rules have been built up for the government of states in their relations with one another. To give a simple example, it is dangerous to have enemies on more than one frontier at the same time. These rules, leaders of nations will ignore at their peril. Niccolò Macchiavelli's *The Prince* is an early example of a source book of technical rules for the statesman.

Then come the normative rules: these indicate, irrespective of consequences, what *ought* to be done in a society of this kind. They are of three types: rules of ethics, rules of law and rules of propriety, or the laws of deference to customary seemliness in the relevant society. We will examine some of these normative regulations later in this book. It is sufficient for the present to dismiss the commonplace assertion that in world politics states do as they think fit, regardless of morals, laws and customs. It needs little argument to demonstrate that there is a *presumption* in the ordinary opinion of mankind that governments *should* conform to normative rules whenever they can. The mere fact that this is a universal expectation has some influence in making states abide by the rules of the game, provided that they can do so without too much damage to their vital interests. It is hard, if not impossible, for human beings to act in continuous disregard of what popular opinion assumes to be right and proper. In fact, it is no exaggeration to say that a good deal of the hypocrisy often laid at the doors of governments derives from their efforts to conform to the rules in circumstances in which they are unable to do so without neglect of their responsibilities to their people. But this point, though normally the subject of passionate debate, needs little further elucidation beyond what is given here and later in this book.[14]

Thirdly, we have referred to the general orderliness of international politics as evidence of their 'systematic' character. This attribution of international order may at first sight seem contrary to common experience, certainly in the twentieth century. The dismal tale of aggression, broken treaties, force and fraud in contemporary politics surely all belie it. But the incidence of these forces can easily be exaggerated. There is certainly a prevailing *expectation of violence* in the international system; otherwise the world's stockpiles of deadly weapons would not exist. But far less violence occurs between one state and another than is generally supposed. There is also an expectation of order. Every day we send letters and cables abroad, dispatch goods and undertake travel to foreign countries on business or for pleasure, without the slightest doubt that our goods and persons will arrive regularly and without interruption from another state's armed forces. The remarkable thing is not that there is violence and brute force in international relations, but that with 140 independent states in the international system, each armed to the teeth, suspicious and jealous of each other, without anything in the nature of a police force to maintain law and order, almost all of them somehow manage to live together *without* constantly shedding blood. The truth is, of course, that while man still has a strong propensity towards conflict and can often profit from it, he nevertheless has an equally strong interest in the more prosaic virtues of earning a living, travelling abroad in peace and keeping himself and his family alive. These help provide him with a stake in international order which makes, not violence, but its opposite, the prevailing rule for the vast majority of mankind in their international relations.

Fourthly, international politics form a system in the sense of a 'complex whole', with the implication that these politics add up to something more than the sum of the political actions of the constituent units in the system. The point is worth dwelling upon. We will often return to it in the later pages of this book. Admittedly, international politics are the consequence of decisions taken by sovereign states which are their own masters except in so far as their freedom of action is limited by international law. But these decisions are made with reference to issues which, for the most part, originate outside the state's borders, and over these issues the policy-maker, even in the most powerful states, has far from perfect control. The policy-maker is in no position to determine the issues about which he has to make his choices. They are presented to him by the unceasing flow of international events. The actual decisions which he makes about these issues are similarly, though perhaps to a less extent, restricted in range by the actions of other states, or, taking all of these actions together, by the 'system'. The foreign-policy maker, in short, does not so much decide what he would like to do, and then does it; his characteristic activity is rather that of 'adjusting to the system'. His foreign policy, considered as a sequence of decisions on issues presented by events happening within the international system, is best conceived as a means of putting the state into communication with its external social environment.

This dominance over policy by the international system, as a manufactory of issues calling for decisions, is borne out when we consider the remarkable emotional revulsion which the international system has aroused in sensitive minds, especially since the First World War, and the failure of the attempts to revise or abolish it which that sense of revulsion prompted. In Britain, for example, radical and Left-wing opinion after 1918 was profoundly opposed to the entire system of international relations, which it judged to have been responsible for the outbreak of war in 1914. The rejection of 'power politics', the balance of power, partial alliances, great armaments, which had characterized Liberal and Nonconformist opinion in nineteenth-century England, was inherited by the post-war rebels against international politics. They proceeded to add to their catalogue of the damned, secret diplomacy, foreign offices, and the whole paraphernalia of *la haute politique*. They looked to Woodrow Wilson as their prophet and the League of Nations as the successor to the old, discredited system. Yet by 1945 this radical revolt against the international system was virtually dead in Britain and survived only fitfully in minorities such as CND (Campaign for Nuclear Disarmament) and the far Left of the Labour Movement. One of the foremost critics of traditional diplomacy, the Labour party, was in office in 1945 with a comfortable Parliamentary majority. There it practised, much more effectively than Conservative Ministers in the 1930s, a balance-of-power policy against the most threatening Power of the day, the Soviet Union, with which leading Labour politicians at the end of the Second World War said they could get on better than could the Tories. Moreover, the Labour party, until the reluctant conversion of its leader in 1967 to the policy of seeking admission into the European Economic Community (EEC), was even less willing than the Conservatives to contemplate the abandonment of that bedrock principle of classical international politics, national sovereignty. In adopting the standard techniques and axioms of foreign policy in the period after 1945 the Labour party (much to the chagrin of its backbench M.P.s) provided an example of how root-and-branch critics of the international system generally accept it when they accede to the responsibilities of office.

Two even more remarkable instances of the pattern of rejection of the international system, followed by return to it, are the present-day super-Powers, the United States and the Soviet Union. Both have experienced the strongest possible emotional and intellectual revolt against traditional international relations at the moment of their earliest encounters with it. Both have been inspired by powerful programmes aimed at reforming or abolishing the international system. Both in course of time have reconciled themselves, in their own national interest as they perceived it, to operating that system, using in the process, techniques of management which would not have seemed unfamiliar to Castlereagh or Bismarck. It is ironic, though not unexpected, that the

United States, whose mission has immemorially been the improvement, or liquidation, of European politics, should in the 1970s have had as a highly effective Secretary of State a man deeply versed in the politics of Metternich.[15]

The United States withdrew in disgust in 1920 from the international system, as modified by the peace treaties, after attempts to reform it by the American President, Wilson, had failed for want of support at home. In 1941 the United States was compelled, for reasons of national defence, to re-enter the system only to make an equally unsuccessful effort to withdraw from it, or to limit its commitments in it, when the Second World War ended. During the Cold War, United States policy alternated between a tendency towards militant intervention in order to solve, once and for all, what Americans called 'the foreign-policy problem' and effect a return to the American way of life, and a reckless impulse to cut loose from all international entanglements and withdraw into the continental fortress. Since the decline of the Cold War in the early 1960s American opinion has been uncertain as to what the country's role in world affairs should be, but the old American aspiration to reform the whole international system has without doubt lost its savour. At the same time no responsible American spokesman believes that, even with its immense military might, the United States can stand alone, without allies and without continuously searching for terms of coexistence with the Communist world. America, like the rest of the world, is condemned to live with the international system as best it can; an experience all the more unhappy in being unrelieved by the hope that it will all soon be changed.

The Soviet Union's adjustment to the international system has been easier. This is partly because in 1917 the Bolsheviks inherited a state which, unlike the United States, had been a leading member of the European system—in those days, *the* international system—for centuries. To Lenin and his colleagues Marxism appeared to prophesy the supersession of traditional international politics by a vaguely conceived federation of proletarian nations. Moreover, the fact that the Communist revolution took place in Russia during an appalling war, which in itself seemed to mark the end of the old régime of international relations, suggested to the Leninists that they were destined to lead suffering mankind into a new order of co-operation and peace. Everyone knows how

Trotsky, the first Soviet Foreign Minister, said that his policy would be 'to issue a few revolutionary proclamations and then shut up shop'; how at the Brest-Litovsk peace talks Trotsky refused to have anything to do with the traditional categories of international relations, war and peace, and sought to transform the world struggle of states into a world struggle of classes within states; how only Lenin's realism saved the Bolshevik régime from extinction by his acceptance of the established means of conducting international relations: international treaties, diplomatic recognition and the exchange of ambassadors, and a national army, of which, ironically enough, Trotsky was made the director. It is well-known, too, how Stalin, in ousting Trotsky in the 1920s, sought for Russia national security above all else; and how he threw the country into the European balance of power, joining the League of Nations and making a choice, though possibly the wrong one, between Britain and France, on one side, and Nazi Germany, on the other, as allies in the fateful summer of 1939. Since the Second World War the Soviet Union has acted in the international system according to all its traditional rules. There could be no better evidence of this than the charge, levelled against it by the Chinese Communists and other dissident groups like the Latin American Solidarity Organization, that it has sacrificed the revolutionary cause to the profits of fraternization with the world's supreme capitalist Power, the United States.

We might conclude, then, that participation in the international system is unavoidable for any state, no matter how burdensome, morally repugnant or contrary to accepted doctrine that participation may be. To state the point in its barest form, participation in the international system and daily adjustment to the pressures it exerts derive from the inescapable territorial propinquity of states, their enforced vicinity. They cannot escape one another's company. With the development of transport and communications, especially by air and artificial earth satellites, hardly any state can function without some relations with its neighbours, and today all its neighbours on this planet are at most only a few hours distant. In the second place, many of the methods of conducting international relations, the technical rules of statecraft, are equally inescapable since they are governed by the nature of the system itself and have been attested by experience.

Hence, in certain respects the system is more powerful than the sum of its parts. Or rather the behaviour of those parts, the various states, is governed not only, and often not mainly, by their own desires and purposes, but by the nature and condition of that whole of which they form parts. Foreign policy might seem to the layman something like an opportunity for setting the world to rights, but it is more likely that the Foreign Minister compares it to entering into a conversation which began before he entered the room and will continue long after he has left it. For these reasons, Morton Kaplan's description of the international system as 'sub-system dominant', by which he seems to mean dominated by its constituent parts, is less than satisfactory.[16] We would prefer to think of it as being at least equally 'system dominant', meaning that in important respects the system as a whole conditions the behaviour of the state-members participating in it.

But this leaves a final question which may be briefly discussed before this chapter is ended. It is: can we really speak of *an* international system? Are there not many international systems today —the Western system, the Communist system, the non-aligned states' system, the inter-American system, and so on? And, even if we postulate an international system today, is it the same system as existed, say, in 1914 or 1939? It must be accepted that to some extent the choice of terms here is arbitrary and must depend upon what the student finds convenient for his own purposes. In this particular study, however, it is considered better to regard the kind of regional groupings we have mentioned as sub-systems of the whole, as indeed they are regarded within the United Nations Charter, rather than as separate and independent entities. States associated together by means of a regional sub-system tend to act from very similar motives to those actuating state behaviour in the wider international system. The cohesion of regional sub-systems, such as the North Atlantic Treaty, and Warsaw Pact organizations, appears to vary in accordance with the political climate in the global system as a whole. And these regional groupings are generally more short-lived than the global system. For all these reasons study of the global system should by all means take account of the tendencies towards regional devolution which have been well marked since 1939; but there can be no question about which has the prior call on the student's attention.

As for the argument that international relations are so different, for instance, in the nuclear age, or as a result of the advent of non-alignment policies in the world, that their study forms a subject quite distinct from that of international relations before, say, 1939, this cannot be judged acceptable. It would imply, for instance, that the foreign policy of France in the 1970s has nothing whatever in common with the policy of France in the 1930s, or that the problems of the United Nations are wholly different from those of the League of Nations. It would mean also that every time a new weapon of war was invented or a new state created, the student of international politics would have to scrap his previous work and begin again on a clean sheet. It is just conceivable that in certain circumstances this might be true, but the implication surely is to rule out international politics as a serious study. We prefer the contrary view: namely, that the international political system, consisting of numerous sovereign states without a common superior above them, has now existed for three or four centuries, though affected by all the changes in the human condition which have occurred during this period; that in its fundamental character and operations it is relatively resistant to purposive reform; and that it plays a vital role in governing the external behaviour of the states from which it is formed.

NOTES

1. See Georg Simmel, *Conflict and the Web of Group-Affiliations*, translated by Kurt H. Wolff, The Free Press, New York, 1955.
2. Bentham, *An Introduction to the Principles of Morals and Legislation*, The Clarendon Press, Oxford, 1879, Chapter XVII, pp. 326–7.
3. I have discussed this point in an article entitled 'National self-determination: the adventures of a moral principle' in *International Relations*, April 1955, vol. 1, no. 3.
4. J. W. Burton's book *World Society*, Cambridge University Press, 1972, is a good example of the high degree of nonspecific generality which tends to result from lumping together *all* human relations of whatever kind.
5. See, as an example from the 1930s, *The Framework of International Society*, by S. H. Bailey, Longmans, London, 1932. The post-1945 Functionalist school drew their primary inspiration from David Mitrany, *A Working Peace System*, The Royal Institute of International Affairs, London, 1943.
6. The UN Charter, Article 71.
7. See the annual *Yearbook of International Organisations* published by the Union of International Associations, Brussels.

8. John Wiley, New York, 1957.
9. P.14.
10. See Chapter Six.
11. See Lasswell's *Politics. Who Gets What, When, How*, Whittlesey House, New York and London, 1936, p. 3.
12. See Chapter Six.
13. See James N. Rosenau (ed.), *Linkage Politics*, The Free Press, New York, 1969.
14. See below, pp. 112–13.
15. Dr. Henry Kissinger.
16. Op. cit., p. 17.

Two

Ancestors of the Modern System

ONE way of describing our present-day international system is to say that it is one answer, though by no means the only answer, to a question which has faced mankind from the beginning of its history: namely, how are the different peoples to live together on the same spacially confined planet—the only home which man has to live in—without destroying one another and while preserving a certain minimum of freedom and independence for each particular community? The modern international system is hardly more than two or three hundred years old: the recorded history of man goes back some five or six thousand years, his unrecorded history perhaps ten million. So that our modern system of international relations has so far been comparatively short-lived, and there is certainly no assurance that it will not be superseded in a similarly comparatively short period by some other formula for the organization of relations between dissimilar peoples. There is an argument for saying that the modern international system, for all its failings, which are only too obvious, has produced the most satisfactory (or least unsatisfactory) combination yet discovered of order in the whole, and freedom for the subordinate parts. Certainly there is evident today no universal urge in the mass of mankind to abolish the existing system and replace it by another. But it is as well to recall that, compared with, say, religion, the family, commerce, war, empire, our international system is for all practical purposes a newcomer to the human scene.

In the present chapter we wish to examine some of the fore-runners of the present-day international system, some earlier answers to the problem of co-existence in conditions of order and freedom. We will then be in a better position to understand how the present system originated and from what previous examples of arrangements for organizing relations between diverse peoples our modern system sprang. It is important to stress that the object of this exercise is not to acquire or rehearse historical knowledge for its own sake: that is decidedly not what the aim of study of international politics is. Our purpose is rather to gain an understanding of the basic features of the modern international system by examining it in the light of earlier models of the same human enterprise. If we try to answer the question, in what other ways have men in past history organized their group relations, and what historical pre-conditions had to exist before the modern international system could emerge into the light of day, we will have gone far to identify the distinguishing marks of that system.

There is another purpose to be served by this inquiry, or rather a useful by-product of this kind of historical investigation: it brings out not only what is unique in our modern international system, which might otherwise not have struck us so forcibly, but also what our system has in common with earlier arrangements for the co-existence of separate peoples. It is a modern fallacy that our own times are wholly unique, or, to use the phrase coined by Ortega y Gasset in *The Revolt of the Masses*, that we live 'at the height of the times'; that all preceding history was a kind of preparation for the present.[1] The more one studies the remoter history of mankind, the more one tends to be persuaded that there is 'nothing new under the sun'.

Our object, then, in this chapter is to outline, as though in thumbnail sketches, the more important formulae in recorded history for the organization of relations between people dissimilar in nationality, race, religion, culture, experience, economic and social character, and so on. This indeed is a curiously understudied subject. Most of the learned works on the ancient world, for example, are accounts of the internal affairs, including the cultural and aesthetic achievements, of the different peoples with which they deal. When, for instance, as in the case of the ancient Assyrian Empire, possibly the most warlike political system in all human history, discussion of relations with other peoples cannot be avoided, this takes the form of detailed accounts of military campaigns, normally followed by short-lived truces. There is generally little in the way of a systematic effort to explain the manner of conducting external relations.[2] The only two substantial modern studies of historical patterns of international relations which appear to have been published are *Culture and Politics in International History* by Abba B. Bozeman (Princeton U.P.,

1960) and *The Political Systems of Empires* by S. N. Eisenstadt
(The Free Press, New York, 1963). A useful short essay partially
dealing with this subject is to be found in Chapter II of K. J.
Holsti's *International Politics. A framework for analysis* (Prentice-
Hall, New Jersey, second edition, 1971).

Looking at the pre-modern systems for the organization of
international relations as a whole, these evidently fall into two
broad groups. One is the pattern of the world state, or rather the
single state embracing or purporting to embrace within one consolidated empire the different peoples of the known world, those
outside the boundaries of empire being related to the metropolis
only by war or armed peace. A supreme example of this, of course,
is the Roman Empire, perhaps the greatest of man's historical
political achievements. The other pattern is the loose association
of independent communities, each of which enjoys some degree of
self-government with perhaps some of these groups being tied to
each other by links somewhat stronger than those prevailing in the
system as a whole. The extent of intercourse and continuous
mutual transactions between the separate communities constituting this pattern has tended to depend on the technical state of
transport and communications, the volume of trade within the
system as a whole and the dependence of the different independent
communities on foreign trade, and possibly also the extent of
migration from one community to another. Typical examples of
this form of multi-member political system are the Greek city-
state pattern in the fourth and fifth centuries B.C., the city-states of
Renaissance Italy and the modern international system.

There are two important characteristics to be noted in the multi-
polar type of political system. The first is that, although this
pattern is sharply differentiated from the world-state type, the
idea of and the aspiration towards the single world empire have
always been powerful forces at least within the contemporary
form of the multi-polar system, that is, the international system as
we know it today. To some extent this has also been true of other
multi-polar systems since the birth of Christ. To unify the world
under a single command and a single group of political ideas has
been a dream since the system began. One may in fact describe the
history of our international system in terms of a conflict between
forces tending towards unification within a single policy, forces
represented in modern times by statesmen as varied as Woodrow

Wilson, Stalin and Hitler, and forces dedicated to the maintenance of the autonomy of the separate states. A possible reason for this is that the modern system grew up against the background of the Roman Empire, which has never ceased to cast its spell over men's minds. St. Augustine, writing in the fifth century A.D., believed that the Roman Empire must be restored, or Judgment Day would come. So did the Venerable Bede in the eighth century. Charlemagne, crowned in Aachen in 800 as ruler of the Holy Roman Empire, considered that the mantle of old Rome had fallen on his shoulders. It is well-known that the Russian Orthodox Church, after the fall of Constantinople in 1453, considered that Moscow was destined to be the Third Rome. There has lived in the mental background of would-be world empire-makers the commitment to restore the glories and peace of Rome, whilst their opponents have conceived of themselves as the champions of national freedom against the pretensions of these ecumenical empires.

The other feature of multi-polar systems is that, while some of them resulted from the collapse of an older world state, as the city-state system of Renaissance Italy sprang ultimately from the fall of the Roman Empire, other factors have combined at different times to preserve the independence of the units of the multi-polar system. For example, in classical Greek times the geographical configuration of Greece provided sites for independent communities with strong natural defences against rival cities in the form of rugged mountains running down to the sea. Moreover, the sheer technical inability of certain world states of the past to win and maintain military control over the whole of the known world inevitably made necessary truces and treaties with surrounding peoples. From this there sprang, *faute de mieux*, as in the case of the ancient Assyrian Empire, a decentralized and multi-polar international system of a kind.

Broadly speaking, it is possible to identify seven major international systems which preceded the one with which we are familiar in the twentieth century. The first of these comprised what we may suitably call the ancient empires of the Near and Middle East. These systems of international relations are well described in Chapter X, entitled 'Political, Social and Economic Organization of the World Empires of the East', of Mikhail Rostovtsev's *A History of the Ancient World*, Volume I.[3] Rostovtsev takes as the three dominant examples of these empires, which flourished in the thousand years or so before the birth of Christ, the Egyptian, the Assyrian (occupying what is now the Kurdish area of Iraq, centred in present-day Mosul) and the Persian. The city-states which developed among these peoples were evidently too small and weak to remain independent. They could not resist for long the forces making for integration and amalgamation. Moreover, the development of 'hydraulic' civilization, depending on the massive and costly control of water supplies for irrigation, facilitated the concentration of power over the city-states into the hands of one individual ruler. He governed as king or emperor, but not as the wielder of any sovereign power which was deemed to be inherent in the people. He was a God-king, the descendant of other God-kings. He was the single and solitary source of power, in that all legislative, executive and judicial authority was concentrated into his hands.

Territories conquered by the central hub of power in these empires were normally left with their own form of government, though they were usually compelled to pay tribute to the all-powerful king. They were also obliged to contribute armed forces to their conqueror's military campaigns and to refrain, on pain of the most dire penalties, from giving comfort and assistance to his enemies. Various methods were adopted to consolidate control by the centre over the subject peoples. The Assyrian monarchs, for example, transplanted their conquered peoples from one part of their empire to another in order to control them more effectively. Another device adopted by the Assyrians as a means of control over their subject peoples was to impose a common religion, the worship of Ashur, in order to strengthen their allegiance, though perhaps only temporarily, to the all-powerful king. Again, the ancient Egyptians, beginning with the Pharaohs of the Eighth Dynasty, planted garrisons among the conquered peoples, with a Governor-General who disposed of the tribute and controlled the auxiliary forces contributed by the vassal peoples as symbols of their subordination.

According to Rostovtsev, the Persians were the first of these ancient imperialists to discover how to unite different peoples into a single empire. They did so partly by effacing differences between the provinces and the dominating core of the empire. The con-quered peoples were incorporated as satrapies, but each was allowed a considerable degree of local independence and no attempt was made to try to impose the Persian language or culture. As Rostovtsev writes:

> The Persians were the first to take decisive steps towards the creation of a real empire, centralised, though heterogeneous, and united. From a number of measures taken by their kings we can see that they looked upon their empire as an indivisible whole: the introduction of a uniform coinage and the construction of great military roads, piercing the kingdom from end to end, are among the most convincing of these measures.[4]

The Egyptian, Assyrian and Persian Empires are thus early examples of world-states, or drives towards world-states, more successful in the Persian case than in the two others. The rulers of these massive Empires had no conception of the equality, taken either in a physical or legal sense, of other peoples or of their moral or lawful right to independence. To them other nations appeared either as potential vassals to be converted into tribute-paying states, or enemies to be kept at a safe distance. Rudimentary treaties had on occasion to be made with hostile states. We know that the kings of Assyria entered into such engagements with the Chaldean, Babylonian and Urartu peoples. But this was only because the God-king's power was, perhaps only temporarily, insufficient to conquer such states and incorporate them within the central Empire.

The pattern is similar, though with some differences, in the Chinese Empire, our second example of pre-modern international systems. The Chinese Empire extended continuously, though interrupted by periods of internecine warfare between warring kingdoms into which the Empire as a whole had been split, from the pre-Han dynasties, beginning with the Shang Yin ascendancy in the eighteenth century B.C., to the Ching dynasty of the Manchu Tartars, which maintained itself from A.D. 1644 to 1912. The traditional and formal attitude of the Chinese towards neighbouring peoples was one of superiority, though this assumption was not based on race, colour, power or wealth, but on civilization, and this perhaps because the Chinese were essentially a settled people and thus had had over many centuries the opportunity to create for themselves one of the most sophisticated and mannered societies known to history. The writings of Confucius typically portray China as a central and celestial Empire surrounded on almost every side by barbarians. The barbarians might someday hope to attain the level of civilized achievement of the Chinese, and if they succeeded in doing so, they might be admitted into relations with the Heavenly Kingdom, but even so only as vassals and on payment of tribute. Any foreigner who was admitted to the court of the Chinese emperor must make his ceremonial obeisance, the *kow-tow*, as a symbol of subordination and must duly pay his tribute. There was no suggestion, nor in truth could there be, of equality between the Chinese and other peoples.

The last sentence, however, perhaps requires one qualification. Michael Loewe of Cambridge University has written in his book, *Imperial China*, that the conception of Chinese superiority described above was not infrequently more of an ideal than a reality.[5] He shows, for example, that when the Buddhist faith first began to penetrate China, Chinese rulers were compelled to admit that it was a creed no less civilized than their own religious ideas. On the level of military power, too, emperors of China were forced to come to terms with and recognize the independent existence of other peoples whom they were unable to conquer, as for instance the Mongols, Tartars, Huns and Japanese. This is another example of the phenomenon we have seen earlier; namely the *de facto* and enforced recognition of the right of other states to exist when they could not be brought forcibly beneath the yoke.

The fact remains nevertheless that at least until the eighteenth century of the Christian era the Chinese were quite unable to accept the notion of the legal equality of states within the international system which is implicit in and basic to modern diplomatic relations. The following extract from the well-known letter of the Emperor Ch'ien-lung to George III of England at the time of the failure of Lord Macartney to establish a diplomatic mission in China in 1793 illustrates the common Imperial Chinese attitude towards other states:

> As to the request made in your memorial, O King, to send one of your nationals to stay at the Celestial Court to take care of your country's trade with China, this is not in harmony with the state system of our dynasty and will definitely not be permitted. Traditionally people of the European nations who wished to render some service under the Celestial Court have been permitted to come to the capital. But after their arrival they are obliged to wear Chinese court costumes, are placed in a certain residence and are never allowed to return to their own countries.

The Chinese determination not to accept permanent diplomatic missions within Chinese territory on the same terms as other states in the international system at that time stemmed from a cultural or psychological source as well as from a legal source. The former was the fear that foreign intruders, unless assimilated as individuals into Chinese life, would have the effect of disturbing local custom, or *li*. While it is almost universal for any people, who have traditionally had little contact with the outside world, to fear foreign contacts and perhaps provide for special rituals to divest them of their dangers to local custom, this primitive xenophobia may well have been especially strong in China's case owing both to the distinctiveness of the Chinese civilization and to the way in which it had developed in the same territory over several thousands of years. As to the second, and legal, source of Chinese opposition to permanent diplomatic missions, it must be remembered that Chinese emperors, with the approval of their subjects, claimed exclusive sovereignty, not merely over territory which they actually occupied and administered, but, in theory at least, over the rest of the world as well. Hence, the Chinese never spoke of *acquiring* new territory; they always thought of and used the word for *recovering* it. Thus, it was incomprehensible to the Chinese that a portion of their own territory could actually be under foreign sovereignty in the form of a diplomatic mission. Nor indeed could they understand how any foreign ruler could claim sovereignty, in the sense of the right to administer it to the exclusion of all others, over territory which was only temporarily under his control. Circumstances might prevent a Chinese emperor from making good his title to territory under foreign occupation, but in Chinese legal theory that title existed none the less.

So forcibly was Chinese resistance to foreign diplomatic missions maintained that in the nineteenth century it had to be overcome by the European Powers—in the first instance by Britain —at the point of the gun. It was the Treaty of Tientsin, signed by Britain and China on 26th June 1858, followed by the Treaty of Peking, concluded in 1860, which conferred on Britain, according to Article 2 of the agreement, the right to representation in Peking 'in accordance with the universal practice of great and friendly nations'. But that had never been the practice of China: it had to be imposed on her by British military force. According to Professor Hsü in a study of the way in which China was compelled to

join the international community by the European Powers in the
nineteenth century, the established Chinese attitude towards the
outside world was that:

> National security could only be found in isolation . . . whoever
> wished to enter into relations with China must do so as China's
> vassal, acknowledging the supremacy of the Chinese Emperor
> and obeying his commands, thus ruling out all possibility of inter-
> national intercourse on terms of equality.[6]

Perhaps it is no accident then that the Chinese Communists, who
brought the whole country under their control in 1949, manifested
for a number of years much the same disdain for membership of
the international system. It seems that it was only the sheer
imperatives of national interest, though not, as in the nineteenth
century, the superior military force of another state, which finally
drove Communist China to accept membership of the United
Nations in 1972 and subsequently normal relations with other
members of the international system.

This story of China's painful first encounters with the international system has a further interest about it in that it relates to
one of the main themes of this book: namely, that states are not
normally members of the international system because of the
gratifications they derive from membership in itself, just as individual men and women derive gratifications from membership of
a social club. Human beings are gregarious and social relations in
themselves answer to those gregarious dispositions. States would,
if they could, prefer to walk by themselves, like cats. Left to themselves the state members of the international system would no
doubt rather cultivate their own gardens than face the perplexities
and shoulder the burdens and dangers of the international
system. But with the world as it is today, most states, especially
the more powerful states, have literally no option but to take part
in the international system since that is often the only way in which
they can fulfil their objectives, whatever those objectives may be.
Equally important is the fact that by participating in the international system a state may ward off the very considerable dangers
and disadvantages which result from not being a participating
member of the system. But we must return to this point later.

As in Imperial China, the lack of any conception of a world
society of equal states is to be found, too, in the kingdoms of

ancient India. Before the Mogul Empire, the collapse of which at the beginning of the eighteenth century heralded the European conquest of India, the sub-continent had immemorially been divided between a group of perpetually warring kingdoms devoid of any conception of balance or equilibrium between them. The sole factor regulating the mutual relations of these warring kingdoms was power—he who possessed it, used it to make good his domination over others. Those who lacked it had no alternative but to submit to those who had it. Such an international system, if anything so arbitrary and disordered can properly be described as a system, corresponds to the erroneous image which most people tend to have of the very different system of international relations which governs our lives today.

The only comprehensive description which remains of Indian international politics before the impact of the West in the early eighteenth century is the *Arthasastra* of Kautilya. Kautilya is generally recognized today as the *eminence grise*, the Cardinal Richelieu, of the Mauryan Dynasty, which controlled what is now Bihar Province, north-west of Calcutta, about 300 B.C. His *Arthasastra*, which was discovered in Mysore in 1904, is in reality a handbook for statesmen, covering both domestic and foreign policy. It might even be described as an ancient Indian version of Macchiavelli's *Prince*.[7]

For the present-day reader there are two striking features of the *Arthasastra*. First, its remarkable modernity; it might have been written in Europe at any time since 1914. Almost all the types of twentieth-century foreign policy are described, as for instance in Chapter 41, entitled 'Decay, Stabilisation and Progress of States'. Here it is laid down that every state can be characterized as having a 'six-fold' policy, and a 'six-fold' policy can in its turn can be reduced to 'Peace', which means 'concord supported by pacts'; war, 'implying armed aggression'; neutrality, implying 'nonchalance'; armed invasion against another Power; and what Kautilya calls 'biformal policy', which involves 'making war with one and suing for peace with another'. Almost all the main ingredients of modern international politics are to be found in this, perhaps the first well-known classification of forms of international action.

The second notable aspect of the *Arthasastra*, in sharp contrast with the view so prevalent of India today as a country of pacifism and renunciation, is its cold, almost mocking realism, or perhaps cynicism. For Kautilya international politics consists of a jungle filled with cruel and merciless animals, with no law, moral scruples or aspiration towards order in the whole. Some of his statements about the international system of his own day are almost caricatures of what we would call today 'power politics' at its very worst. As an example, Chapter 46 of the *Arthasastra*, entitled 'Strategies of Peace', contains the following passage:

> When, with a view to overcoming the enemy, who is rocked by internal disorders, an agreement or pact is made of a general nature to catch the enemy in his weak points and conquer him, the pact is called a general peace pact.

Thus, a summary of the international systems of the ancient world which we have so far briefly considered—the old empires of the Near and Middle East, Imperial China and ancient India—is to be conveniently found in Abba Bozeman's *Culture and Politics in International History*, in which she writes:

> The idea of a balance of power could not have been entertained in Persia and China because it was utterly incompatible with the dominant images that sustained the absolute supremacy of the Shah of Shahs and the sole ruler of the one and only Middle Kingdom. Nor could it have been accommodated in ancient India, even though the territorial organisation of the realm with numerous separate kingdoms is comparable to that of Renaissance and modern Western Europe. For this pluralistic order did not suggest the conclusions upon which the west Europeans were to agree eventually, namely that it would be unethical and unwise to persist in bids for absolute power and that the national interest would be served by maintaining an equilibrium in inter-state relations.[8]

Another way of stating this same general point is to say that before the advent of the modern system of independent states, security for the individual state tended to be sought through the weakening, and if possible the total overthrow, of hostile states. After the coming of the modern international system, security has tended to be sought through certain means for organizing the world international system as a whole, of which the classical balance of power is one.

When, however, we come to the Greek city-state system of the fifth century B.C., the pattern of the ancient world seems at first sight to be broken. It is true that the Greeks, considered as one Hellenic people, exhibited much the same sense of unity against a lawless and dangerous external world as had all the ancient empires. That was sufficiently shown in the Greek wars against the Persians in 490 B.C. to 480 B.C. That unity was symbolized by affinities of language, religion, descent and culture between the Greek city-states. But between themselves and in their own world the Greeks practised a state system which had many features in common with our own. Many striking parallels have in fact been observed between the bipolar international system which was in operation during the 'Cold War' period following the Second World War and the conflict between Athens, with her hegemony over her allies, and Sparta, the leader of the Peloponnesian League, at the outset of the great war between the two which began in 431 B.C. and is described by Thucydides. There was moreover an impressive similarity to latter-day techniques of Cold War international policy in the rivalry between Athens and Sparta for mastery of the 'Third World', or the group of states committed neither to one side nor the other. The conflict between Athens and Sparta was fought, not only between the armed forces of the two cities and their allies by land and sea, but also in the form of revolutionary struggles for power (known as *stasis*) within the territory of uncommitted states. These tactics, to which the name 'informal penetration' has been given, reflect the familiar two levels—that of intra-national and international policy—on which the giant Powers have conducted their competition for supreme power in the years since 1945.[9]

Moreover, the Greeks employed many other institutions and practices which would be familiar to the modern diplomat. The principle of the diplomatic immunity of envoys, for instance, was well-established among the Greek city-states, though these were not usually regarded as negotiators in the modern sense, but as messengers, and the idea of the permanent diplomatic mission was unknown: the Greek word 'messenger' ($\dot{\alpha}\gamma\gamma\epsilon\lambda o\varsigma$) suggests the role of the classical Greek envoy. Alliances and treaties were also integral parts of the Greek diplomatic system, and arbitration for the settlement of disputes between the city-states was fairly well established.[10]

Nevertheless, the tendency towards the creation of a single

hegemony over, and integration between, the Greek city-states was strong. It might have resulted in the formation of a centrally controlled and united Greek nation had the geography of the country been somewhat more congenial. Athens and Sparta during the Peloponnesian War were somewhat like Prussia and Austria in the 1860s struggling for the leadership of the German nation in its efforts to create a single German state. This tendency towards Greek unity was stronger in Athens, just as it was in Prussia a hundred years ago. Athens had made herself head of the Delian League formed from the Greek states which had banded together to resist and ultimately to defeat the Persian invaders. Her naval strength had been the foremost military factor in the repulse of the Persians. After the Persian wars the Athenians had used that naval power to dominate the Aegean Sea. In 454 B.C. the Treasury of the Delian League, to which each member state made its financial contribution in return for naval protection by Athens, was removed from Delos to Athens, thus symbolizing the transformation of an alliance into an empire in embryo. The allies in effect became tributaries of Athens and the right to secede from the Athenian connection was extinguished. Rebellions against what now speedily became Athenian domination, such as those of Samos and Byzantium, were crushed with the greatest severity. All the allies were obliged to refer their suits at law in the last resort to Athens for settlement in the Athenian courts. Athens imposed her own democratic form of government on the allied Greek states and fomented revolts against non-democratic régimes. Hence, by 431 B.C., when the great war between Athens and Sparta began, the allied league had become an Athenian empire. According to Thucydides, 'what made war inevitable was the growth of Athenian power and the fear which this caused in Sparta'.[11]

Sparta, who dominated the cities of the Peloponnese, with the notable exceptions of Argos and Achaea, ruled her own league with only a slightly less heavy hand. The Peloponnesian League could hardly be called a Spartan empire. It was strictly a multilateral defensive alliance with Sparta no more than *primus inter pares*. Tributes were not collected from the lesser allies, as in the Delian League, but when joint military campaigns took place, members of the Peloponnesian League were expected, if necessary, to contribute some two-thirds of their military forces to the common effort. Sparta also tended to interfere less than Athens in the internal government of allied states, but nevertheless tried to ensure that conservative oligarchies should prevail. The obedient political élites in the different subordinate states tended to look to Sparta as their master and protector for their defence both against foreign attack and against revolution from below, rather than to the Peloponnesian alliance as a whole.

But if Sparta ruled with a somewhat lighter hand than the Athenians, this was no doubt mainly due to her notoriously precarious domestic situation. The central fact dominating all Spartan politics and policies was the potentially explosive situation on which the Spartan state was based, in the form of the suppressed population of helots, some 200,000 in number, with only 4,000 adult males constituting the dominant Spartan minority to control them. This subjugated mass were the original local population of Messenians who had been conquered by the immigrant Spartans.

To sum up, then, one might say that, although the ancient Greeks lived their lives within a multi-state system which in many respects resembled the modern international system, the driving impulses towards unification and control from a single centre were strong during the classical period. The Peloponnesian war between the two great coalitions led by Athens and Sparta respectively (431 to 404 B.C.) was in one sense a war for the unification of the Greek people, in much the same way as the war between Austria and Prussia in 1866 was a war for the unification of the German people. Had Athens won the war, it is likely that, after a suitable time for political and economic recovery, she would have brought all the Greek states within her enlarged empire, though whether such a highly volatile and polemical people as the Athenians could have held together a united Greece for any considerable period is another question. As it happened, it was Sparta that won the war, and Sparta, like Austria in the 1860s, lacked both the skill and the domestic stability to unite and govern the Greeks in peace. Eventually the Greeks were united together but this was part of other empires, first the Macedonian and Alexandrine, then the Roman, later the Byzantine, and these empires were essentially not multipolar systems but integrated unities like those of the old world.

This dissolution of the Greek multi-state system therefore brings us to the Roman and Byzantine empires, since these formed, as it were, bridges with the mediaeval period of European history from which our modern system of international relations was later to spring.

The Roman Republic, as it spread around the Mediterranean shores, was essentially a highly centralized political system. Territories acquired by the Republic through military conquest were tied to the centre by separate bilateral treaties according to the Roman principle of *divide et impera*. Subsequently, though not in the earlier centuries, all their inhabitants were granted Roman citizenship. These conquered territories were eventually formed into provinces, an expression which originally signified the sphere of duty of a magistrate. Later, distinguished generals were appointed to the governorships of Roman provinces, but nevertheless the Senate in Rome, which was mainly composed of former magistrates, strictly supervised provincial administration. The Senate also appointed the governors of the provinces, fixed their terms of office and received accounts of their administration from them on their return to the capital. The governor and his staff otherwise enjoyed complete control of the province in civilian and military affairs; they administered justice, maintained order and supervised the use of taxes.[12]

Under the Roman Empire, formally established by Augustus Caesar in 27 B.C., control of the provinces from the centre was even strengthened. Provincial governors were given a fixed salary, but military control was strictly in the hands of the Emperor, as the permanent and virtually indisputable Commander-in-Chief, the provincial governors being appropriately known as *legati Augusti* (the Emperor's lieutenants). At the same time, the inhabitants of the provinces were given a distinct voice in the government of the Empire, not, certainly, by anything like self-determination of the province as a whole, but by being allowed to sit in the seats of power in Rome and even, on occasion, to become Emperors themselves. The Roman imperial system of provincial government in this respect tended to resemble the later French practice of according representation in the National Assembly in Paris to their overseas colonies. In the practice of Rome, however, the whole system was firmly balanced under the divine authority of the Emperor. All law for the Empire as a whole was made in Rome. Its usual name was *ius gentium* and it was, in theory at least, an amalgamation of Roman and provincial law. In practice, however, the primacy of Rome over all its extensive domains was underlined by the fact that Roman courts and Roman judges decided and administered these laws of the Empire.

In the Byzantine Empire government was even more highly centralized than in Rome. The rulers of this Empire took Constantinople as their capital after the sacking of the Eternal City by the Goths in the fourth century A.D., and regarded themselves as the true successors of the Roman Caesars. They felt themselves to be even more free than the rulers of Rome from all sense of responsibility to other states and to any wider international system. The Byzantine Empire can in fact almost be described as the European equivalent of the omnipotent Chinese Empire which finally collapsed in the 1900s, though far more ruthless and power-hungry. Of the Byzantine Empire at its apex of power Miss Bozeman has written:

> The ruling circles of Byzantium regarded the state as the highest value in society. They did not admit that the actions of the state were subject either to law or to morality. Nor could they attribute any political value to such concepts as 'humanity' or 'the unity of mankind', since they saw the world around them in terms of disconnected and conflicting parts. In the tradition of Byzantine statesmanship no moral approbrium was attached to war and no intrinsic value inherent in peace. Both have their time and place in accordance with the interests of the state. As the paramount manifestation of the Byzantine state in the realm of competitive power politics, diplomacy was as amoral as the state itself. The chief purpose was to protect the state, ensure its survival and promote its power by any method which promised success.[13]

The political vocabulary and ethics of Byzantium, in other words, were only slightly different, if different at all, from those of Kautilya's *Arthasastra*.

This brings us to the last of the great pre-modern systems of international relations with which we wish to deal in this chapter, namely the mediaeval system from which our present-day international system, directly or indirectly, sprang. The mediaeval system of politics in Europe was 'middle' in linking the old order with the new. In part the mediaeval system inherited the political ideas of some of the great empires of the past. In the Holy Roman Empire, founded in A.D. 800 with the crowning of Charlemagne as Emperor in Aachen, and in the still surviving Greco-Byzantine Empire based on Constantinople there was no sense of equality of status with other contemporary political entities. In an essay on mediaeval diplomacy in *The History and Nature of International Relations*, C. J. Hayes has explained that:

> Neither the Holy Roman Empire nor the Greco-Byzantine Empire would recognise as equals the sovereigns of the kingdoms that were growing up about them; and without a theoretical equality of independent sovereign states international relations are not possible.[14]

Again, the same note of equality is struck; without the firm acceptance of the principle of sovereign equality it hardly seems that the modern international system could have come into existence.

But there was also another link with the old empires in the sense that through the Papacy, the central religious institution of the Middle Ages, Europe had temporarily a single and uniform religious orthodoxy, the One True Faith, that extraordinarily powerful factor in cohesion in all societies, calling to mind the worship of Ashur or the mystical gods of the Nile Valley. The Popes of Rome certainly never controlled in either theory or practice every aspect of the government of the numberless provinces, dukedoms, cities, independent estates, which constituted the political landscape of the Europe of the Middle Ages. Nevertheless, the prevailing theory of government was that the local ruler was in some, not always well-defined, sense a viceroy of the Pope, and that all the local rulers taken together were brotherly co-operators in a single task—the governing of that *magna civitas Christiana* which was Europe.

At the same time, the Middle Ages in Europe looked forward to the centuries ahead and to the eras of modern politics. This was especially true in two respects. In the first place, the great, loosely amalgamated empires of mediaeval Europe, of which the Holy Roman Empire was the foremost example, were gradually breaking up. The principle of political fragmentation was at work and eventually the various pieces were to be gathered together and bound up again, but this time into the tough national states which we know today. Each of these national states was to have in due course its own more or less distinct national interests, and these were to prove in time to be the foundations of those states' national policies in their relations with each other. In the second place, as the Middle Ages waned, politics tended to become increasingly secularized. As control over local policies by the Roman Church gradually faded, the new and formidable principle of *raison d'état* came to replace religion with essentially secular prescriptions for the practice of government. But this vital transformation we must examine more fully later on.

We may therefore say that the two pre-conditions for the emergence of the modern international system are, firstly, the notion that states have their *raison d'être* in being themselves rather than parts of a disciplined whole, and, secondly, secular government, or the idea that the object of government is not the establishment in Heaven or on earth of the Kingdom of God, but the maintenance and defence of the interests of that everyday thing, the sovereign territorial state. When these two conditions are firmly accepted by the minds of men and in the practical acts of government, the stage is set for the ushering in of the modern international system.

Finally, it is always vital to remember, in an age of intense criticism of the present system of international relations, that compared with some earlier international systems which we have sketchily examined in this chapter, the modern system has strong merits on its side. The international system of today has often been considered dangerous, criminally wasteful in its expenditure of human life and resources in its wars, and generally out-of-date for modern conditions. But in the long perspective of history, that system comes out tolerably well, and in many ways better than many of the earlier systems which we have mentioned. Compared with ancient Assyria, Persia and Greece, it is more orderly than it deserves to be, with its total lack of a single government above all the different states.

Compared with the Roman and Byzantine Empires, it allows the small state to live out its days in relative freedom from the great devouring Leviathans. For better or for worse, the small states of today, so far from being the mere hewers of wood and drawers of water for the great states, can virtually live, thanks to the nature of the international system, unhindered by the depredations of the Great Powers. They can even pull the lion's tail from time to time and get away with it.

NOTES

1. Authorized translation, Allen and Unwin, London, 1932, Chapter III.
2. *The Cambridge Ancient History*, Vol. III, Cambridge University Press, 1925, is one example.
3. Translated by J. D. Duff, The Clarendon Press, Oxford, 1926.
4. Op. cit., pp. 151–3.
5. Cambridge University Press, 1966. Chapter IX, 'Relations with Foreign Peoples'.
6. I. C. Y. Hsü, *China's Entrance into the Family of Nations*, Harvard U.P., Cambridge, Mass., 1960.
7. See *Essentials of Indian Statecraft, Kautilya's Arthasastra, for Contemporary Readers*, by T. N. Ramaswamy, Asia, London, 1962.
8. Princeton University Press, 1960, pp. 495–6.
9. These techniques are well described in Andrew Scott's *The Revolution in Statecraft*, Random House, New York, 1965.
10. M. N. Tod, *International Arbitration among the Greeks*, The Clarendon Press, Oxford, 1913.
11. *History of the Peloponnesian War*, translated by Rex Warner, Penguin Books, 1954, Book 1, Chapter I, p. 25.
12. See R. W. Moore, *The Roman Commonwealth*, Hodder and Stoughton, London, 1942, pp. 44–57.
13. Op. cit., p. 338.
14. Edited by Edmund Walsh, Georgetown University, New York, 1922, p. 72.

Three

Origins and Growth of the System

WE ended the previous chapter with a reference to the political organization of mediaeval Europe in so far as it foreshadowed the contemporary régime or formula for the conduct of international relations. It did so in the twofold sense, firstly, that from the mediaeval order sprang the secular conception of government— that is, the idea that the object of government is earthly advantage and not necessarily the greater glory of God or preferment on Judgment Day—and, secondly, that mediaeval Europe repre- sented the fragmentation of former imperial wholes, which left elements to be regrouped into the later national states.

There is, however, a striking forerunner of the later European multi-state system to be found in the political and diplomatic system of Renaissance Italy.[1] The opulent Renaissance cities of Venice, Milan, Florence and Naples, together with the Papacy, mirrored in small scale the later European world of the Great Powers. Many of the diplomatic practices of the Europe of the last two or three centuries were introduced by these Italian city-states, as for instance the permanent diplomatic mission with its immu- nity from the local legal system. But one of the most significant in- ventions of Renaissance Italy was the idea that the diplomatic envoy had a strictly utilitarian and secular function, which was wholly contained within the notion of service to his own sovereign. The textbook entitled *De Officiis Legati* ('on the duties of an envoy'), written by Ermolao Barbaro during his Venetian embassy in Rome, whither he went in 1490, explains the new Renaissance principle of diplomacy: 'the first duty of the ambassador is the same as that of any other government servant: to do, say and advise whatever may best serve the preservation and aggrandize- ment of his own state'.[2]

The present-day reader would no doubt consider such a defi- nition of the diplomat's role to be hardly novel. Today the diplomat would be judged as untrue to his calling and disloyal to his employers, the government and taxpayers, if he did not define his business in somewhat similar terms. In Barbaro's time, however, such words must have caused many people shock and indignation. After all, throughout the Middle Ages all government and activities carried on by government had a strongly religious association about them. It is doubtful whether in those times any aspect of human life or behaviour was entirely free from essentially religious overtones. The public man, in whatever capacity he acted, owed—at least in theory—his ultimate allegiance to the Pope in Rome and through him to God. The idea that any public duty could be performed wholly or solely in relation to a state, kingdom or monarch must have seemed to the generality of people deeply repellent, though for the most part it is taken for granted today. Such is the extent of the changes in thought about government effected by the public servants and scribes of the Renaissance.

But we can go much further than this and say that in the contemporary international system which we have today there exists, besides the oscillations between tendencies towards unification and tendencies towards the preservation of the different individual units, a bipolarity between belief in the world-wide creed, and belief in the self-sufficient virtues of the independent secular state. When, in the twentieth century, leaders of opinion like Woodrow Wilson have summoned mankind to renounce the nation-state and national interests and bind themselves together in a world-wide community of power in which the interests of the whole world would take precedence, in the minds of ordinary men and women, over the interests of the part, they were in effect repudiating the diplomatic principles of Barbaro which the Renaissance system proclaimed and later bequeathed to the European state system as a whole. This conflict between the whole and the part in international relations can be seen even more dramatically in the political programme and strategy of Marshal Stalin in the period between the two World Wars. At the Central Committee of the Soviet Communist Party in Moscow in 1927 Stalin proclaimed his famous axiom: 'he is an internationalist who unhesitatingly, unconditionally and without vacillation is ready to defend the USSR'. And also: 'it is impossible to defend the world movement unless the USSR is defended'.[3] Again, there is seen here the subordination of national loyalties (other than those owed by

Soviet citizens to the Soviet Union) to the world faith, the latter being understood as unflinching service to the Soviet Union as the state in which the one true faith has been materialized. In the 1930s, therefore, Communists outside the Soviet Union who wished to remain within the brotherhood of the Third International found that, like the disciples of Christ, they were called upon to put aside family, kith and kin and follow the Master. We can understand, in the light of this, the horror and indignation of those who, like George Orwell in the Spanish Civil War in the 1930s, found that in reality the Communists were fighting, not in the first instance for the freedom of Spain or other such national causes, but for the triumph of a world-wide faith, the prophet of which had his headquarters in Moscow. George Orwell discovered to his deepest dismay that the principles of international action had retrogressed to the time before Ermolao Barbaro.

Bearing in mind, then, the politics of mediaeval Europe and the new principles of government introduced by the Renaissance, it is clear that the modern international system can be regarded as having emerged into the light of day when two of its basic characteristics took shape: the secular principle, or the spirit of *raison d'état*, which first became established in the minds of thinking men about the sixteenth and seventeenth centuries, and, secondly, what we have called the 'fragmentation' principle, or in other words the waning of the idea of a united Europe as a dominant object of policy. The latter development we have to place at a later date, perhaps as late as the beginning of the nineteenth century. Hence, the answer to the question, when did our modern international system originate or, when did it emerge in the form with which we are familiar today, is essentially twofold. Namely, that if we think *raison d'état* to be the most distinctive mark of modern government, we should be inclined towards placing the origins of the system some four hundred years ago, say, in the sixteenth century, whereas if we are thinking of modern international relations as dominated by national interest, with little or no deference towards any ecumenical centre, we should incline to regard the beginning of the nineteenth century as having inaugurated the age of the modern international system.

Let us look at the idea of the emergence of *raison d'état* first. In the sixteenth century, with the consolidation of the great monarchical states of Austria, England and France, the notion was coming to be accepted that by sovereignty was meant a monarch's or state's freedom from all external restraints, legal, moral or religious, and that the purpose and justification of government was the advancement of that territorial entity, the state. This is the principle argued in the sixteenth century by Niccolò Macchiavelli and Jean Bodin in their revolutionary works. It is well expressed in Bodin's celebrated apothegm: *majestas est summa in cives ac subditos legisbusque soluta potestas* ('sovereignty is supreme power over citizens and subjugated peoples and is bound by no other law'). The last three words in that expression encapsulate the principle of *raison d'état*.

Raison d'état was never in theory, though it may have been so bandied about in the practical arena of politics, equivalent to the crude and ruthless maximization of the power of a particular state.[4] It has generally and more accurately been regarded as a certain political and indeed moral obligation: the duty of a government to study intensively and without pause what is required to preserve the security and satisfy the needs of the state in an anarchical international system and a certain inescapable complex of space relationships *vis-à-vis* its neighbours. The question in the forefront of the sovereign's or government's mind must be: what kind of policy at a particular juncture of affairs does physical security, immunity from foreign attack or control, the well-being and advancement of the people necessitate? The imperative ('must') in that sentence implies that a ruler may, if he so cares, neglect those necessities of state, but that if he does, he does so at his own cost and will in the course of time be succeeded by another sovereign who takes his obligations more seriously: or, if that does not happen, the state will perish and its land and resources will be inherited by another state which takes a more conscientious and prudent view of the necessities confronting it. But recognition of certain determinate necessities of state assuredly does not mean an invariable policy of expansion or aggression at the expense of another state. Sometimes it may dictate withdrawal or even surrender. *Raison d'état* prescribes the compulsion to act in accordance as the interests of the state determine at any given moment in history. The individual statesman or the government may from time to time misinterpret the interests of the state, but this does not affect the permanence and ubiquity of the principle at stake.

In the second place, *raison d'état* involves the clearest possible perception of *other* states and of what the necessities of a situation require of them and their governments. The wise ruler, acting from the principle of *raison d'état*, will endeavour to be as familiar with the interests of other states as he is with those of his own. He must recognize the fact that the governments of those other states will be acting on the basis of the best available understanding of the interests of their own states. And that those governments cannot be expected, any more than he himself, to be bullied out of defending the interests of their states unless they are in the desperate situation of having no alternative before them other than that of relinquishing their obligations. At the same time, just as we have insisted that *raison d'état* does not necessarily demand a belligerent attitude towards other states, neither does it always assume incompatibility between state interests or conflict between states, rather than co-operation. It is, for all we know in a particular instance, just as likely that 'reason of state' may demand co-operation with other states as it may require conflict. But neither conflict nor co-operation are presupposed: the primacy of *raison d'état* is. Statesmanship lies in discerning where unities of interest exist and how co-operation may be built upon them. No one but the occasional lunatic, or mentally deranged leader, wants conflict for its own sake.

Hence we may find in this argument the explanation of the paradox sometimes dwelt upon by Professor H. J. Morgenthau, namely that the government acting from considerations of national interest may show more respect for the moral values of Western civilization, such as tolerance, restraint and ability to see both sides of an argument, than a government acting in pursuit of different goals, as for instance the imposition of some kind of moral or political order on the world. The practitioner of *raison d'état* respects the right of other states to exist and to defend their national interests because he knows that to deny that right (which is bound to be intensely claimed) is to waste his own resources on fruitless and unnecessary tasks. He also recognizes, as we have pointed out above, that in order to safeguard the interests of his own state, he must often seek the support of other states, and that support is not likely to be gained by those who are blind to the interests of those whose support they need. *Raison d'état* is also closely associated with the principle of non-interference in the internal affairs of other states, difficult as it may be to observe this principle at the present day, when the internal and external affairs of states are so inextricably confused. *Raison d'état* discourages interference in the internal affairs of other states since one of the most cherished areas of sovereign self-government is the state's own private domain, which it is an elementary object of *raison d'état* to protect. Above all, the practitioner of *raison d'état* is bound to have a declining interest in violence and war in the relations between nations, as weapons of mass destruction have become more and more diabolical with the progress of twentieth-century technology. It is significant that in the nuclear age it was Mr. Nikita Khrushchev, always a zealous champion of the necessities of state of the Soviet Union, who used to call most insistently for peaceful co-existence between the Communist and non-Communist worlds on the ground that, like the animals in Noah's ark, we would all run the risk of drowning in the most horrible way possible unless we learned somehow to contain our differences and live together in peace.

Finally, and following on from the above, it by no means signifies that to act from *raison d'état* in international relations is necessarily to act immorally, or even amorally. The secular ruler, wishing to observe the axioms of 'reason of state', is probably more, not less, likely to suffer from moral questionings than the ruler wholly preoccupied with his place in some divine ordering of things. The religious or theocratic ruler has his own reasons for thinking that during his daily work he is in very truth performing God's mission. He can have no doubt about the long-term moral rightfulness of his vocation, even though from time to time he may have doubts of a technical character, that is to say, he may doubt whether a particular action in operation or contemplation most expediently advances his larger life purposes, about which he can never be in any doubt. The secular ruler or sovereign, on the other hand has never ceased to be plagued by moral questionings, especially after the advent of Christianity, which presented its followers with endless problems of choice between doing a little evil so as to avoid having to do a greater evil, on one side, and retiring wholly from the political scene and watching from the sidelines even more evil being done by others. The secular ruler is bound to compare the moral values of his own people with those of another people, to reflect whether and how to do evil, which he hopes will be limited in its effects, in the hope somehow, somewhere, of doing good to others, and to weigh the moral right of his own people to prosper and be free from external interference against the moral right of other people to be left alone and allowed to cultivate their own gardens. In short, the principle of *raison d'état* does not end the moral problems of statesmanship; on the contrary, it initiates them.

Accordingly, we are bound to regard the advent of the principle of *raison d'état* as one of the possible historical starting points for the international system which we have today. If we accept this particular criterion for determining the date of origin of the international system, we would have to see our state system of today as emerging in about the sixteenth century. But there is another important criterion, which takes us back to the waning of the Middle Ages. That is the acceptance by Europe temporarily of a system of fragmented, dispersed, decentralized power, and the apparent abandonment, again temporarily, of the idea of a united Christian Europe, in which arrangement each state acquires its significance from being a member of a team rather than from being an entity in its own right. This criterion, as already stated, could give us a date of origin for the international system somewhere at the end of the eighteenth or beginning of the nineteenth century. The two criteria, then, secular politics and the dispersion of power, are essential marks of the contemporary international system. By referring to them, we can see the two historical poles between which modern international politics sprang into being. It is still a matter of debate, however, whether we should push the actual date of origin of the system towards the earlier or the later date. Much will depend upon which of the two principles is considered more vital for the birth of modern international politics.

One of the principal exponents of the idea that it is the second of these two criteria, namely the disintegration of a postulated united Europe, which most accurately defines the modern international system, is F. H. Hinsley of Cambridge. In his book *The Power and the Pursuit of Peace* Hinsley argues that a system of sovereign states could not come into being until the mediaeval conception of a single Christian and European republic (*magna civitas Christiana*) had given way to a system of separate states with interests more or less sharply differentiated from each other.[5] In more specific terms, Hinsley writes that the outlines of our

modern system became discernible when the Turkish threat to
Europe began to decline towards the end of the seventeenth
century and European affairs at last ceased to be those of a
united but beleaguered fortress besieged by the rulers of Constantinople. It could be argued indeed, Hinsley maintains, that
this process of the fragmentation of Europe, which began with
the decline of the idea of a single Christian republic, was not
really completed until 1815, when the defeat of Napoleon I at
Waterloo at length put an end, once and for all, to the vision of a
recreated and reunited Christian Europe.[6]

Professor Hinsley regards this process of the emergence of the
modern European multi-state system as having culminated in the
mid-eighteenth century, though not as having been definitely
completed until 1815. He examines three levels on which it is
possible to see this transformation taking place: the level of
writers about international affairs, the level of international law
and the level of diplomatic practice. As for the first of these, a
transition can be seen from seventeenth-century writers such as
William Penn, Bellers, Leibniz, St. Pierre and Fénelon, who
continued to think in terms of the rebirth of the supposed 'single
civitas' of the mediaeval period, to one such as Jean Rousset de
Missy, who invented the term 'droit de convenance' to describe
the concept of the balance of power, not, as heretofore, a device
for the maintenance of order in the whole European society, but
as an instrument used by sovereign states as a matter of ex-
pediency and in order to preserve their independence. Rousset
was writing in the 1730s. After the 1730s, Hinsley writes:

> The idea of Europe as a whole was restored but there was a shift
> of emphasis, from concentration on Europe's unity to concentra-
> tion on the autonomy of states. Rousset was close to making that
> shift. In another ten or fifteen years, in the writings of men like
> Montesquieu, Voltaire, Hume and Rousseau, we have for the
> first time abundant evidence that is has been made.[7]

A similar shift of focus can be seen in European thought in the
mid-eighteenth century in the field of international law. In
essence this change represents, if we can speak in highly simpli-
fied terms, the movement from a naturalistic to a positivistic
theory of international law. In Hugo Grotius in the early seventeenth century the rules of international law were identical with

the rules of any Christian society in which the Bible and 'right reason' (in that order of importance) were the true sources of legal right and wrong. International law had no other purpose, Grotius considered, than to serve the good of the whole:

> Just as the laws of each state have in view the advantage of that state, so by mutual consent it has become possible that certain laws should originate as between all states, or a great many states; and it is apparent that the laws thus originating had in view the advantage, not of particular states, but of the great society of states. And this is what is called the law of nations, whenever we distinguish that from the law of nature.[8]

The Swiss lawyer Vattel, however, writing some 130 years later, had an entirely different conception of the international society and international law, one more in accordance with the usages of the contemporary international system. Vattel begins, not with the single Christian republic of Europe, which is by now a part of history, but with the national state, and the collectivity of states he describes as follows:

> Nations or states are political bodies, societies of men who have united together and combined their forces in order to preserve their mutual welfare and security. Such a society has its own affairs and interests; it deliberates and takes resolutions in common, and thus it becomes a moral person having an understanding and will peculiar to itself and susceptible at once of obligations and rights.[9]

It is evident that we are here approaching the modern shibboleth, that in affairs of state necessity may sometimes know no law. For Vattel continues:

> The first general law . . . is that each nation should contribute as far as it can to the happiness and advancement of other nations. But as its duties towards itself clearly prevail over its duties towards others, a nation owes to itself, as a prime consideration, whatever it can do for its own happiness and advancement . . . When therefore a nation cannot contribute to the welfare of another nation without doing an essential wrong to itself, its obligation ceases in this particular instance and the nation is regarded as lying under a disability to perform the duty (to others).[10]

This is, assuredly, speaking with the accents of the present age, though still with some echoes from the past.

As to the third level, the practice of diplomacy, it is significant that the Treaty of Utrecht, signed in 1713, was the last great European international convention to refer to the old *Respublica Christiana*. By the mid-eighteenth century there was coming into existence that approximation towards an equality of power between the separate states of the European system without which the multi-state system is inconceivable. F. H. Hinsley, to cite him once again, writes:

> The condition of near-equality between several states, replacing a long-standing situation in which Europe had been dominated by two conflicting leading states (Austria vs. France), each suspecting the other of the goal of universal monarchy, and dividing the rest of Europe into their two rival camps, is the key to the development of the system in the high eighteenth century.[11]

There is an obvious parallel here to the tension between the biplolar system of fifth-century Greece B.C., which we described in the previous chapter, and the impulses tending towards multi-polarity in that system.[12] There is a similarity, too, in the tendency towards polycentrism in the world of the early 1970s as a development away from the two-camp system of the Communist and non-Communist countries which prevailed in the two decades or so following the Second World War.

There is clearly much persuasive force in Professor Hinsley's argument. But it should be recalled that historical developments such as the emergence of the world-wide international system of states, which is the subject of the present book, never occur in any very clear-cut manner. The intimations of great changes in human society may be signalled long before men become aware that they are happening. Residues of former systems and 'manners of attending to the arrangements of society'[13] linger on when a new order is already in being, perhaps even when it is fully mature. Thus it is important to stress that the birth of modern international politics, while it is certainly visible in the intellectual changes noted by Hinsley in the eighteenth century, can perhaps more accurately be discerned in the advent of the notion of *raison d'état* as much as two centuries earlier. We must, of course, separate political thought from political practice. The erosion of political forms resulting from public criticism may take decades or centuries to work itself out, and older practices may continue to receive lip-service even when goals and motives of political activity have undergone revolutionary change. Nevertheless, it would be wrong to ignore, in the advent of nationalist particularism in the mid-eighteenth century, the influence of the long exposure men had had by that time to the powerful attractions of 'reason of state'.

It is doubtful, too, whether the conception of the 'single Christian republic' was ever quite the common cause of states and government which it has so often been represented as having been. The call of locality has always surely been strong, the appeal of a whole civilization relatively weak, especially in ages when communications and transport were primitive. As early as the first decades of the fourteenth century, for example, Pierre Dubois was advocating a united Christian crusade against the East. But, according to C. J. H. Hayes, this was by no means conceived in the old spirit of subordinating the individual European states to the abstraction of a united Christian Europe. Hayes writes:

> Dubois had in mind the truly mediaeval purpose of recovering the Holy Land from the Mahommedans and for this purpose he urged the cessation of war within Christendom and the co-operation of all Christian peoples. But he departed fundamentally from earlier mediaeval ideas when he advocated as head of his league . . . neither the Pope nor the German Emperor but the King of France.

This, Hayes continues, 'is fierce nationalism; this is rampant imperialism. It is essentially modern, not mediaeval'.[14]

At the other end of the time spectrum we need not go as far as Hinsley in attributing the full maturation of the international system to the final defeat of Napoleon Bonaparte in 1815. In the first place, despite all the antique trappings of the Bonapartist régime, it is overstraining the truth to see in Napoleon the last fling of mediaeval Europe. The French Emperor was no doubt at times captivated by that brand of mission, but the whole thrust of his régime was essentially modern. Nor, of course, is it correct to describe the Napoleonic régime as the last effort to force the different European states back into a single common mould—

under French auspices, as it goes without saying. Another Frenchman, Charles de Gaulle, seems to have shared somewhat the same ambition during the Fifth Republic in the 1960s. So, it seems, did Adolf Hitler. And so perhaps did Marshal Stalin in the years immediately following the cessation of fighting in Europe in May 1945. As we have pointed out in the previous chapter, in our international system tendencies to unify the whole have always alternated, and sometimes clashed, with tendencies to maintain the independence and autonomy of the several parts of the whole.

To sum up, then, we may identify two criteria for declaring that the modern international system has made its appearance in man's political history; and we are concerned with this process of birth, not so much for its intrinsic historical interest, but as a means of defining what the international system is and what constitutes its principal properties. The first of these criteria we have described as the secularization of political activity resulting from the advent of the principle of *raison d'état*; the second, the fragmentation of the mediaeval conception of a single European state into a constellation of near-equal sovereign states, each with its distinct and separate interests to protect, and no longer regarding as the foremost object of its policy the preservation and advancement of a united Christian family under the Pope.

Perhaps the most accurate way of conceiving the origins of the international system is as a lengthy process extending from the mid-sixteenth to perhaps the mid-eighteenth century. At the earlier extreme along this historical spectrum, the modern system began to take shape when the rulers of Europe first started to think of their business as essentially material and earthly, rather than religious, or in other words as the conduct of the affairs of the secular state: all which was not God's domain was Caesar's domain. At the later end of the spectrum, and nearer to us in time, there was the acceptance of Europe, no longer as a single estate, the interests and welfare of which had to be defended against the infidels by sovereign and people alike, but as a collection of separate entities with interests unique to themselves. These entities were regarded as associated together by principles of law and morality which echoed the older unity of the whole, but which might from time to time have to give way to the even greater necessities of the sovereign state.

NOTES

1. For an account see Bozeman, op. cit., pp. 459–89.
2. See Garrett Mattingly, *Renaissance Diplomacy*, Cape, London, 1955, p. 117.
3. *Soviet Documents on Foreign Policy*, Selected and edited by Jane Degras, Vol. II, 1925–1932, O.U.P., London, 1952, p. 243.
4. Perhaps the best-known lengthy account of *raison d'état* is Friedrich Meinecke's *Macchiavellism: the doctrine of reason of state in modern history*, first published in 1924 and translated by Douglas Scott, Routledge and Kegan Paul, London, 1957.
5. Cambridge University Press, 1963.
6. Op. cit., Chapter 8.
7. Ibid., p. 162.
8. *De iure belli ac pacis*. The Classics of International Law, ed. by J. B. Scott, Carnegie Endowment, p. 15.
9. *Droit des gens*, tr. by C. G. Fenwick, The Classics of International Law, ed. by J. B. Scott, Vol. III, p. 3.
10. Vattel, op. cit., p. 6.
11. Hinsley, op. cit., p. 176.
12. See above, Chapter Two, pp. 44–7.
13. The phrase is Professor Michael Oakeshott's.
14. 'Mediaeval Diplomacy' in E. A. Walsh (ed.), *The History and Nature of International Relations*, Georgetown University, Georgetown Foreign Service Series, New York, 1922.

C

Four

The Impact of Change

THE international political system, set against the background of the many forms of international organization which preceded it, has therefore been relatively short-lived, and is, at most, less than three centuries old. It is none the less older than any conflict or any other type of mutual relationship that has occurred between its member-states. Hence it is more to the point to regard such occurrences in the relations between states as having taken place within the context of the international system, than to think of the system as having been formed from these occurrences. Moreover, the international system has by no means remained unaffected by the tides of history. Change has been continuous and never more so than during the twentieth century. Two of these major changes will be considered in this chapter; taken together, their effects may be described as having constituted an enlargement or expansion of the system. Before discussing these changes in detail, however, some general points should be made about their consequences for the international system as a whole and its method of functioning.

The first of these consequences has been negative. It is that the two changes we are referring to do not appear to have affected what may be called the basic dynamics of the international system. International politics seem to have continued, and still continue, much as they have since the origins of the international system. The second effect is more positive, though possessing some negative aspects. This is that in so far as the international system has felt the impact of historical change, the effect has been to import certain frictions into the workings of the machine. The machine does not appear to be working as smoothly or as efficiently as it did before these changes occurred. 'Noise' has entered the system, so to speak, and one effect of this is that the international system of states has been made the focus of more academic study in the past fifty or sixty years than ever before. But this is not surprising; we are rarely conscious of the bones in our body until they begin to ache.

The first of the two changes we refer to is the advent of the principle of nationality, which occurred in the first century of the life of the international system: hence the latter's name. The principle of nationality has been active ever since. The advent of nationality implies, in the first instance, the replacement of the divine right of kings as the essential and legitimate basis of sovereign authority within the different states, by the divine right of nations: by nations meaning certain psychocultural groups whose members share various cultural affinities and exhibit a determination to become one day a state, the legal equal of other states within the international system. Secondly, once the nationality principle became embedded in the international system a practical criterion for drawing boundaries between one state and another was supplied; boundaries became recognized as lines dividing people of one nationality, as defined above, from people of another. It now becomes a fundamental ideological axiom of the international community that the political map of the world should conform, as far as contrivance can make it do so, with the ethnographic map of the world.

We are thus able to visualize a process of transformation within the international system in which three major stages predominate. Firstly, there was the stage during which nationality was not officially recognized by the various governments as relevant to the constitution of the states, and during which the monarchs considered themselves as 'fathers of the people' in the mediaeval fashion, as did the governments constituting the Holy Alliance in 1815. Secondly, there was the stage during which the mature European states in the mid-nineteenth century accepted nationalism as their basic constitutive principle and regarded themselves, in the manner of Mazzini's celebrated image, as forming a great concert, each nationality playing its own tune and making its contribution to the 'virtues of diversity'.[1] And thirdly, there was the stage at which President Wilson called for the ordering of the world system on national lines and for the formation of mutual guarantees among the different states for the protection of national boundaries and national homelands.

The principle of nationality may be regarded as predominantly rational or predominantly irrational; but perhaps its strength and vitality lie in the fact that the national principle is in reality both at the same time. It has been argued—on behalf of the rational interpretation—that, just as Karl Marx saw the history of social classes as one of the products of technological progress in manufacture, so the nation came into existence, uniting petty principalities, minor city-states and dukedoms, as the largest governable body able to afford security to the people forming it against the most destructive basis of weapon-power at that time, namely gunpowder. When men saw the independent cities of the Middle Ages falling like the walls of Jericho before the bombardments of gunpowder, they clamoured for the larger protection afforded by the nation-state. This, the rational or pragmatic function of the state, has been well described by John Herz.[2]

Lord Acton, on the other hand, writing of nationality as a historian, drew attention to the irrational sources of the phenomenon. It was, he wrote, the partitions of Poland at the end of the eighteenth century which first undermined confidence in the prevailing system of dynastic absolutism, when, according to Fénelon, 'a princess carried a monarchy as her wedding portion'.

> For the first time in modern history (wrote Acton) a great state was suppressed and a whole nation divided among its enemies. This famous measure . . . awakened the theory of nationality in Europe, converting a dormant right into an aspiration and a sentiment into a political claim . . . Thenceforward there was a nation demanding to be united in a state . . . for the first time a cry was heard that the arrangements of states were unjust.[3]

Not perhaps for the first time. Nevertheless, the fate of Poland and the violent emotions which it evoked in Europe, certainly played their part in making nationality an informing principle of the international system. In 1919 the rebirth of Poland was the centrepiece for the general liberation of the suppressed nationalities of Europe to which President Wilson gave his blessing. In 1945 the subordination of the independent life of Poland to the Soviet Union set alarm bells ringing round western Europe as to the future security of the national states of the world outside the Communist pale.

It is well-known that the French Revolution of 1789 gave a powerful impetus to the principle of nationality and to the doctrine of national self-determination, which aspires to the incorporation of nationality in a political form. The armies of the French Revolution carried these electrifying ideas from one country in Europe to another. They found in them a weapon of the utmost power for splitting open the dynastic multinational empires which stood in their path. The period between the defeat of Napoleon in 1815 and the outbreak of the First World War, all but a hundred years later, saw the widening acceptance of the nationality principle in liberal Europe. This, despite the fact that it took the First World War to shatter the fetters of the Romanov, Hohenzollern, Habsburg and Ottoman empires and set free the nations imprisoned within them. Since the Second World War this explosive principle has been applied in the extra-European world, with the resulting creation of a host of new African and Asian states out of the old and proud European empires.

The assumption of liberal thought on international relations has been that the attainment of national self-determination is somewhat more than a moral right, though less than a legal right. It was also considered to be the *sina qua non* of a peaceful international system. J. S. Mill, for instance, argued in his *Considerations on Representative Government* that in the long run there could be no place for free institutions outside the borders of the national state, and free institutions in the liberal mind were indispensable to well-ordered and peaceful international relations. In Mill's thinking, once the aspiration for independent national statehood was firmly implanted in the minds of any community, it would never be satisfied with the existing order of things until that aspiration was realized.[4] This is the thesis underlying the claim of the NATO states since at least 1955 that until the Germans are freely united in a national state once more, there will be a grave element of unrest and instability in the heart of Europe.

But this claim, that the national basis of inter-state relations predisposes those relations towards peace, has often been challenged. Scholars, such as Professor Kedourie, who write in the tradition of Lord Acton, see no reason why the nationalist leader should not regard his own people, like any people outside the sacred circle of the nation, as cannon-fodder in wars of his own making waged on behalf of his greater power and glory.[5] The twentieth century is far too familiar with the merciless excesses, against fellow nationals as much as against foreigners, and ruthless aggression against neighbours, which certain types of nationalism can inspire, to accept Mill's view of the virtues of nationalism as an instrument of peace in the world. The very insistence, contained within the principle of national self-determination, that national enclaves beyond the nation's borders must one day be brought within those borders is bound to engender national strife. And this, particularly whenever the national principle collides with other principles, such as a state's need to be viable, have defensible frontiers, good communications and so on: from this collision sprang the crisis of Czechoslovakia in 1938. The imposition of Communist rule on eastern Europe by Marshal Stalin in 1945, though no doubt an affront to political morality in any Western sense of that term, has at least had the advantage of extinguishing the time-honoured squabbles over frontiers and national minorities which characterized east European political life in the period between the two wars. It also had the effect of putting an end to the imbalance of power created in European politics by the formation of a united national German state in Europe in and after 1871.

But whatever the intrinsic merits or demerits of the national principle, its effects on the working of the international system have undoubtedly been profound. First, there has been the purely quantitative effect; in other words a dramatic increase in the number of states participating in the international system. National self-determination, after all, represents the making of new states through a process of the breaking of old states; the core of the system enlarges itself by fission. The apogee of this process has been reached in the period since 1945, when the 51 states represented at the conference in San Francisco for the negotiation of the United Nations Charter has increased to the 140 members of the United Nations today (1975), an increase of about 150 per cent. During this process of expansion many 'mini-states' have been created consisting of tiny populations and often insignificant natural resources which throw doubt on the whole principle of sovereign equality of UN member-states, regardless of size or power. The paradox of the 'mini-states', however, has not much troubled majorities in the United Nations General Assembly, which continue fervently to vote for national self-determination for any colony, no matter how small or however precarious the prospects for survival of the self-determined state.

It might be argued that the greater the number of member-states in any international system, the greater the number of potential quarrels between them. According to one well-known formula, the number of potential quarrels in any society increases, not in arithmetic, but in geometrical proportion to the number of members in the society.[6] But this seems to confuse quantity with quality, or rather with intensity. A certain society may experience a great number of quarrels between its members, but each quarrel, and certainly all of them together, may be less in intensity and destructiveness than one big quarrel which splits the society into two, fairly equal armed camps. It may not be too fanciful in fact to discern in the international system a 'law of conservation of tension', as it may be called, according to which there always seems to be a stable and unchanging level of friction between the members of the system. If the tension is not expressed in one part of the system, it tends to remain available for use in another part. We will return to this 'law' in a later chapter. For the present it is sufficient to note that a conflict between two very large and powerful states is obviously a much more serious matter than many trivial disputes between a large number of minor states.

What we are able to say with some confidence, though this is qualitative rather than quantitative in character, is that the greater the number of states in any international system, the more the representation of those states in international organizations will tend to be based on the principle of sovereign equality rather than on the principle of national interests. That is to say, for example, that in the United Nations, the most widely representative organ in the present international system, the verbal participation of all member-states has been widened so as to cover all matters of international concern, without their interests in any one of them having been deepened. All state-members of international organizations have an equal right to speak and to vote, but this is far from saying that all, great and small, have a real interest in or a real capability to affect the outcome of the issue in debate. In the international system of nineteenth-century Europe invitations to international conferences were normally extended only to the 'Powers principally concerned', as the diplomatic formula had it. The rest, who could not affect the outcome anyway, merely had to stand and wait. Today, resolutions issuing from meetings held under the auspices of the United Nations reflect the pattern of opinion among the totality of member-states, though only a minority of those states really have the capacity to implement those resolutions, and they may find themselves on the losing side in the vote. The result tends to be a divorce of the responsibility for deciding UN resolutions from the actual power to influence outcomes in the practical world. In more concrete terms, the United Nations passes as resolutions on controversial issues, such as *apartheid* in South Africa, statements of opinion which alienate those states with effective power to change the situation in countries like South Africa, while frustrating the great majority of states who seem to believe that democracy on the one-state, one-vote model has, or should have, the power to change the course of history.

The second major consequence of the absorption of the national principle by the international system is in regard to the moral attitudes of states towards issues arising within that system. Whatever sacrifices of personal values national loyalty may impose on the individual nationalist, which he may readily accept, there is no question that collectively the nation tends to be a self-regarding animal, prone to disregard the costs of its own well-being in terms of the welfare of other nations. Nationalism has in fact been characterized as organized selfishness. Nations are apt to respect no law higher than their own self-glorification, and governments are liable to feel more secure in power the more they are able to satisfy the nation's demand that its own security and welfare always justify prime consideration.

Moreover, nationalism has become such a powerful force in politics during the past hundred years that all other social developments seem as though they have been drawn into it as a means of buttressing and fortifying its strength. Franz Borkenau in his book *Socialism, national or international* has shown that, since the social reformer must act through the state—in fact, almost by definition, he is bound to wish to make more positive use of the state machinery for the purpose of social betterment than the conservative—he tends to become a more committed nationalist than the conservative.[7] This is why, of course, in Britain since 1945 the Left wing in politics has on the whole been opposed to British membership of integrated European institutions, whereas the Right wing has generally been somewhat more in favour. In Borkenau's vivid phrase, 'nationalism has been socialized and socialism has been nationalized'.

This segregation of all human activities into nationalist compartments, no matter with what cosmopolitan objectives they began, is in sharp contrast with the supposed Christian unity of the European governments before the advent of nationalism. No doubt there never was a time when these governments in their day-to-day affairs regarded themselves as 'brothers in Christ', but at least such was the professed ideal of the *ancien régime* in Europe and many of Europe's rulers at that time were indeed brothers in the literal sense of the word. The possibility certainly existed that state power could be restrained, and restrained with a feeling of rightfulness, by a sense of Christian brotherhood. For the modern nation, on the other hand, the cry goes out, governing both theory and practice: *salus populi suprema lex*. And in consequence, as Winston Churchill once pointed out, the wars of nations have turned out to be far worse than the wars of kings.

The second major change, after nationalism, which has overtaken the modern international system is the geographical expansion of that system. In less than forty years the so-called European 'comity of nations' has become world-wide. This is partly the result of the working out of the principle of nationality beyond the confines of Europe, and partly due to the growth of a world-wide economy and the ceaseless development of transport and communication, partly also because of the weakening of the central European core of the system through two World Wars and their respective aftermaths.

The modern international system of sovereign states is co-extensive with the great globe itself as is strikingly reflected in the composition of present-day international organizations. Forty-five per cent of the membership of the old League of Nations was European. The League was, one might almost say, a European regional institution with a Latin American appendix. Of the existing United Nations organization only 21 per cent of the membership is European. In the United Nations Security Council only two of the permanent members, Britain and France, are in all respects European, while the mere names of the other three, China, the Soviet Union and the United States, suggest the world-wide character of the organization. Moreover, since 1945 the membership of the Security Council has been enlarged from 11 to 15 largely in order to make room for more African and Asian states. Even the Miss World Competition, held in London every year, has been known to be dominated by beauties from the non-European world.

This migration of power from its old European centre outwards has been remarkably recent. The four-Power conference in Munich in September 1938 for the revision of the frontiers of Czechoslovakia could be described as the last great act of the European great Powers. That meeting was, as it happened, the culmination of the consistent effort of the British representative, Neville Chamberlain, to restore what he called the 'comity of Europe'; both Russia and the United States he regarded with almost equal suspicion since both were outside the confines of Europe. Since then the main centres of decision in the international system have been non-European, or largely non-European. Europe, it could be said, once used to make decisions the effects of which were felt outside Europe. Today, or more particularly since 1945, decisions have tended to be taken outside and the effects have been felt inside Europe. Even alliances which are mainly European in composition, such as the NATO and Warsaw Pact systems, have not only been dominated by certain extra-European states, but have tended, again in accordance with our so-called 'law of conservation of tension', to force international tensions outside Europe. It is true that, with the economic revival of Europe during the 1960s and the enlargement of the European Community from six to nine member-states in 1973, doubts have arisen as to whether Europe will continue to be merely the object, rather than the subject, of world-wide diplomacy. But even if those doubts were to be resolved favourably for Europe, it is still hard to imagine the continent within any foreseeable future resuming its old place as the paramount club of the nations.

Seven main stages in the expansion of the international system from its European base can be discerned. First, there was the admission of the United States into the international system by the signature of the Treaty of Paris in 1783, by which the victory of the thirteen colonies in their struggle for independence from Britain was recognized. The United States, however, played no significant part in European affairs until after the civil war in the 1860s and did not enter the European system as an active partner until 1917. Secondly came the recognition of the rebellious Latin American states by George Canning, the British Foreign Secretary in 1823. Thirdly, the Ottoman Empire together with Rumania was admitted to the European system by the Treaty of Paris which concluded the Crimean war in 1856, although it was not until the negotiation of the Treaty of Lausanne in 1922–1923 that the reformed Turkey received its sovereignty and autonomy as a fully mature member of the international system.

Fourthly, Japan joined the international system as a result of being opened up to foreign trade by the American 'black ships' under the command of Commodore Perry in 1853. This was followed by the extraordinarily rapid modernization of the country after its emergence from mediaeval seclusion, the constitutional counterpart of which was the Meiji Restoration in 1868. In 1895 Japan overthrew another member of the international system, China, and in doing so laid claim in the traditional manner to recognition as a Power within the system. This was followed by Japan's defeat of Russia, an old colossus of the diplomatic scene, in 1905; but strictly speaking, it was in 1902 that Japan joined the European, which was then the world-wide, balance of power through her celebrated alliance with Britain. China, the fifth entrant in our succession, joined the international system as a result of diplomatic relations and the unequal treaties being imposed on her by Britain in the mid-nineteenth century. As late as 1919, however, when China attended the peace conference in Paris at the end of the First World War, she was still subject to capitulations and this remained the situation until 1943. At the Washington conference in 1921–1922 China was regarded as a ward of the Powers rather than as a Power in her own right. Then the civil wars in China in the 1920s, followed by the invasion of the country by Japan in 1937, deprived China of an equal place in the international system until she was placed among the United Nations in the Second World War.[8]

The sixth and seventh stages in this historical globalization of the international system were the admission of the Arab states, former dependencies of the Ottoman Empire, as a consequence of their graduation to maturity through the machinery of the 'A' mandates system adopted by the Allied and Associated Powers in

1919; and the vast expansion of the system which came with the decolonization of the old European empires in Africa and Asia and the formation of a host of new states in the years following 1945.

This enormous and speedy geographical expansion of the international system can be described as having militated against the cohesion of that system. The sense of there being a single system, a 'concert of Europe' or 'comity of nations', has to a large extent been dissipated, and processes and procedures for dealing with frictions in the system have been robbed of much of their effectiveness. In particular, there are four ways in which this seems to have happened.

In the first place, in the classical European diplomatic system which received its final *coup de grâce* during the Second World War it was established custom for tensions and conflicts at the core of the system to be resolved by suitable adjustments of resources and territory at the periphery. The appeasement (in the old, respectable sense) of a Power in a quarrel with another Power in the system, or the rewarding of a state for deserting its friends and joining an opposing alliance, could be achieved through compensations at the expense of the world beyond the confines of Europe. Thus, after his dramatic defeat of France in 1870–1871, Chancellor Bismarck suggested that the French should console themselves by annexing Tunisia, which they did ten years later. When the British and French clashed dangerously at Fashoda in 1898 they eventually ended their quarrel by mutual guarantees of their spheres of interest in Egypt and Morocco respectively, and on that foundation they built the Entente Cordiale in 1904. Britain and France, in other words, rewarded each other with tributes paid by the Egyptians and the Moroccans. In April 1915 these two Powers bribed Italy to join the Entente side in the War by promises of parts of Anatolia and Africa when peace was restored. Their failure after the War to make good these promises was an important factor in Italy's estrangement from the democratic Powers under Mussolini. To reduce that estrangement Britain and France at the Stresa conference in April 1935 sought Italian help in building security in Europe by intimating their disinterestedness in regard to Abyssinia and their acquiescence in Italian designs on that country.

This last example, however, is highly significant. It was possibly the final occasion in European history when this kind of compensation could be arranged. Mussolini's reported astonishment that the British government could have attempted, so shortly after the Stresa conference, to throw him out of Abyssinia by League of Nations sanctions shows how strange to the old brand of European politicians was the new idea fostered by the League. This was that a weak or backward country was not necessarily available for annexation by a great Power simply because it was situated in an area where the great Powers had customarily compensated themselves in order to smooth their mutual relations at the centre of the system. Today, what was a new idea in 1935 has become the established rule of the globalized international system.

Secondly, the old European international system was held together, if we may be quite frank about it, by a common feeling of opposition and superiority to the 'lesser breeds without the law' in Africa and Asia, a frame of mind which echoed the European crusades against the infidel Turk long ago. This common European front made itself felt in European solidarity against the nineteenth-century risings in China against Western imperialism. It is significant that one of the few occasions when an international army was formed among the European Powers before 1914 was when the Powers had to stand together to defend their hard-won privileges in China against the Boxer Rebellion in 1900. This common front appeared again at the Algeçiras conference in 1906 when France, backed by Britain, and Germany realized that they differed far less between themselves than they did from the savage world of native Africa, fit only for colonization. Again, the vindictive attitudes of the victorious Allies towards Turkey at the end of the First World War, reflected in the Carthaginian, though fortunately abortive, Treaty of Sèvres signed with Constantinople in August 1920, and the attitudes of the Stresa Powers towards Abyssinia in 1935, suggest that in the period up until the 1930s the European Powers strove energetically to defend their world-wide predominance by fostering a common front among themselves against those who lay beyond the charmed circle of the European family.

Today the reverse is the situation. Instead of the dominating European Powers combining to exploit the rest of the world, there is a schism between the European or Europeanized Powers, with each side doing its best to curry favour with the extra-European (or the Third) World in the hope that it will join one side or the other against its rival. The struggle for the goodwill of the non-European world has become a dominant issue amongst the great Powers of the international system. This is in sharp contrast with the pre-1939 situation, when the solidarity of the great Powers was directed *against* the African and Asian worlds, and this confrontation of Europe versus the rest proved a substantial factor in such unity as Europe then enjoyed. Or, to put the same point another way, race, which was never an issue in international relations even as late as the 1930s, has become a substantial bone of contention since 1945. The paramount Powers, who shared the common conviction that they were one and all congenitally superior to the coloured races, now try to out-shout each other professing that their attitude to the race question is the only enlightened one. When President Eisenhower and Mr. Dulles in 1956 expressed horror at the Anglo-French invasion of Egypt through fear that it would ingratiate Moscow with the Third World they broke, not for the first time, the old common front of great-power unity against the coloured peoples of the world.

Thirdly, and closely associated with the above, is the argument of some that the geographical expansion of the international system has tended to weaken the old religious basis and sanction behind the system of international law. As indicated in the previous chapter,[9] in the mind of writers like Grotius the Bible was one of the most powerful sources of international law. They considered that a judge in a court applying international law would be as justified in searching sacred Christian texts for evidence of the existence of a legal rule as he would be in examining other sources, perhaps even more so. Those religious foundations of international law naturally weakened with the general decline of religious conviction among the Christianized peoples. But, beyond that, the geographical spread of the international system outside Europe brought non-Christian peoples into the system who could only regard international law as, at best, either binding because it was traditional or because it was based on the reciprocal convenience of the various states. The experience of international law by the Chinese in the nineteenth century may be recalled. It was an American missionary, W. A. P. Martin, who introduced international law to the Chinese by translating in 1864 Wheaton's famous treatise on the law of nations into Chinese. Martin, consistent with the typical old Western view of international law as having an essentially Christian basis, regarded Wheaton's textbook as a means of religious conversion. Writing to a friend in 1863, he described his translation as 'a work which might bring this atheistic government to the recognition of God and His Eternal Justice and perhaps impart to them something of the spirit of Christianity'. This was not, however, how the Chinese received Martin's book. A Prince Kung, reporting on Martin's translation for the Imperial throne, wrote that 'in this book there are quite a few methods of controlling and bridling the barbarian consuls, which may be useful to us'. When a revised edition of the book was published, a Chinese foreign affairs expert wrote in the foreword: 'this book can serve as a useful aid to China in planning its border defence'.[10]

Of course, this is by no means to say that non-Christian peoples have been or are today any less scrupulous in their observance of international law than Christian communities. It does mean that as the international system stretched beyond its old European core, at least one of its former sanctions tended to fade away.

Finally, with the geographical dispersion of the international system a new crop of sub-systems within the whole has developed, creating problems of cohesion both within these sub-systems and within the world-wide system itself as allegiance has oscillated from one system to another, from the region to the world and back to the region again. In none of these sub-systems, which we will be considering in some detail in a later chapter, has integration ever been anything like complete. In perhaps the most integrated of these sub-systems, the Communist bloc of states, disintegration began to set in with the Sino-Soviet conflict, and even in the Soviet bloc itself there have in recent years been strong indications of centrifugal forces at work. Nevertheless, the modern state has had in the period since 1945 two different kinds of society in which it has to live: the global society represented by the international system as a whole, and the more intimate regional sub-system formed by the state and its immediate neighbours, though the Commonwealth is a notable example of a distinct sub-system, with its own organs of consultation, which is not, however, regional in character. This means that the question of how the global system and the particular sub-system can be co-ordinated together raises problems for most states which were never envisaged in the old, internally consolidated European order.

Hence the momentous changes and developments experienced by the international system have not always been for the benefit of mankind, nor made for good relations between its various sections. But we are not interested here in constructing a kind of profit and loss account, which must involve the making of moral judgments in which the scholar has no particular skill. What we have done, by taking two of the most outstanding of these developments, the advent of the principle of nationality and the extra-Europeanization of the international system, is to show that while that system has felt the impact of far-reaching changes, its basic *modus operandi* has remained much the same. If *raison d'état* was a leading consideration at the birth of the international system, it remains the same today; and so on. However, in so far as there has been basic change, the effect has been to introduce 'grit' into the wheels of the international system—to reduce its efficiency and cohesion. In spreading on a world-wide scale the system has acquired variety and novelty. But its joints creak and ache more than men ever remember them having done in the past.

NOTES

1. The phrase is Professor Elie Kedourie's; see his *Nationalism*, Hutchinson's University Library, London, 3rd edition, 1966, Chapter II.
2. In *International Politics in the Atomic Age*, Columbia University Press, New York, 1959.
3. *Essays on Freedom and Power*, selected by Gertrude Himmelfarb, The Free Press, New York, 1948, Chapter VI, p. 171.
4. Chapter XVI, 'Of Nationality, as connected with representative government', in J. S. Mill, *Utilitarianism, Liberty, Representative Government*, Introduced by A. D. Lindsay, Dent, Everyman's Library, London, 1910.
5. See *Nationalism*. It is curious to read in this book that nationalism is a doctrine 'invented in the early part of the nineteenth century'.
6. See below, p. 260.
7. G. Routledge and Sons, London, 1942.
8. Even so, at the Yalta conference in February 1945, at which China was not represented, President Roosevelt, in accepting Marshal Stalin's territorial demands in the Far East at China's expense, undertook to secure Chiang Kai-shek's agreement later.
9. See pp. 60–1.
10. Hsü, *China's Entrance into the Family of Nations*, p. 135.

Five

Centuries of War and Peace

IN the previous chapter we discussed two of the most important changes which have overtaken the international system since it first became recognizable as a distinct social and political order. It is now appropriate, within the general framework provided by these changes, to examine the experience of the international system during the nineteenth and twentieth centuries in order to bring out more clearly the process by which the system has come to be what it is today. Two questions in particular will concern us. Firstly, why did the system function without catastrophic shocks in the nineteenth century—the century of quintessentially *European* international relations—or, in other words, why was that a 'century of peace'? And secondly, why did the century of peace terminate in 1914 and bequeath to us a 'century of total war'?

The peaceful and warlike natures of the last and the present centuries respectively are well reflected in the interest intellectual circles took in the study of international politics before 1914 and after 1918. Before 1914, certainly in the Anglo-Saxon countries, international studies as we know them today, and even the idea of international relations as a distinct field of intellectual speculation, hardly existed. For all the interest social investigators like Sidney and Beatrice Webb and their circle in Edwardian England took in international affairs, it might seem as though those affairs were not in motion. An even more striking example is the intellectual currents which surrounded, say, Rupert Brooke in the decade or so before 1914. As described by Brooke's biographer, Christopher Hassall, the poet was the centre of a coterie of intellectuals which met in Cambridge and included the most talented and politically conscious men and women of his day: J. M. Keynes, Bernard Shaw, H. G. Wells, Leonard Woolf, D. H. Lawrence, the Webbs and many others of the same mental stature were among them. They talked about every subject under the sun, and the contemporary state of society was never far from their conversation, but they hardly ever discussed international affairs.[1] The international system, like the bones of a healthy person, was ignored because it gave so little trouble. To a generation like ours, on the other hand, which has known Stalin, Hitler, and the nuclear weapon, there can never be a hiatus of that magnitude in our conversations or thoughts. The bones have begun to ache throughout the whole body.

We mean, of course, by the nineteenth century the hundred years which ended, not in 1899, but in 1914, the First World War having been, as the historian Barbara Tuchman once called it, a 'band of scorched earth lying between that time and ours'.[2] The age which began in 1914 truly inaugurated the epoch of contemporary international politics. When the British Foreign Secretary, Sir Edward Grey, said in August 1914 that the lights were going out all over Europe, he might have meant that the continent was about to be convulsed in a mighty war, or that the old Europe would die in the coming struggle. He could more properly have meant that Europe as the essential stage of international politics, or perhaps more truly the only stage, would give way in time to the great globe itself. Combined political, economic, social, military, psychological and intellectual forces were striving together to alter the physical reach of international politics.

The year 1914, or rather the war which began in that year, saw the beginning of the practice of total war, the total mobilization of the national economy for war and later, in some countries, for peace as well. It saw also the beginning of ideological crusades, democratic-type international organizations, the democratization of foreign policy, which thereafter moved from the private Cabinet room and the Chancellery to the market place and public meetings, the use of the fifth column for the purpose of breaking up the social unity of opposing states, the diplomacy of mass persuasion and political warfare, and all those types of international strategy which have come to be known as the 'informal penetration of states'.[3]

To be more precise, we must really look back to 1917 as the year in the First World War when the curtains began to rise on the political world we inhabit today and when its still shadowy outlines first became visible. In 1917 came the Bolshevik Revolution in Russia, which signalized the awful philosophical divide between East and West which has dominated the present age; and not only

that, but the social war at the heart of the capitalist states which
has since become a basic theme in modern life. In 1917, partly as a
consequence of the Russian Revolution, there came the defeat of
great Russian armies by the Germans, bequeathing to Germany
the dream of a *Drang nach Osten*, not through Constantinople and
Baghdad, but through Russia into the world island of Euro-Asia.
The Leninist seizure of power in October 1917, too, touched off
the civil war in Russia, which put into the heads of the Western
allies the idea of setting Japan loose on Russia in her Far Eastern
territories, thus committing Lenin and his successors to a permanent state of anxiety and defensiveness in relation to East Asia.
In April 1917 came the crushing defeat by Germany of France's
long-prepared Nivelle offensive on the Aisne, portending France's
permanent future military inferiority to Germany. In November
1917 the Italians were overwhelmed at the battle of Caporetto,
exposing the whole of southern Europe to German expansion and
laying ultimately the basis for the Pact of Steel of the 1930s, in
which Mussolini gave Germany support in Eastern Europe provided Hitler did not raise the question of the Austrians in the
South Tyrol. And in 1917, among the other events of that *annus
terribilis*, came the momentous entrance of the United States into
the European balance of power, a development which was ultimately to shatter the exclusive domination of the international
system by the European great Powers.

But, to revert to the comparative success of that system in the
hundred years before 1914, that success was registered in the fact
that the five great Powers of the European system—Austria
(Austria-Hungary after 1867), Britain, France, Prussia (Germany
after 1871) and Russia fought no general war among themselves.
Such wars as the great Powers did fight in Europe were either the
inconsequential, though bloody, Crimean war of 1854–1856, or
short-term, highly professional operations like Bismarck's campaigns against Denmark in 1864, against Austria in 1866 and
against France in 1870–1871, none of which gave any indication
of shaking the international system to its foundations. Wars of the
most intense savagery were fought by the European Powers in
Africa and Asia as part of what they called their civilizing mission,
but at its European core the international system was not only for
the most part at peace, it was also free from the kind of tensions
between the states which in the twentieth century have thrown

doubt on the whole future of the international system and indeed of civilization itself.

It goes without saying that this relatively smooth operation of the international system owed practically nothing to international agencies deliberately designed for the maintenance of peace and security, to use the oft-repeated United Nations phrase. The traditional diplomatic agencies, the network of permanent foreign missions throughout the world and all the rules and procedures which went with them played a vital role in the continuous process of adjustment and readjustment by which the great Powers dealt with their differences; but it would have been quite impossible for them to do so had not the disposition towards peaceful compromise existed. The same may be said of the international organization (if anything so informal can be so described) of the Concert of Europe and its ability to iron out differences between the Powers which required collective solutions, as well as the various courts of arbitration which had existed from the time of ancient Greece for the settlement of legal disputes between the states. These bodies were almost all of the most casual and rudimentary character as compared with the gigantic and complex international organizations created after 1918, such as the League of Nations and the United Nations. Their success or relative success as subsidiary aids in keeping the peace for such a long period was by no means due to any such intrinsic factors as the efficiency of their own machinery. They worked, quite simply, because the international system as a whole was oriented towards the maintenance of peace at the core. It was a peace-biased system, where the international system after 1918 was for a variety of reasons war—or tension—biased. Why this was so we most now examine.

To begin with, the mere fact that there had been a great European war, lasting for 23 years, before the nineteenth century started, a war of conservative European Powers against the French Revolution and its Napoleonic aftermath, was a powerful factor in the restraint of militarism between 1815 and 1914. The war had in effect been a great political and social revolution. Napoleon I had passed through the Europe of the old régime like a hurricane, upsetting thrones and empires and leaving behind a nightmare of chaos. One of the chief reasons why Bonaparte's nephew, Napoleon III, was so mistrusted in the third quarter of the nineteenth century, and why he was so isolated in the moment of crisis in 1870, was that he reminded men of the torment his tremendous forerunner had inflicted on Europe; Louis Napoleon was regarded as at best a restless, unreliable man of intrigue. The monarchical governments of Europe in the last century and the aristocratic and prosperous middle classes which provided their support were in fact welded together after the battle of Waterloo in an international compact against further social revolution. The Congress system based on the Quadruple Alliance of November 1815, which periodically met together in the years 1815 to 1822, gave this repression of revolution a short-lived institutional machinery, but joint repression there was none the less. The balance of power continued to be hated by radicals and socialists right up until the Second World War, not so much because it seemed a formula for international anarchy, but because it appeared to them as a bulwark of social reaction.

During the First World War this international compact against revolution from below, this use of the international system to preserve the social and political *status quo*, collapsed, never to rise again. Its grave was dug by Lenin and Trotsky, on one side, and President Wilson, on the other. When the Bolsheviks, after the Treaty of Brest-Litovsk in March 1918, first used the diplomatic bag to send revolutionary propaganda to Berlin, the first capitalist centre to recognize them, and when at the Paris Peace Conference in 1919 Woodrow Wilson tried to seduce the Italian people away from support for their own government during his dispute with the Italian delegation at the conference over Fiume, the knell of the international system as an engine of social repression sounded. There has been no resurrection.

But if fear of a recurrence of the revolutionary wars of 1792 to 1815 helped to keep the international system at peace in the nineteenth century, why did that fear not continue to operate in 1914 when the march of millions to Armageddon began? One reason is that those wars with France had been fought a hundred years before, time for three generations to live and die, time for admirals and generals to strut about in coloured uniforms and to forget what war was really like. Carl von Clausewitz's famous treatise on war, which appeared in the 1830s, is really about playing soldiers and moving armed forces on a map, not about killing and being killed. Moreover, few, if anybody, thought in 1914 that the war would be a real war, with deaths by the hundreds of thousands, the falling of thrones and the sweeping away of long-standing social systems. It was expected to be a 'jolly little war', as the German Emperor described it, with the troops home with the falling leaves of autumn, after the final cavalry break-through with banners flying and brass bands and football matches with the enemy after the battle. And behind the belligerent governments in all countries there were wild men who had no stake in the existing order of affairs, men who yearned for 'that day, that dreadful day, when Heaven would boil in flames'. There were nationalists wanting to break free from Habsburg and Russian and German Empires, frightened conservatives in Ireland, men of the *revanche* in France, social revolutionaries in the cities, all waiting and praying for the great day. Generals and socialists, patriots and incendiaries, all felt that they had no longer any need for those bulwarks against disaster which Europe had built for itself in the frightened years which followed Waterloo.

But there is a futher question. If fear of war helped to keep Europe at peace in the nineteenth century, why did not that same fear, after the far more terrible war of 1914–1918, keep Europe at peace for longer than twenty years until 1939? The answer lies in quite another set of factors which we will examine later in this chapter.

A second major development which biased the international system towards peace in the Victorian age was the extraordinary and quite unparalleled economic expansion of that century. The industrial revolution, which began in England in the late eighteenth century, spread over all Europe, transforming the great Powers, even Austria-Hungary, even Russia, and changing men's mental attitudes to the social world they inhabited. Expansion showed itself in all the economic indices: of gross national product, of national income and output per man, of production of iron, steel and coal, foreign trade, investment at home and abroad, of population, personal incomes and savings. In Germany in the twenty-four years between 1876 and 1900 average real income per head rose by 33 per cent, in Britain by 82 per cent. The statistics are endless and all point in the same upward direction.[4] Indeed, one might say that the First World War would never have assumed the character which it did had the belligerent nations not passed in the previous century through the industrial revolution.

Along with material progress came self-confidence, a conviction that material progress marched hand-in-hand with moral progress, and a feeling of the inevitability of national and personal enrichment. In the first half of the last century England became the industrial power-house of Europe, and, more than that, the banker and workshop of the world, building its railways, roads and canals, exporting all over the world its own products, skill and savings. Money-making became, as Matthew Arnold once said, the religion of England, or rather it was blessed and sanctified by the religion of England. Men and nations seemed to have in fact no time or inclination for militarism, in Europe at least. The great Powers might on occasion have to use the sword, or at least rattle it, when threatened by revolt of the helots in their overseas empires, but the idea that civilized nations should spend vast sums of money on war when they could far more profitably invest it in commerce and industry seemed as absurd as it did to that famous Birmingham business man of the 1930s, Neville Chamberlain.

The industrial classes increasingly ruled nineteenth-century Europe and these frock-coated men were essentially a pacific breed.[5] They were internationalist in sentiment not only because peace was good for trade, but because in their time there was growing up in Europe and, as the Europeans spread themselves beyond their own continent, in the world, an international economy *par excellence*. Until the last decades of the century it was an era of free trade and the Gold Standard, certainly wherever Britain's influence prevailed. Its symbols were the abolition of the Corn Laws in Britain in 1846, the Cobden Free Trade Treaty between Britain and France in 1860, most-favoured-nation agreements, Gladstonian budgets with their close control of government spending. The case for British free trade was never shaken until the fearful economic whirlwinds which struck world commerce in 1929–1932. And freedom applied not merely to commodities, but to men and money in that age without passports or financial controls. In the first chapter of his *The Economic Consequences of the Peace*, published in 1919, J. M. Keynes describes the international economy of the world before 1914 and sums it up with the words: 'the internationalization of economic life was almost complete'.[6]

The business community in all the European Powers had a stake in peace because peace was good business. Norman Angell, writing the first of many editions of his book *The Great Illusion*, first published in 1908 and a best-seller for many years afterwards, thought that peace was indeed such good business that rational man could never be so mad as to abandon it.[7] But after the 1870s and 1880s firebrands in Germany and Italy, but also in France and the Habsburg Empire, began to question that proposition. The thought grew, and it was taking hold of wider areas of European public opinion by 1914, that perhaps there were grander visions in life than making money. These were the 'ancestral voices prophesying war', murmuring in the unconscious of Europe.

The bourgeois character of mid-nineteenth-century Europe was reflected in and strengthened by the fact that there was a rough equality of power between the five principal members of the international system, and that Britain, the pre-eminent industrial state, was *primus inter pares*.[8] There was a rough equality of power in the sense that none of the five could over-power the rest, or even another state, without the other three coming to that state's assistance. Russia, for instance, could not utterly defeat Austria-Hungary in the Balkans, or even Turkey, without fearing British and, after 1871, German opposition. After his defeat of France in 1871 Bismarck had constantly to conciliate Britain and Russia for fear that they would side with France and form a coalition against him. His nightmare of opposing alliances was certainly no illusion. Moreover, Britain was *primus inter pares* in the sense, first, that London was without doubt the world's greatest financial centre.[9] The financial support of London was valuable to any state and its denial could be disastrous to any state. Britain, too, was wealthy enough to feed her friends and allies with subsidies; that assistance had helped her to win the wars against Napoleon. Britain enjoyed naval supremacy by virtue of her two-Power standard, which she yielded only to the United States as late as 1921, and this allowed her to determine the outcome of many political issues in foreign affairs. British naval power meant that no armed action was possible in the Atlantic, Baltic, Mediterranean or Black (until 1871) seas, or even around many of the shores of those seas, without the acquiescence of London.

Britain's land policy was, of course, the balance of power, that is, the organization of coalitions against the strongest and most threatening European Power of the day. This was related to Britain's naval strategy in that the maintenance of the two-Power naval standard was possible so long as the continental Powers did not unite their forces and outstrip Britain at sea. The resulting equilibrium, with Britain first among equals, tended to weaken in the last ten or fifteen years of the nineteenth century. Britain lost her predominance in the output of iron and steel, the basic structural materials of the time, to Germany and the United States in the 1880s. The sheer burdens of empire, especially with the race for African colonies in the 1880s and 1890s, made it difficult for Britain to keep ahead of the changing pattern of power in Europe. The result was that when the two great armed camps formed in Europe towards the end of the century, the Dual Alliance between Germany and Austria-Hungary in 1879, becoming the Triple Alliance when Italy joined it in 1882, and the Franco-Russian Alliance created in 1891–1892, Britain played no part in their formation and was quite unable to hold the balance between the two. When war finally came between the two alliances in 1914, the British government found that neutrality was not a real choice for the country since at the end of the war, which Britain, as they judged, was quite unable to prevent, the British Empire would be totally at the mercy of whichever alliance proved victorious. It is no exaggeration to say that Britain went to war in 1914 chiefly in order to make sure of a seat at the eventual peace conference. But since a place among the great Powers was regarded by most British people as a natural complement of their power, many of them were puzzled to know after 1918 what they had really been fighting for.

But the most important transformation in the international system in the years before 1914 resulted from the unification of Germany. Once Germany was united after 1871 and industrialized, there existed in a superb central position in the heart of Europe a military and productive capability roughly equal to that of all the rest of Europe put together. In the First World War, at least until 1917, Germany, with no considerable assistance from her allies, was able to hold the rest of Europe and the forces of all their colonies at bay. The unification of Germany in effect meant that thereafter the European equilibrium was no longer a matter of European terms alone. A new world had to be called into existence to restore the balance of the old. Britain had to form an alliance with Japan in 1902 in order to offset the naval rivalry, first with Russia, then with Germany; and finally the deadlock in the great European war in 1917 could not be resolved without the entrance into the conflict of the United States. Britain, in short, could no longer alone construct an operative balance of power against Germany since Germany was now too strong. Napoleon had been beaten in Russia in 1812; Germany beat Russia in 1917. Napoleon was eventually defeated by allied forces held together by British sea power; Germany in the First World War almost starved Britain into surrender by use of her submarine power. If the history of the European balance of power since 1900 has proved anything, it is that Germany is destined either to dominate or be dominated. She is too big for any lesser role.

Finally, among the factors making for peace in the nineteenth century was, as we have seen in the previous chapter, the existence of a world of opportunity outside Europe in which tensions at the centre of the international system could be intermittently relieved. When the great Powers came to the brink of war between themselves, tempers could be assuaged and a settlement sweetened by the annexation of a colony here, the adjustment of an imperial frontier there. But towards the end of the nineteenth century the open spaces outside Europe were plainly filling up and the Powers, thwarted in their search for compensations in Africa and Asia, returned to confront each other at the centre, and usually in no friendly state of mind. Russia was worsted by Japan when expanding in Manchuria in the first decade of the twentieth century; the Romanovs then returned to Europe to confront their old enemy in the Balkans, Austria-Hungary, the jailer of the Slavs. France clashed with Britain at Fashoda in 1898, then with Germany in Morocco. Italian efforts to make a colony out of Abyssinia were frustrated at the battle of Adowa in 1896. Is it any wonder that the great Powers began to turn their guns against each other in 1914 when targets for their weapons in the world outside Europe started to run short?

To sum up, then, we may say that there were four chief factors tending to make the international system peace-biased in the hundred years before the First World War: the élitist pact among the five great Powers (six after Italy joined them in 1871) against revolution from below; the spread of the industrial revolution and the attitudes towards peace and war which industrial progress engendered; the equilibrium of power in the international system with Britain as the undoubted *primus inter pares*; and the availability of land for annexation and exploitation in the non-European world. The disappearance, or the lessening influence, of these factors in the twenty or thirty years preceding the First World War partially account for the lack of stability in the international system in the twentieth century. But there were additional circumstances which aggravated that instability and which arose largely from the nature of the twentieth century itself.

Why was the peace of 1919 to 1939 so short-lived? Why was the international system during those twenty years so conflictful? There have been theories in abundance in answer to these questions. These range from the idea that it was the fault of wicked or stupid men, to the strangely unhistorical view of E. H. Carr that it was all due to the democratic nations having read the wrong books and picked up the wrong political philosophies.[10] We wish here to offer an explanation in terms of the malfunctioning of the international system which is the subject of this book.

Theoretically, Germany, the state most threatening to the international system and its equilibrium in the mid-nineteenth century, lost the First World War in 1918. Actually, she won it, or came within an ace of winning it; or rather she won the war against all her enemies as they stood in August 1914. She defeated Russia. She defeated or helped Austria to defeat Italy. She almost defeated France, almost starved Britain into surrender, and all this practically single-handed. It is symbolic that in November 1918 the German army returned as an exhausted, though still integrated, force to a homeland desperately short of food but nevertheless physically unscarred by the war. It is hardly surprising that once the Germans had recovered from the shock of defeat they could not understand how it had taken place. They had to resort to such fairy tales as the 'stab in the back' legend in order to make some kind of sense of it all.

The victory of the Allies in November 1918 was for all practical purposes a fake, however tragically real the price of the German surrender had been. The Germans gave up the War before they had truly reached the limit of their resources because they knew that while the Entente Powers were as exhausted as themselves, the United States, as the American Commander-in-Chief, General Pershing said during the armistice negotiations, could fight and undoubtedly would fight on indefinitely. Better for the Germans to throw in the towel rather than see their country fall, as Winston Churchill put it in 1945, 'like a headless trunk on the table of the conquerors'.[11]

The peace which was a fake could not be enforced, even if the will to enforce it had existed on the side of Britain, the chief and, with France, the only guardian of the peace. Britain was unwilling even to try to enforce the peace against Germany for several reasons: she feared the onset of Bolshevism in Germany if that country was pressed too hard; she feared economic collapse in Europe, which would be fatal to the sagging British economy, if war fever were permitted to continue raging; she miscalculated the balance of power on the continent, many of her leading men believing—*sic quem deus vult perdere prius dementat*—that the threat to peace in Europe would come, not from Germany, but from France. Both the political Right and the political Left in Britain dissented from the morality of the 1919 peace treaties, the Right considering that no great state like Germany would passively accept the creation of a belt of weak states in Eastern Europe, formed to a large extent from her own territories, while the Left almost uniformly regarded the treaties as a 'capitalist peace', the product of a despised and outmoded social order which socialism was destined to extinguish. Here indeed can be found clues to the causes of British attitudes, all along the political spectrum, to the defence of Eastern Europe in 1938 and 1939.

Another Entente ally of the First World War who was unenthusiastic about the enforcement of the peace treaties was Italy. Robbed in 1919, as the Italians thought, of the territorial gains promised to them when they joined the Entente in 1915, they never accepted the rightfulness of the peace of 1919, except in regard to South Tyrol, where they gained 300,000 German-speaking people at the expense of Austria. But here they feared an alliance or amalgamation of German and Austria which would put Berlin in Vienna's shoes as champion of the South Tyrolese Germans. Therefore the Italians under Mussolini considered that their interests lay in diverting Germany's attention towards the East, towards revision of the Polish Corridor and the Polish-German 1919 frontier in Silesia; this was to have been encouraged by the four-Power pact initiated by the Italian *Duce* in 1934. Thus Italy was driven towards revision of the 1919 peace treaties by her wish to protect that part of the treaties which she did not want to see revised, namely the new Italo-Austrian frontier.

But even if the Allies wished to enforce the 1919 peace settlement, how could they have done so? The Americans, whose intervention on the side of the Allies in 1917 was essential to Germany's defeat, had gone home, leaving the European allies to enforce a victory they had not even been able to win on their own. The Allies could have marched into Germany to enforce the peace, as France and Belgium did in 1923, but sooner or later they would have had to march out again, leaving the Germans virtually the moral victors. The Allies wanted American economic assistance in the aftermath of the War, but the Americans would give assistance only on the condition that Allied controls on Germany were relaxed and Germany's sovereignty and territorial integrity were respected. United States funds supplied to Europe under the Dawes Plan, initiated in 1924, were dependent upon Germany having full control of her national economy, that is, on the Ruhr occupation being terminated. Moreover, the Allies, and in particular Britain, could not but fear that if Germany were pressed too hard she might bolt into the Soviet camp, as indeed she did at Rapallo in 1922, to the general dismay of the West. In fact, when Britain and France at length won Germany for the West again at the Locarno conference in 1925, they found they could only do so by declaring that they would offer no special resistance if she broke out towards the East in an effort to revise the Versailles treaty.

The situation in the inter-war years was thus that the balance of power which finally defeated Germany in November 1918—if indeed she was really defeated—disintegrated in the early 1920s, leaving the Allies without the means of enforcing the treaties that they had made at the end of the War. Germany might be induced to accept the 1919 settlement in the West at Locarno, but the Allies could not enforce, or even profess that they would enforce, the peace settlement in Eastern Europe. Nor did they particularly want to; Britain did not approve it, neither did Italy. France, of course, did; the East European settlement was one of the chief pillars of her security system. But still there were strong forces in France who thought otherwise—'better Hitler than Stalin' and even 'better Hitler than Léon Blum' expressed their sentiments. When the East European settlement of 1919 was eventually challenged by the Nazis in 1938–1939, it plainly could not stand. It could have been preserved, if at all, only by the containment of Germany by means of an effective balance of power. Even if such a balance of power could have been constructed, it would not have been the balance which won the War in 1918 and made the peace in 1919. In place of the United States among the combination of forces ranged against a resurgent Germany in the 1930s there was the Soviet Union, and between that country and Britain and France there was little but measureless mistrust on both sides. Besides, Soviet Russia had grievances as great as those of Germany against the 1919 peace settlement, an important factor in the Nazi-Soviet Pact signed in August 1939. Russia, as the British and French efforts to join her to themselves in a peace front in the summer of 1939 showed, could only be brought into the European balance of power by making over to her the very countries in Eastern Europe which she was supposed under the peace front to be defending.

But yet another circumstance militated against the formation of an effective balance against resurgent Germany in the 1930s, and that was the memories of the catastrophic effects of the First World War. It is commonplace, of course, to say that the democracies were loathe to form a deterrent force against the dictatorships in the 1930s because they feared another war on the pattern of 1914–1918. It is somewhat more to the point to say that, after the great economic depression of the early 1930s, European governments adjusted themselves mentally to the inevitability of a second world war. The great question was: where would the blow fall? Who would take the shock and strain of the first onset? Who would act as the stone of attrition, engaging the enemy force from the first day while other nations prepared themselves behind the lines? Attitudes towards the coming war were somewhat like those of soldiers in the First World War who are said to have prayed: 'Dear God, give us a victory, but not in our sector'. The international history of the 1930s can in effect be told in terms of the efforts made by each of the European great Powers to ensure that the first blast of war should be discharged as far as possible against some other Power. British and French politicians often hoped that, if there must be war, it would come in the form of a savage clash between Nazi Germany and Communist Russia, thus destroying two of their most troublesome enemies at the same time. In reply Stalin uttered his famous warning, so little heeded, in March 1939 to the effect that he could not be expected 'to pull other people's chestnuts out of the fire for them'. Mussolini calculated that by staying out of the Second World War when it finally broke out in September 1939 he would be able to join in the struggle later on and pick up some cheap gains from countries which others had defeated for him. Even the German Chancellor, Hitler, who seemed of all the politicians of the day to be least afraid of war, gave the appearance of hoping that by a parade of German military frightfulness the opposing citadels would fall into his lap without his having to pay an inordinate price in German blood. Such attitudes, strongly influenced as they were by recollections of the hateful attrition warfare of 1914–1918, encouraged policies of waiting to see how events would develop rather than taking a firm grip on affairs.

The European system thus remaining unbalanced, the forces on which the peace of 1919 depended could not be maintained. Moreover, by the 1930s the European international system was supplemented by another, the new sub-system of the Far East, and the balance of forces there could not easily be co-ordinated with those at work in the principal European theatre. There took place, in other words, a bifurcation of the international system, rather as the Roman Empire once separated into Western and Eastern branches.

Until the First World War China and Japan played no very significant roles in the international system, while the rest of East Asia was merely the passive object of European diplomacy and imperialism. After 1918, and with an interval of reconstruction following the devastating earthquake in 1923, Japan, or rather the Japanese Right wing, embarked upon a programme later to be known as the 'Greater East Asia Co-prosperity Sphere'. This was envisaged by the Right as an amalgamation of China, Manchuria and Japan, with Japan as the predominant partner and Western interests continuing to exist within it, but solely on Japanese sufferance. This design did not succeed at once. Many Japanese liberals in the 1920s feared that the country's trade with the West would suffer if Japan developed aggressive policies in the Far East, though this argument carried less conviction after the Great Depression in 1929–1932, which played havoc with Japan's export trade. But it is possible to trace the stages in the implementation of Japan's imperialist policy from 1914 until 1945.

The grand design of the Greater East Asia Co-prosperity Sphere was foreshadowed by the notorious Twenty-One Demands issued by the Japanese government to China in 1915; they amounted to a call for a virtual Japanese protectorate over China. At the Paris Peace Conference in 1919 Japan inherited German properties in the sacred Chinese province of Shantung, together with German islands in the Pacific north of the equator. By the four-Power naval agreement signed with Britain, France, Italy and the United States at Washington in 1922 Japan acquired virtual immunity against any hostile naval assault against the home islands while a Japanese army was operating in East Asia. Then in 1927 came the Tanaka Memorial, repeating in essence the Twenty-One Demands and claiming a practical overlordship in China. This was re-stated in the Japanese Foreign Office's Amau Declaration in 1934. Between these two policy statements came the Japanese attack on Manchuria in September 1931, followed by the creation there of the state of Manchukuo, ostensibly independent but in reality under Japanese control. Japan's final attack on China itself in July 1937 was precipitated by the seeming end to the long civil war in China and the creation in that country in 1933 of the first settled Chinese government since the fall of the Manchu dynasty before the First World War. In 1938 the Greater East Asia Co-prosperity Sphere was officially declared in Tokyo. Meanwhile, the civil commotions in China had been touched off again by the Japanese invasion of the country in 1937, but this time it took the form of a struggle for supremacy between the Nationalists and the Communists, culminating in the victory of the latter in 1949. For the first time since at least 1900 China had by 1949 a strong central government and an obedient people, with the remnant of the Nationalist force fled to Formosa where it continued to cherish dwindling hopes of a return to the mainland.

The implications for the European balance of power of the emergence of this Far Eastern sub-system of international politics may be stated under three headings. First, it created critical problems for Russia, one of the classical weights in the European balance. The danger which overhung all Russian foreign policy after the rise of Japan was that of becoming embroiled in a war on two fronts, the European and the East Asian, at the same time. Secondly, it increased in Nazi Germany the idea that, with this split in the international system, her moment of opportunity had arrived. It is true that, strictly, no military alliance was formed between Germany and Japan, and the two fell violently apart after the Nazi-Soviet Pact of August 1939, which was a bitter shock to Tokyo. Nevertheless, so long as Japan was pulling down Western authority in the Far East, few in Germany doubted that this meant that the democratic European states could be thrashed in the two theatres of politics at the same time. Above all, the emergence of the Far East, as a sector of international politics with strong and challenging local power of its own, created the gravest complications for Britain, the dominant external Power in the Far East. There was no question that after the outbreak of the Sino-Japanese war in 1937 Japan had to be appeased by Britain, since Britain was at the same moment grappling with a menacing European situation and receiving no assistance from the United States in either theatre of diplomatic operations. And yet there was equally no doubt that to appease the Japanese militarists when they shouted about their natural rights in East Asia was in reality to stoke up the fires for the incendiarists and revisionists in Europe. Thus the bifurcation of the international system in the period between the two Wars did nothing to preserve an effective balance of power in either system.

Two other major factors of weakness may be discerned in the international system as it appeared before 1939. The first was the portentous economic stresses and strains of the times. With falling international trade, vast unemployment and under-use of resources, the collapse of the stock markets, the banks, and, above all, the international, long-sacrosanct Gold Standard, many doubted whether the world capitalist system itself could survive. Young men and women in the democratic states read books like John Strachey's *The Coming Struggle for Power*[12] and wondered whether the world was not on the brink of the Messianic age after the final demise of capitalism. In Germany, Italy and Hungary massed battalions of youth surged forward gladly to meet their fate in the flames of conflict. The civil-war character of international relations in those years was at once intensified. People thought of civil strife and international strife in the same language and strove for, and were not contented until they found, a common set of causes. The Left saw in Fascism and Nazism nothing more nor less than the final stand of the capitalist class against the dispossessing revolution. The Right, on their side, thought of the world economic crisis as the more or less deliberate work of international financiers and Jewish-Marxist conspirators to frustrate whom required the cold-steel efficiency of jackbooted patriots.

D

There is no need to inquire here into the real causes of this world-wide economic collapse, except perhaps to say that many of the remedies which governments applied, especially in the democratic states, turned out to be worse than the disease. It is the implications of economic collapse for the effective operation of the international political system which are more immediately relevant. To begin with, the economic problems facing all the state-members of the international system—they included unemployment, falling prices, diminishing international trade and hence balance-of-payments difficulties—bred a 'sauve qui peut' mentality among governments. In circumstances in which they had to make a choice between the interests of the international economy as a whole, however conceived, and their own national interests, even when narrowly conceived, it was always the latter which won the day. And the fact that that choice tended to be made in this way was, of course, a reflection of the simple fact that in the last resort Ministers are answerable, not to a world constituency, which is as yet far from existing, but to a national electorate which in times of slump or depression tends to be frightened, xenophobic and more than usually self-centred. Hence, political nationalism, which was in itself all too prevalent in the inter-War years, was strengthened by economic nationalism.

Again, the economic problems faced by the *status-quo* countries in the 1930s discouraged them from making an effective resistance to aggression and from the formation of an appropriate balance of forces against threats to the international order. Conciliation of the aggressors seemed, in the perverse logic of the times, to be the political prerequisite of economic recovery because it did not necessitate public spending on armaments; and public spending of any kind was, according to the received economic theory of that day, the high road to ruin when the economic weather was bad. In the revisionist states, however, that is, Germany, Italy and Japan, precisely the opposite conclusions were drawn. Their recipe for recovery, as was that of President Roosevelt in his New Deal programme, was to pour money into public works and in so doing create effective demand. No matter that rearmament programmes made no direct contribution to public welfare; so long as people found their way back into jobs and workers in the arms industries fed their wages into the national economy, widening circles of effective demand were created. In any case, armaments could be and were used to force the depressed democracies into making one concession after another in the field of foreign affairs.

In 1936 J. M. Keynes published his *General Theory of Employment, Interest and Money* in which he argued that in times of falling demand the state should, contrary to the postulates of classical economic theory, spend its way back into prosperity.[13] This is called the 'Keynesian revolution' and Keynes is justly celebrated for it. On the other hand, considering that Hitler and Roosevelt had actually been practising these techniques for as long as three years before Keynes's book saw the light of day, one wonders whether the 'revolution' was quite as radical as that name suggests. However that may be, it remains the fact that while the economic depression of the early 1930s made the opponents of the international order bolder and stronger, it made the defenders of that order more timid and weak.

As a final source of weakness in the international system before the Second World War, there was the ineffectiveness of the major instrument for the collective enforcement of peace during those years, the League of Nations. Much has been written about the weaknesses of the League of Nations, and it is worth-while in considering them to remember, as we have already stressed, that international organizations for the maintenance of peace tend to reflect conditions, social, political, economic, in the international system rather than to determine them. If peace could not be maintained in the 1930s it was due to the fact, in the first instance, that the coalition of forces which won the War in 1918 could not be preserved, as we have already explained. In terms of sheer physical strength the League and its member-states could not have bolted and barred the door against war when Italy and Japan, members of the Allied coalition in the First World War, seemed to have more sympathy with Germany than with the League states, when Soviet Russia was hostile and at the same time seemed to be weak, and when the United States was even more solidly isolationist than it was during the first three years of the First World War.

Of all these weaknesses, it has been generally recognized in the West since 1939 that the absence of the United States from the League, owing to the non-ratification by the US Senate of the peace treaties of 1919, was the greatest. What is not often remembered today is that the defection of the United States from the European balance of power in the 1920s not only robbed Britain and France of a most powerful ally, it also set them at one another's throats and compounded their differences. With the United States absent from the League of Nations, British Ministers tended to think that the obligations of the Covenant should be diluted in order to attract into the League a naturally isolationist American public opinion. The effect was precisely the reverse on France; the French, perhaps with more realism than the British, considered that, with the United States unlikely to make any effective contribution to the enforcement of the peace, the obligations of the League Covenant should be proportionately strengthened.

Besides, it is notorious that all international organizations for the maintenance of peace are profoundly influenced by the nature of the war at the end of which those organizations are born. It was so in 1945, with the creation of the United Nations Organization (UNO), as it had been in 1919, with the creation of the League. Politically and strategically this meant that the League Covenant was framed for facing the wrong kind of war, or in other words a war like that which broke out in August 1914. After 1918 the victorious nations readied and prepared themselves to face that kind of war, though it was less likely to occur in future. But after 1918 it became increasingly clear that another war would begin, if at all, from foundations already laid by propaganda, by subversion, by the breaking of public morale in the opposing forces, rather than by the crossing of international frontiers by columns of armed men, such as the League Covenant envisaged in Article 16. Against the sapping and undermining of the bases of peace by totalitarian régimes, long before the outbreak of actual hostilities, the League had little or no premeditated defence. Like Singapore in January 1942 it could be surprised from the rear while its garrison looked out to sea. The reoccupation of the Rhineland by Germany in 1936 was a vivid example; the League Covenant was not provided for such a contingency, yet it changed the balance of power in Europe far more than did the Italian attack on Ethiopia in the previous year, which did stir the League to action in accordance with its Covenant.

The League of Nations, too, was framed to deal with the wrong kind of threat to the economic order which underpinned the international political system. If one phrase could be used to describe the economic thinking permeating League committees and conferences in the period between the two Wars, it was the

cult of the old, multilateral free-trading world as it existed before
1914. Britain and the United States, if not France, who had won
the War between them, shaped the economic ideology enshrined
in the Covenant. Whether through a sentimental nostalgia for the
old European life before the earth shook in 1914, or because of the
sheer persistence of ideas absorbed by politicians thirty or forty
years before, delegates at the League's economic committees were
captivated by the uncontrolled international economy of before
1914 as though by a powerful spell. Time and again in the inter-
War period Ministers would sit in their Cabinet rooms contriving
to put one more stone on the pyramid of nationalist economic
defences they had built against the storms which blew in from the
international economy. Then they would hasten to Geneva and
there deplore in League assemblies the fettering of free commerce
by nationalist shackles and politically inspired controls. In
economics, as in politics, the League of Nations was handicapped
in dealing with the realities of the times by a burden of conventional
wisdom which had ruled in the years before the League saw the
light of day.

Hence, the factors disposing the international system towards
instability and ultimately to war were deeply embedded in that
system in the twenty-year inter-bellum period. Perhaps the most
important of these factors was that the combination of forces
which had determined the outcome of the War in 1918 were not
strong enough, and moreover lacked the will, to keep the peace
after victory. In 1939 essentially the same war had to be fought
again, this time to ensure that the victory over Germany, forged
at so great a cost in 1918, was finally definite and assured. To make
matters worse, the international system fell apart; a Far Eastern
sector made its appearance and the forces of order could not work
effectively on behalf of the *status quo* in both sectors at the same
time. We have mentioned too the economic *malaise*; the world
economy was in crisis and this weakened the diplomatic consensus
essential to any peaceful adjustments of the existing order of
affairs. Finally, the substratum of ideas on which international
organization, notably the League of Nations, was based was ill-
adjusted to the hard realities of the times. The League itself was
grounded upon unsatisfactory arrangements for maintaining an
effective balance of power against forces anxious, like Samson, to
bring the whole edifice down in ruins.

It is not our intention here to present a similar account of the functioning of the international system since the Second World War. One reason is that in the remainder of this book we will be concerned to explain the international system which we have today. It is worth noting, however, that, when compared with the 1919–1939 period and its many weaknesses, which we have described earlier in this chapter, the contemporary system has been characterized by certain strengths. In the first place, the system has been stabilized by the central spine it has acquired in the form of the continuing Soviet-American relationship which to a large extent still dominates the international system today. It is true that this unique relationship has passed through many phases, from the intense mutual fear, perhaps hatred, of the early years of the Cold War to the quite remarkable determination to solve disputes without recourse to war which both sides exhibit today. It is true, too, that this relationship (and the first signs, since 1972, of its extension on the American side to China) by no means exhausts all the patterns and forms of international relations which the world has seen since 1945. Nevertheless, when considered alongside the complicated apparatus of arms balances and deterrence systems which have grown up with it, the Soviet-American relationship has given the international system more stability of structure than it has had since the nineteenth century. And by organizing the lesser states on each side in rival bands, the two super-Powers have managed to impose more order in international relations than the system has previously enjoyed in the twentieth century.

What is equally striking is that while certain revolutionary developments have taken place in the international system since 1945, in many respects these have not fundamentally affected the basic character of that system. Indeed, it might even be said that the fundamental features of the system have been confirmed rather than weakened.

This is clear if we look for a moment at the two facing poles of the Soviet-American relationship. On the one side, it seems that the revolutionary thrust of Soviet Communism has given way to an almost bourgeois acceptance by Russia's leaders of the present world system of states. For the Leninists of the 1920s it seems that the expression 'peaceful co-existence' meant little more than an ephemeral pause in the revolutionary dynamic before the next great leap forward towards the Promised Land; or, in the Leninist phrase, embracing the enemy the better to strangle him. It is doubtful whether Soviet leaders regard their relations with the rest of the world in the same way today. Since Marshal Stalin died in March 1953 they seem increasingly to have subordinated their mission of social revolution to a prudent concern with the traditional objectives of foreign policy, national security, the immunity of the home base from foreign attack, the maintenance of Soviet influence in areas of local conflict, such as the Middle East, outside the confines of Soviet territory, and so on. The Soviet Union, like a rich man, has an extensive stake in the international system and, to the chagrin of Chinese Communists, among others, seems anxious not to jeopardize it by heavy involvement in revolutionary causes.

On the other side of the post-1945 ideological divide, American public opinion seemed for a long time to nourish the idea of a campaign to rid the world of oppression and suffering and then perhaps the wish to retire into the American way of life. The notion of permanent involvement in the international system was accepted only gradually and grudgingly. Moreover, America's role as one who puts the rest of the world to rights was abandoned only gradually, too; it was reflected in America's slowly increasing tolerance of Communism in the world, provided that it was non-aggressive. This seems first to have been publicly acknowledged in President Kennedy's speech at the American University, Washington, on 3rd June 1963, although it was for all practical purposes recognized in October and November 1956, when Mr. John Foster Dulles, the leading advocate of an American 'roll-back' of Communism in Eastern Europe, abandoned the whole idea of 'liberation' when the Soviet authorities crushed the Hungarian revolution without interference from the outside world. There is no reason why the United States should not reach the same conclusion about Asia, and President Nixon's efforts in 1972 to improve relations with China may be regarded as a sign that this process has already begun. Hence, in the ten years since the Cuban missiles crisis in 1962 to President Nixon's visit to China in 1972 the United States has gone far to show that she accepts the idea that the object, which is the traditional object, of foreign policy is not to try to change the basic nature of other states, but to co-exist with them, if that be possible.

The resultant Soviet-American *détente*, with some of its most important foundations in the nuclear stalemate and the migration of the world's chief tension centres from Europe to Asia, facilitated polycentrism in the two armed camps. The result of this was that new alignments, or potential alignments, were formed between individual states on either side of the dividing line of the old Cold War in Europe and before long the whole *raison d'être* of the two armed camps was being called into question. An all-European *rapprochement* began to make itself evident in the late 1960s, expressing itself in the idea of an all-European security conference and arms control arrangements which some hoped in the course of time would gradually replace the NATO and Warsaw Pact structures. In this situation national interests and national sovereignty seemed to count for more, bloc loyalties for less. This was more likely to be so as the demand for higher living standards, and hence for reduced spending on national defence, grew with the slowing down of Western economic progress in the 1970s. Resentment, too, increased at the alleged efforts of the bloc-leaders on both sides to keep their allies locked indefinitely in a sterile and increasingly irrelevant military confrontation.

The same desire for national freedom, symbolized so dramatically in the 1960s by President Charles de Gaulle of France, had always characterized the so-called Third World, formed by the countries in Africa and Asia which were decolonized after 1945. This provided the second major feature of the post-Second World War international system after the Soviet-American relationship. The approach to foreign policy of Third-World countries was powerfully influenced, if not dominated, by the fierce cult of national sovereignty and independence. The Panch-Shila, or five principles of co-existence, adopted by non-aligned Third-World states at their conference at Bandung, Indonesia, in April 1955, is the *Magna Carta* of the traditional international system. There was certainly no great haste shown by these new entrants into the international system to shed their independence and to rush into political, economic or strategic alliances with other countries, even within their own group. It is true that, as in the 1960s the tension centres in the international system moved from Europe to Asia, leading Third-World states, notably India, were compelled to reconsider their non-alignment policies. But it was clear that if ever they abandoned these policies it would be mainly on grounds of national interest and national security, the same reasons, in other words, which actuated their general foreign policies. The international behaviour of Afro-Asian states since 1945 has certainly shown a deep desire for a more equitable share-out of the good things of life within the international system, but not for an essentially new international system.

When we now come to the advent of nuclear weapons, a third major development in the post-1945 international system, it is clear that while these weapons have radically altered the climate of international relations, they have had, so far, less effect on the structure and functioning of the international system. Some writers have argued that these terrible weapons have finally made the sovereign state obsolete, but it seems more likely that the actual outcome has been precisely the opposite.[14] In the first place, nuclear weapons have not appeared to accelerate federalizing tendencies anywhere in the world. The nuclear age since 1945 has rather been conspicuous for the creation of a whole host of proudly independent states, with no conspicuous drives towards federation. Where federation or integration has been moving forward most rapidly in the post-1945 world in Western Europe, though only there at a very slow pace, it could hardly be argued that any of this was due to nuclear weapons; on the contrary, both the British and French governments, which alone possess nuclear weapons in western Europe, seem ready to pool every other symbol of their national independence before they come to nuclear weapons. Whether as stabilizing or destabilizing forces in the international system, these weapons seem rather to consolidate than to change the international system. As stabilizers, nuclear weapons are credited with having produced a climate of security favourable to continuing confidence in national sovereignty. As destabilizers, their effect has been to strengthen the case for national nuclear forces since, whenever national security has really been in danger, the most obvious and effective means of defending it was through an adequate system of national defence, including the most up-to-date weapons.

We may conclude therefore that the international system in the world since the Second World War seems to have been free from many of the dangerous weaknesses from which it suffered before the War; that it has been more firmly structured and better balanced. We can never in international relations be confident about the future, but there is at present (1975) some reasonable grounds for hope. At the same time, developments within the international system since 1945 seem not to have weakened, but rather in some ways, to have strengthened the basic character of that system.

NOTES

1. *Rupert Brooke*, Faber, London, 1964.
2. *The Proud Tower*, Hamilton, London, 1961, p. xiii.
3. See on this Andrew Scott, *The Revolution in Statecraft*, Random House, New York, 1965. Also below, p. 238.
4. See *The New Cambridge Modern History*, Vol. XI, *1870–1898, Material Progress and World-Wide Problems*, especially the Introduction by F. H. Hinsley, Cambridge University Press, 1962.
5. A good description of the type is given in Thomas Mann's *Buddenbrooks* and Charles Dickens's *Dombey and Son*.
6. Macmillan, London, 1919.
7. Heinemann, London.
8. The nineteenth-century *Pax Britannica* was essentially a commercial peace backed by unobtrusive British naval power. The contemporary *Pax Americana*, on the other hand, is essentially political; it seeks to maintain the political *status quo* in the world when it is subject to subversive attack.
9. See E. H. Carr, *Nationalism and After*, Macmillan, London, 1945, Chapter I.
10. See Carr's *The Twenty Years' Crisis*, first published in 1939 by Macmillan, London.
11. I have argued this point more fully in *Freedom and Necessity in British Foreign Policy*, Weidenfeld and Nicolson, London, 1971.
12. Gollancz, London, 1932.
13. Macmillan, London.
14. Perhaps the best-known of these writers is John Herz, author of *International Politics in the Atomic Age*, Columbia University Press, New York, 1959.

Six

The Political Process

WE have so far considered the circumstances from which the
international system, as we know it today, sprang; the major
developments in its history and the effect of these on the functioning of the system today; and some of the reasons for the oscillation
of the system from peace to war in the nineteenth and twentieth
centuries. It is now time to turn from the developmental to the
analytical aspect of the subject and we must begin with an
examination of the nature of the political process taking place in
the international system. To put the point another way, how can
we characterize the *essence* of the political activities which proceed
in the system of interacting sovereign states? It will be remembered
that in the first chapter of this book some definition is offered as to
what we are to understand as political activities.[1]

Before we come to the international political process, however,
we must note that in the international system, as indeed within
virtually any social system, there are many processes at work at the
same time, just as Jesus Christ said that in His Father's house
there were many mansions. There is, most obviously, a process of
expansion and contraction going on in the international system
from day to day and year to year, both in the system as a whole and
in its constituent parts, the states. There is, or has been a process
of expansion in the geographical sense in the system. Its geographical reach has expanded in two senses: first, with the great discoveries, especially of the last century, the area controlled by the
state-members of the international system has increased until it
now embraces the entire globe; and, secondly, that whereas the
members of the system, the states, were predominantly confined
to Europe only a hundred years ago, now they are distributed
over the whole surface of the planet. It is by no means beyond the
the bounds of possibility, in this age of scientific miracles, that in
the next century the international system, following the steps of

the first astronauts, will take leave of its restriction to this planet and extend to outer space.

But there has also been in the last two centuries a contraction in the international system as a whole, not in the geographical, but in a time-space sense: meaning that, owing to the vast improvements in transport and communications, the time it takes for messages to pass between the two state-members of the system most geographically remote from each other has become a matter of seconds or fractions of seconds, and the time it takes men or goods to move, a matter only of, at most, twenty-four or thirty hours. In the case of communications, the time problem is almost infinitesimal. It is now technically possible for a Soviet Prime Minister or American President to give a speech in his own country and to have reactions to it from abroad placed on his rostrum for him to read before he comes to the end of it.

The vast effects of all this on the conduct of international affairs, though often remarked upon, have never been systematically accounted for, but it is at least clear that those effects have been registered throughout the international system. The elimination, or drastic reduction, of the time-lag between action and reaction; the enormous increase in the sheer volume of information which is now made available and on which political decisions need to be based; the removal of all areas of the international system from the class of those which are too remote to be taken account of—there are today no 'far-off countries of which we know nothing'; the increasing fusion of negotiation and the making of policy, the traditionally detached spheres of diplomats and Ministers respectively: all these are merely a few of the consequences of what have been called 'contact inventions'.[2] And to these there must be added the immeasurable psychological consequences: the unending strain and ceaseless pressures upon decision-makers in such a system; the intellectual problem, where the flow of information is so vast, of distinguishing between what is important and what is not; the difficulty of forming a policy-position and of holding it long enough to be effective in circumstances in which response and counter-response follow each other at such lightning speed. There is also the larger philosophical question, when the pace of technological change alone is so rapid, of knowing what there is in earlier practices and ideas which needs to be discarded and what can safely be retained.

But there is also an obvious process of expansion and contraction in the state-members of the international system. Numerically, of course, there has been an extraordinary increase in the absolute numbers of sovereign states in the world since, say, 1939. This has only been very slightly offset, if at all, by the gradual process of integration among the different states. Moreover, it is a normal law in the world of sovereign states that, like any other social organism, or like life itself, they are prone to a rhythm of growth and decay, perhaps also birth and death. We are apt often to visualize states as though they were individual animate beings and the misleading consequences of so doing must be resisted as far as possible. Nevertheless, as we will see later, there is such a thing, for example, as a 'circulation of élites' in the international system; as we are often told, the Great Britain of yesterday could become the Spain of tomorrow. With changes in the balance of natural resources, in the technique of production or commerce, or the arts of war, a moderately-sized state may become a colossus: indeed there has been a movement in that direction by the oil-producing states of the world. 'Count no state happy until it is dead' could be the Solonian apothegm of international politics.

Hence, processes of expansion and contraction are always at work in the system and in the different states. But there are also other processes certain of which we must take note as they exist alongside the political process, which is our proper concern. There is the international economic process, the never-ceasing to-ing and fro-ing of goods and services, people and money, from one state to another, from one group of states to another. There is the process of economic change and technological progress, and of alterations in the relative wealth of this country as compared with that. Possibly we can speak, too, of a social process, one which provides for, among other things, the migration of social practices from one state to another; or changes in the social structure of one state or a number of states such that the relations between them and other states are affected; or conflicts between the social classes in a particular state which may have profound consequences for that state's dealings with the rest of the world. We could even speak of an ideological process at work between states, meaning by that, shifts in the winds of political or economic doctrine which erode the certitudes and switch the mental assumptions of states, or the entire world, in novel directions. In more religious times there were, of course, international theological processes, of which the Reformation and the Counter-Reformation are prominent examples. The international system, in short, is a congeries of processes, of which, however, at the present time it is the political that most engages our attention.

But let us for the moment dwell on some of the implications of the word 'process' in order to understand better what we have in mind when we refer to the 'international political process'. It is as well at the outset to recall four different, if interconnected, nuances which attach to this word 'process'.

First, there is the idea of continuity, as for instance found in the expression 'the process of time'. How often have newcomers to the system of international relations thought that, so to speak, 'time would have a stop', and that that stop would constitute a kind of resting place where all the problems, struggles, injustice and oppression of this harassed world would reach some end. Nations struggling for what they regard as their rights, or battling against oppression, or braving themselves for a career of conquest, have shared the eschatological vision of Avilion:

> *Where falls not hail, or rain, or any snow,*
> *Nor ever wind blows loudly; but it lies*
> *Deep-meadow'd, happy, fair with orchard lawns*
> *And bowery hollows crown'd with summer sea.*

But in the political world, and especially in the international political world, all such chiliastic thinking is illusion. There is in fact no end to the story, no final victories or defeats. The most that men can do in any generation is to hand over their endless task to the next generation in no worse condition than that in which they inherited it. One of the many dangerous hallucinations, mistaken for reality by the so-called 'social science' *genre* of students of international politics, is the idea that the ever-new conjunctions and problems of those politics can be pinioned, as it were, within an Iron Maiden of permanent theory. The truth is that, like Heraclitus, man can never step into the same stream of international politics twice. In the political process 'tomorrow is a new day' and brings with it new challenges.

Secondly, the expression 'process', whether applied to a system made up of things or of people, implies a certain interconnectedness of events and actions. Everything leads to everything else: the garment of life is without seams. No event or action is wholly uninfluenced by what went before or is wholly without influence on what follows. This may seem perhaps sufficiently obvious so as not to need to be stated. But in international politics in particular it cannot be overstated, with the kind of continuous and dynamic processes in operation which we have described in the previous paragraph, that actions will often have consequences never anticipated when those actions were set in train. Or, to state the point more simply, in meeting the problems of today we must be careful to see that the situation resulting from what we do today is not positively worse than before it was done. In 1939 British people tended to think that the most vital thing was utterly to defeat Nazi Germany; what happened after that was scarcely worth thinking about. But in words now forgotten the Prime Minister of the day, Mr. Neville Chamberlain, reminded them that what they should think of was not merely the action which had to be done, but the situation likely to emerge once the action was achieved. 'In modern war', he said, 'we cannot tell who will be our enemies and who will be our friends at the end of it.' He no doubt meant that the war against Nazi Germany could never be won without the assistance of the Soviet Union, yet the price of that assistance, which people bent on waging the war might forget, could be the frustration of the very purposes in Eastern Europe on behalf of which the British people were going to war. Later, after the war had broken out and the United States had joined in it, it was left to Mr. Churchill to try and persuade President Roosevelt that, in the act of winning the war, thought must be devoted to the question of the state of political forces in Europe after the fighting stopped. He enjoyed in this very little, if any, success at all. There is, in brief, hardly a crueller irony in inter-national relations than that the conditions required to make an achievement possible sometimes nullify the anticipated good effects of that achievement. We cannot pluck any single thread from the seamless garment without affecting every other thread which goes to make it up.

Thirdly, there inheres in the idea of 'process' the notion of an accepted *method* of achieving desired results, a method which is widely recognized and is capable of being transmitted to new entrants into the system. It is with this aspect in mind, no doubt, that we speak of a 'process of manufacture'. It is possible that all the actions of states party to the international system may seem to the onlooker to be as arbitrary as, for example, the actions of baseball players or cricketers on the field seem to the British and American people respectively. But when the rules of the game are explained to the spectator, and when he is told what the players are trying to do and what prevents them doing what they want, a certain pattern of controlled activity becomes clear in which the participants take their parts as though in an orchestra. Similarly, to the uninitiated, the international system may seem to be something akin to undisciplined chaos. In fact, there runs through the whole of the system a network of orderly rules and regulations.

We have formulated, earlier in this book, a simple scheme for the consideration of rules in any social process: the basic idea was the distinction between technical and normative rules, the former specifying the means to be adopted to achieve a certain end, the latter stating that some ends are preferable to others.[3] The normative rules are further divisible into legal, moral and ethical. The extent to which all these rules are deferred to in the practical life of international politics is controversial: we will look at that question next. In the meantime something should be said about the sanctions operative in the international system in the event of breaches of the rules. It is a common view that no such sanctions exist in international relations, and that if any state or government is able to break the rules and 'get away with it', that is the end of the matter. But it is not as simple as that: it never is. Technical rules, of course, carry with them one obvious sanction in case of breach, and that is failure, the shallows and miseries of unsuccess. But can the same be said of the three types of normative rules— the rules of law, the rules of propriety and the rules of right and wrong? What does the intending violator of such maxims of international politics have to fear? Certainly not the police or the locked cell. But there is such a thing as standing and prestige in the community of states. A sense of honour in relation to the pledged word sounds perhaps Edwardian today. But in reality states depend, not so much on the public opinion of mankind, but certainly on the goodwill of other states. The individual can, if so inclined, shut himself up and ignore his neighbours. For the state there is no such 'keeping itself to itself'. The success of its business with other states (and it is usually business of a deadly seriousness) depends on whether those states think it is worth doing business with. Reputation is not a bubble but an asset of solid worth.

It does not, of course, follow that to recognize such rules do exist in the minds of peoples and governments implies that in fact they are observed all or most of the time, or even ever, for that matter. We have little in the way of positive evidence as to the regularity of the observance by member-states of the international system of these four groups of rules. It has, however, been authoritatively stated by the late Professor J. L. Brierly that international law is probably more regularly complied with by states than municipal law is by individuals.[4] The essential point, nevertheless, is not the regularity with which the rules of any social system are observed, but the general acceptance by members of that system that they *ought* to be observed. And as to that acceptance there can be no reasonable doubt. The mere existence of diplomatic criticism and the almost universal proclivity of people to indulge in it are sufficient proof of this. We cannot say, as all of us do from time to time, that such-and-such a policy is inexpedient, meaning that it violates the technical axioms of the international system, or that it is wicked, improper or illegal, unless we assume that technical and normative rules are relevant to action in the international system. In fact, it might be true to say that most people's discussion of their own and other states' behaviour is more permeated with technical and normative censure than their discussions of almost any other form of social behaviour.

Fourthly and finally, when we think of the word 'process' as applied to interconnected, continuous and regulated sequences of actions in the international system, we think of the movement of events or people which can be described as coherent and seemingly purposeful even if no one actually willed it. A crowd, for example, which is seen from the top of a high building, may seem to move in accordance with a single pattern, yet the separate individuals which make it up are probably actuated by quite unique and independent motivations. Thus, a 'process of politics', national or international, may be conceived from the outside as a dynamic sequence moving through the force and impetuosity of the several interest groups constituting it without there necessarily being much in the way of conscious design or external manipulation.

A suggestive version of this kind of image of politics is presented in A. F. Bentley's famous work, first published in 1908, called

The Process of Government.[5] Here the conception of a political system is that of the interplay of innumerable organized pressures, the interaction of which goes to produce a certain pattern or balance of forces which none of them foresaw or willed.[6] Bentley argues, as against the view that this or that government *did* this or that for this or that reason, that there comes about an accidental consequence or set of consequences, unwilled and unpremeditated, resulting from the ceaseless impact of pressures, one against another. These notions were reflected half a century later, as the title of the later book suggested, by David B. Truman in his book, *The Governmental Process.*[7] Truman's book is a plea, which may now seem positively commonplace, to shift the focus of political study from institutions, the United States Congress, the British Houses of Parliament and so on, to the infinitely complex pressures making up the web of society. Political institutions, we may say— and the proposition is abundantly true for international institutions, such as the United Nations—do not 'allocate values', as it is sometimes said. They rather register a purely temporary equilibrium reached, more by accident than by design, between the parties to the political process, and that equilibrium, like a truce on the battlefield, facilitates a temporarily legitimate allocation of spoils, or values. But tomorrow the battle will be fought again, and it, too, will have its short-lived truce.

One may say, then, that in the word 'process', as in the expression 'international political process', there are intimations (1) of continuity and endlessness; (2) of the existence of a complex of interrelated parts, the idea of the seamless garment; (3) of the technical and normative regulation of action, or at least the *idea* of that kind of regulation; and (4) of the equilibration, repeated again and again without cessation, of subordinate and organized social pressures.

It will next help us to bring out more clearly the nature of international politics if we compare them with the kind of political activities going on within the boundaries of a single state. Obviously, there are many similarities and differences and the clarification of these will enable us to grasp more clearly what international politics are and what they are about. Obviously, both national and international politics are 'processes', bearing the implications we have already discussed. Clearly, too, they are both 'political' in some such senses as the following. First, they both involve the exercise of power in the form in which political activities generally appear to us, namely that of a minority regulating the actions of a majority through the promulgation of demands which are accepted by the majority for reasons which range along a spectrum from consent at one end to enforcement at the other. To some extent, the parallelism between the two forms of politics is already beginning to break down here, in that in national politics the number of those subject to the political authorities is obviously much greater than, say, the number of states in the world which habitually defer to the will of the United States. Nevertheless, the basic pattern of politics, as demand followed by some degree of compliance, is common to both.

There are two further senses in which the internal and the international political processes are truly political, as that word is commonly understood. One is that in the political situation the use of power—that is, the capability of making one's will felt in other decision-making centres, as we have defined it[8]—is directed towards the satisfaction of certain essentially *public* interests. The well-known definition of these given by H. D. Lasswell is perhaps sufficient to be going on with for the time being: they are income, safety, deference, or wealth, security and prestige.[9] Politics may, of course, on occasion be steered towards the satisfaction of private ends by unscrupulous politicians, but the mere fact that politics of that kind are condemned by most people would seem to imply that politics are essentially public matters, the affairs of the *polis* or the *res publica*.

The second point to make about political activities, as we know them today, is that the public issues with which the politician or government is concerned are essentially deliberative, and not inquisitive, questions. Of course, the politician, or more likely the assistants in his office, must seek objective information on which his decisions are ultimately based. He may also have to put to himself profound questions as to where the national interest really lies or whether a recommended course of action is consistent with his or the community's sense of right and wrong. In these respects the politician's work is certainly inquisitive, like scientific research. But the information he seeks on such questions has to serve in solving an essentially deliberative question. The question for the politician is not 'What is truth?' That is the academic's or scientist's domain. Nor is it, as it is for the moral philosopher, the

question 'What is right?' In the final resort the politician is left
with his own ultimate question 'What shall we *do*?' That, of
course, includes the question 'Shall we do nothing?' And again,
as a consequence of the speeding-up of communications which
we mentioned earlier in this chapter, that question has to be
answered, not next year or in the next decade, but tomorrow or
even this afternoon.

The question for the politicians, 'What shall we do?' soon re-
solves itself into the question, 'What *can* we do?' It is an elementary technical rule of international politics never to embark upon
any international action without a reasonable assurance that the
means exist to follow it through to the end. Evidently this is not
merely a matter of having the right kind and quantity of physical
resources; it is more often a matter of consensus, or at least
acquiescence, on the part of those formally subject to the political
will. Hence, in answering the question, 'What can we do?' one is
really answering the question, 'Is there a certain equilibrium of
social forces in the community which permits the question, "What
can we do?" to be answered?', since no government is advised to
embark upon a policy in favour of which a distinct balance of
forces does not exist in the country. But it is vital to remember, as
we have stressed earlier in this chapter, that the existing equilibrium of forces in the community is always in process of change
or decay. A government which has a fairly accurate picture of
'what the public will not stand', to quote Walter Bagehot's
famous phrase, can direct the existing consensus in the community
towards the fulfilment of its aims, even though the cost of doing
so may be high. If the equation of social forces is in constant process of change, this means that tomorrow the equation of social
forces may permit the politician to do things which the equation
of social forces of today does not permit. Or, to put the point
another way, political problems are rarely, if ever, 'solved'; it is
more true to say that they may be 'settled' and, even so, only for a
limited period of time. No sooner is a particular policy feasible
because the equation of social forces has moved in its favour than
it becomes obsolete because the forces which supported it have
dwindled away as new causes, demanding new policies, have to be
satisfied.

But now let us consider the ways in which internal or domestic
politics are distinguishable from the politics between the state-

members of the international system. The most obvious difference, of course, is the presence of an overriding government within the state and the conspicuous absence of any such government between states. If we remember the point which we have just made in reference to A. F. Bentley's and David B. Truman's work, namely that in reality what government in a state does is not so much positively to organize the people towards certain ends, but to register a kind of temporary agreement, tacit or otherwise, reached between the dominant social forces in the state, then the presence or absence of government as an institution may perhaps not seem all that significant. But, although there is thus more similarity between domestic and international politics than most of us are inclined to think, the fact remains that the two processes are, after all, distinct.

One striking way of bringing out this distinction is to consider the simple model of political activity suggested by the French political writer, Bertrand de Jouvenel, in his *The Pure Theory of Politics*.[10] De Jouvenel, in his attempt to strip political activity of all its inessentials and to give us the 'essence' of that activity, indicates in this book 'three features fundamental to any political system', though they are not, as it happens, all present in the international political system. The first of these is some method of selecting between different 'instigations', or proposals for action by the community, when it would be intolerable to try to implement more than one at the same time. De Jouvenel points out that if such 'instigations' are really incompatible 'at the level of the set'—that is, if followed by the community as a whole—they may be destructive of public welfare. He gives the example of a besieged city which cannot with safety follow at one and the same time the advice of one leader that it should surrender and the advice of another leader that it should continue to fight.

Hence, secondly, one, and one only, of the competing instigations must prevail through the process of selection and that one must be proclaimed as something entirely new, that is, as an authoritative command, which it was not previously. 'The proclamation', in de Jouvenel's words, 'must be such that the "call to do" now uttered is unmistakably recognized by all as utterly different in nature from an instigation which they would be free to respond to or not. This is now a command and the abstract difference must be brought home by the visible majority'. Of course, de Jouvenel is here thinking of the method of selecting between competing instigations as it is found in liberal democratic states. There is no reason why the words 'visible majority' in that sentence should not be replaced by 'examination of the entrails of the sacrificed animal', or 'the decree of Augustus Caesar', or Hitler's statement after 30th June 1934 that he was 'for twenty-four hours the supreme judicial power in Germany'. All that is required is that the final pronouncement of the victorious instigation should be regarded as authoritative and final. Thirdly, after this process is completed and the command has been issued, there may still be freedom to advocate competitive instigations (a point on which de Jouvenel is not entirely clear), but there is no freedom to argue any such competitive instigation *as though it were an authoritative command*. There is a certain echo here of the conception of John Austin, the nineteenth-century British jurist, of law being the will of a determinate superior, that is, a command in de Jouvenel's sense of the term.

We can now see more clearly the contrasting characteristics of the international political process. We perceive that the international process is essentially a 'process of processes', that is, that the instigations (or, more simply, the proposals) of the different states in the international system are pre-selected. They have, at the national level, already passed through the three stages of selection indicated by de Jouvenel before they confront one another in the role of competitors at the level of the international system. International politics is in effect a rivalry between competitive instigations from the various national capitals which have already proved victorious in the domestic or intra-national system: they have already, in their several states, passed from being instigations into being commands. One implication of this is that the authors of those instigations which have won out at home and become commands there, that is, the different governments in the world, will naturally wish to preserve that domestic victory; and hence they will tend so to act in the international system that their instigations will continue to remain commands in the domestic system for as far ahead as one can see. This is indeed another way of saying that foreign policies are always influenced by domestic considerations in so far as those with authority to formulate foreign policy, that is, the different governments, try to act outside their states' borders in such a way as to preserve their supremacy within the domestic system.

All this has an important bearing on the concept of national interest which has become central to the study of international relations. We will deal more fully with the definition and use of this concept later.[11] Here it is enough to say that one factor in the definition of national interest in any concrete international situation is the wish, as we have said, of the policy-making élite to retain their official authority at home by preserving the victory of their own 'instigations' within the state. Hence, any given conception of the national interest which underlies a foreign policy will tend to reflect, not only what the actual needs of the state demand in the international situation in which it finds itself, but also the necessity to preserve the domestic authority of the policy-makers. This need not mean that governments will deliberately subordinate the national interest, however they define it, to their own interests as vote-catching politicians. It does mean, however, that any foreign policy (or instigation) which becomes the official policy of a state (that is, which becomes a command, in de Jouvenel's sense) must have proved more acceptable to the effective political fraction in that state than rival policies. To that extent, whether this process is apparent to the conscious minds of governments or not, all foreign policies of all states must reflect *both* the objective needs of the situation, as Ministers and permanent officials perceive them, and the consensus-building needs of that country.

We have described the international political process as a 'process of processes', or in other words two-tiered. So is the intra-national political process, but in a different sense and with different consequences. The domestic process is two-tiered in the sense that a government, urging its victorious instigation, now the country's command, in the international system, is made up of men whose 'instigations' have at some time previously won out at the party-politics level of rivalry between 'instigations'. The Ernest Bevin, in other words, must become his party's favourite son, or one of them, before he can compete with the Anthony Eden to become the nation's favourite son at the Potsdam conference. But there is this vital difference between the two-tiered system of domestic politics and the two-tiered system of international politics: if a Prime Minister or President can win the support of the nation, he can almost afford to ignore the party; *its* future will depend on *his* capacity to win favourable votes from the national people. But it is no good for a government in its international relations to think that it can afford to sacrifice national support to the support it may win from world opinion. Plainly, no government can, so to speak, cut off the channel of support from its local opinion, no matter how rapturous the welcome it may receive from the rest of the world. President Wilson in 1919 was the supreme example of a world statesman ultimately frowned upon and rebuffed by his own countrymen, a statesman to whom the plaudits of the world were irresistible, but who was unable—the world political structure being what it then was—to make those plaudits the fulcrum of a bid for world power.

The other, and possibly more important, distinction between the two political processes—the national and the international—springs from the fact that the authority sought by the aspirant to political office in the domestic political system is essentially lawful, legal, legitimate; it is the source of what de Jouvenel calls 'command'. Those subject to government authority in the state feel a certain compulsion to obey, which ultimately derives from a theory of political obligation which is accepted as legitimate in the country concerned. There is a recognition that the enforcement of sanctions against persons who defy authority of the 'command' type is correct because the offenders have broken a rule of law accepted as binding on all. We have to keep saying that a theory of political obligation is *accepted* as legitimate in a given country and that a rule of law is *accepted* as binding for the simple reason that, when all is said, government, legal authority, command, *are* matters of acceptance or rejection. Once the psychology of deference to legal authority is established in a country, the miracle by which a few can govern millions begins to work. Once that habitual submission gives way to doubt and questioning, the unthinking obedience of today becomes the sullen refusal of tomorrow.

This legitimate power of authority within the state de Jouvenel calls 'potestas', the remote and awful majesty of kings, the traditional charisma of 10 Downing Street or the White House, which elevates the words of politicians who enter these places from the status of 'instigations' to that of 'commands'. The office-holder obtains 'potestas' in a successful political career after he has cast his personal spell (de Jouvenel's 'potentia') over his followers.

They first knew him as a source of 'instigations', but through them he has risen to be a spring of commands, and these are effective over many people who perhaps would never have accepted him as a bearer of 'potentia'.

Now 'potentia' is essentially non-legal. It is not illegal; it merely has nothing to do with law. It has to do with feelings, with respect, admiration, perhaps even love, and with interest, calculation, self-advancement. As such, it is the power which one state may exert over another in the international system. State power in the international system is non-legal except in some rather marginal circumstances. It is true that on occasion one state may appeal to another to comply with its will from an essentially legal footing. Britain in 1972 asked Iceland to refrain from extending its waters under national control to 50 miles from land, on the ground that this, in British eyes, would be an infringement of the legal rules concerning the sea which were binding on both. In such an instance there is much the same reliance upon 'potestas' as when, for instance, an Inland Revenue collector calls upon the subject to pay his taxes. But this is not the most common method of wielding power internationally, and in any case the resort to legal argument in appeals to other states to comply is rarely if ever used alone.

In the everyday functioning of the international system the appeal of one state to another to comply with the former's will is essentially an appeal to the good sense of the other state, or to the common interests of both. The tone in which the appeal is couched is something like the following: 'would you not agree that in the long run you have more to gain from accepting our proposals than by resisting them? After all, we may be able to make things difficult for you, if you refuse to comply, and life for you could become impossible if you persist in opposing our will. And if you agree with us, there are certain benefits which we can bestow on you which will be very advantageous'. To revert to Bertrand de Jouvenel's terminology, this is merely another way of saying that in the international system no instigation is ever raised—or at least is very rarely raised—to the status of command at the level of the set.

It may be objected that there is one well-known exception to this in the shape of the authority of the United Nations Security Council. By Article 25 of the UN Charter resolutions adopted by the Security Council when acting under Chapter VII of the

Charter, which deals with 'threats to the peace, breaches of the peace and acts of aggression', are *ipso facto* binding upon all member-states even when adopted only by a qualified majority of the Security Council. By Article 2(b) of the Charter this quite extraordinary reserve power of the Council extends even to non-member-states since it is stated in the Article that:

> The Organisation shall ensure that states which are not members of the United Nations act in accordance with those Principles so far as may be necessary for the maintenance of peace and security.

But, in contradistinction to this argument, it should be remembered that only very rarely indeed has the Security Council been able to assert these powers—at the outbreak of the Korean War in June 1950, for example, the Council did no more than *recommend* to member-states that they put their armed forces under UN control in defence of South Korea. From this it may be inferred that the international process is normally a competition between non-legitimate instigations, none of which has been raised to the level of command.

We are inclined to say that this is because the state-members of the international system are, after all, themselves sovereign sources of law and hence cannot be subject to the law-making power of any other state. But there is another and more precise way of putting it. We must first go back to the reasons why the subjects of a state put up with the elevation of an instigation to a legitimate command with which they are obliged to comply, in the manner explained by de Jouvenel. They do so, it would seem, because, like Americans with their 'self-evident truths' in the Declaration of Independence of 1776, they adhere to a certain theory of political obligation which tells them why they should comply with government laws. If the prevailing theory of political obligations fails to command general approval, there occurs civil war, a state of affairs not unlike the normal condition of international politics. We read in John Locke's *First Treatise on Civil Government* of an unsuccessful attempt made by Sir Robert Filmer to make sense of the divine right of kings as a theory of political obligation, the argument being that, just as children are subject to their father, who provides security and subsistence, so God made man subordinate to kings. Locke calls this a 'strange kind of domineering phantom', which he says 'cannot appeal to rational and indifferent men'. Afterwards he himself in the *Second Treatise* constructs a theory of government as the protector of human rights and this, he argues, can appeal to 'rational and indifferent men'.[12]

Similarly, in France at the end of the eighteenth century writers sought for a rational theory of the state which would make sense of habitual obedience to government since it was no longer possible to repose faith in the theory of the *ancien régime*. Jean Jacques Rousseau began his famous treatise with the ringing words:

> Man is born free; and everywhere he is in chains. One thinks himself the master of others, and still remains a greater slave than they. How did this change come about? I do not know. What can make it legitimate? That question I think I can answer.[13]

Revolutions, in fact, may be described as periods of time in which old theories explaining the legitimacy of government fail, or, in Locke's words, no longer appeal to 'rational and indifferent men', and new formulae have to be worked out before the chains of government can lie easily and tolerably on the subject once again.

In the international system, however, there is no such thing as a commonly accepted theory as to why the various states should defer to a single focus of authority in the world, except within the limited confines of the UN Charter which describe the authority of the UN Security Council, as we have explained above. The Western liberal has one theory of what moral and political qualities should inhere in a single world government, and what moral and political ends that government should serve. The Communist has quite another; the African and Asian have others, and so on. If there could be a consensus among the states as to how a single world government could be legitimized, the problem of creating such a government would be solved.

The point is illustrated in a well-known essay by the late Professor Martin Wight called 'Why there is no international theory' which was first published in 1960.[14] In this essay Wight seems to confound two kinds of theory: theory of explanation, that which tells us what reality is really like, how things work, and so on, and theory of legitimacy or justification, or that which seeks to establish the rightfulness or acceptability of certain ideas or practices. Whatever one may think of the quality of the explanatory theory now available depicting the international system, that it exists, and exists in abundance, is not open to doubt. The libraries are filled with books purporting to explain how and why states act as they do in their relations with one another, how and why order in the international system from time to time breaks down, producing war or other forms of conflict; and so on. There are also fragmentary efforts to describe what *could* be the legitimate basis of a single world authority. But there cannot be in the literature of international politics any parallel to the continuous and coherent histories of theories of political obligation within the state. The reason is the obvious one, that within the state central authority does exist; man is 'everywhere in chains'. The question is, how can we make this acceptable to 'rational and indifferent men'? But we have no world government and have never had anything like it since the fall of the Roman Empire. Therefore we have no accumulated speculation on what the legitimate basis of that world government should be, whereas we do have a distinct tradition of inquiry into the moral foundations of government within the state.

Reverting now to the differences between 'potestas', the power of lawful authority within the state, and 'potentia', the non-legal power which precedes, and sometimes co-exists with, 'potestas' within the state, these differences shed a certain sombre light on the nature of political power within the international system.

First, simply because 'potestas' is essentially lawful authority, its scope is normally limited. Whether in the form of the rule 'render unto Caesar the things that are Caesar's and render unto God the things that are God's' or in the form of a social contract which stipulates what government is for and what it should not seek to control, it is essential to state authority that there is a realm in which its writ does not run. Indeed, that must be the situation if the writ of state authority is to run anywhere at all. Thus, one can speak of government authority being abused, of government acting *ultra vires*, of Ministers deciding matters beyond their competence. This is not perhaps quite so evident in a unitary state like Britain, in which the legislature is all-powerful, as it is in a federal state like the United States in which the powers of the several governing authorities are stipulated in a written constitution over which a Supreme Court acts as a guardian. But even in Britain a government could so overstep conventional ideas as to what are the proper limits of law that its whole authority might be called into question. All-powerful as the British Parliament undoubtedly is, it cannot in fact, though it has the formal, legal power to do so, regulate wages by statute or even forbid people to smoke. In any case Britain now has an Ombudsman whose duty it is to protect the ordinary person against public authorities which try to exceed what they may lawfully do.

'Potentia', on the other hand, is entirely without any such limits. One can never say that there can be, is, or should be a limit to, for instance, a leader's personal hold over his followers. There is no reason in theory, though it is quite clear that there is in practice, why the followers of a leader may not so increase as to embrace the whole world population, or why such followers should not bind themselves for ever, body and soul, to that leader, like Dr. Faustus to Mephistopheles. But such a conception is totally alien to the nature of lawful authority or 'potestas'. The same is the position in the field of international relations. When the United States or the Soviet Union, for example, calls upon another state to comply with its will, there may be countless reasons why the super-Power does not in the event have its own way; but if there is a disposition in the other state to submit there can be no limit to the extent of that submission. The United Nations, to take another example, imposed Unconditional Surrender on Germany in May 1945 and there was nothing in the law of nations to prevent them exacting any conditions whatever from the defeated state. Again, we are in the realm, not of finite law, but of infinite submission.

Another difference between these two types of authority, 'potestas' and 'potentia', has to do with the nature and quality of resistance that might be offered to either. Resistance to 'potestas' is unlawful; it has to be prosecuted in courts of law and under accepted rules of procedure, or with 'due process'. It is subject to lawful and stated sanctions, and there will normally exist in most stable states a system of appeal against the imposition of such sanctions, right up to the highest courts of the land. Resistance to 'potestas' may also be considered immoral by the public opinion of the community, but in most civilized countries the courts concern themselves only with allegations of actual illegality. Resistance to 'potentia', on the other hand, is normally regarded as immoral, among other things. The politician who opposes the party leader, for example, tends to be described, not as a law-breaker, but as a traitor to the party, or a schismatic, a 'splitter', a friend of the party's enemies, and so on. He is therefore prosecuted with the full *saeva indignatio* of the party, and is not usually protected by any rules corresponding to the due process of law, except that the party may not legally impose on him penalties contrary to the law of the country. Again, there are parallels in the international system. When the United States Secretary of State, Mr. John Foster Dulles, described the non-aligned states in Asia and Africa in the 1950s as 'immoral' because they declined the Secretary's proposal that they should join defensive military alliances against Communism, he was saying in effect that no punishment was too bad for them. Had the charge rather been that of breaking some rule of international law, at least that charge, and the sanction demanded for it in the event of the charge being proved in the law courts, would both have been limited.

Thus, in characterizing power in international relations as non-legal, or as 'potentia', in contrast to 'potestas', we are ascribing to it qualities which make it more awesome and dangerous than the kind of authority wielded by the sovereign state over its own citizens. This raises the question whether the political process in the international system is not better thought of as 'power politics', to use the commonplace expression, whatever that phrase may mean for different people. Does the image conjured up in the mind by the phrase 'power politics' correspond more or less with the realities of political activities as they proceed in the international system?[15]

To some extent and in some respects it does, to some extent and in some respects it does not. There are some connotations of the term 'power politics' which do, and others which do not accurately describe the international system. In so far, for example, as 'power politics' means that the parties to the political process are predominantly motivated by the lust for power, or what H. J. Morgenthau, the chief exponent of this view, calls the 'impulse to dominate', this does not faithfully describe the international system.[16] It may so describe some states at some periods in their history; these are what we have earlier called the 'power-misers' of the international system.[17] But it is surely better to think of political power, not so much as the object of all action in the international system, but as the indispensable condition for the performance of almost any action in that system. This is the con-

ception of power in international relations which we have presented in Chapter One of this book.

Nor is it correct to say, as some wish to imply by the term
'power politics', that all relations between states in the international system are governed by ratios of physical strength,
measured in military or other physical terms. A great deal of the
influence which states can exert within the decision-making
centres of other states has nothing to do with military strength,
but may in fact derive more from military or economic weakness.
Just as a bank can sometimes not afford to let a debtor go bankrupt
because, among other reasons, it has invested too much credit in
him already, so a powerful state is sometimes bound to go on
helping a small and weak country in order to secure some benefit
from its previous help, or for fear that that small and weak country
may totally collapse and fall into the big state's rival camp, or for
other reasons. The United States's experience with the weak
states of South East Asia provides many examples of this kind of
thing.

There is also the unconvincing argument that the politics of the
international system, as conveyed in the term 'power politics', is a
bellum omnium contra omnes, a war of all against all, as Thomas
Hobbes in the seventeenth century described the condition of
men without a common superior 'to keep them all in awe'. The
plain fact is that the states of the world do not fight each other
all the time. Some states have never fought each other; some, as
for instance Britain and New Zealand, are so unlikely to fight
each other in the future that for all practical purposes the possibility of war between them does not have to be provided for in the
forward planning of both countries. Karl Deutsch has used the
expression 'security communities' to describe such states, with
some slight difference in meaning.[18] There is a persuasive argument to the effect that in the world peace will never be secure
between the nations until war is literally as unthinkable between
them as it is between members of security communities in the
international system today.

Having thus discussed shades of meaning of the expression
'power politics' which are irrelevant to, or positively misleading
in, the study of our subject, we may now look at such nuances of
that expression which do convey some of the real essence of
international politics.

In the first place, it would be true to say that the climate of feeling in the international system, the 'political weather', the aggregate of hopes and fears which the human race entertain about its future, tends to revolve around the relations between the greatest military Powers rather than around relations between the smaller state-members of the system. This is not because the great Leviathan states lead more interesting lives, or that they are more virtuous or gifted, than the ordinary run of states. The plain fact is that the giant Powers have it in their hands to determine, not only what kind of future the other states will have, but whether they can reasonably expect any future at all. Hence the world's diplomats, governments, United Nations' officials and such like, consider local crises such as the Arab-Israeli conflict in the Middle East partly as human tragedies and at best costly in life and wealth for the states immediately concerned. But they also more critically regard them as possible Sarajevo assassinations which could embroil the greatest Powers in the Third World War, an intolerable fate for the rest of us. It is true that with the neo-isolationism which began to tinge the attitudes of the super-Powers—especially the United States—in the 1970s, the danger of their involvement in local crises tended to lessen. Nevertheless, the mere fact that the super-Powers have it in their hands to raise any minor, low-level conflict anywhere into a nuclear Armageddon involving us all, is bound to mean that all international relations today have the appearance of being variations on a major theme written by the super-Powers.

Again, there is in the expression 'power politics' an implication of violence, or at least the expectation of violence, pervading the political system, and of that violence being self-perpetuating: one act of force leads to another, and so on. This is a true description of the state of the international system. There is not a *bellum omnium contra omnes*; there are many security communities in the sense described above. The remarkable thing, too, is not that blood is shed, but that so little is shed in international relations, considering the tensions and quarrels that there are in the world, the combative spirit of man and the absence of means to prevent violence in the international system if the states determine to commit violence. Nevertheless, the very existence of armaments on a massive scale even in the smallest country and the devotion to defence of perhaps one-ninth of the world's goods and services testify to a permanent expectation that tensions between states may have a violent outcome.

In a famous passage in the *Leviathan* Thomas Hobbes argued that in a society without government there exists an expectation of war which in fact constitutes the cause and the condition of war:

> Hereby it is manifest that, during all the time that men live without a common power to keep them all in awe, they are in that condition called war; and such a war as is of every man against every man. For war consisteth not in battle only, or the act of fighting, but in a tract of time wherein the will to contend by battle is sufficiently known. And therefore the notion of time is to be considered in the nature of war as it is in the nature of weather. For as the nature of foul weather lieth not in a shower or two of rain, but an inclination thereto of many days together, so the nature of war consisteth not in actual fighting but in the known disposition thereto during all the time that there is no assurance to the contrary. All other time is peace.[19]

Thus, in international relations, too, the expectation of violence leads to the provision of arms and where arms exist the possibility that they may be used also exists.

But what accounts for the expectation of violence in some, though by no means in all, parts of the international system? The simplest answer is that violence between the state-members of the system, sometimes on a horrifying and massive scale, has been a recurrent event throughout the entire life of the system. Historically nothing has occurred to rule out violence, even on the greatest possible scale, or rather to convince states that they need make no provision against it. At all times the armourers thrive, as in a rainy climate do the umbrella manufacturers, not necessarily because man is irrational, but because he must draw logical inferences from his circumstances. It would be as imprudent for a state to go about defenceless as it would be for a man to go out on an overcast day without an umbrella. But this does not mean, of course, that the state, and the man, will not do all they can to contrive to live in a more favourable climate.

The state of the international system, in short, is that of an 'insecurity community' in that war is a contingent liability, in some place, at some time, against which provision has to be made by each state on a self-help basis, since this obligation can be

E

delegated to no other agency in the international system. If a time were to arise in any national state (and it has already done so in many) in which the citizen had to walk abroad armed because he could not rely upon any public provision of security, there would exist conditions approximating to the normal state of affairs in the international system.

Finally, the expression 'power politics' would seem to imply a relatively low moral tone prevailing within any political system, and there is certainly an echo of this in our international system. States, being composed of human beings, cannot ignore their own moral inhibitions. Most people, even perhaps in the most barbarous states, would probably wish to act in accordance with the moral law as known to them, if they were free to do so. We all readily quote the famous American phrase, 'My country, right or wrong!', as though it typified the utterly amoral nationalist. In fact Stephen Decatur's complete phrase was the very different: 'My country! May she always be in the right in her international controversies, but my country, right or wrong'. The fact is that, despite the desire of most people to do the right thing internationally, circumstances in the international system may make it hard for them to do so, or that is how it may seem.

One such circumstance has to do with the relation between morality and freedom. Taking his cue from the writings of Immanuel Kant in the eighteenth century, the modern moralist would no doubt agree that we cannot be said to be morally responsible for our actions if we are not causally responsible for them. It must be presumed, in other words, that the individual is free not to sin; if he is not free and he does sin, the moral responsibility will generally be thought to lie with whoever is denying him that freedom. Now, there can be little doubt that, in the political life, Ministers and sovereigns are less free to act as they will than private individuals. In the 1930s King Edward VIII of Britain could not marry the woman of his choice and remain on the throne. But in the international sphere of action they are even less free than within the territorial boundaries of their own states, if only for the obvious reason that the condition of their achieving their objects is normally the consent of other states, and that may not be forthcoming. Governments in the international system are apt to find themselves doing what they must, rather than what they would, and that is why we tend to think of their moral responsibility being rather less than that of people having full control of their affairs.

There is also the circumstance that in the international system the stakes at issue between the different parties are often inordinate, embracing not merely the lives and welfare of many millions of people, but even, on occasion, the fate of mankind itself. If two men play at cards on the condition that the winner will take the life of the other at the end of the game, most people might feel that a little cheating was not inexcusable, though they would deplore the appalling dilemma in which both the players had been placed. Christian ethics appear to hold that man's moral character actually improves with deprivation, as in Christ's famous saying, 'Blessed are the poor in spirit'. On the other hand, the celebrated apothegm of Thucydides when he is describing the effects of prolonged war, shortage of food, disease and civil violence on the Athenians seems more true of human nature: 'men', Thucydides wrote, 'are reduced to the level of their circumstances'. When physical security fails, moral restraints unfortunately tend to fail with it. This is perhaps not as it should be, but as it is. The same point was made by the philosopher Henry Sidgwick in two essays called *National and International Right and Wrong*, published just after the First World War, when in all the belligerent countries people were questioning the moral rightfulness of the war.[20] Sidgwick argued in these essays that Christ's injunction 'turn the other cheek' might be satisfactory to a religious prophet living within the physical security of the Roman Empire, but that it might not apply to the Roman soldier in Britain or France guarding the imperial frontier, who had to provide for that security.[21] There is quite clearly here, and in every kind of political system, a direct relationship between the physical security which people enjoy and their freedom to keep within the moral law.

Thus, the expression 'power politics', in the different senses defined here, may to some extent serve as a synonym for 'international politics'; in some ways the two terms do mean the same thing. But there are ways in which the loose cliché 'power politics' (for it is as such that this expression is often used) can be seriously misleading in the understanding of the international system. What is beyond doubt is that the description of the political process in that system which we have given in this chapter affects the entire role of violence, morality, the feeling of right and wrong, war and peace, as human experiences in international relations. To use the terminology which we have used in this chapter, there is no way in the international system in which the preferred 'instigation' in a number of competitive 'instigations' can be raised to the level of command. In that fact lie, at one and the same time, the recipe for catastrophe and the guarantee of freedom.

NOTES

1. See above, Chapter One, pp. 17–19.
2. See W. F. Ogburn (ed.), *Technology and International Relations*, University of Chicago Press, 1949.
3. See above, Chapter One, pp. 25–6.
4. *The Basis of Obligation in International Law and other Papers* by J. L. Brierly, edited by Sir H. Lauterpacht and C. H. M. Waldock, The Clarendon Press, Oxford, 1958, p. 69.
5. University of Chicago Press, Chicago.
6. There is a parallel between this conception of the political process and Tolstoy's idea of historical progress, as for instance in *War and Peace*.
7. Knopf, New York, 1951.
8. See above, Chapter One, p. 20.
9. *Politics. Who Gets What, When, How?*, Whittlesey House, New York and London, 1936, p. 3.
10. The Cambridge University Press, 1963: see especially Part IV, p. 30. The author wrote the book in English.
11. See below, pp. 191–99.
12. See edition of the *Two Treatises* by Peter Laslett, Cambridge University Press, Cambridge, 1960.
13. *Le contrat social*, translated with an introduction by G. D. H. Cole, Everyman's Library, J. M. Dent, London, 1933. The words quoted are preceded by a short introduction. By 'chains' Rousseau meant, of course, the bonds of government.
14. Reprinted in *Diplomatic Investigations*, edited by H. Butterfield and M. Wight, Allen and Unwin, London, 1966.
15. See *Power Politics*, first published by Georg Schwarzenberger in 1941, which has now (1975) reached the third edition; also *Power Politics*, by Martin Wight, published by the Royal Institute of International Affairs in 1946.
16. Morgenthau, *Politics among Nations*, Knopf, New York, 6th edn., 1972.
17. See above, Chapter One, pp. 20–21.

18. See K. W. Deutsch, *The Analysis of International Relations*, Prentice-Hall, Englewood Cliffs, New Jersey, 1968, pp. 193–6.
19. Chapter XIII: See the edition with an introduction by Michael Oakeshott, Blackwell, Oxford, 1955.
20. Allen and Unwin, London, 1919.
21. Ibid., p. 39.

Seven

The Anatomy of Statehood

IF we define a system as a certain intelligible and continuous complex of relations between certain determinate particulars, as we wish to do, we must indicate in the case of the international political system, precisely what those 'particulars' are. What are the units in the system which make up the whole? Evidently, in the present state of world politics, we have no alternative but to identify these entities as the sovereign states of the world, of which there are now some 140. The word 'state' has, of course, a double meaning: it may refer to the law-making machinery for controlling the social behaviour of a people within certain recognized national frontiers, or it could refer to the hereditary territorial organization as a whole, consisting of a people organized by a single focus of authority. The state in the latter sense—as when we speak of the states of Europe or Africa—necessitates state in the former sense in order to constitute an active and independent member of the world system of states. State in the first of these two senses—as in the expression 'man versus the state', 'state education', 'state ownership of the means of production', and so on—is a single noun: in the second sense it may be either singular or plural. However, it is 'state' in the second sense to which we are referring here.

In recent years there has been much debate among professional students of international relations as to whether we can continue to regard the state as the irreducible basic unit in the international system, the chief animal in the international zoo, so to speak. Some writers have argued that the traditional image of the state, as a social unit of 'billiard-ball' hardness, has been rendered obsolete by the advent of new methods of penetrating the state's old exclusiveness. Thus the economy of the modern state, even the most autarchic of states, is tied in with the world economy; economic changes in one country can have the most profound effect upon others, no matter how much the latter may try to insulate itself against adverse currents from outside. Again, the day is long past when the government of any state could hope to close its people's eyes and ears to ideas and intellectual influences in the world outside; the frontier is no longer, if it ever was, an impenetrable barrier against the immigration of political ideas from abroad. And finally the modern national frontier offers no protection against weapons which can now fly through the air with unerring accuracy to the other side of the world. Along with all this, modern politics have found means of weakening or breaking up another state without invasion from the outside at all. There can be the 'fifth column', the guerrilla force, the saboteur, who can work from within to destroy a state, either acting independently or in close accord with military forces moving in from the outside. Thus, it is said, the modern state can no longer behave as an integrated whole in the international system today.[1]

There is another argument against the claim made on behalf of the modern state that it represents the most important social unit in the international system. This is the argument that, with the increasing complexity of international relations, the ever-thickening network of contacts in various fields between states, the proliferation of permanent organizations for the conduct of international business, and the widening disparity between the strongest and the weakest states in the system, the power of independent initiative has left the sovereign state and shifted to the super-Powers, or to international organizations, or to genuinely international non-governmental organizations, or to revolutionary organizations such as guerrilla forces in the different developing countries. All countries, it seems, suffer from the illusion that they are free to make their own decisions; in the overwhelming majority of such cases, contrary to popular assumption, their decisions are made for them, either by the more powerful states or by abstract forces which they are unable to contain.[2]

It is convenient to deal with the second of these arguments first. No doubt the modern state is hedged in today by all manner of restraints, as compared with, say, the situation a hundred years ago, though it would be difficult if not impossible to prove this. No doubt, too, that when nations express their fear of losing their freedom of choice if they join a supra-national arrangement along with other states, they are in fact regretting the loss of something which they never really possessed. There is always a considerable hiatus between the independence which sovereignty is legally supposed to confer and the practical freedom to do as they like which states enjoy. But even if the power of independent initiative has left the nation-states of this world, it is doubtful whether it has been appropriated by the other commonly acknowledged rivals to the states as the chief entities in the international system.

Let us consider the super-Powers first. Writing in 1946 Martin Wight prophesied that in the post-War era then beginning effective sovereignty would be held by hardly any other states than the super-Powers, that is, at that time the United States and the Soviet Union.[3] It is true, of course, that the rivalry between America and Russia dominated international politics after the end of the Second World War, and that, so physically powerful were these giants, any military sequel to their quarrel must embroil the whole world. Nevertheless, the remarkable thing about the two or three decades since 1945 is the extent to which the super-Powers have been 'muscle-bound', in the sense of being virtually unable to use their military power to strengthen their diplomatic pressure. Clearly, the super-Powers' fear of general nuclear conflagration has served to deter both of them from becoming too closely involved in any local problem. Their attitudes towards the Middle East crisis in the late 1960s and early 1970s are good examples of this. Again, the dominant armed conflict in the world in the 1960s and early 1970s, the war in Vietnam, showed in the most striking way that even the greatest military Power of the day can sometimes do virtually nothing against a small developing country, provided the troops of the latter are prepared to go on fighting for many years and they have enough sentimental support in the world outside. Certainly the lesson which the American public and Congressional opinion seemed to draw from their experience in Vietnam was that they should be on their guard in future against being dragged into military operations in a small country, however all-powerful their own military and economic resources might seem.

There is no question that the super-Powers dispose of immense military resources for the strengthening of their foreign policies, and their economic wealth provides them with a wide repertory of diplomatic persuasion. But it would be quite mistaken to infer from this that either super-Power is in a position to throw its

weight about in world affairs and do what it will. The mere fact
that since 1945 the international system has been polarized between the two giant Powers means that the allies and friends of
each are accessible, in some degree, at least, to the influence of the
other. It also means that the existence of a rival super-Power
makes a giant state nervous of alienating small countries for fear
that they may turn to the other side. Moreover, at the present
time the classic technique of 'gunboat diplomacy', that is, the
frightening of small states into submission by a show of force, is
less practicable than ever before. The climate of the times is
against it, especially when 'gunboat diplomacy' is practised by
white states against coloured states, as the Suez crisis demonstrated
so vividly in 1956, and there exists today a United Nations
emotionally disposed against the bullying of small countries. The
United Nations may be physically powerless, but the noise it can
create around the world is not something even the greatest Power
cares often to incite.

One cannot repeat too often that in the international system
there is no simple correspondence between physical capability
and freedom to do as one wishes. The great Power also has great
responsibilities; its leaders realize (or their competitors for office
soon make them realize) that what they say will be heard, attended
to, pondered upon, everywhere, and that what they do is bound to
have repercussions around the world. There is also the fact that
the giant Power, unlike the small state, is normally slow to move
into action because of its sheer size and bulk, and for the same
reason its leaders know that for a super-Power to switch its course
in foreign policy is a ponderous operation, not lightly to be embarked upon. George Kennan once described the American
democracy as being 'like a palaeolithic monster which is slow to
arouse but which, once aroused, lays about itself with such force
as to wreck its own habitation'. The same may be true, though, of
course, the psychological factors are different, in the case of the
Soviet Union.

Next, we should have even less difficulty in disposing of the
second entity which allegedly rivals the sovereign state as an actor
in the international system, namely the contemporary international organization. Among the six states which formed the
original members of the European Communities, enlarged to
nine in January 1973, there was undoubtedly a wish to transcend

the sovereign state as a unit of human organization, and there was a practical movement towards that end in the form of the actual erosion of sovereignty in the various treaties creating the Communities. But the remarkable thing is how little this integration process has been taken as a model outside western Europe, and also how slowly the process is moving even in western Europe, where the conditions seem to be more favourable than anywhere else in the world. France under President de Gaulle (1958–1969) showed no inclination to accept the extinction of her sovereignty in the Communities; very much to the contrary. De Gaulle's successors, Georges Pompidou and Valéry Giscard d'Estaing, were men of no less caution. As for Britain, the strong fears expressed in that country about membership of the Communities, both before and after actually joining in 1973, suggested that Britain would hardly ever be in the van of European federalists even if it remained in the Communities. Supranationalism, for all the interest it has aroused among intellectuals who have lost enthusiasm for the sovereign state, has been far from sweeping away the great mass of people or politicians in western Europe.

When we consider the more traditional international organizations, whether global like the United Nations, or regional like NATO or the League of Arab States, it is even more evident that the state has not been displaced by the international institution as the main centre of initiative in the international system. The effectiveness of the United Nations, as has been stated over and again, and not least by its Secretaries-General, does not rest upon any intrinsic power within that organization to affect events on its own account, but on the readiness of member-states—that is, including the greatest Powers but other states as well—to work together for the common good. As the record of the United Nations has repeatedly shown, the organization, except in very uncommon circumstances, has no power to force its will upon anybody. In any case, what we conversationally call its will is in fact none other than the joint wills of the states which make up its voting majorities, and often even they do not consent to be bound by the resolutions they have voted for. The same is true for the Specialized Agencies of the United Nations and for the various regional organizations which have been formed for co-operative purposes in the world since 1945. It is better to regard all these bodies, not as substitutes for the states as originators of initiatives in the international system, but as devices for mitigating the inconvenience resulting from the unwillingness of the peoples of the world to abandon the states in which they live.[4] International organizations, in other words, reflect state initiatives rather than determine them.

Another way of conceiving the role of international organizations in the international system is to see them as part of the whole world environment in which the state lives and in which it has to make its various decisions. They constitute actualities outside the state's borders, of which the state must take account and to which it must adjust. Or, to state the point another way, they are one of the external 'inputs' which are fed into the policy-making process.

Something similar may be said of certain other participants in the international system, or actors on the international stage, to which some students today wish to assign a role as important as, or perhaps more important than, the sovereign state. These are the many transnational groupings of people and organizations, most of them having little or no connection with national governments, which express the essentially international character of life today. International business corporations and companies are an obvious example: these often have budgets larger than those of many of the states in the international system and are suspected of playing an autonomous role in the rise and fall of governments, especially in the developing countries. But whenever and wherever people are engaged in similar activities in different states, whether in the course of business or pleasure, there is a natural tendency towards transnational co-operation, which is often embodied in some more or less institutional form, such as an annual conference and permanent offices in some world capital. Since the First World War it has become standard practice for political parties and trade unions throughout the world to develop international links for mutual support and advice. All this is part of the stuff of modern life. To that extent the world has outgrown the idea and practice of the sovereign state.

But it is, nevertheless, hard to regard these non-governmental international associations as major determinants of the shape taken by international politics, though, as is the case with inter-governmental organizations, they play an increasingly important role in creating the environment in the midst of which the making of foreign policies by the different states takes place. This in-

creasingly complex pattern of cross-national affiliations is part of
the world in the late twentieth century. Governments acting on
behalf of states in the international system can no more ignore
these affiliations than can anyone else. But there seems little
doubt that governments still possess the power to regulate and
control this unofficial international activity, if it becomes important to state policy to do so. Only in very exceptional circumstances
can guerrilla organizations, for example, virtually usurp the
functions of the state, as they seem to have done in some Arab
countries in the Middle East. The state has by no means abdicated
in the face of threats to its primacy from world-wide or region-
wide pressure groups. The lives of the majority of the people in
the world, for better or for worse, are still spent within the confines of their own state, which still creates the framework of their
daily activities from birth to grave. Where this is not so, as in some
of the less advanced developing countries, it is the village or the
tribe which is the social unit with which most people identify, and
certainly not the world organization far beyond their mental
horizons.

   This brings us back to our first question: how real is sovereignty
in the world today? Are people saying anything significant when
they talk of the issue of national independence and how it may be
jeopardized by schemes for international integration? We can
certainly say that prejudice against joining one's fortune with that
of another state exists and is widespread in the world today. It
almost seems as though it is a condition of social organization
that people enclosed, for example, within the circle of the state
should feel some hostility towards the rest of the world—'every
primitive tribe has its White Australia policy', wrote the sociologist Edward Westermarck—and this in itself must make the idea
of a merger with another community essentially unattractive.
Certainly, too, there is a universal conviction that, despite all the
obvious limitations on the freedom of choice of governments,
something meaningful is taking place when the executive in a state
formulates foreign and domestic policy. If it were the case that the
broad lines of policy were dictated to governments by forces beyond their control, there could hardly be the controversy over the
policy which generally takes place whenever there is a major issue
to be decided or choice to be made. Controversy implies that there
is *some* freedom of choice open to states in the international system,

although care must always be taken to see that this is not exaggerated. If a state decides to throw in its lot and integrate with another state, the area of controversy within the state would presumably be reduced, and hence real freedom of choice would be lessened. That most people are more or less aware that this is the necessary sequence of events, implies that they think of sovereignty as something real, though they may exaggerate the extent to which it is real.

We are safe, then, at least for the present, in assuming that the states are the principal units in the international system, the chief animals in the international zoo, so to speak, in that the events which make up the continuum of international politics result from decisions taken by those states, however varied in weight and importance those decisions may be, and however much they may be influenced by extra-national agencies, such as international organizations, international businesses and so on. But it would be wrong to read too much into that fanciful phrase 'the chief animals in the international zoo'. In a real zoo there is a sharp distinction between the zoo as an organization designed by men for their own study and entertainment, on one side, and the animals designed by nature through a process of natural selection, on the other. The animals in the zoo may adapt themselves to the system of the zoo, but it is not essential that they do so. The fat old gorilla who sits in the corner gorging himself on bananas and taking no other interest in his surroundings is just as much a part of the zoo as the chimpanzee who sits at the table drinking tea with his keeper. But the international system of states is not, in the sense of a zoo, an aggregate of entities formed outside the system. On the contrary, the states of the world are themselves shaped by the need to participate in the system. Indeed states may be defined as entities moulded, whether deliberately or not, for the purpose of taking part in a certain kind of system. They are means of organizing people for participation in the international system. So far, Political Science, in its concentration on the nature of the state seen from the inside, so to speak, has tended to ignore this international aspect of the state. But there are good reasons for attempting to define the state in terms of the international context in which all states live.

One such reason concerns the bases of social cohesion in the modern state. In Britain we are inclined to take social cohesion in the state for granted, though with the increase in coloured immigration into this country some have feared that Britain's age-old social unity would weaken; there are also the centrifugal tendencies in Northern Ireland, Scotland and Wales. But Britain's situation is in any case exceptional; so far from social cohesion being the norm in other states of the world, most of them are divided within themselves on religious, racial, linguistic, class or tribal lines. Unity in such states, and the habitual deference to the state authorities which makes the maintenance of law and order possible, are to a large extent dependent upon the fact that the state is a member of a dangerous and highly competitive international system. Could the modern state, or the majority of modern states, hang together at all unless they faced, and were continuously being made by their governing authorities to feel that they faced, a hostile and acquisitive society beyond their borders? Edmund Burke in the eighteenth century defined the state as a partnership in prestige, but there can be no prestige except in a society wider than that of the individual state, that is, world society. Again, H. R. G. Greaves has defined the state as a 'co-operative organization for the promotion of the welfare of its members'.[5] But pre-eminent among the elements which constitute welfare, is the defence of its members' interests *vis-à-vis* the outside world. Hence, as we have said, the state can be regarded as a 'co-operative organization for the collective participation of its members in the international system of states'. When we ask: 'What is the state for?' we must answer that it exists in order that its people may participate in the international system. What did the Smith régime in Rhodesia hope to gain from its unilateral declaration of independence in November 1965? Presumably entrance into the international system as an equal sovereign state, in the expectation that it could do certain things and receive certain things, especially the sanctification of its white-biased political régime, which were not available to it as a colony.

But we must relate 'state' to 'international system' for another reason. This concerns the attribute of sovereignty, which all state-members of the international system are deemed to possess. Sovereignty has, of course, an internal and an external connotation. Internally, it generally means supreme competence to make law within the determined frontiers of the state to the exclusion of any other law-making authorities. We normally inquire: Where is sovereignty in this territory? With whom does it lie? Who is sovereign? Generally speaking, it is easy enough to answer: in Britain, for instance, sovereignty lies with the Queen in Parliament with Lords and Commons assembled. In federal states these questions are more difficult to answer.

Externally, however, sovereignty does not mean 'supremacy', but 'equality'. The stress is not on being higher than anyone else in law-making power, but on being on the same level as other law-making authorities, that is, other states. Britain and France, for example, are not as sovereign states supreme over anybody except their own people and, this, within their own frontiers. They are considered to be equal in respect to each other and to other members of the international system. This is in effect to say that states, in so far as emphasis is being laid on their sovereignty as one of their key attributes, are defined by reference to the international system in which they are participants. A sovereign state, then, is nothing more nor less than an entity which participates in the international system on a level of legal or formal equality with all such similar members of the system.

There is a further point to be borne in mind about sovereignty. As we have already stated, sovereignty does not mean freedom to do as the state pleases, any more than being legally mature within any domestic system of law means that you are free to do as you like. Sovereignty, as a concept in the study of international relations, is essentially a legal expression which refers to a status of equality with other sovereigns within a distinct system of law, that is, international law. It means competence to enter into international legal contracts on a basis of equality with other member-states of the international system; having one's legal rights respected on a non-discriminatory basis with other states; and freedom to act within a certain nexus of rights and obligations, opportunities and restrictions, laid down by international law. When a colony becomes an independent state and the flag of its former metropolis is lowered for the last time, the people of the new state can only tell what it means to be a state, what they can do, or must do, what they cannot do, or should not do, when they consult the rules of international law, which incidentally were in operation long before the new state was born. Only those rules can tell them how their new status differs from the old. It is beside the point to inquire at this stage whether international law is effective, or whether the equal rights obtained under it by a state acquiring sovereignty for the first time are likely to be respected. What we are considering here is the body of assumptions on which a certain political system rests, not whether that system operates effectively.

Hence, to return to our main point, we are insisting that the sovereign state as we know it, that is, a certain hereditary organization of people inhabiting a defined territory and controlled by a distinct system of law, could not exist outside the international political system. It certainly could not be defined as it is defined, that is, as sovereign, except with reference to that system.

The question may then be asked whether the state-members of the international system, all 140 of them, are not too heterogeneous—too varied in power, size, culture, history, and in a hundred or more other respects—to form a coherent subject of study. Where a group of entities is very numerous it is possible to make fairly valid predictive statements about them. It is a fair assumption, for instance, that if we know that one out of ten in a given population suffers from rheumatism, provision should be made in national planning to accommodate 10,000 rheumatic patients in a total population of 100,000. But in this sample of some 140 or so states forming the international system, the diversities tend to outweigh any possible similarities. We cannot say, for example, that if five states go nuclear over a ten-year period, ten will go nuclear over the next twenty years. Or, to put the point another way, how can we talk about *the* state when the known examples of states vary so much from one to another?

One answer to this question we have already given: namely that all states belong to a common *genus* in so far as they all participate in a certain recognizable international system. What, we may ask, have all these pieces of wood in common, apart from the fact that they are wooden? Perhaps it is the fact that they were all designed to fit together to make an article of furniture, or a picture, or a jig-saw puzzle. States in their common membership of the international system are not dissimilar.

The other way in which we can make a study of states, as portions of our study of the system, is to look at them in three different ways. First, we can inquire what they have in common and what this implies for the nature of the relationships between them; secondly, we can see if the existing states of the world can be classified in groups which have common features differentiating them from other groups; and thirdly, we must try to examine states individually, considering each as *sui generis* and having its own unique style of life and form of behaviour within the system. With such a three-fold method of study we should be able to penetrate more deeply into the nature and *modus operandi* of states.

To begin, then, with the common features of states. We must place high among these the primary fact that the word 'state' implies a certain relationship between government in that social entity and the governed. Within the frontiers of a sovereign state the government exercises ultimate compulsive authority; it has a monopoly of legal force over its subjects. It is true that many other social groups, such as trade unions, social clubs, political parties, are so organized as to give their directing authorities— their chairmen, presidents and executive committees—the power to enforce rules against members by imposing some form of fine, denial of group facilities, and ultimately expulsion from the organization. In that respect, as H. R. G. Greaves has pointed out, the state is merely another kind of social organization.[6] Nevertheless, the authority wielded by a state over its members is so different from the authority encountered in other social organizations as to be almost of a different kind.

In the first place, the authority of the state is pervasive: there is no escape on this planet from the state's all-seeing eye and control, and even emigration from one state only brings the subject under the authority of another state, which alone may determine whether the immigrant will be welcome. Secondly, it is absolute and final: in the end there is no appeal against the authority of the state and even appeals against the state to an international organization, such as the European Commission on Human Rights, are often uncertain in their effects. Moreover, a state against which an appeal has been successfully launched in such an organization is not necessarily lacking in means of retaliation against the author or authors of the appeal. Finally, the authority of the state is supreme; that it to say, it covers powers of life and death. The authority of the state makes the taking of life legal. In fact, the legality or otherwise of killing, and the precise circumstances of that legality, can only be determined by reference to the official laws and courts of law of the state.

All this means that the state cannot but raise profoundly disturbing moral questions for the individual, which are not raised in everyday life in private society. In our everyday lives, and in the non-state groups and organizations which make up the web of private society, we are free to refrain from actions which offend our sense of right and wrong. In the final resort we can resign from the club or trade union if it acts in a way morally displeasing to us. But there is no such contracting out in the case of the state and in our role as citizens: as subjects of the state we may be compelled to do things to foreigners, in time of war for example, which may be deeply repellent to our consciences. Day by day we are forced to be parties to the imprisonment of people, and possibly to their execution through capital punishment, which may be equally repugnant to our sense of right and wrong. Yet we are forced to comply.

Hence, the compliance of the governed with the decisions of the government in a state must rest on foundations peculiar to itself. We must remember, too, that the dealings of sovereign states with one another are profoundly affected by this division of the state sociologically into the leaders and the led. A government, for example, in its dealings with the governments of other states, will generally seek not to lower or diminish the compliance it normally expects from its own people; normally it will endeavour by its acts and policies in the international system to increase that compliance. It must, in other words, try to use its external policy for the purpose of reducing, if possible, resistance to its rule at home. But there is also the problem of making government seem right and morally acceptable in the eyes of its subjects. As Macchiavelli pointed out long ago, there is, and is bound to be, something inherently evil about government if only because, as we have earlier remarked, people have to do things, or participate in the doing of things, at the instigation of government, which are deeply disturbing to their consciences. One way of dealing with this moral dilemma is to think of the alternative to doing or participating in doing those things as being even more evil than those things themselves. Obviously, in wartime a nation can harden itself to perform dreadful actions like the bombing of Dresden in 1943 or of Hiroshima in 1945 because it can bring itself to believe that, without such actions, the situation in the form of the imposition of the enemy's will on itself would be even more dreadful. But, in peace or war, it can be stated as a general rule that people can accept the moral level of their own state, no matter how low, so long as they can persuade themselves that the world outside the state's borders is even more immoral. In brief, what most of us do most of the time is to take morality from the external world and give it to the state, *our* state. So long as the world outside looks an immoral and dangerous place, we can stomach the immorality which is an inescapable part of living in any state, at any time.

A second important common feature of states is that they are all essentially territorial entities; they are space-bound, their physical limits are determined in terms of space. It is true that states are not entirely different from other social groups in being territorial entities: cities, towns, counties, provinces, are also territorial. But states are charactericially so, and moreover if other social units, such as those we have mentioned, are territorial, it is by way of being parts or aspects of states.

The essential territoriality of states determines certain peculiarities of statehood. One of these is that the bond of association in the state, or the habitual submission of the governed on which statehood is built, has deep roots in the attachment of people to a certain piece of soil. Land, even in a highly industrialized society, is capable of inspiring the strongest emotions, many of them no doubt unconscious, in people's minds, and the sacrifices involved in the kind of service men and women have rendered to their states throughout history are often the product of passionate attachment to a certain piece of territory, which becomes identified in the mind of the patriot with the exceptional virtues his people are supposed to possess. The invasion of one's territory by foreign armed forces arouses the kind of primitive alarm and hostility which birds and animals manifest in defence of their territorial domain. The establishment and maintenance of the integrity of a nation's territory is one of the strongest motivations in foreign policy, as India's attitude towards Portuguese Goa and Spain's attitude towards British Gibraltar have shown. Title to territory has in fact, and not surprisingly, provided throughout history the classic subject-matter of international disputes, often leading to war.

Moreover, people who wish to form a nation-state must have, not merely a piece of earth on which to build it, but a territory which can provide the viable basis of a state. That is to say, it must be defensible and not easily exposed to conquest by neighbours and it must provide a livelihood for those wishing to inhabit it. To take merely one striking example, the state of Liberia in West Africa was founded in the 1840s as the outcome of a quixotic plan to transport all the negroes in the United States back to their African place of origin. The problem was to find an unsettled territory on the coast of Africa and populate it with black emigrants from North America. The difficulties of subduing the wilderness of the territory eventually chosen, however, were such that the first two batches of imported negroes perished and only at the third attempt was a successful lodgment on the coast effected.[7] To constitute a state, in short, demands more than people and a certain strength of will: it also requires physical properties in the destined territory which are capable of making a settlement possible.

But a nation's will to make a state in that particular geographical location must be there, too. The land must not only be defensible and capable of supporting a community, but it must stimulate in the people's minds the feelings and ideas necessary, if the efforts and sacrifices essential to the making of a state are to be forthcoming. The present-day state of Israel is a good example of a highly vulnerable territory from the military point of view, a thin strip of land clinging to the coast and surrounded by numerous implacable enemies. Israel's struggle to survive in its chosen environment has had far-reaching effects in giving the country the character of a nation-in-arms, and that may not be altogether wholesome for its long-term development. But would the Israelis have it otherwise? Before the First World War the British Government offered the Zionists land in East Africa in which to build a Jewish national state, and the Jews had to ask themselves whether they could ever say: 'Next year in Kampala, or Nairobi' with the zest with which they said: 'Next year in Jerusalem'. At the Zionist Congress in Basle in 1903 Dr. Chaim Weizmann led the movement to turn down the British offer with the words 'nothing but Palestine can satisfy the immemorial longings of the Jewish people'.[8] And that surely is only common sense; if people are called upon, as the Israelis have been, and more than once, to fight and die for their country, it must be a country, or in the simplest sense a territory, for which their love knows no limitation.

But there is a further point to be made about territory as the material foundation of statehood, and that is the way in which people and ideas, or ideologies, which are transplanted to a particular territory begin to shape themselves in accordance with the nature and requirements of that territory. Land, it seems, has an immense capacity to assimilate and mould people and ideas to suit its own needs. The example of the Jews in Israel, again, illustrates this. One of the most remarkable features of life in Israel since the state was founded in 1948 is the nationalization of even the physical features of Jewish immigrants, who come from all over the world. It seems as though, generation by generation, a new and distinctively Israeli personality is growing up in the country, one which is well adjusted to the physical environment. The same is, of course, true for the millions of immigrants who have settled in the United States; within a generation or two a combination of rejection of the immigrant's old background far away, and the attractions of the new one, helps to forge a new people. No doubt this is due in large measure to the assimilative forces of society, especially education, but the society itself reflects the physical nature of the environment in which it develops. As for the effects of territory on ideas, it is well-known how Marxist Communism has been transformed as a result of being established as the ruling ideology in China and Russia respectively. No doubt, again, the pre-Communist history of these two countries, their level of economic development and their cultural and intellectual traditions have all played a part in making Soviet Communism markedly different from Chinese Communism. But the country itself as a physical entity, and the demands which it makes upon those who have settled in it, have probably done more to mould the practical shape of Communism in those two countries than all the discussions about the theoretical aspects of the Marxist faith among the *cognoscenti*.

When we now turn to consider the implications of the territoriality of states for their practical behaviour in the international system, it is evident that these are many. We must begin with the obvious fact that states, being territorial agencies, are fixed on the map; they have no, or very little, physical mobility. It is true that frontiers are very often changed and this may have the effect of literally moving a state from one spot on the earth's surface to another; thus Poland in 1945 was shifted some hundred miles or so west of the Soviet Union. But that is altogether exceptional; the physical immobility of states remains one of their most distinct characteristics.

Territorial immobility implies an inescapable relationship with one's neighbours. A state cannot escape from, nor ignore its neighbours, in the same way that a family can pick up its belongings and depart for a more congenial environment. A state's position with respect to its neighbours—and this is perhaps the most obvious fact about statehood and it could be the most important condition of all international relations—is that of enforced vicinity or involuntary propinquity. And not only that, but enforced intercourse with neighbours, especially as distance is conquered by science and technology, means that trade, travel and pollution increase. It was an axiom of the ancient Indian philosopher, Kautilya, that all states contiguous to a given state were automatically hostile, whereas other neighbours on the far side of such states were automatically friendly.[9] There is no reason why this should be regarded as an iron law of nature. But it is at least a matter of common experience, that the juxtaposition in space of two communities which are unable to change their situation, creates problems of which both are bound to take account: neither side can ignore the implications of enforced contiguity. For this reason the image of a 'game', which is sometimes used to describe relations between states, seems in some respects unsatisfactory.[10] There is one option which most players of games have, which states do not enjoy, and that is to bring the game to an end. On occasion it is true that players of Christmas party games, for example, are conscripted for the game against their wish by importunate children or tedious elderly relatives, and their resulting feelings of resentment may affect their attitude towards the game. But this is the normal condition of international relations. When Mr. John Foster Dulles in 1954 warned France of an 'agonizing reappraisal' of American foreign policy unless France ratified the European Defence Community treaty, he was voicing the intense resentment of a country conscripted for international politics against its will and painfully aware that there was no chance of being soon demobilized.

Clearly, there are important consequences for the foreign policies of states which follow from the principle of enforced vicinity. The most obvious is that participation in the international system is inescapable for practically every state, no matter how small or how remote from the main tension centres of world affairs. Not only must states have dealings with their most immediate neighbours, but they cannot avoid playing some part in the whole system of states whatever their objects and interests may be. The point was stated, in his usual homely way, by Abraham Lincoln in his First Inaugural Address in 1861, when he was endeavouring to persuade the Americans, in north and south, not to fight the impending civil war. Man and wife, he said, may divorce and go their separate ways, but states are not able to part. They may fight, but after fighting they must continue to face the problem of how and on what terms they will live together afterwards. Is it any easier, Lincoln asked, to determine those terms after fighting than before fighting?[11]

There is an important point made in those words about the nature of the international system as a social organization. If we divide social groups into two kinds—we may call them the hedonistic and the pragmatic—the former, like social clubs, mothers' meetings and such like, arise in response to the social instinct, that is to say the gratifications which people seem to derive from the mere act of belonging, from being in the company of other people. The pragmatic association, on the other hand, such as the trade union or the Stock Exchange, may afford somewhat similar gratifications to their members, but primarily they are formed to satisfy some non-social object of their members, such as defending their standard of living or making money. The international system is essentially not the hedonistic type of association. States do not join the international system because they 'feel lonely'; they appear indeed to have little in the way of a gregarious instinct. It seems rather as if the states, if they could have their own way, would prefer to cut adrift from the international system and go their own way. Taking part in the international system is always irksome. It means acquiring commitments which can be inconsistent with one another, and which at best may be positively dangerous. It means making concessions to other states when one would like to have it all one's own way. It may imply making serious inroads, if not into one's actual independence as a state, then perhaps into one's sense of being independent. But the international system is also pragmatic in the sense that states, being pinned to the map, as it were, cannot avoid participating in the international system. Moreover, being pinned to the map creates needs, especially for security, which demand associations with other states, defensive or otherwise. It is a curious fact that almost the only occasion when states 'feel lonely', as individuals often do, is when they are diplomatically isolated and need the assistance of other states to protect them against threats from the international system. If they were not fixed to the map, they could physically remove themselves from such threats.

But there is another implication for policy within the international system which derives from the physical immobility of states. This is that it can never be a sound rule of foreign policy to seek to eliminate another state. 'Never destroy another state', wrote Fénelon, 'under pretext of restraining it'. This was once a well-established axiom in classical European diplomacy. It was reflected, for example, in the care taken by the European Powers, especially Britain, to restore France to the 'comity of Europe' after the defeat of Napoleon in 1815; by the time of the Congress of Aachen in 1818 France, the poacher, had joined the game-keepers. With the coming of total war and popular democracy in the twentieth century, however, the idea began to spread that, after the defeat of an enemy in war, an 'unstate' could be made out of him by destroying permanently his ability to wage war and ostracizing him for ever from the respectable society of nations. This latter-day conception of '*Carthago est delenda*' was reflected in the notorious Morgenthau plan for the pastoralization of Germany after the Second World War, which President Roosevelt for a short time adopted, to the horror of some of the older hands in the Foreign Office in London. It was reflected, too, in the many newspaper articles written in Britain during the War entitled: 'Can we do without Germany?'

There is an obvious distinction to be drawn here between the German state, in the sense of a certain apparatus of government, together with its armed forces, civil service and national administration, on one side, and the German state in the sense of an organization based on a certain determinate territory. A state in the first sense may be utterly destroyed without a great deal of difficulty, which happened to Germany in 1945; all its people may even be killed or sold into slavery, and its soil ploughed with salt, as was the custom in ancient times. But the territory remains and into that space political forces may penetrate which are even more hostile and dangerous than the previous régime. This became brutally clear at the end of the Second World War. Vengeful as the Western Powers felt towards Germany in 1945, regarding it has having plunged the world into a terrible war, albeit under the Nazi régime, it soon became clear to them that any attempt to destroy Germany utterly must have the effect of inviting Communist forces into the resulting power vacuum, and those forces might well be as harmful to the Western Powers as the Nazi régime which they had destroyed at such heavy cost.

We may in conclusion describe states, the subject of this and the following chapter, as means of organizing people for the purpose of participation in the international system. If there were no international system, or if participation in it was not compulsory, there would be no states as we know them. Just as a football or cricket team has no significance outside the system of play in which it participates, so the state is what it is because it is organized for the purpose of taking part in the international system. In the analysis of states we have asked three questions: what common features distinguish them, how may they be classified, and to what extent can their behaviour be explained in terms of their uniqueness as individual social wholes? Having discussed the first of these questions in the present chapter, we can go forward to deal with the other two in the next.

Notes

1. For this argument see J. Herz, *International Politics in the Atomic Age*, and Andrew Scott, *The Revolution in Statecraft*.
2. See K. J. Twitchett and K. Cosgrove (eds), *The New International Actors*, Macmillan, 1971.
3. *Power Politics*.
4. I am indebted for this conception to Professor C. A. W. Manning.
5. *The Foundations of Political Theory*, Allen and Unwin, London, 1958, p. 14.
6. Op. cit., p. 14.
7. See the interesting account of the foundation of Liberia in George Padmore, *Pan-Africanism or Communism*, Dobson, London, 1956, Chapter II.
8. For an account see Weizmann, *Trial and Error*, Hamilton, London, 1949.
9. Narenda Nath Law, *Inter-state Relations of Ancient India*, Luzac, London, 1920.
10. See C. A. W. Manning, *The Nature of International Society*, Bell, London, 1962, Chapter XIII.
11. *Abraham Lincoln, Speeches and Letters*, J. M. Dent, Everyman, London, 1936, p. 172.

Eight

A Taxonomy of States

ANY attempt to classify the state-members of the international system into groups with similar characteristics must be to some extent artificial. There is, first of all, the problem of determining acceptable criteria in terms of which one group of states can be distinguished from another. There is also the question of where the dividing line should be drawn between states which might just as well fall into one group or class as into another. The same problems arise in the construction of taxonomies of all human associations. Nevertheless, it would seem to be a rule of orderly study that when the student is confronted by an otherwise undifferentiated mass of data, he should try to classify it in certain recognizable groups. It has also been habitual in everyday discussion of international relations and to some extent in the professional language of diplomacy, too, to speak of states as though they were divisible into distinct categories. There is some purpose to be served in attempting to make these categories somewhat more clear-cut and orderly. It is important to insist, however, that the taxonomy of states which is attempted in this chapter is much more than an intellectual exercise which may or may not be worth doing for its own sake. What we are interested in is how far and in what way a state's membership of a particular class or category affects its behaviour and policy in the international system.

We are therefore proposing five different types of states and will attempt to explain how this typology in itself is related to the play of international politics. The first and perhaps foremost of these five types is determined with reference to the state's geographical location. This is in conformity with our discussion in the previous chapter of the territoriality of states as being one of their most distinctive characteristics. The situations of the various states on the surface of the globe are obviously susceptible of analysis in many different ways, but it is useful in the present context to examine those situations in terms of a range or spectrum between extremes, with intermediary forms extending from one extreme to the other. Thus, we are able to speak of varying bipolarities of geographical or geopolitical location.[1]

One such bipolarity, which is sufficiently commonplace, is that of land, land-locked or continental Powers, at one extreme, and sea, oceanic, thalassic or maritime Powers, at the other. These two types, in other words, are, first, those whose contact with the international system is through other, contiguous states, and, secondly, those which encounter other state-members of the international system chiefly across a space of water. The two extremes of Britain or Japan, and Czechoslovakia and Malawi are obvious examples, with France, Belgium and other such countries having both continental and maritime outlooks. The needs and attitudes towards the system of international relations of these two types of state are wholly different from each other and have led to conflicts and controversies throughout history. Of the many causes of the long-standing tensions between Britain and France, the fact that Britain is traditionally a sea-going state and France a continental state is perhaps one of the most important. It is not too fanciful to say that one who stands in the heart of London can hardly help being conscious of shipping, the docks, the river, and down that river is the sea, leading away to the Mediterranean, India, the Far East, on one side, and North America, on the other. In the centre of Paris, on the other hand, one can hardly but be conscious of Europe, its art, architecture, culture, religion, extending from Paris, one might say, until it reaches Russia, as far as the Urals, as General de Gaulle phrased it. In fact, it is only in the context of the continental character of France that de Gaulle's expression takes on any meaning at all. Certainly in those two conceptions of where Britain and France stand in relation to the rest of the world is contained in miniature the whole, long story of the love and hate between the two of them.

Again, this geographical factor was of vital importance in Anglo-French relations in regard to Germany in the period between the two World Wars, and especially in the 1920s. It is common knowledge that Anglo-French differences over the treatment of Germany during that period played a major role in the destruction of the Entente which defeated Germany in 1918, and hence paved

the way to the Second World War. France assumed on the whole
a pathologically suspicious, even vindictive, attitude towards
Germany, suspecting her of illicitly evading the provisions of the
Versailles Treaty of 1919 and of planning for *revanche*, while the
British were more forgiving, believing that fair play (a British
rule of life) prescribed a policy of raising a country to its feet after
its conquest in a bitter war. As usual in international relations,
there were many different factors responsible for this fatal Anglo-
French divergence in attitude towards the German problem, but
certainly the factor of geographical location played a dominant
role. Britain, as an island Power, could afford to, and had a strong
inducement to, leave Germany alone while she herself attended
to her world-wide and imperial interests over the seas. The British
hoped that in God's good time the obvious advantages of peaceful
trade and industry would soften the bitterness in Franco-German
relations and that accordingly they would both 'see sense' and
live peacefully with one another. The French, however, with their
continental situation, could never afford to stand aside from the
German problem; they had to live with it and in consequence felt
that they had to *solve* it. They could solve it either by trying to
crush Germany completely, as they attempted to in the years
leading up to the Franco-Belgian occupation of the Ruhr in 1923;
or by succumbing totally to Germany, as the official leadership
did in 1940. The image of imperial France, the forger of European
unity, gave way to the image of France as a collaborator with
Germany in building the Nazi version of European unity. After
Germany's defeat in 1945, a not dissimilar pattern was renewed:
Britain again withdrew, not entirely, but leaving the west European states to conclude that they must make the best of their own
situation without British participation in their problems, while
France again, through the Schuman plan of 1950 for integrating
the heavy industries of western Europe, began to dream of a new
scheme of European unity under the leadership of France, as of
old.

Britain's differences with friendly states arising from her
situation and mentality as a sea-going Power, while they were
essentially land-Powers, is also illustrated by Anglo-American
relations. The United States is, of course, not a land-locked state
and it may indeed be described as part of a very large island. Still,
the concerns and interests of the American people, certainly until

the last twenty or thirty years, have been predominantly continental and introspective, and this has been reflected in the
alternating attractions to the American people of isolation and
intervention in the international system. The United States has
only since 1945 become a sea Power of world dimensions, and even
today her foreign trade per head of population remains small in
comparison with the maritime states proper. The resulting differences between the British and American situations have, along
with many other factors, aggravated political differences between
the two countries. This has particularly been the case in regard to
the diplomatic recognition of states and governments. The
American view, certainly since Woodrow Wilson first won the
presidential election in 1912, has been that a foreign political
régime must exhibit some of the essential features of a democracy
in the Western sense. It must in some way reflect the people's
will, before recognition can be granted. In British eyes, on the
other hand, the sole test has been the extent of the foreign government's effective control over the territory in which it claims
jurisdiction. The rule has not been invariably applied, but it is the
general principle. Because of these differences in approach to the
question of recognition, British Ministers continuously disagreed
with Washington over the recognition of Communist China after
1949 and never went along with the American undertaking in the
1950s to 'roll back' Communism from Eastern Europe, where
Russia had imposed it after 1945, and the West had no alternative,
short of going to war, to reverse the position. The British, being a
sea-going and commercial people, are habituated to ask themselves when arriving at a strange country across the sea: who
is the local authority? Who wields effective control here and who
can establish the conditions necessary for peaceful trade? The
Americans, on the other hand, having built for themselves a
continent-wide nation-state 'dedicated to a proposition', as
Abraham Lincoln put it in the Gettysburg address, have always
asked themselves on encountering a new political régime in
another country: What proposition is it dedicated to? Or, in other
words, does this régime share the kind of ideological beliefs which
we can ourselves accept? Of course, there are other factors,
especially the American experience of rising and falling revolutionary governments in Latin America, which have influenced
the United States' concept of recognition, but the habit of the

continental mind has certainly been an element of importance.

Sea Powers tend to be concerned with the security of maritime communications in peacetime and the practice of blockade in time of war. Land Powers are concerned with the defence of land frontiers and the establishment of political stability behind those frontiers. It is interesting to see in this connection how, in the same state, departments of government having to do with maritime and continental affairs respectively, have differed in their approach to international questions, in the same way as maritime and continental states. In Britain, for example, the Foreign Office and the Admiralty both favoured the adoption of the Balfour Declaration issued by the Government in November 1917 on behalf of a National Home for the Jews in Palestine. The Foreign Office considered that it might have consequences favourable to the Allied cause in the United States and Russia, the Admiralty wished to see what it hoped would be a friendly state in the Levant alongside the British sea route through the Suez Canal to the Far East. The India Office, however, opposed the Balfour Declaration owing to its concern for political stability in the Indian subcontinent; it feared that British support for the National Home for the Jews in Palestine would have an unsettling effect on the millions of Muslims in the British Empire, and especially in India.[2]

The pattern was repeated in the negotiation of a settlement with Turkey at the end of the First World War. The British Foreign Office and Admiralty, for sufficiently obvious Departmental reasons, favoured the total expulsion of the Turks from Europe, as indeed had been agreed in the abortive secret arrangement in February 1915, by which Britain and France conceded that Constantinople and the Straits should pass to Russia at the end of the War. The India Office, then under the control of the powerful Cabinet Minister, Edward Montague, was able to frustrate this project, again on the ground that it might have the effect of inciting the Muslim population of India to revolt. Perhaps the prevalence of these attitudes in the maritime and continental branches of the same government are in line with another generalization which might be made about land and sea Powers: namely, that the latter have an interest in the maintenance of a balance of power and the discouragement of political unification in adjacent land masses, whereas land Powers tend to seek the consolidation of land masses either by conquest, voluntary federations or, in an earlier age, dynastic marriages. The policies of Britain and Japan with regard to Europe and China respectively are thus in strong contrast with those, say, of France and the United States.

A final distinction which can be made between maritime and continental states concerns their attitudes towards, and policies for, the organization of peace and security in the international system. The land Power will tend to think in terms of the exchange of guarantees for the defence of the existing territorial *status quo*; it will do so obviously because its own frontiers and those of its allies are part and parcel of the *status quo*. The sea Power, on the other hand, may not wish to involve itself in the defence of the territorial *status quo* in every particular; its focus of attention covers a wider area than that of adjacent land masses and it must keep its land forces available for action in those wider areas. Thus there was the sharpest distinction between British attitudes towards the maintenance of peace in 1919, on one side, and those of France and the United States, on the other. President Wilson's ideas on the new League of Nations seemed to go little beyond the mutual exchange of guarantees to sanctify the *status quo*, and they found their expression in Article 10 of the eventual League Covenant. France, for obvious reasons of her own, took the same view, and so did the continental states of Eastern Europe, France's allies, which were created or re-born in 1919. Britain, on the other hand, deprecated the commitment to use force to protect in every detail the settlement reached under the peace treaties. She favoured peaceful revision of the *status quo* as time went by and conditions changed, and, with this in mind, secured the insertion of Article 19 in the Covenant, which provided for peaceful change, though not in the position in the Covenant which the British wanted. She sought also to place the main emphasis in the League Covenant, not on the enforcement against all comers of the territorial peace settlement, but on the peaceful settlement of disputes.

So much for the bipolarity of land and sea Powers. A second geographical or geopolitical range of variation spans the two extremes of what we may call accessibility and remoteness. States, in other words, may be classified according to whether they are situated near to, or remote from, the classic epicentres of crisis and conflict in the international system.[3] There are certain tension centres on the world map where the ambitions of states cut across and rival each other; they may be points at which great trade routes cross each other, or sites, the control of which gives a state a definite strategic advantage over other states; or regions rich in scarce raw materials or sufficiently populated as to provide valuable commercial markets. One of the best-known founders of the study of political geography in Britain, Sir Halford Mackinder, in his famous article 'The Geographical Pivot of History', first published in 1904, identified seven such epicentres of inter-national politics, all fringing the world island of Euro-Asia, the control of which, in Mackinder's view, was tantamount to control of the whole world.[4] The seven were: the Low Countries, Belgium and Holland; Eastern Europe; South East Europe together with the Dardanelles Strait leading from the Black Sea into the Aegean Sea; the North African littoral; the Middle East and Persian Gulf; South East Asia; and the Yellow Sea and its shores. At the time of the Cuba missile crisis in 1962 one might have been tempted to add the Caribbean, but the mere fact that the United States Government made it quite clear (and the Soviet Government ultimately acquiesced in this), that it would under no circum-stances regard the Caribbean as an area of dispute between itself and the Soviet Union, was sufficient indication that the region could not be called an epicentre of world politics in the sense of a cross-roads of great Power ambitions. Otherwise, if we add the North Pole as an epicentre of the air age, it is remarkable how stable these points of high tension in the international system have remained for over seventy years.

The chief point to bear in mind, however, is the result, in terms of experience and diplomacy, of a state being sited at, or near, one of these historic epicentres, as contrasted with the effects of a state living in a relatively remote location. The 'epicentre state' has to fear the tornado of great wars raging across its territory, like Belgium in the two World Wars of this century; or the depreda-tions of the great Powers, like Poland in Eastern Europe or the countries of North Africa or South East Asia; or it may fall under the domination of one or other of the great Powers to which its relation then becomes virtually that of a client state, like Egypt or Jordan during the period of British paramountcy in the Middle East, or Thailand or South Vietnam during the time that the United States was trying to keep South East Asia free of Com-munist control. The states of Latin America, on the other hand, together with some of the states of Central Asia, such as Afghanistan, have been relatively fortunate in that having a situation detached from the main highways of world politics or, being securely within the sphere of interest of a great Power, they have never seriously been the object of the ambitions of another great Power. What we have called a 'remote' state is therefore either remote in the physical sense of being removed away from the principal epicentres of world politics, or remote from the scene of struggles for control between two or more major Powers.

There is a third and final kind of geographical bipolarity, though in this case we are thinking of cultural factors as much as of the purely geographical. We refer here to the range between 'integrated' and what may be called 'marginal' states. The former are those countries which have a relatively cohesive culture. There may be class differences, or perhaps racial differences, in the state, but these are not felt to be destructive of the sense of unity in the community. The country, to speak figuratively, knows where it has come from, and whither it is going. It may, too, have the self-confidence which comes from having a cultural past which is both distinctive and valuable. Britain—at least until the crisis of self-confidence which came with the economic problems of the 1950s and 1960s—was pre-eminent in this category. So was, and is, China, and perhaps France, too. These states do not seem to have experienced strong temptations to be other than what they always were.

Marginal states, on the other hand—it is important to remember that we are talking here about a range or spectrum of states and not merely two sharply distinguished types—are those which, mostly by reason of geographical position, are juxtaposed between coherent and integrated culture-systems. Three good examples from modern times are Russia, Germany, and Japan. Russian political life has notoriously felt the competing pulls of Europe and Asia at least from the time of Peter the Great. The classic dispute between the Slavophils and the Westernizers in Russia a century ago reflected this split-mindedness, so did the famous dispute between Stalin and Trotsky in the 1920s. From the vantage point of Europe Russia looks, at least partly, like an Asian state, not a surprising thing considering that a large part of the Soviet Union actually lies in Asia. From the point of view of Communist China, however, Russia still seems to remain an

F

exponent of nineteenth-century European imperialism, against which the Chinese Communists regard themselves as having a mission to defend in Asia. There was a time in the nineteenth century when Russian foreign policy fluctuated between interest in Europe and interest in Asia. The truth today seems to be that Russia cannot afford to be disinterested in either.[5]

Germany's marginality in relation to Eastern and Western Europe resembles Russia's marginality as between Asia and Europe, the latter now including the East and West German states since 1955. By every test Germany before 1939 was a European state, though its not having had the long exposure to Roman rule which Britain and France had experienced made it an unusual European state. But once Germany was united in 1871 and developed with industrialization into a great, if not a world, Power, the problem arose, with its central position in Europe, as to the direction in which the country would lean, whether to East or West. The defeated Germany of 1919 tried to make its peace with both, with Soviet Russia at Rapallo in 1922 and with the West at Locarno in 1925. Hitler's attack on Russia in June 1941 seemed to demonstrate that his dream of expansion into a *Lebensraum* in Eastern Europe and Russia was a genuine one. Had Russia collapsed as Hitler (and many people in the rest of the world) expected, there is reason for thinking that Germany would have become, perhaps permanently, an Asian Power. Hitler's failure in 1945, however, ensured that the solution to the seventy-year-old German question—will it be East or West?—has been provided, for the time being at least, with the division of Germany into two parts, one politically belonging to the West and the other to the East. Nevertheless, Western, or Federal, Germany cannot so easily disinterest itself in the East, as can Britain, France or Italy. Both the main West German political parties, the Christian Democrats and the Social Democrats, have practised an *Ostpolitik* when in office since Dr. Adenauer's retirement in 1963. If *Ostpolitik* were to succeed and the two German states were finally to be reunited, neither Western Europe nor Eastern Europe (that is, the Soviet bloc) could permit Germany to play East against West or the other way about, as in the past. This is perhaps another way of saying that the only basis on which German reunification is possible in the foreseeable future is that of an agreement for a lasting peace between Western Europe (possibly through the

European Community) and the East (necessarily dominated by the Soviet Union).[6]

Modern Japan is possibly an even better example of the marginal state, than either Russia or Germany. It is well-known that Japan's response to the impact of the West was not, like China's, one of haphazard and futile resistance, but one of acceptance and assimilation. The Japanese, after the visit to their country of Commodore Perry's 'Black Ships' in 1853, lost no time in modernizing their economy, their political constitution and their educational system along Western lines. By 1902, when Japan formed its alliance with Britain, by 1905, when it defeated one of the most formidable Powers of the European system, Russia, and by 1919, when Japan appeared at the Paris Peace Conference as one of the Allied and Associated Powers which had won the War, it was evident that the country had found its way into the inner circle of the great Powers. During the 1920s Japan was quiescent in international policy, partly owing to the great national disaster caused by the earthquake in 1923. But with the world-wide financial crash and economic depression of 1929–1933, which cut to shreds Japan's profitable export trade in raw silk, the Japanese military, backed by sections of the business community, began to wonder whether they had been wise to hitch their waggon to the Western economic star. One effect of this was the formation of the Japanese plan in the 1930s for the creation of a Greater East Asia Co-prosperity Sphere, to consist of Japan, China and Manchuria.[7]

This represented a decisive switch in Japan's attitude from the West towards East Asia. The Co-prosperity Sphere, of course, could not survive the impact of the United States war machine in the Second World War and once more, in 1945, Japan turned again to the West, though this time in a much more thoroughgoing fashion than before. The remarkable thing was that Japan's political and business leaders and its public opinion seemed, both under American occupation at the end of the War and after Japan's sovereignty was restored with the peace treaty signed in 1951, to harbour no regret for the past, nor desire to return to the previous way of life. The traditions of old Japan seemed to be totally buried; but perhaps they were only dormant, springing intermittently to the surface in student violence and anti-American demonstrations. The revival of China in the diplomatic world, especially after

President Nixon's visit there in March 1972, left open the question of which way Japan would turn next. If the partial Sino-American *rapprochement* remained in being and developed, Japan might be able to continue riding the two horses of her Asian and Western policies. But if China and the United States were to remain enemies, Japan's position as a marginal state between the two worlds would be subject to the greatest pressure.

Having thus dealt with the basic classification of states in geographical terms, we can now proceed to our second category, which is possibly even more commonplace than the former, and this derives from the relative political status of the state in question. We are familiar, again from everyday usage, with the 'pecking order' of the state-members of the international system, with the great or Leviathan states at the top—we would perhaps think of them as super-Powers—with the 'mini-states' at the bottom, and an indeterminate collection of middle-range states in between. Just as in the domestic social system, few count themselves as either plutocrats or working men and women, preferring to be thought of as 'middle class', the same seems to be true of states. Professor Schwarzenberger has used the term 'aristocracy' to describe the state-members of the international system as a whole and the term 'oligarchy' to refer to the acknowledged giants of the system.[8] W. T. R. Fox has used the engaging names 'squirrels' and 'elephants' to distinguish the mass of states from the great Powers.[9] Sometimes the hierarchy of power is sanctified in the constitutions of international organizations, more votes being given to the richer and more powerful states or permanent seats on the organization's executive council for the greater states and non-permanent seats for the lesser. The Governing Body of the International Labour Organization, for example, represents the ten most highly industrialized countries. The Covenant of the League of Nations, drawn up in 1919, assigned permanent seats on the Council to the great Powers, that is, the chief Allied and Associated Powers, though these were not named. When Germany joined the League in 1926, she was at once given a permanent seat on the Council; the same was done with Soviet Russia on her entry into the League in 1934. When the United Nations Charter was drawn up in 1945 it assigned permanent seats on the Security Council to the five greatest Powers in the victorious allied coalition and these were named in the Charter; they were the United States, the Soviet Union, Britain, France and China. The passage of time since 1945 has shown the artificiality of this classification since by no test can Britain or France today (neither could France even in 1945) be grouped in the same power category as America and Russia; no doubt it will be some time before China ranks with the two super-Powers. Moreover, there are states in the United Nations which have joined since 1945, perhaps India and Japan, whose claim to permanent seats on the Security Council is as good as, if not better than, those of Britain and France.

The men who framed the Charter no doubt had in mind 'states of the second rank', or at least in the intermediate range between the giants and the pigmies, when they laid down the criterion of eligibility to be satisfied by states elected to the non-permanent seats on the Security Council, of which there were six in 1945, and ten today. Thus it is stated in Article 23 (1) of the UN Charter that when the General Assembly elects members to the non-permanent seats it shall especially pay 'due regard . . . in the first instance to the contribution of Members of the United Nations to the maintenance of international peace and security and to the other purposes of the Organization, and also to equitable geographical distribution'. There is an implication here, as in the composition of the permanent members of the Council, that responsibility should somehow be associated with power; that is, that no state should be able to take part in a Security Council decision which is binding on all other member-states unless it can make a direct contribution from the basis of its own strength in implementing it. This criterion of eligibility, however, has tended to be ignored in the practice of the United Nations. The small state, or even the 'mini-state', seems to have been just as frequently elected to fill a non-permanent seat on the Organization's executive body as the middle-size state. This is partly due to the fact that election to those seats has become a matter of prestige and rivalry among member-states, and also to the increasing influence of the less powerful African and Asian states in the United Nations.

When we consider the qualifications on the basis of which a state's place in the international hierarchy of power is determined, it is evident that they can be reduced to three. First, there is actual and measurable strength, reckoned in terms of size of population, though always in terms of the skills, education, relative youthfulness and health of that population; size of exploitable territory, which needs under modern conditions of warfare to be on a considerable scale if the state's economic power is not to be knocked out of action in the first phase of hostilities; gross national product per head of population, productivity per head of population, industrial production, proportion of national income available for new investment; and other such standard indices of national strength. The practical result of all these factors is that the Powers at the head of the hierarchy should not be capable of being overthrown without a world war and without a whole combination of other Powers fighting against them. The more one moves down the ladder of power the less proportionately would these conditions need to apply.

Secondly, we may say that the position of a state in the international 'pecking order' is governed by the extent and diversity of the state's interests or its stake in the international system. One would expect a minor state to have strictly local interests, a Power of the middle-range, regional interests, and a Power at the top of the ladder, an acknowleged super-Power, should have world-wide interests. In this context we must be careful to define an interest, not merely as the assertion of a claim for consideration, but the assertion of a claim which other members of the international system are not in a position to ignore. If Britain, for example, has an interest in the Suez Canal in the sense that no system for the administration of the Suez Canal can be enforced in the face of British dissent, then that claim can be described as a true interest, in the diplomatic sense of the term. This takes us back to what was said in the first chapter of this book on the nature and definition of 'power'.[10] Power was there defined as the capacity to make one's will felt in other decision-making centres. If a decision cannot be made by states in their negotiations with each other without some other state's will being taken into account, that state can be said to have power, which, as we have said, can be local, regional or world-wide in extent. A state's power is thus reflected in the interest in particular local, regional or world-wide issues which it claims. If a number of states do agree on an issue without consulting and securing the approval of that state, such an agreement would not be worth the paper it is written on. If, again, a state has such diverse and true interests in every part of the globe such that its will cannot be ignored in the settlement of any issue arising in any part of the world, that state should be regarded as a world Power. And accordingly for all the others down the scale.

But this brings us to the third and final criterion of status in the international system; namely recognition of that status by other members of the system. The world system of states is essentially a continuous self-assessing process: states are all the time taking stock of each other, sizing each other up in order to determine what degree of recognition to accord each other. Power, we have described as the capacity to influence the decision-making of others. Hence it follows that recognition of power status, which we have in mind here, is a process of according deference to another state depending upon the extent to which its wishes have to be taken into account in reaching one's own decisions. Deference, of course, does not in the political situation refer to admiration, affection or approval; it means accepting the cold fact that one cannot advance towards one's objectives without the co-operation of the state deferred to. The story is told that towards the end of the Second World War, Mr. Anthony Eden, then the British Foreign Secretary, told General de Gaulle, the leader of the French exiled forces in London, that he had given the British more trouble than all the other exiled governments put together. To which de Gaulle is said to have replied: 'And why not? We are a great Power'.

Recognition is naturally a reflection of the other two criteria of status mentioned above, that is, crude, measurable physical strength and the geographical extent of the state's interests in the international system. But it may be based upon many other considerations. In 1958, when the African state of Guinea opted out of the French Union, even though it meant the cutting off of French economic assistance, its President, Sekou Touré, was received with red carpets wherever he went abroad. This was not deference to Guinea's insignificant material strength; obviously, people wanted to know whether other new African states would follow Guinea's example, with perhaps far-reaching effects on the whole balance of power in Africa. That example might have signalled, though in fact it did not, a bitter struggle for the allegiance of the new African states between the Communist and non-Communist centres of world influence. Hence, for purposes of academic study, our ordering of the shifting hierarchy of power in the international system should begin with the standing

accorded to each other by the state-members of the system themselves. At the Munich conference in September 1938 none of the
four states represented, Britain, France, Germany and Italy,
seemed to think of Russia as a great Power, even as a Power with
effective interests in Eastern Europe, the frontiers of which were
under debate at the conference. A year later, though Russia's
actual physical capacity had undergone no marked change, the
British and French, on one side, and the Germans, on the other,
were competing with each other for an agreement with the
Russians. Deference therefore comes first; when we have taken
note of that we can then try to account for the reasons why
deference in a particular case is accorded to a state.

There are two further observations to be made about status in
the international system. One is that position in the hierarchy
varies from time to time, or rather that the deference which states
accord to each other is continuously under review; the death of a
President, a great natural disaster such as an earthquake, a find of
rich oil reserves, and many other events, can cause a reassessment
of the standing to be granted to a particular state. There is such a
thing, in other words, as a circulation of élites in the international
system, and sometimes this can be quite rapid. The transfer of
leadership among the democratic nations from Britain to the
United States in the course of the Second World War, even so, is
unique. A second fact of importance to notice has been the
diminution in the number of first-rank Powers over the past century and a half. At the Vienna Congress in 1815 there were five
leaders of the international system: Austria, Britain, France,
Prussia and Russia, though France, owing to her defeat in 1815,
was for the time being recessive. Spain in 1815 was definitely in
decline. At the Congress of Berlin in 1878 the pattern was much
the same, with Germany now united under Prussian auspices and
a united Italy was joined to the Powers. At the Paris Peace Conference in 1919 the effective supreme Powers were three—Britain,
France and the United States—with Italy and Japan nominal
Powers, and Germany and Russia temporarily recessive. By the
end of the Second World War in 1945 there were now only two
effective great Powers, the Soviet Union and the United States;
Britain, China and France were nominal, or 'courtesy' Powers.

This 'law of concentration of power', if it can be so dignified,
has been noted by Professor Toynbee in his *Study of History* as

being characteristic of earlier civilizations. There is a recurrent pattern, he contends, in which the numerous centres of power at the core exhaust themselves by war, to be succeeded by fewer power-centres at the periphery—precisely the turn of events in Europe since 1939.[11] At the point at which the dwindling process has reached in the post-1945 world a dangerous condition of what may be called 'penultimate power' is reached; that is to say, if the chief rivals for world power have shrunk to two, the question haunting the minds of those two must be: who will be the final Power standing on the chess board? In all previous power conflicts in the international system a state which suffered military defeat could rely upon bystander states to rescue it from utter destruction: Britain thus rescued France from utter destruction in 1815 and did the same for Germany after 1918. But after 1945 this was no longer the state of affairs: a total defeat of the Soviet Union by the United States or of the United States by the Soviet Union, assuming that the 'victor' would not be reduced to a cinder along with his victim, would no doubt be a defeat, on one side, and a victory, on the other, a state of affairs which would for all practical purposes be permanent. This situation of penultimate power added an extra dimension of fear to the two rivals for world domination: each felt, as never before in history, that if defeated by the other, there was no hope of resurrection, at least through the friendly intervention of other Powers. However, with the advent of *détente* between the United States and the Soviet Union, and with the rise of Communist China, India, Japan and possibly a united Europe of the nine Community states, it could be that this concentration of power in the international system is going into reverse.

A third commonly used criterion for the classification of states is the economic. A distinction has normally been drawn in the world, since the Second World War, between 'developed' and 'developing' countries, or since the equator is a rough-and-ready line of division, between countries of the northern hemisphere and countries of the southern hemisphere. In the European international system before 1939 a somewhat similar distinction was drawn between what were then called the 'have' and the 'have-not' states. We will return to this distinction later in the present chapter. It is enough to say here that the pre-1939 distinction between the two groups referred to the two European Powers, Germany and

Italy, and to Japan, all of whom claimed to be worse off economically than such countries as Belgium, Britain, France and Holland because they had not done so well out of the colonial share-out. The colonies of the European Powers themselves were not then included in the 'have-not' group because, as they were not yet members of the international system, their voice did not count in the contemporary classification of states. Today the developing countries (to use the well-known euphemism) are for the most part the former colonies which now face more or less serious problems of economic advancement. There is, however, one resemblance between the rich-poor division of today and the have-have not split of the period before the Second World War, namely that it is, and was, more than a mere division of states; it was a sharp conflict of interest. The Second World War sprang out of the have-not division of the 1930s; some have argued that a third world war could spring from the rich-poor division of today, thought it is hard to see this happening.

A developed state, as we would call it today, usually means one which has a mainly industrialized and urbanized population, with a high proportion of the working people employed in manufacturing industries and services, a high rate of capital formation, diversified foreign trade, a relatively high gross national product and annual output per head. A developing state, by contrast, tends to be industrially backward, with a low rate of capital formation, a mainly rural population with a low level of literacy and technical skill, and low output per head relative to that of other countries. It is important to emphasize that all of these criteria are strictly relative. By the standards of Western Europe, Greece and Turkey might be considered developing countries. By the standards of Ethiopia or Nepal they might be considered developed.

Two generalizations may be hazarded about these two groups of states, the developed and the developing. One is that it seems easier to indicate the lines of international behaviour a developing country will tend to follow than it is to indicate those of a developed state. It would not be surprising to find that a developing country was: non-aligned or neutralist in its foreign policy, eschewing involvement in the military alliances which sprang up in the wake of the Second World War; was stridently anti-colonialist and opposed to all forms of race discrimination; supported the United

Nations and all schemes for channelling the wealth of the richer nations to the poorer nations, preferably through impartial international agencies; supported disarmament and schemes for easing the tensions of the Cold War; and called for a new deal in world trade so as to reduce or eliminate discrimination against the exports of the developing countries. In other words, although the developing nations, like other nations, have their own individual interests and policies, there is among them a high degree of solidarity on many basic international questions.

One conclusion, which might be said to flow from this, is that the lower down the scale of economic development a state happens to be, the more its international outlook and policy will tend to correspond with those of other states at a similar level of economic development. As we move up the scale of economic development, the harder it will be to predict the wants, preferences and aversions of the states concerned. This is in conformity with the commonplace economic rule, that the more a person's income rises above the level of bare subsistence, the more difficult it is to forecast his wants; or that basic needs of the human being are relatively inelastic in relation to the price of their satisfaction, whereas the demand curve for luxuries is relatively elastic.

This leads straight into our second generalization about the behaviour in the international system of developed and developing states respectively. It is one of the assumptions of this book that the behaviour of states within the international system is a reaction to two forms of pressures: those which come from outside, from the international system itself, and those which come from within the state. The former may be called 'systemic' forces, the latter 'idiosyncratic' forces. One may be inclined to place British foreign policy near to the systemic pole of the spectrum: this would be accounted for by the long-established British sensitivity to events far away from the home islands, the cohesion of the British people, which hardly as yet makes it incumbent on British Governments to reflect in their foreign policy sharp internal conflicts, and possibly the accepted idea in Britain that the making of foreign policy is strictly a matter for the informed élite to determine after close study of the international situation confronting them.[12] The new, developing countries, on the other hand, have had a much shorter experience of international affairs. At the same time, their policies are bound to be dominated by certain basic internal economic problems, which they cannot afford to forget; and their social unity is bedevilled by tribal and other deep-seated divisions. For many of these states foreign policy tends to be rather more an external projection of internal requirements than a rational reaction to international events. To that extent, to revert to our terminology, their behaviour in the international system is 'idiosyncratic' rather than 'systemic'.

Our fourth method of classifying states is by reference to their internal political and constitutional structure. One obvious taxonomy of political structure is the following: unitary states, such as Britain, in which sovereign authority is strictly centralized in the hands of a single organ; federal states, such as the United States and the Federal German Republic, in which there is a distinct division of powers, normally stipulated in a written constitution, between central and local authorities; and pseudo-federal states, of which the Soviet Union is the best-known example, and in which the constitution purports to describe a genuinely federal state, but where supreme power is as effectively concentrated in the hands of some central organ of power as in the unitary state. Obviously, as in all varieties of political organization, these represent 'ideal' rather than actual types. Nevertheless, one might normally expect the making of international policy to be rather more of a 'stream-lined' affair in a unitary or pseudo-federal state than in a genuinely federal state; this might well affect the problems a federal, as distinct from a unitary or pseudo-federal, state, might have in entering into any scheme of integration with other states. The genuinely federal state, too, is apt to have a 'federal' attitude to affairs in the international system, that is to say that it may tend to understate the force of nationalism in other states and to believe that other people should have no difficulty in reproducing its own federal experience, even though, as we have said, its own federal structure may be an obstacle to its own membership of still larger federations. Thus, the United States after 1945 persistently called for a European, or West European, federation until the implications of the European Economic Community for American foreign trade began to be brought home. It is also no accident that in Europe, the Federal German Republic seems to have had less difficulty than the unitary states in Western Europe, notably Britain and France, have had in accepting the idea of the political unification of Europe.

Cutting across these differences between political constitutions is the distinction between authoritarian and relatively liberal states. The former are often actuated by what may be called 'mechanistic' ideologies, that is, beliefs which assume that day-by-day political activities should conform to some large-scale and premeditated plan, while the latter prefer 'voluntaristic' thinking in the sense of the belief that man by his own free will can determine his own fate despite the pressures of larger social or economic forces.[13] The traditional liberal assumption was that the liberal state (or republican state, as it was known in the eighteenth century) was more likely to be peace-loving in the international system than the authoritarian state or the state in which human rights were denied. This argument seems somewhat less convincing today, after fifty or sixty years' experience of 'mass democracy', though it is fully enshrined in the United Nations Charter and such wartime documents as the Atlantic Charter, signed in August 1941. Nevertheless, there might be general agreement to the proposition that sudden switches of the lines of foreign policy, or diplomatic revolutions, are somewhat easier to accomplish in the authoritarian state than in the liberal state, in which public opinion still counts as a force. Stalin, who told the Germans in August 1939 that it would 'take a few days' to explain and justify the Nazi-Soviet pact to the Russian people, would presumably have required somewhat more time had he been the Prime Minister of a Western democratic state.

Finally, states may be classified according to their attitudes towards the prevailing *status quo* in the international system. They may be relatively satisfied or relatively dissatisfied, and accordingly they could be called '*status quo*' or 'revisionist' states, 'haves' or 'have-not' states, '*die Mächte der Beharrung*' or '*die Mächte der Erneuerung*'. These are indeed crude distinctions, reflecting, as so often in political studies, the vague, emotional phrases of the market-place and the hustings; they need to be handled with the most careful qualifications. In the first place, a state may be satisfied with regard to the international system as a whole, but dissatisfied with the state of affairs in a particular area or region; or it may be the other way round. The United States, for example, has on the whole been satisfied throughout the period of the Cold War with the situation in the world in general, but was intensely dissatisfied with the position in a particular area, namely Eastern

Europe. So dissatisfied was America in fact that in 1952–1953 the American government seemed dedicated to the idea of 'liberating' the people of Eastern Europe from Soviet control. On the other hand, the Soviet Union has seemed highly satisfied with the situation in Eastern Europe since 1945, but has used its influence to secure changes in the existing social system elsewhere. Secondly, a state may be entirely satisfied by comparison with another state, but highly dissatisfied with respect to a third. The Soviet Union, for example, was regarded in Western eyes as a 'have-not' state throughout the period of the Cold War, but nevertheless appeared in the guise of a 'have' state throughout the same period in the eyes of Communist China, and possibly of Albania, North Korea and North Vietnam, too. Thirdly, no state, no matter how successful its recent encounters with the international system have been, will tend to count itself wholly satisfied. France, a supreme victor in 1918, certainly was not, nor was the United States at the summit of her power in 1945, although she had contributed to the making of the world which she then faced.

The fact is that all the state-members of the international system are all the time seeking the redress of their dissatisfactions, which always exist. In the ensuing struggle a coalition tends to form around those states which, so to speak, have seized the initiative and are actively engaged in re-shaping the world according to their desires and interests. A counter-coalition will then tend to form around the states which also want to change the system but want to change it in a different way and in accordance with a different scheme of values. The result will be some sort of victory for one of the two coalitions, and when that happens all the temporarily repressed dissatisfactions in that coalition come to the surface, and a new coalition and counter-coalition are formed in order to determine which of the new round of dissatisfactions is to prevail. It is not so much that states can be conveniently classified into 'satisfied' and 'dissatisfied' groups. The question is the extent to which one of the dissatisfied states can publicize its dissatisfactions and make common cause with others, as against those states which prefer to repress for the time being their own dissatisfactions in a counter-coalition.

The classifications which we have discussed so far in this chapter are what may be called 'alternative' systems for the grouping of states under common heads. They are quite distinct and different from the 'derived' systems of classifications in which one group forms out of another group at a higher level so as to constitute a pyramid. Thus, in the major biological classifications invented by Linnaeus, the genus, the lowest branch, is a sub-division of the species, which in its turn is a sub-division of the variety, which in its turn is a sub-division of the order. In the classifications used in this chapter, on the other hand, a state, for instance, may be a land Power and at the same time a developed or developing Power; it may be liberal or authoritarian in politics, revisionist or *status quo* in its attitude to the prevailing international system, and so on. These classifications, in other words, are somewhat like different pairs of spectacles which the observer puts on one after the other to examine the same objects. He finds that different colours or other properties of the things seen come into his field of vision as the spectacles are changed.

Classifications of states (and those suggested in this chapter are not intended to be any more than illustrative examples) can take us a certain distance in the analysis of state behaviour, certainly further than study of the common features of states, the first level of analysis, as proposed in the previous chapter. But in the final resort, and as our third level of analysis, there is really no alternative to the consideration of the state as a quite unique entity. Apart from certain superficially similar physical features, it remains true that no two states, and no two people, are exactly like each other. We may enumerate all the standard aspects of foreign policy, as set out in any textbook on the study of foreign policy, but in the end the nature of that state and its attitudes towards other state-members of the international system will elude us unless we have done something to penetrate its unique cast of mind, the product of quite unique historical experiences. The Russian has ideas and emotions about the Chinese, for example, which are quite different from the ideas and emotions the French have about the Germans or the Canadians about the Americans, though these are all pairs of contiguous neighbours. Only by attempting, difficult though it certainly is, to see the world of states through Russian, Chinese, French, German, Canadian, American eyes *seriatim* can we hope to know anything about the basic springs of action of each of these peoples.

NOTES

1. The word 'geographical' is used here, not as meaning that geographical facts *determine* political events, but that they are an important *conditioning* influence.
2. See Leonard Stein, *The Balfour Declaration*, Vallentine, London, 1961.
3. In seismology an epicentre is the point of outbreak of an earthquake.
4. Reprinted by the Royal Geographical Society, London, 1951.
5. See E. H. Carr's essay 'Russia and Europe' in R. Pares and A. J. P. Taylor (eds.), *Essays presented to Sir Lewis Namier*, Macmillan, London, 1956; also Georgine Ogden, *Russia and Europe*, unpublished Ph.D. thesis, University of London.
6. On the whole question of Germany's marginal position and political outlook see Lionel Kochan, *The Struggle for Germany*, Edinburgh University Press, Edinburgh, 1963.
7. See above, pp. 95–6.
8. *Power Politics*, Stevens, London, 3rd edn., 1964, Chapters VI and VII.
9. *The Super Powers*, Harcourt, New York, 1944.
10. See above, Chapter One, p. 20.
11. O.U.P., London, 1934, Vol. III, pp. 302–3.
12. British attitudes towards the European Community, as reflected in the national referendum on the issue, held in June 1975, seem rather an exception to this pattern, but it is an exception which surely proves the rule.
13. See T. D. Weldon, *States and Morals*, Murray, London, 1950, for a development of this distinction.

Nine

The Motives of State Behaviour

WE have dealt in the two previous chapters with the nature of states, the foremost members of the international system, and the problem of classifying them. The questions now arise of how states are brought into contact with the international system and the forces which motivate them as participants in that system. The first of these questions is relatively easy to answer, the second is steeped in controversy, as indeed all discussion about the motives of human beings is bound to be. There are in fact two answers to the first of these questions. One is provided by the attribute of territoriality which we have described as a striking distinguishing feature of states as social organizations.[1] The fixed geographical location of states provides them with neighbours from which they cannot escape and with which they must sooner or later have relations. In his famous work *The Expansion of England*, based on lectures given in Cambridge and first published in 1883, Sir J. R. Seeley showed, not only how improvements in transport and communications had the effect of giving the western coasts of Europe, including Britain, new neighbours in the Americas, but how the New World changed the entire internal and external histories of those states, especially in the seventeenth and eighteenth centuries.[2] Hence we can regard the international system which we have today as a global network of continuous communications arising from the principle which we have earlier called the enforced vicinity of states.

The second answer is that states may be defined, and it is our preference in this book so to define them, as organizations of people for the purpose of participation in the international system. States somewhat resemble football or cricket teams; outside the context of the football or cricket match such teams have no *raison d'être*; their whole existence presupposes a sequence of encounters in the field. In much the same way, states, in the form in which we know them, have no significance outside of that complex of activities which we call the international political system. In taking part in that system states are, as the saying goes, 'doing what comes natural'. But, in a much more direct sense, states participate in the international system for what they can gain from such participation. We have distinguished earlier in this book between the 'hedonistic', or gregarious association, which corresponds to the desire or instinct of people to be together and to do things together, and what we have called the pragmatic association, which is formed to serve some specific and normally utilitarian object, such as the protection of living standards in the case of trade unions or the abolition of legal discrimination against women in the case of organizations of women.[3] The pleasure or reward which comes to individual members in the pragmatic association derives perhaps partly from purely social gratifications, but more especially from more tangible benefits. Aristotle was no doubt thinking rather of pragmatic than hedonistic associations when he described friendship as an 'exchange of benefits'; most people would probably regard that as a somewhat self-centred manner of regarding friends. It is true, however, that the 'friendships', *ententes*, and 'special relationships' of states are rather more pragmatic than hedonistic associations, since states, unlike individual persons from whom they are constituted, do not appear to have a 'herd instinct', or 'solidarity feelings'. They belong to, and participate in, the international system, quite bluntly, for what they can get out of it, and if they derived no material gain from it, they would probably not continue to belong merely for the pleasure of being 'one of the crowd'.

What the states get out of participation in the international system is of two kinds: the negative benefit and the positive benefit. The negative benefit is the avoidance of the adverse consequences which might flow from non-participation. It is an unfortunate fact about international politics that whenever two or more states get together and talk privately, the interests of third states tend to be in jeopardy. Or, at least, third states tend to suspect that such may be the result, and hence they are often willing to pay quite a high price merely to find out, sometimes by espionage and all its modern mechanical refinements, what is being said, whether about themselves or not, by other states behind their closed doors. The French proverb '*les absents sont toujours torts*' has a special application to diplomacy. This is perhaps one reason why member-states today are generally loathe to resign from international organizations, even when these are failing badly, but are willing to put up, like South Africa, with a great deal of abuse or cold-shouldering in the organization from other member-states. It was a common form in the inter-War years for member-states which resented resolutions adopted by the League of Nations to rise there and then and leave the organization for ever. Germany, Italy and Japan were three of the most notorious examples. Since the foundation of the United Nations in 1945, however, only one state, Indonesia, has retired from the organization, and that was only for a short period. There are surely many reasons for this, but no doubt one such reason for remaining in the world organization is to prevent things happening in it which may be detrimental to the state contemplating resignation. The United Nations, a state may complain, is wholly ineffective. But does this mean that that state would prefer to see the United Nations doing something effectively but which is contrary to that state's interests? If not, how can that state prevent developments in that direction taking place in the world organization, except by remaining in it and using its influence at least in a negative sense? For the United Nations to do nothing, most of us would surely agree, is better than that it should from our point of view do something disastrous.

On the other hand, there are, of course, positive reasons why states wish to participate in the international system and in the major international organizations within that system. This brings us to the second question which we posed at the beginning of this chapter, namely, what kind of forces motivate the states in the international system; what makes them 'tick'? What effects are states, or governments acting on behalf of states, seeking to achieve through their participation in the international system? We must remember here that no state can provide for the welfare of its people without participation in the system or without continuous co-operation with other states. Some people appear to think that states which seek the co-operation of other states are somehow virtuous or 'peaceloving' or 'progressive'. The plain fact is that all states, no matter whether weak or powerful, no matter whether their aims are good or evil, are bound to seek the co-operation of other states. Hitler, for example, was one of the greatest co-operators in history; he co-operated at Munich with Britain, France and Italy for the dismemberment of Czechoslovakia; like us all, he was ready to co-operate with anybody—on his own terms.

Most of us, even those professing no special knowledge of international relations (or perhaps most especially those), feel that we know the answer to the questions about motivation raised in the preceding paragraph. Many would say that these answers are self-evident and that no special inquiry to find them is needed.

For this reason, one of the primary tasks which academic investigation can do is to clarify some of the ideas generally held about the motivations of states, and hopefully bring these ideas more into relation with reality, rather than pretend that there are startlingly new discoveries about the subject to be made. With this in mind, it is useful to begin by drawing some basic distinctions between things often confused.

The first and perhaps most elementary of these distinctions is that between the avowed, or publicized, or declared, objects of state policy in international relations, and the real objects. We all know that a very wide gap normally exists between what Ministers say about their policies when speaking at public meetings or on radio or television, and what they actually have in mind. Both students and practitioners of diplomacy must, as a kind of first-form lesson, learn to differentiate between one and the other, and must in general recognize that international politics, and for that matter domestic politics, too, are carried on in a kind of symbolic language which is often not at all indicative of the real purposes and situations involved. An excellent example was the euphemistic words used by the national executive committee of the British Labour Party in 1954, when it was faced with the formidable task of persuading the annual conference of the Party to approve the principle of the rearmament of the Federal German Republic, the whole idea of which, for obvious reasons, was highly distasteful to the Party and to the trade unions. The executive committee finally decided to ask the conference to approve the principle of a 'German contribution to collective security'. If one substituted for the last phrase 'collective defence' (which in fact the Germans *were* going to contribute to), it would be easy to imagine the difference in the resulting emotional impact on a Party most members of which identified collective security, not with an

armed alliance like NATO, but with the lofty idealism of the
League of Nations and the United Nations. Not that the British
Labour Party is more prone than any other party to use this
loaded symbolic language. It is in fact inherent in the human
situation, especially the political situation.

We call this kind of communication 'rationalization', the
couching of the irrational in rational form. But it is as well to
remember that rationalization need not be taken as meaning only
the substitution of a fictitious and respectable reason in place of
the actual, but less respectable reason. It can mean, and often does
mean in practical political life, the rearrangement of motives in
one's conscious mind and in one's manner of explaining one's
actions, in such a way that the respectable or less important
motivations are placed first in the list and the real, but not so
flattering motives, lower down. Moreover, rationalization often
occurs not, as many people think, because the rationalizer has no
scruples and does not mind what lies he tells in order to keep other
people's esteem, but because he has more scruples than he can in
fact handle or live up to. Hypocrisy, it has been said, is the tribute
which vice pays to virtue. That is to say that rationalization, in so
far as it is a form of hypocrisy, arises not so much from defiance
of the moral rule, but from a very clear awareness that there are
indeed moral rules which have to be complied with as far as
possible.

More particularly, this is likely to be the situation in international relations in so far as people expect those relations to be
carried on with as much regard for the moral rule as in inter-
personal relations, or perhaps even more, whereas in international
relations the moral rule tends to be, if anything, more difficult to
follow than in private life. Possibly because states tend to be
visualized by many people as though they were living individuals
('la belle France' or 'poor little Belgium') the expectation seems to
be that they will behave like living individuals, or rather perhaps
like the most saintlike individuals. A state's failure to live up to
these lofty standards is often met either by shock and indignation,
or by weary cynicism, whereas a similar failure by an individual
person might tend to be excused by some reference to the 'weakness of the flesh' or the general shortcomings of, after all, mortal
men.

It is often forgotten that states are in the nature of things less likely than the ordinary person to be altruistic and other-regarding; and this for many reasons, only two of which we need to mention here. First, it seems to be a general rule of human behaviour, that the larger the human group, the more difficult it tends to be to follow the moral law. A corporation or business company, it has been said, has no soul to damn or body to burn, and certainly in a large group, such as a nation, it is often easy for the anonymous individual to deny moral responsibility for the actions of the group and to hide away from moral reproach in the solidarity of the mass. Indeed, it could be argued that the individual is able to live on a tolerably high moral level in the smaller human circle, such as the family, assuming that that is what he does, because he can act out his more immoral propensities in the larger group situation. The second reason is that the international system, with its lack of central executive organs, is so structured that if a state does not look after its own interests, it can be fairly sure that no one else will. The international system is unfortunately not yet a welfare state in which the strong look after the weak, though some day it may become one. It is, truth to tell, rather more like a warfare state, in which the rule is, look after yourself or no one will look after you. It is a strange fact that in this world a state can usually only get assistance from other states by proving that it does not need it, or that, with a little assistance, it will overcome its enemies by its own right arm.

Nevertheless, after having made full allowance for the force and frequency of rationalization, we must be careful not to exaggerate its role. Some people imagine that governments *never* say precisely what they mean, but this is clearly wrong. Every public authority is bound to put the best face it can on its behaviour or policy, but not to the extent of concealing entirely all that it intends. Obfuscation, or otherwise concealing one's meaning and intentions, may in some situations pay off, but carried too far it can be positively inexpedient. We have stressed the fact earlier that states normally achieve their objects, or as much of them as they can, not as a general rule by forcing other states to give way, but by securing their co-operation on the basis of common interest. The question which states are most often in the habit of putting to one another is: 'Do you not agree with me that it is in your interest to co-operate with me in doing so-and-so?' But that can only be done, if not on a public platform, at least in private discussions, by disclosing one's objects, but, of course, not necessarily the *price* one is prepared to pay to have those objects implemented. It is usually good tactics, when buying a house or persuading a possible spouse to wed, not to be in too much of a hurry to say how urgently you need the house or the spouse; but it would be bad tactics to show no interest whatsoever in the deal. Hence a British White Paper on Foreign Office reform, issued in 1943, described the object of British diplomacy as being 'to make British foreign policy *understood* abroad and as far as possible accepted'. You can do neither of those things by persistent and unmitigated lying.

The second distinction we would like to make, is that between private and public objects pursued by governments on behalf of states in the international system. The Minister or other representative of a state may have all manner of private axes to grind in his dealings with other states; he may be powerfully swayed by personal likes and dislikes, just as Sir Anthony Eden and Mr John Foster Dulles are said to have been moved by strong mutual aversion in the Suez crisis in 1956. But if he is going to fulfil satisfactorily the logical requirements of his office, he must distinguish between these personal likes and dislikes and the public objects and interests which he has been placed in power to defend. His aim should be to identify and satisfy, in so far as he can, the necessities of state for his country at any one time, though these necessities are naturally modified by the need to maintain a certain public consensus to support him in his work.

Policies advanced by governments in the international system are, or the force of circumstances tend to make them, necessities of state multiplied by a certain factor which represents what in practice the making of consensus in that community demands. The Foreign Minister must at all times ask himself, not 'what would I like to do?' but 'what is it necessary for my country to do in existing circumstances in so far as it is possible to form a consensus of electoral opinion strong enough to enable me to pursue those necessities of state?' Needless to say, the position is not qualitatively different in a totalitarian state; all we would need to do is to substitute for 'a consensus of electoral opinion' some such words as 'a consensus among the state's effective political fraction', and that fraction could in certain conditions be counted on the fingers of one hand.

With regard to the factor of consensus in helping to define the meaning of 'necessities of state', it is worth while to consider how wide of the mark we are when we speak, in a parliamentary democracy of the Western type, of people choosing their leaders through the electoral process. We picture to ourselves the different election candidates presenting themselves and their policies to the electorate for the latter to make their choices, just as the salesmen in the market display their goods in the hope of attracting the housewife's choice. But there are reasons for thinking that in the political situation the process is quite opposite. Does not the election candidate or the political leader in general choose his people, rather than they him? Does the leader not identify himself with those wants, needs, interests, which he finds prevalent in the community, or, in other words, the prevailing necessities of state? He has to subordinate, or make the best possible job of looking as though he is subordinating, his private feelings and objects if he is to command a following in the community. That is why Sir Robert Peel was once described as an 'uncommon man of common opinions'.

This leads us further into our analysis of the motivations of state behaviour. The distinction between the private and the public objects of governments is connected with another important feature of their behaviour, namely its relative continuity, especially in the field of foreign policy, despite changes in the political complexion of governments and sometimes even quite catastrophic internal revolutions. Professor A. J. Toynbee once wrote that changes of government at election time in a democracy were, in their bearing on the state's foreign policy, something like the change that takes place at half-time in a football match. The team which during the first half was defending one of the two goals now begins to attack it, while the team which was in the first half attacking it, now begins to defend it. Interpret that word 'goal' as 'foreign policy objective' and you have an apt description of the political situation in a country when a new government comes into office. Much the same is true, though to a less marked extent, for home or domestic policy.

This is a fact of common experience and needs no detailed examination, but if we look briefly at the effects on foreign policy of great political and social revolutions in states, it is apparent that these revolutions tend to affect the language of diplomacy rather than its substance, or, to return to the distinction we made earlier in this chapter, to affect the avowed objectives of the states concerned, rather than their real intentions. The Great French Revolution of 1789, like the Napoleonic Empire, could not alter France's long-standing preoccupation with the security of her Rhine frontier. France's place in the international system did not significantly alter with the fall of the Bastille. Again, in 1917 Russia did not cease to worry about her frontiers with the East European states or her access to the Levant or her position in the Middle East or the Indian sub-continent when she fell to Communism. Indeed, since 1945 much of the Soviet Union's international policy can be better understood in Tzarist than in Communist terms. Similarly with China: it almost seems that the Communists who won the civil war in China in 1949 have made even more use of the old Chinese conception of the 'Middle Kingdom' than their imperial ancestors. Certainly in regard to Tibet, the Himalayan kingdoms and India, South East Asia and Russia, the Chinese Communists can hardly be said to have abandoned the old pretensions and ambitions of the imperial ages.

The same sense of continuity is clear, too, in the experience of the genuinely democratic Western states. The alternations in office of the two major political parties, Labour and Conservative, in Britain since the Second World War is a most striking example. Before 1939 the Labour Party almost unanimously denounced the balance of power as a security policy; it was a capitalistic device and never had any ultimate outcome but war. During its period in office, however, between 1945 and 1951 the Labour Party very effectively practised the balance of power in committing Britain firmly to the North Atlantic alliance, which has been the bedrock of official Labour policy ever since. In 1950 the Labour Government was criticized by the Conservative opposition for allegedly 'dragging its feet' over European integration. When in office in the following year, 1951, the Conservatives dragged their feet in exactly the same way. Labour looked quizzically at the Conservatives' attempt to join the European Economic Community in 1961, then they themselves when in office in 1967 followed precisely the same policy and again, though not without the most painful internal divisions, in 1975. The Labour Government disgusted the Conservatives by their decision, announced in 1968, to withdraw British forces east of Suez by 1971. Mr. Heath, the then Leader of the Opposition, undertook to reverse that policy

when he came to power in June 1970, but his resolution soon
waned. Mr. Heath did, however, renew Labour's application to
join the EEC when he became Prime Minister in 1970; this was
now opposed by the new leader of the Opposition, Mr. Wilson,
if not in principle, at least with regard to the terms of entry
negotiated with the six EEC states by Mr. Heath and his team of
Ministers. But when Mr. Wilson came to office in 1974, he was,
within a year, recommending to Parliament and the Labour
Party entry after a renegotiation of the terms which many considered to be quite superficial.

The reasons for this relatively continuous character of foreign
policy in one-party, as well as in Western democratic, states,
despite changes of government, are clear enough. They are: the
relatively stable external environment, including the fixity of the
geographical features of states, both those which favour and those
which oppose the existing *status quo*; the existence of commitments and obligations to other states, which it would be damaging
to the state's standing in the international system to repudiate;
and the relative continuity in the foreign policies of other states.
Almost the universal experience of new governments or revolutionary régimes, when they embark upon ruling a country for the
first time, is to discover that the 'facts which live in the office' (in
Walter Bagehot's phrase) are somewhat different from what, as
aspirants to office, they thought they would be. This fact was much
exploited in the 1960s and 1970s by both political parties in
Britain, which have each affected dismay and disgust to find on
entering office that the economic situation of the country left
behind by their predecessors was far worse than they themselves
had ever imagined. But another major reason for the relative continuity of foreign policy, despite changes of government, arises
from the distinction we made earlier between private and public
objects of policy: the public objects, being necessities of state for
the country concerned, are what the government must aim at if it
is to perform the rational requirements of its job, and these are
clearly independent of internal changes of régime in the state
concerned.

It is a short logical step from the distinction we have tried to
draw in the preceding paragraphs to the difference between what
we may call internally generated and externally derived motives
or goals of state behaviour. This is another aspect of what we have

described earlier in this book as 'idiosyncratic' and 'systemic' forms of state action.[4] An 'idiosyncratic' behavioural form is one in which the principal impetus towards action comes within the state itself; the 'systemic' form is one in which the chief pressures come from the international system as a whole. We are thinking in fact of the true origins of the drives towards state behaviour, and whether these are largely derived from the internal play of forces within the frontiers of the state, or from the external environment. Another way of expressing the same point is in the form of free will versus necessity. Do states, in other words, behave, or do they merely react to the circumstances in which they find themselves?

This is indeed a far-reaching philosophical and psychological problem which arises in the study of all forms of human action, collective or individual: which are we to be in our assessment of the moving forces in human action, rather more voluntarists, or rather more determinists? In the study of psychology there has been the long-standing controversy between what used to be called the 'instinct' school (to which the psychoanalysts belong) on one side, which takes as its starting point the presumed existence of a certain set of propensities in the human mind which seek an outlet in action, though the subject's way of expressing them may be culturally conditioned, and, on the other side, psychologists of the various schools of behaviour, who argue that human action is infinitely plastic, being wholly the result of external conditioning, and that we are in fact as adult individuals precisely what society has made us. It is not necessary in a book of the present kind to venture far into the intricacies of this argument. But we can perhaps agree that it is possible to draw up certain rules or guides, as it were, when we are thinking of the practical implications of the voluntarist/determinist debate for the study of state behaviour.

First, there is a tendency for most people, and the less familiar people are with the realities of international politics the stronger the tendency, to overstate the scope for freedom of action of the various states in the international system. The eternal experience of governments on entering office, and there are an infinite number of memoirs of Ministers to show this, is to find that the facts of the situation are not only, as we have just said, different from what they imagined, but are also much more demanding and imperative, less easy to ignore, more constrictive of free choice, than they previously thought. This is especially important when we remember, secondly, that in the field of international politics governments are not free to choose the issues about which they have to make their decisions; they are not free to decide the ground on which they have to stand and fight. How unfortunate Mr. Harold Macmillan was in May 1960, when, having devoted himself, with all his considerable force, to persuading his two Western allies, France and the United States, to go to Paris for a summit meeting with the Russians, he found that Mr. Khrushchev had changed his mind and did not want the meeting after all! And how odd it was that Charles de Gaulle, having been welcomed back to supreme power in France in May 1958 in order to defeat the Algerian nationalists, should have realized so soon that the situation demanded the giving of self-determination to those same nationalists!

The fact is, of course, that by far the majority of issues which foreign-policy decision-makers have to decide come from abroad: they result from the actions of other states or peoples, as in the two examples given above. Any examination of the in-tray of any Foreign Minister in the world will proably show that most items awaiting a decision by him derive from the actions of other states: even when the Minister has initiated one of these items himself, his further treatment of it must consist of considering responses, or 'feedback', to it from other states. These responses he himself generally has an irritatingly limited power to shape or control. For all these reasons, those who have had practical experience of the conduct of foreign policy, would probably smile at the assumption of the inexperienced onlooker that a powerful man like a President, Prime Minister or Foreign Minister can virtually do what he likes if he really wants to, and that he therefore should be scolded when he fails to do what the critic thinks he ought to.

Another obvious, though important, rule to bear in mind is that freedom to choose, or perhaps we ought to say a sense of freedom to choose, may tend to be greater on some issues than on others. In Professor H. J. Morgenthau's well-known theory of international politics there is an apparent contradiction between his thesis, that states, almost as a law of their being, act from national interest, 'measured', as he puts it, 'in terms of power', and Morgenthau's fears that unless the people of a state recognize that this is the true reality of international affairs, they will make the wrong choices

and hence injure their national interests. The first of these pre-
cepts appears to mean that states have no option but to pursue
policies which, on balance, increase their power relatively to other
states; they are bound so to do because human beings, as Morgenthau argues, have an impulse to dominate, which is called a 'bio-
psychological drive', 'the constitutive element in all human
associations'. But if this were so, it would seem to be unnecessary
to have to warn democratic peoples against thinking that states
act from other motives, such as ideology, idealism or the desire to
establish world peace. Morgenthau's whole purpose in writing
his *Politics Among Nations* in 1948 seems to have been to impress
such a warning on the American people in particular, since they
were peculiarly prone to forget it.[5] But if the United States, like
other states, was bound to act from power considerations, what
did it matter what they *thought* they were doing?

Professor Morgenthau's reply to this objection on one occasion[6]
was that *in times of crisis* the United States had always in the past,
and would always in the future, act from self-interested considerations, just as a person thrown into a river would think only of saving
his life; but at other times the United States indulged in fantasies
about the nature of international politics which were more or less
deeply injurious to American national interests. We need not
dwell here on the further objection which then arises, namely
whether it is wise to construct an entire theory of international
politics on the basis of premises which are valid only in exceptional
times. Nevertheless, there is some point in saying, to revert to our
discussion of the limits of freedom of choice in international affairs,
that in times of crisis those limits may tend to be narrow.[7] In
September 1939, for example, it hardly seems that Britain had any
other choice than to resist, even at the risk of war, the German
invasion of Poland, unless she were willing totally to abandon her
independence, which it was a primary objective of her foreign
policy to preserve. On the other hand, many would probably
agree that in June 1950 Britain did have definite freedom of choice
whether or not to take part in the Schuman plan for a European
coal and steel community. That this view is a prevalent one in
Britain today (1975), is evident in the common argument that
Britain *ought not* to have 'missed the bus' in 1950, which implies
that there was then a genuine freedom of choice.

However, without examining here in detail why the British

Labour Government made a negative response to the Schuman plan in June 1950, the proposition may be ventured that when any major decision of foreign policy is examined in detail, the alternatives to what the government actually decided to do often seem less and less convincing. Or, to put the point another way, as observers of the event, after the event, we are not at liberty to argue that a government which did A ought to have done B, unless we have first thoroughly explored why in fact it did A and not B. We must, of course, remember that making decisions involves weighing the course of future possibilities and that is never as easy as it seems later on. 'What is now the past', F. W. Maitland once said, 'was once the future'.

If freedom of choice in the making of policy does vary from one situation to another and from one issue to another, it may also vary from one state to another. There is a commonplace assumption that the more powerful the state, considered in physical terms, the greater its freedom of action; 'the strong do what they can, the weak suffer what they must'. After all, what must we consider that power in the international system is sought for, if it is not to widen the range of options confronting the state in its external policies? Certainly Britain since 1939 has found the range of choices confronting her in international policy to be sensibly narrowing as both her physical resources available for the implementation of policy and her standing in the international system diminished. It seems now a far cry from 1925, when a British Foreign Secretary could say in the House of Commons that:

> The British Empire, detached from Europe by its Dominions, linked to Europe by these islands, can do what no other nation on the face of the earth can do, and from east and west alike there comes to me the cry that, after all, it is in the hands of the British Empire and if they will that there shall be no war there will be no war.[8]

But in reality there is no precise general equation between a state's power and its freedom of choice in international affairs. A man bearing supreme responsibility in a state, an absolute monarch or democratic Prime Minister or President, may well look back on his carefree days of consorting with Falstaff and grieve over the hard constrictions of his political position. So the great state, simply because the scale of its operations in the international system is so much grander than that of the minor state, is often forced to cut its commitments in one area in order that it can maintain those in another. It was a brave President Nixon who could say 'we will act to defend our interests whenever and wherever they are threatened any place in the world'.[9] Evidently he had forgotten that, only four years before, the mighty United States was powerless to retaliate against the petty state of North Korea when the North Koreans seized the American spy-ship *Pueblo* and detained it for a whole year. Three years after Nixon's statement President Ford was virtually admitting that all America's efforts to save Cambodia and South Vietnam from Communist control had failed.

Having thus cleared the ground by exploring some of the basic preliminary distinctions which need to be drawn, we can now come nearer to our central question: what motivates state behaviour? What effects are states habitually seeking to achieve in their relations with other states in the international system? It is as well to begin by dismissing, or reducing to their proper proportion of importance, two commonly stated answers to this question. One is power, or the desire for power. As explained in the first chapter of this book, states, unless their governments are quite irresponsible, must be *concerned* about their power, in our previously defined sense of the ability to make one's will felt in other decision-making centres.[10] Since the greatest states can do nothing by themselves and depend at all times on the more or less freely given co-operation of other states, power is bound to be the *indispensable condition* of the achievement of whatever objectives states set for themselves, including the objective of not being *overpowered* by any other state. But this is far from saying that states invariably make the acquisition of power an objective of policy to be attained for its own sake, though some states in what may be called a psychopathological condition clearly sometimes do.

The second common answer to the question: 'what are states seeking from their participation in the international system?' is the national interest, the contemporary form of the older expression *raison d'état*, which we discussed in a previous chapter.[11] There we considered *raison d'état* as the modern alternative to the religious or theocratic principle of government. Here we are considering it as the comprehensive basis for a theory of the motivation of states. As such, we cannot but regard the idea of national interest as the force behind international policy either as false, or at best, unhelpful. It is false if it means that states, in fact, do what is good for them, what is in their real interest. The most that we can say is that governments, acting on behalf of states in the international system, do what they *believe* to be for the nation's good. That statement is of some value; it tells us, as we have explained in Chapter Three, that modern governments are not concerned, or, if they are concerned, are so to a very limited extent, with the use of their power to achieve religious objectives or universal moral principles which may have a distinct religious basis. But, beyond that, there is little help to be drawn from the concept of national interest in our attempt to understand the rationale of decision-making in the international system.

It is a truism to say that governments in their foreign policies are acting in the service of their nations' interests, as they see those interests, and to the extent that the domestic consensus, on which the governments depend, allows them so to act. When foreign policy is discussed in a modern Cabinet or other executive committee of the state the question at issue is hardly ever that of whether or not the government should take the nation's interest as the supreme test of the acceptability of any particular proposal. It is true that on occasion a member of the government may argue against a policy which, in his view, is harmful to the international community, though it might be beneficial to the nation 'in the short run', but the form his argument would probably take would be that 'in the long run' what was good for the world, was good for the state. It is hardly conceivable that such a Minister would persist in arguing a case manifestly beneficial to the rest of the world, or to another state, if it was clearly and without qualification injurious to his own state. If he did, he would no doubt be reminded by his colleagues that the taxpayer did not give him his salary for talking that kind of language.

If, therefore, debate and controversy do not arise in a modern Cabinet, or in the legislature, or in the nation as a whole, on the rightfulness or otherwise of national interest as the overriding object of policy, what *does* debate focus upon? The answer is not the further question: what is the national interest in a particular set of circumstances? It *is* the question: what *interests* (in the plural) do we have to sacrifice if we adopt in these particular circumstances policy A, or B, or C, and so on? The sacrifice of interests (even if the interests happen to be only the time and trouble spent by Ministers and permanent officials in considering a particular question) is inherent in the making of decisions and the taking of action. There can be no action in the international system (or anywhere else, for that matter) except at certain cost, or, as the economists say, at a certain opportunity cost, and this cost consists of the other actions which cannot be done if the action contemplated in the present instance is performed. Britain, for instance, cannot send arms to South Africa without offending coloured countries with which it is expedient to remain on good terms; at the same time, she cannot refuse to sell arms to South Africa without jeopardizing security in the south Atlantic or driving South Africa into alliance with another supplier.

The image we must have in mind therefore is of a certain pattern, mosaic, constellation or syndrome of separate interests, meaning by this last term the requirements, needs and expectations of a state from its participation in the international system. A state's interests clearly have two sources—here we are developing what we have said previously in this book about the two-fold character of foreign policy[12]—the external and the internal—the world, or systemic environment, on the one hand, and the complex of demands which arise within the country and which somehow the government must satisfy, or at least make a show of satisfying. The external source of foreign-policy decisions may be sub-divided further into: first, the world environment in the general sense, that is, the international political system in which the states, for better or worse, are condemned to live, and, secondly, the particular state of international 'play' at a particular moment in history. Britain, for example, has had an interest for hundreds of years in preventing the unification of Europe against her as a hostile force; at the same time, she has a particular, and no doubt transient interest, in maintaining a military garrison in West Berlin as an outcome of the Second World War.

The pattern or mosaic of particular interests which foreign policy must serve may not constitute an internally consistent unity; indeed it would be very remarkable if it did. There may, and there no doubt always will be, three kinds of inconsistency in the pattern of interests of a state: internal inconsistency, in the sense

G

of a conflict between demands arising within a state, as for instance when farmers profit from a certain policy, which they wish to see continued, whereas industrialists want to see the policy changed because they lose money by it, or the other way round; chronological inconsistency, as it may be called, when, for instance, a waning interest, like that of the coal industry, competes with that of a rising industry, like that of nuclear power; and external inconsistency, as when one country's interests conflict with those of another, or perhaps with the interests of the international system as a whole. These inconsistencies of interest arise partly because men are not all alike and do not all have the same needs—the villager does not necessarily welcome flights over his land of big jets which benefit the aircraft industry—and partly because resources are not available in infinite amounts—if British trawlers fish around the shores of Iceland, there is necessarily less fish available for the Icelanders.

We may now look at some possible classifications of national interests. One obvious general grouping is in order of their importance. Some interests are considered to be more vital than others, meaning that some are judged to be more worthy of sacrificing other interests to, than others. Some interests are so vital that a state may be willing to sacrifice all that it has in order to defend them; this is implied in the expression 'better dead than red', though the rhetorical value of that phrase as a fine declaration may be more than its value as a real intimation of the intentions of those who use it. Hence, one diagrammatic description of interests may be in the form of a series of concentric circles surrounding a 'core', which would stand for the 'vital interests' referred to above. As we move, circle by circle, from the core to the outer rim of the design we come to 'negotiable' interests, namely, those which are available to surrender to another state or other states in order to secure from those other states recognition of the interests nearer to the 'core'. The more distant from the centre a given circle of interests is, the less willing the state, or its government, is to pay a high price in terms of the sacrifice of other interests, in order to secure it. This is explained in Diagram 1.

When negotiation takes place between two states, what is normally happening is that each state hands over to the other what it considers to be a lower-priced interest in order to secure a higher-priced interest in return. This agreement is, under favour-

Diagram 1

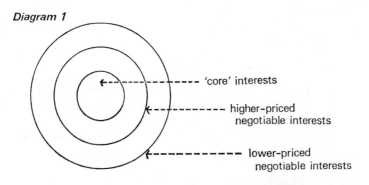

able circumstances, possible because what is considered lower-priced by the one side may be regarded as higher-priced by the other side, and *vice versa*. The essential thing is that the state sacrificing an interest should regard it as low-priced, whereas the other side should regard it as high-priced. Thus, in the famous Anglo-French Entente of 1904, Britain secured recognition from France of British predominance in Egypt, a high-priced interest from the British point of view, but a low-priced interest from the French point of view. In return France secured British recognition of French predominance in Morocco, a low-priced interest from the British point of view and a high-priced interest from the French point of view (Diagram 2).

With the advent of the Entente, British interests in Morocco were less securely protected since Britain had acknowledged French supremacy there. On the other hand, British interests were more securely protected in Egypt. For France it was the other way about.

As an example of an attempted settlement, which so far (1975) has not been achieved, there is the long-standing Arab-Israeli conflict in the Middle East. A diagrammatic exposition of this deadlock on similar lines to our diagram for the Anglo-French Entente of 1904 might take the form as shown in Diagram 3.

No successful outcome has yet been possible in this famous controversy, and this, it seems, is because both sides attach equal, and higher, values to the territorial question and equal, and lower, value to the recognition question. Considered in the simplest terms, which means stripping away a vast number of incidental considerations, it would seem that Israel must either attach a

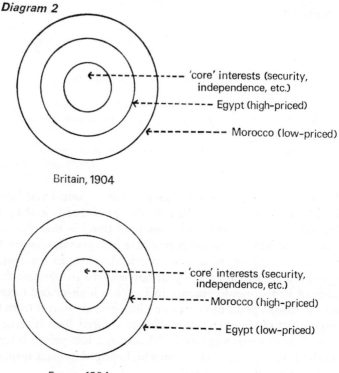

Diagram 2

'core' interests (security, independence, etc.)

Egypt (high-priced)

Morocco (low-priced)

Britain, 1904

'core' interests (security, independence, etc.)

Morocco (high-priced)

Egypt (low-priced)

France, 1904

lower value to keeping the territories she gained from the Arab states in 1967, or attach a higher value to recognition and guarantees from the Arab governments. Or alternatively, the Arab states must attach a lower value to their interest in recovering the territories lost to Israel in 1967, or a higher value to their interest in refusing full recognition to Israel, which means, in turn, that they must give less importance to their various pledges to support the cause of the Palestinian Arabs and organizations. The immense difficulties facing either side in the revision of the priorities among their national interests in this way are at once obvious.

We may also classify interests by order of location. Some national interests may be locally or regionally situated; others may have a more general or global location. All states have some interest in the maintenance of order throughout the international system, in an 'effective' United Nations, though the precise

Diagram 3

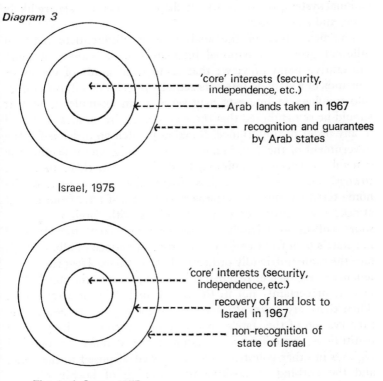

'core' interests (security, independence, etc.)

Arab lands taken in 1967

recognition and guarantees by Arab states

Israel, 1975

'core' interests (security, independence, etc.)

recovery of land lost to Israel in 1967

non-recognition of state of Israel

The Arab States, 1975

meaning they would give to that word 'effective' varies enormously from one state to another, and in reducing the world-wide burden of armaments, and also no doubt the political tensions which are deemed to justify those armaments. But it is reasonable to suppose that for practically all states these general interests will tend to form part of the outer or peripheral circle of interests, for the simple reason that, in the case of most states in the world, there is usually very little that they themselves can do to further general interests of this kind. On the other hand, local interests, such as the security of a nearby frontier, a military base under the state's direct control, or the condition of trade in the region of the world in which the state is situated—all these will tend to be sited nearer the inner ring of 'core' interests. We have in fact argued in a previous chapter that the higher the power-ranking of a state in the international system, the more widely dispersed its interests are likely to be, and *vice versa*.[13]

The next stage of the analysis is to differentiate between different groups of national interests from a somewhat more substantive point of view: that is, to what kinds of claims or demands of a state do interests actually refer? The following five-fold typology of interests may serve as an example, though it should be remembered that these classes are by no means ranked in any order of importance. Ranking in such an order is for the government of the day, in a given community and reflecting the general consensus of opinion, to decide. First, then, there are *strategic* interests, that is, those involved in the security of the home territory and its overseas possessions, if any, from armed attack; the security of communications with foreign markets, sources of supply, friendly states and commercial partners beyond the state's own frontiers; the security from attack of allies which face the same unfriendly or hostile Powers themselves; the main-tenance of a global or regional balance of power in the state's own favour, or certainly not in the favour of hostile or rival states. Then there are *political* interests, which may be defined as the preservation of the state's own form of government, its political institutions, practices and customs; the defence of political régimes in other countries which are well disposed to the state, and the curbing or positive undermining of hostile régimes abroad; the maintenance of a certain ratio of military and economic strength between the different states of the world and perhaps the defence or achievement of a certain type of political order in the international system which is consistent with the state's own political ideals and standards. Thirdly, there are *economic* interests, by which we mean the protection and, if possible, the improve-ment of domestic living standards, the solvency, stability and growth of the national income from year to year, the level of international trade and investment, government or private, in the rest of the world; and the achievement of desirable economic goals such as full employment, stability of the world's currencies and the equitable distribution of wealth in the world as a whole.

Fourthly, we can speak of a state's *legal* interests, by which we would mean the defence of a certain international treaty system which safeguards the rights of the state concerned and the preser-vation of such legal agencies for the maintenance of the existing legal order in the world, as the International Court of Justice at The Hague. Finally, since 1918, though not perhaps before 1914, we have been able to speak of *ideological* interests, by which we mean, at most, the promotion of a certain 'way of life', or style of politics, which is nationally endorsed at home, so that it extends throughout the international system on the widest possible scale, or, at least, the protection of that system of values against the encroachment of alternative or hostile political ideals. It can, of course, be argued that, when people talk of fighting for their ideology, they more often than not have in mind the defence of their standard of living or some other material benefit. But there is no doubt that, if only for reasons of habit or xenophobia, most of us would prefer, if we could, to see all the world acting according to political principles which we ourselves accept.

In the formulation of the state's pattern of interests (which may not in any particular case correspond at all with the order of interests suggested in the two preceding paragraphs) we must distinguish between the roles of the professional bureaucrat, the Foreign Office or State Department official, and that of the politician who is responsible to whatever electorate is the lawful one in that particular country. Since the First World War it is true that in many states these two roles have been increasingly confused, as the politician (thanks in the main to modern high-speed travel) has taken over more of the diplomat's traditional functions. However, it is the difference between the diplomatic and executive functions, if they may be so called, with which we are concerned, and not so much with who happens to be performing them.

The permanent official's role in relation to national interests is essentially one of definition and articulation. When any international issue, especially one which could become serious, comes before a government for decision, the official (or the politician if he is acting the official's role) must spell out in an ordered form the interests of the state in that issue. He must, of course, go much further than this and assess for the Minister the case for and against particular courses of action in so far as they affect the various national interests, but action by any state in the international system must begin, and in practice generally does, with the drafting in the office of a paper setting out the state's various interests in a particular issue on which a decision has eventually to be reached. The question on which the Cabinet, if the issue gets that far, would like the permanent official's advice is: which of our interests as a nation-state, if any, are likely to suffer if events develop thus or thus?

The Ministerial or Cabinet role is that of evaluating one interest, or group of interests, against another, and of *choosing* which interests may have to be sacrificed if other, more highly-valued, interests are to be effectively protected. He does not do this, or rather the logic of his political position necessitates that he should not do this, simply on the basis of his personal preferences, or according to how he happens to be feeling on that day. As we have stated before, interests constitute a constellation of imperatives of state so defined as to command a domestic consensus strong enough to support a government in office. As Mr. Harold Wilson put it in a speech on the debate about British membership of the European Community:

> What the referendum means is that it is not enough for any politician or political leader to say what he believes . . . it must be for the country to decide what is best for the mass of the people and for their children.[14]

A government may so define the state's constellation of interests as to destroy the basis of consensus behind it. In that event it will no doubt fall and be succeeded by a government which accepts a definition of the state's constellation of interests that facilitates a consensus broad and strong enough to support a government in power. But we must bear in mind that when we are thinking of a Minister or Cabinet defining interests in such a way as to command an effective consensus we mean that that Minister or Cabinet is in effect deciding which of its national interests it will sacrifice in favour of others since, as we have already said, there can be no action, and no government decision to act, without sacrifice. Government in any community, we might say, consists of deciding which public interests are less important than others, or, to put it another way, defining priorities.

We have come to the end of our examination of the motivation of state behaviour in the international system. Bearing in mind the distinctions which were made at the beginning of this chapter, we can certainly say that states are actuated in the modern age by, and seek as far as they are able to implement, a certain conception of national interest. How indeed in a secular age could it be otherwise? But we have carefully to relate that conception to the process of consensus-formation in the state. Above all, we must look beyond the over-all conception of national interest to the constellation or pattern of separate interests which lie behind it. We must accept as the central problem of decision making in the international system, not so much the question, 'what do we want to do as a state and how are we to do it?' but the question: 'how can we minimize the losses resulting from whatever we do, and how can we feel our way towards a policy which, when all our minds are made up about it, does rather less damage to all our interests than any other choice which we might have made?'

NOTES

1. See above, Chapter Seven, pp. 147–9.
2. Macmillan, London.
3. See above, Chapter Seven, pp. 151–2.
4. See above, Chapter Eight, pp. 171–2.
5. Knopf, New York, 6th edition, 1972.
6. In conversation with the present writer.
7. A 'crisis' could be defined as a period of time in which existing policies are subjected to such challenges that their continuing validity is brought into question.
8. Austen Chamberlain, 182 H.C. Deb. 5s. Col. 322 (24 March 1925).
9. State of the Union Message, 20th January 1972.
10. See above, Chapter One, pp. 20–1.
11. See above, Chapter Three.
12. See above, Chapter Eight, pp. 171–2.
13. See above, Chapter Eight, pp. 166–7.
14. *The Times*, 12th April 1975.

Ten

The Expansion of States

IN an earlier chapter of this book we examined some of the characteristics commonly shared by state-members of the international system.[1] In the present chapter we propose to discuss another of these characteristics, this time one which has played such a dominant role in the history of international relations as to justify separate treatment. This is what may be called the propensity of states to expand; that is, to enlarge their physical selves, their territory, or their interests abroad or their influence beyond their own borders. 'Every great country', wrote an Italian historian, 'every active people, naturally tends to expand'.[2] To this tendency the name 'imperialism' has been given, though in the period since the Second World War that word has been so saturated in negative connotations that its value as an academic concept has come to be questioned.

The tendency to expand, or the principle of growth, may characterize all social organisms. It is possible to conceive even a life-cycle of social organisms, which writers like Spengler and Toynbee in the twentieth century have ascribed to entire civilizations: a cycle of birth, growth, decay and demise. When applied to modern empires, it is clear that the cycle has been comparatively short. The overseas German Empire lasted a bare 35 years, from 1885 to 1919; the Italian Empire, 34 years, from 1911 until 1945; the Japanese Empire, half a century, from 1895 until 1945. The British Empire, the most extensive in history, lasted two centuries, but, once begun, its decline was extremely rapid, taking no more than a little over two decades to be totally extinguished. Surprisingly enough, the dissolution of the Empires of these states does not seem to have affected the living standards of their peoples; in fact, decolonization has been accompanied by an improvement in those standards beyond the wildest expectations entertained during the imperial era. The relationship between empire and the domestic standards of living of the metropolitan Powers has not yet been spelled out or even seriously examined.

However, we are concerned in this chapter with the expansionist phase of the life-cycle of states, if indeed such a life-cycle exists. Man may be, as Aristotle wrote, a political animal; the state, as all history bears witness, is an expansionist or imperialist animal. The international system, as we know it today, consists of giant Powers whose expansionist drives in the period since 1945 have been all too evident, smaller states like Belgium, Britain, France and Sweden, whose expansionist phases are now in the past, and new states which owe their existence to the retirement from empire of earlier metropolitan states, and which are often not reluctant to exhibit much the same acquisitive drives as their former masters. Indeed, it is a basic peculiarity of the inter-national system, and a source of some of the most severe conflicts within it, that it is at one and the same time a multiplicity of equal sovereign states, and a collection of imperialist, or potentially imperialist, or ex-imperialist, entities. Disequilibrium is built into the international system because there are two contradictory principles at its core: the principle of growth and expansion, militating against the independence of its member-states, and the principle of national self-determination, militating against the imperialism of its member-states. If we suppose that the former victims of imperialism should in logic be immune to its tempta-tions, we should consider the Philippines in respect to Sabah, Indonesia under President Soekarno in respect of Malaysia, India and Pakistan, in respect to Kashmir and the Rann of Kutch, and Iraq in respect to Kuwait. There are many other examples.

This seeming built-in tendency of states to expand has come to acquire intensely immoral connotations, though this is only a development of the past twenty or thirty years.[3] Hence students have generally been disposed to ascribe imperialism either to certain contemporary conditions, which can be expected to pass away for ever, or to certain inherent drives in man himself, which characterize man as an essentially sinful being. It seems hard for people to accept the notion that the state itself is an imperialistic animal, just as the beaver is a dam-building animal, or rather perhaps that their own state is an imperialistic animal. In fact, most of the modern theories of imperialism tend to place its cause outside the nature of the states; three of these we propose to

examine in the following paragraphs. These theories are evidently
open to such *prima facie* objections that one is bound to consider
whether the roots of expansionism, or imperialism, do not lie in
the nature and structure of the state itself as a form of social
organization.

First, there is the most widely-known of these theories, the
Marxist-Leninist idea that imperialism—in the sense of the drive
for the acquisition of foreign territory—occurs in a late stage of
the capitalist system, that is, in the phase of finance capitalism.
The origins of this theory are to be found, of course, in the work
of the British Liberal writer, J. A. Hobson, whose book *Imperialism*
was published in 1902.[4] Hobson had naturally been influenced by
the anti-imperialist thought of men like Richard Cobden and
John Bright, who considered that imperialism was not only a
cause of war, but an obstacle to the proper functioning of the
world-wide liberal economy. However that may be, Lenin, whose
classic work *Imperialism* was published in 1916, fully acknowledged his indebtedness to Hobson.[5] Lenin's idea was, in brief,
that, with the progressive combination of capitalist businesses, a
falling rate of profit in the home market begins to make itself
evident. This is intensified by the fact that, with technological
progress, manufacturing plant becomes more mechanized and
capitalized, and the proportion of labour, on which 'surplus
value' is made in manufacturing industry, is reduced. At the same
time, the workers, as a result of the Marxist law of the increasing
immiserization of the proletariat, lack the purchasing power to
buy up the products of capitalist industry, which now have to be
increasingly exported if the declining rate of profit is to be halted.
Fierce competition, which often results in bloody wars, therefore
takes place between capitalist nations in their struggle to win
overseas markets for their otherwise unsaleable goods. *Pari passu*
with this there occurs the accumulation of lifeless capital at home
causing international rivalry for the export of these funds to the
colonial areas of the world. With colonies thus becoming profitable
as markets for otherwise unsaleable goods and also as areas of
profitable investment, the machinery of state in the capitalist
countries enters the scene as an agency for finance-capitalists in
their search for markets and opportunities for investment. After
all, in Marxist theory the state is nothing more than a committee
for administering the affairs of the bourgeoisie.

This Marxist-Leninist formulation seemed to explain certain things which were left unexplained in pure Marxist theory. First, it helped to explain, or seemed to explain, why the workers in fact tend to get better off in the capitalist state, whereas Marx himself prophesied their increasing destitution. Lenin's answer to this conundrum was that the workers, like their capitalist masters, benefited from the exploitation of colonial peoples; to that extent, Marx's law of increasing proletarian immiserization was falsified. Secondly, Lenin's *Imperialism* helped to explain why the Communist revolution in Russia in 1917 occurred, not, as Marx forecast, in the most advanced capitalist state, but in one of the least advanced. Russia, in the Leninist scheme of things, was depicted as the 'weakest link in the capitalist chain'; it was, in other words, not only the world's most vulnerable bastion of capitalism and most prone to fall to the Communist revolution, but also an exploited colonial, or semi-colonial, country itself, France being its chief exploiter; and hence was the most advanced of the colonial world to rebel against capitalist-imperialist control. In the words of Lenin, Russia in 1917 was no more than a 'colonial dominion'.

This Marxist-Leninist analysis of capitalist-imperialism was applied by many Left-wing writers in the period between the two World Wars to the phenomenon of totalitarian Fascism and Nazism. A typical example of this kind of study was *Behemoth: the structure and practice of National Socialism*, by Franz Neumann, published in 1942.[6] This portrayed Hitler as the puppet or henchman of the capitalist-imperialist interests in Weimar Germany who feared a dispossessing revolution when the world capitalist economic system began to quake in the early 1930s, and who hoisted the Nazis into power as a way of saving themselves from it and of expanding Germany's power in order to win back the foreign markets they had lost in the Great Depression. If this was how the Hitler revolution took place in Germany in the 1930s, German finance-capitalists must have thought of themselves as having acted in the role of the Sorcerer's Apprentice after the Führer was firmly seated in the saddle of German politics.

The Leninist thesis about imperialism has been subjected to a damaging examination by, among others, Raymond Aron in his *The Century of Total War*.[7] Aron in this book points out some of the obvious facts which seem to contradict Lenin's argument:

first, that advanced capitalist states tend to find their best custo-
mers, not in poor colonies with low purchasing power, but in one
another; secondly, that likewise the best return on invested capital
comes from money sunk, not in undeveloped countries in which
the basic foundations of a modern society, like roads, railways,
bridges, have yet to be created, but in advanced states, in which
moreover the axe of nationalization does not so habitually hang
over foreign enterprises as it does in the developing countries;
and, thirdly, that the decade or so leading up to the First World
War, an allegedly imperialist war if there ever was one, was a
period of unbounded prosperity for capitalist Europe, and also a
period in which trade rivalry was more intense between Britain
and the United States (who were allies in the ensuing war) than
between Britain and Germany (who were enemies in the war). To
these objections to the Leninist analysis put forward by Aron
there may be added the equally obvious fact that empires existed
long before the period of advanced monopoly capitalism. The
great empire in the New World created by Ferdinand and Isabella
of Spain in the sixteenth century and reputedly animated by the
desire for gold and converts to the Christian faith is but one example from the modern European period, to say nothing of the
great empires of the ancient world. The Leninist thesis could
hardly apply to any of these, and we are therefore bound to ask
whether there is not some other common root of imperialism to
which we must look.

Another theory which purports to explain imperialism in contemporary terms—that is, in terms of determinate and presumably
transient historical events and conditions—is that which represents it as a logical development of nationalism. It is argued that
nationalism begins in the form of a demand for national independence, for separation and secession from a larger, multi-national
state. But no sooner is the separate national state formed, than the
same spiritual vitality—the *sacro egoismo*—which was the driving
force behind the struggle for independence, is diverted, naturally
and almost automatically, into expansion: the forces released by
the struggle for national freedom cannot be contained within the
national shell. Hence the story of the international system could
be related in the form of four acts of a drama: first comes the
demand for national self-determination, then the achievement of
national self-determination, followed by the pressure of the newly

self-determined state against its neighbours, and finally there comes the demand of those neighbours for self-determination against it. The history of international relations can thus be regarded as an endlessly repeated cycle of thrust, resistance, thrust, resistance, and so on.

Some support for this idea, that all nationalism is potentially imperialism, and that all imperialism is nationalism pressed to its most logical conclusion, is provided, of course, by the fact that some of the more recently consolidated national states—such as Germany and Italy in Europe, and Japan in the Far East—almost immediately turned towards colonial expansion after their unity and statehood had been attained. The leaders of such countries seemed to be impressed, and perhaps oppressed, by the fact that those countries were late arrivals on the scene of international relations and late arrivals on the imperial scene, that the 'open spaces' of the world were being rapidly filled in, and that they would have to move quickly to acquire a respectable colonial empire, this being regarded as almost indispensable for a proud national state, as, say, a smart suit is for the 'man about town'. Moreover, the intense collective pride aroused by successful nationalism no doubt supplied much of the motivation behind imperialism. Thus, it has often been pointed out that United States imperialism in the period of the war with Spain (1898–1899) was the outcome of a nationalistic hysteria in America which was stirred up by popular, sensationalist newspapers caught up in battles for circulation.

The difficulty is, however, that it requires but one example of imperialism before the age of nationalism, that is, before, say, the eighteenth century, to destroy the argument that imperialism is equivalent to nationalism writ large. Again, we may use the examples of the Spanish Empire in the Americas in the Golden Century of Ferdinand and Isabella, or the Anglo-Dutch and Anglo-French colonial struggles of the seventeenth century. In all these cases, and, of course, there are infinite other examples, the sense of empire being an expression of what we would today call nationalism was entirely absent. Indeed, it is possible to stand this argument on its head and say that imperialism, so far from being the offspring of nationalism, could just as well be conceived as its opposite. Nationalism, or rather its political expression, national self-determination, can be regarded as a violent rebellion against imperialism, and imperialism as the denial or suppression of nationalism.

The third of our selected theories of imperialism, unlike the two previous ones, seeks to place its origins, not in certain historical conditions, but in the acquisitive capacity of man, a permanent inclination of human nature, and evidence for this is certainly all about us, both in the contemporary world and in the records of the past. When we make the seemingly innocuous statement, which is normally made without question in modern industrialized society, that if taxes are raised too high, the incentive to work will be reduced, we are in effect taking it for granted that men will not do what they have no inclination to do, unless their acquisitive instincts (we call them such) are thereby satisfied. Appeals to the citizen's sense of civic duty will not, we assume, act as a sufficient incentive to work unless there is some cash benefit, and perhaps the promise of more cash benefits in the future. There are many examples of this famous and familiar theme in literature and history. Thucydides in his *History of the Peloponnesian War* retails the well-known dialogue between the Athenians and the Melians in the sixteenth year of the war with Sparta, when the Athenians were asked why they wanted to conquer Melos and they replied that it was a 'law of nature' that the strong should conquer the weak and that was all that needed to be said about it.[8] Again, Thomas Hobbes in the *Leviathan* placed acquisition and acquisitiveness as the first principal cause of conflict:

> So that in the nature of man we find three principal causes of quarrel. First, competition; secondly, diffidence; thirdly, glory. The first maketh man invade for gain; the second, for safety; and the third, for reputation.[9]

Likewise, at the end of the eighteenth century Alexander Hamilton argued for a federation, rather than a confederation, for the thirteen American colonies, on the ground that only thus would the union of the colonies be strong enough to contain the primitive lust of men for profit and gain.[10]

That man is covetous is only too obvious; that he takes pride in the expansion of his nation, prophesying that:

> *Wider still and wider*
> *Shall thy bounds be set;*

God who made thee mighty
Make thee mightier yet

has been a pertinent factor in international discords since the international system began. We must never lose sight of the basic human material from which our subject is formed, unflattering to ourselves as it sometimes is and familiar as it sometimes seems. But it is one of the difficulties in psychological analysis of international relations that, if it is assumed that man is acquisitive and hence imperialistic in his political life, we have to explain how it comes about that he is often indifferent, if not positively opposed, to imperialistic ventures. It is well-known, for example how in the eighteenth and nineteenth centuries many British leaders of opinion, from Adam Smith to Bright and Cobden, were bitterly opposed to imperialism and wished to discard British colonies overseas. If we are to follow the argument from psychology, it would seem that we must assume that a nation can be acquisitive and self-denying at the same time, or rather that a nation which is acquisitive in respect to colonies can short-sightedly ignore the even greater material benefits of doing without them.

It is not a fundamental objection to the psychological analysis that nations have sometimes rejected imperialism and at other times embraced it, but it does seem to suggest that additional sociological or historical data need to be brought into the analysis in order to make it satisfactory. The same difficulty arises when we consider how a national people, like the British, for example, in 1945, after two centuries or more of continuous imperialist endeavour, can fall into a mood of rejection of Empire and can disestablish their Empire very rapidly and almost with a feeling of relief. Perhaps this, too, can be explained in terms of the 'acquisitive instinct', but not without a ballast of historical sociology, perhaps enough to outweigh the original psychological proposition.

The theories which we have briefly mentioned, as we have seen, evidently have such *prima facie* weaknesses about them that one is driven back, after all, to consider whether the state itself is not an expansionist entity, whether to overspill its borders, literally or metaphorically, is not a tendency built into the state itself. Perhaps the question should not be, why the state outgrows its original limits, but what prevents it doing so as a natural form of development? If we are to consider imperialism as a peculiar form of state activity, as a behavioural form of the state itself, we should begin with a distinction between what may be called the 'automatic expansionist tendencies' of the state—those that is, in which will, feeling, ideas and intention play little or no part—and what we may call the 'myth of empire', the idolization or deification of empire as a self-conscious and deliberate object of effort.

The automatic impulses towards empire are connected with the physical growth of states and the contacts brought about as a result of that growth. The state is a developing organization, unless it is to stagnate or die: its population grows, its social structure and economy become more complex over time; its trade, internally and externally, becomes more diversified and voluminous. This growth increases the sum of the claims or interests which governments have to promote and defend in the international system, and yet often without any conscious or formulated desire for that increase. The interests of individuals in foreign trade, the defence of foreign markets and investments, in fact become national interests because they are sources of income and economic security for many more besides the actual traders and investors. And developing interests which are blocked in one area try to find an outlet in another.

Here we must remember, too, another and this time negative reason for the retention of colonies and other foreign possessions, that is, the losses which might be sustained if colonial possessions, which may not be of great positive value to the community as a whole, were abandoned or allowed to pass to another state. The German Nazis used to ask in the 1930s why, if British colonies were, as the British said, of so little value to them, they did not hand them over to a have-not state like Germany. The question, if serious at all, ignored the fact that, even if a country has little positive to gain from colonies, it may have something to lose by abandoning them, or rather certain groups among its people may have something to lose. The interested minority is bound to have more influence on the government's colonial policy than the indifferent mass who merely pay an always obscure proportion of their taxes for the upkeep of colonies.

It is also an unfortunate fact that often a state, if it is to protect its existing position in the international system, must extend its frontiers or its influence, or feels that it must do so, even if the new acquisitions are worthless in themselves or even negative in value. The search for a defensible frontier goes on. Often, too, the collapse of one empire creates an *imperii absentia*, a vacuum of power into which states are drawn as though they hardly had any option to do otherwise. A good example of this is the way in which the United States, despite its traditional association with the anti-imperialist cause in the world, acquired the Philippines and Cuba in 1898. Some American Senators spoke of the Philippines as doors which opened the way for American exports into the vast untapped markets of China, and Marxists tended to draw the conclusion from such statements that these commercial aspirations were the true motives behind the annexation. But we should not fail to understand President McKinley's dilemma: it was not in the American tradition to govern colonies overseas, Americans were unaccustomed to it and there were problems and difficulties about the whole idea of an overseas empire ruled from Washington, as American experience of this kind of thing has shown ever since. But Spanish naval power in the Pacific and the Caribbean had collapsed; what power was to take its place if not American power? What was to be done with Cuba and the Philippines after the Spanish left? McKinley did not know, but he did know that America could no longer stand aside; the Americans had pulled down the roof in the Pacific and were to be ever afterwards involved in building and holding firm another roof. President McKinley later said that he prayed all one night for an answer to this dilemma and one came at length when God said: 'annex the Philippines'. Perhaps that fairy tale made the God-fearing American people more prepared to accept a burden which many of them thought they would be better off without.

Similarly, the Allies in 1919 inherited Germany's colonies at the end of the First World War. Perhaps they were pleased to have them; the Australian delegation at Paris certainly left no doubt that they meant to have their share. Perhaps each of the Allies resented the others getting their hands on the German possessions. At any rate, they had little choice; the colonies could certainly not go back to Germany; public opinion in the Allied states would never stomach that. And, by the standards of political judgment of that day, there was no thought of giving them independence. Again, in 1945, was it ambition or necessities of state which drew

Stalin's forces into Eastern Europe? There is a good case to be made out for the argument that it was more importantly the latter.[11] Yet another example of what we have called imperialist expansion without a self-conscious imperialist motive is A. T. Mahan's account of how Russia's restricted access to the sea has tended to deprive her people of the wealth of maritime trade. Hence the rulers of Russia through the centuries were driven to acquire outlets to the sea, not necessarily because of territorial greed, but as a cardinal imperative of state. This is how Admiral Mahan put it:

> It would be a curious speculation to consider how far the systematic forward designs often attributed to (Russia), as in the rumoured will of Peter the Great, simply reflect the universal consciousness of her evident needs and consequent restlessness.[12]

It is an equally 'curious speculation' to consider to what extent Russia's international behaviour in the period after the Second World War has been similarly shaped by 'consciousness of her evident needs and consequent restlessness'. We should always remember that, as a geographical fact, the Soviet Union is a state which looks infinitely dangerous from the outside and at the same time infinitely vulnerable from the inside.

Secondly, there is the Imperial idea, the Imperial myth. This is the sense of mission, providence, vocation or destiny, which lives in all great empires. Haushofer, the architect of the German so-called science of geopolitics, wrote that 'once the sense of mission is lost, the building of great empires comes to a stop'. After the foundation of the Roman Empire in 27 B.C. by Octavianus, who became Augustus, the word *'imperium'* was identified by the Romans and the world with the law and order which the Empire brought with it: Rome's great work was *parcere subjectis et debellare superbos*. The spell of the Roman Empire dominated Europe for centuries after the barbarians sacked the Eternal City: its vigour can be seen reflected in the First Empire of Napoleon Bonaparte. The Holy Roman Empire of Charlemagne was an attempt to re-create the glories of the first Roman Empire. The Tzars of Russia are said to have considered themselves as having inherited the mantle of the original Rome in the myth of Russia as the Third Rome, after Constantinople fell to the Turks in the fifteenth century. The Orthodox monk Philoteus is said to have

addressed the idea to the Muscovite ruler, Vassillii III. The idea
of mission, or fateful obligation, was a familiar theme of British
imperialism, too, carrying with it the concept of the White Man's
Burden, the whites' responsibility, at whatever cost to themselves,
to bring the presumed blessings of civilization and the comforts
of the Christian religion to the lesser breeds without the law. Lord
Curzon, the Conservative statesman and one-time Viceroy of
India, never for one moment considered empire as having been
intended for the enrichment of Britain or the British: that might
be its consequence, but it was never its purpose. Empire was for
Curzon a considerable burden which history and Providence had
imposed on the advanced nations of the world. Those nations had
immense responsibilities to discharge in relation to the more
backward peoples of the world, in somewhat the same way as the
socialist of the present day thinks of the rich nations as having a
similar moral obligation to help with the advancement of the
poor.[13]

It is an interesting question whether the Imperial idea or the
Imperial myth has generally preceded or followed the building of
empire: whether it served to motivate or to justify imperialist
enterprises. In the case of ancient Rome there is some reason for
saying that the Empire was celebrated and was depicted in arts
and literature as one of mankind's greatest achievements, not
perhaps after the Empire had reached its greatest geographical
extent, but certainly after its broad outlines had been established.
In the preface to his history of the Roman Empire, Livy (59 B.C.–
A.D. 17) tells us that his work was inspired by anxiety concerning
the moral inadequacy, as he saw it, of his contemporaries to
shoulder their imperial responsibilities. His purpose, as he described it, was to bring out the contrast between the old Romans
who had laid the foundations of the empire and later generations.
He writes that he must in his history inquire into 'the ways of life
and public contact, the leaders and the acts of peace and war by
which the empire was founded and made great'.[14]

Much the same is true of Britain. The British Empire was built
up in three main phases: the period up to 1713, the end, that is, of
the wars of Spanish Succession, when the most important gains
were overseas trading posts and strongpoints; the period up to
1783, the date of the final loss of the first British Empire in North
America, which was followed by a period of stabilization of

British control in Canada and India; and thirdly the creation of the great African British Empire in the middle and late nineteenth century. But the period of glorification of empire, as it may be called, the vulgarization of the imperial idea, came in the fourth quarter of the nineteenth century, when the overseas Empire was reaching its greatest extent, a focal point being the Diamond Jubilee of Queen Victoria in 1887. It was when the British Empire began to be seriously challenged abroad, especially by Russia and Germany in the 1880s and by Liberal opinion at home, particularly after Mr. Gladstone's first administration in 1868–1874, that the 'imperial interest' became established and the idea of imperial federation and an imperial customs union began to be talked about.[15]

It is true, of course, that there have been empires—those, for example, belonging to states, such as Germany, Japan and Italy, which entered the race for empire comparatively late—the growth of which more or less coincided with the adoption and the popularization of the myth of empire. But it would be safe to assume as a general rule that *Imperialism*, in the sense of an emotionally tinged ideology, tends to develop when the need arises to justify imperial conquests and acquisitions, rather than when these are actually taking place. If this is so, it would help strengthen the main thesis of this chapter, namely that the expansion of states is probably a consequence more of automatic propensities within the nature of the state itself, than of a will to empire or of other contemporary conditions which may change as the state changes. It seems rather as though nations find that they have, or are making, an empire, and they then convince themselves that this is worth having and certainly worth defending.

One may say, then, that states will tend to overrun their borders—though this may not be in a literal or physical sense—unless there exists some definite obstruction which stands in the way. Or, to put the same point as we have done earlier in this chapter, the question which might properly be asked is not 'why do states expand?' or 'what causes imperialism?' but 'what prevents states following their tendency to expand?' or 'what is it that sets a limit to imperialism?' To the last two questions there can be three answers, or rather three forces constraining imperialist drives, and these may act separately or all together in particular instances. There may be some kind of internal weakness in the state which denies it the resources to maintain an establishment of dependencies outside its borders. During the Wars of American Independence in the eighteenth century Edmund Burke, the champion of the American colonies, used to say that, with eighteenth-century methods of transport and communications, even the most powerful despot had to 'truck and huckster' with his most distant subjects; there is always a limit to what even super-Powers can do in the modern world. That internal weakness may, of course, be a weakness of the will or inclination of the people of the state concerned. Or, secondly, there may be a veto on a state's expansion, imposed by more powerful states. When the colonies of Spain and Portugal in South America revolted against foreign rule in the 1820s, it was British sea power, supporting the Monroe Doctrine of 1823, which prevented the colonies being forced back under the yoke. In the same way, it is to be presumed that it was the opposing forces of the Western Powers which nullified any Soviet desire to expand their control in Eastern Europe after the end of the Second World War in 1945. Or, thirdly, there may be resistance to expansion on the part of the subject peoples themselves, and if this is supported, as it generally has been since 1945, by major Powers abroad and by institutions such as the United Nations which purport to represent the international community as a whole, it may be virtually impossible for the would-be imperialist state to overcome.

These forces which, along with others, have historically served to curb the expansionist tendencies of states and have inhibited the growth of empires go far to explain the different forms which imperialism has taken throughout its history. The tendency has been, especially since the First World War, for a shift to take place from 'direct', or overt, to 'indirect', or concealed, forms of imperialism. The most obvious direct form of imperialism is, of course, the classical European overseas empire of the middle and late nineteenth century in which there was a formal assumption by the metropolitan Power of the administration of the dependency, which was thereafter regarded for purposes of international law as falling under the jurisdiction of the metropolis in precisely the same way as its own territory within its own frontiers. It may be that, as a matter of convenience, administration of the dependency is exercised by local chiefs, a system which used to be called 'indirect rule' in the high noon of British imperialism; but in the

final resort supreme executive, legislative and judicial power lies
with the metropolitan state. In a legal sense the boundaries of the
dependency are assimilated with those of the metropolis.

Then there are various forms of what may be called mitigated
imperialism, or concealed or disguised imperialism. In these the
legal status of the dependency and that of the metropolis are not
fused together, but nevertheless the metropolis secures the benefits
of the imperial relationship, and the situation of inequality which
is inherent in the imperial relationship is brought into existence
between the two parties concerned. Many of these forms of mitigated imperialism shade into one another and international law
is vague about them. But if a scale is imagined on which, at one
extreme, the lesser state and its people are most like a colonial
dependency and at the other they are most like an independent
member of the international system, it would no doubt run (or
used to run before the Second World War) somewhat as
follows.

First comes the old-fashioned form of the Protectorate. Lord
Curzon, who probably knew as much about empire as anyone in
his lifetime, defined the Protectorate as:

> a plan adopted for extending the political and strategic, as distinct
> from the administrative, frontier of a country over regions which
> the Protecting Power is, for whatever reason, unable or unwilling
> to seize and hold itself, and while falling short of the full rights
> of property or sovereignty, it carries with it a considerable degree
> of control over the policy and international relations of the pro-
> tected state.[16]

The metropolitan state, in the case of the Protectorate, normally
assumes a legal obligation to defend the protected country from
external armed attack and to secure the proper treatment of
foreign subjects and property inside its borders. There has never
been, however, any accepted rule in international law on the extent
to which interference by the metropolitan Power in the internal
administration of the protected state is justified.

Moving along our imaginary scale of the classic forms of imperialism we come (again the language is hardly now 'in polite
use' in diplomacy, though the real form still exists in practical
politics) to the Sphere of Influence. Well-known examples are the
Monroe Doctrine, pronounced by the United States President in

1823 and strengthened by the so-called Roosevelt Corollary embodied in President Theodore Roosevelt's Message to Congress in December 1904, the agreement reached between Winston Churchill and Premier Stalin in Moscow in October 1944 for the mutual distribution between them of Spheres of Influence in Eastern and South-Eastern Europe after the liberation of those areas from Nazi control, and the so-called Brezhnev Doctrine in 1968, in which the Soviet Union and other Warsaw Pact countries claimed a right to intervene in any country in Eastern Europe in which the socialist system was threatened. In the Sphere of Influence, as classically understood, no external Power except one may, by law, custom or tacit or written understanding, assert itself in the territory so described; commercial exploitation and political influence are regarded as the peculiar right of the one interested Power. The local government is normally left undisturbed; indeed its sovereignty may be specifically reaffirmed in the agreement, if there is one, establishing or recognizing the Sphere of Influence, but the degree to which the local administration actually enjoys any genuine independence tends to vary from one situation to another.

The Sphere of Interest, on the other hand, is normally regarded as a somewhat less developed or restrictive form of external control than the Sphere of Influence, though it is only perhaps in the most formal diplomatic contexts that the distinction between the two terms, if not between the two forms, would be recognized today. Traditionally, in a Sphere of Interest the external Power would be accorded—again through recognition by other Powers— a dominant, though not exclusive, commercial and/or political influence. The most common situation has been one in which a number of external states, in return for certain services rendered to the local authority, would share out among themselves certain privileged rights within the territory in question.

Leases and concessions are generally more specific forms of privilege awarded to an external state or its nationals in the territory of another state. These may not carry with them any explicit authority over the government or foreign policy of the country granting the privilege, though, in the present age of acute sensitivity to encroachments on national sovereignty, it is easy for a privilege-granting state to feel that its independence has very definitely been undermined in the process of parting with leases and concessions. A good example where the Sphere of Interest merges into the concession is the exploitation of oil reserves in the Middle East and North Africa by consortia of foreign firms of differing nationalities. The experience of such firms at the hands of local nationalist governments, from the nationalization of the Anglo-Iranian Oil Company by the Iranian Government in 1951 to the nationalization of the Iraq Petroleum Company by Iraq in 1972, is indicative of the sensitivity to which we have referred.

Finally, at the furthest extreme from the formally and fully subordinate colonial dependency, is the 'client' state, or what used to be called in the more impolite days of the Cold War a 'satellite', one form of which is the 'neo-colonialist' state, as defined by the late Dr. Kwame Nkrumah when he was President of Ghana. A client state was traditionally a small and relatively powerless country which accepted financial assistance, military protection or advice, and technological help from a greater Power in return for offering to that Power such facilities as military and naval bases, favourable positions in the exploitation of important local raw materials, or possibly general diplomatic support of the superior Power: the last of these has become peculiarly important in an age of multinational organizations such as the United Nations which have a parliamentary-type system of voting. The post-1945 'satellite' is much the same except that, in so far as the term has been used by the Western Powers to refer to the lesser countries in the international Communist sub-system, there is the implication that an alien political régime has been imposed on the subordinate state which its population would probably reject if they had the power to do so. The 'neo-colonialist' state, as that term is commonly used in the Afro-Asian world, means somewhat less than this, but it does suggest that the foreign Power has such a strong economic grip on the lesser state, usually a recently decolonized country, that its political independence is to all intents lost, though formally it may still exist.

Lord Curzon, in his 1907 Romanes Lecture on 'Frontiers', which further develops some of the distinctions drawn above, saw a tendency in history for the looser forms of imperial relationship to be transformed into the tighter forms, or, using our own terminology, for the forms of mitigated or disguised dependency to move towards the pole of overt or direct dependency. He wrote:

Of all the diplomatic forms or fictions . . . the uniform tendency is for the weaker to crystallise into the harder shape. Spheres of Interest tend to become Spheres of Influence; temporary leases to become perpetual; Spheres of Influence to develop into protectorates; protectorates to be the forerunners of complete incorporation.[17]

As a 'striking illustration of this tendency' Lord Curzon in this lecture contrasted Lord Salisbury's Siamese Declaration of 1896, which affirmed the 'single and uncontested authority of Siam over the unguaranteed Siamese territory lying outside of the Menam watershed', with Lord Lansdowne's Declaration of April 1904, by which this territory was openly divided into British and French Spheres of Influence in which the two Powers conceded to each other liberty of action. Curzon continued: 'Lord Salisbury's was the first step; this was the second; and if at any time there is a third, its approximate character can be foreseen'. By that last phrase Curzon seems to have been referring to outright annexation.

Since the end of the First World War, however, it appears that this tendency has rather been in the opposite direction, that is, for indirect or disguised control to be preferred to direct administration and for external states to exercise the substance of authority over a lesser country without either incurring the expenses of administration or suffering the odium of annexation. This is to some extent indicated by the fact that some of the older terms for the imperial relationship, such as the Protectorate, the Sphere of Influence and Sphere of Interest, are no longer in polite conversation in the diplomatic world. This does not, however, mean in itself that the real forms of international relationship represented by those terms are now obsolete.

Three reasons may be suggested for this apparent reversal of Curzon's pattern of imperial development, or for the movement of imperial control since 1919 to be from the tighter to the looser types of management. The year 1919 is a significant date, in that public opinion in many countries, and especially in the victorious states which had fought the First World War, was anxious to cash the cheques of idealism which the warring governments had so freely doled out for propaganda purposes during the war. The public seemed to want international politics lifted to the levels of altruism which the Allied Powers had said that they stood for. It was also a time when America's traditional anti-imperialism was making itself felt in the Paris peace negotiations in the person of President Wilson and when the Russian Bolsheviks were exciting soldiers all over the world, as they waited for their demobilization, with their denunciations of the war as a product of capitalist-imperialism. For these reasons it proved impossible for the Allied Governments simply to annex Germany's colonies and the non-Turkish portions of the Ottoman Empire. This was not what the Allied peoples thought they had fought for. The League of Nations mandates system was therefore introduced as a form of disguised or mitigated imperialism. It made the annexation of German colonies and the Arab portions of the Ottoman Empire tolerable to a re-educated world opinion.

The first of the reasons we have mentioned for the movement in the twentieth century from overt to covert forms of imperialism is the spread of the idea of national and racial equality in the world since 1914. Even in 1919 it was possible to write into the League Covenant a reference (in Article 22) to peoples who were described as 'unable to stand by themselves in the strenuous conditions of the modern world' and who hence should become mandated to the 'advanced' Powers. That kind of language is politically quite impossible today: the implication of the modern euphemism 'developing countries' is that there is no inherent barrier, cultural, educational, racial or social, to the advancement of the poor people of the world to the level of the richest and most powerful nations, provided that impartial aid is channelled to them through United Nations agencies and the world trading system is revised so as to give them a square deal. So far from economic or cultural backwardness constituting a reason for deferring the grant of complete independence to the 'developing' countries, it has been urged over and again by non-white delegates at the United Nations that only by achieving full independence and expelling all foreign influence can these countries really experience the economic 'take-off'. But once the idea of the equality of all peoples has been widely accepted and embodied in a solemn document such as the United Nations Charter, it becomes virtually impossible to continue using the term 'imperialism' in any other than a derogatory sense since, however 'imperialism' may be defined, there is bound to remain some residual sense of inequality in the term. One such definition may be: a form of control exercised by one nation over another such that relations of inequality are brought into existence between the two and the unequal nation feels that it enjoys the right of national self-determination on which the international system, as it is at present, is based. Another such definition, this time from *Chambers's Encyclopaedia*, states that 'political inequality is of the essence of Empire, and the inequality must apply to races or nations or peoples'.

Secondly, and again since 1914, there has spread within the international system the idea of the Rule of Law as between equal sovereign states, expressed through universal international institutions such as the League of Nations and the United Nations, which has been entrusted with the supervision of all colonial administration, whether carried out by great Powers or small, and the controlled advancement of all dependent peoples towards independence and nationhood. The mandatory régime of the League of Nations was by way of being a half-way house between the old imperial system and the present age of the national equality of all states everywhere. The mandatory régime was in one sense one of those 'fictions of equality' to which imperialist Powers have generally resorted as a means of disguising the fact of their overlordship over weaker peoples. But in its United Nations form, as set forth in Chapters XI and XII of the UN Charter, there have been far more rigorous arrangements for the international supervision of dependent territories, and this mainly because the world organization, in marked contrast to the old League, has come to be dominated by African and Asian member-states which were themselves dependencies not long ago.

A third important historical factor tending to reverse Lord Curzon's conception of a movement from looser to tighter forms of imperial control has been the internal modernization and Westernization of certain Middle East and Asian states, notably China, Egypt, Japan and Turkey, some of which were themselves powerful and extensive imperial states in the past. Under the reformed régimes of these states they proved strong enough either actually to overthrow a great imperialist Power and hence establish the right to rank, theoretically at least, with the élite of the international system, as Japan did when she defeated Russia in 1905; or to drive out all elements of Western domination, as Turkey did in 1921–1923; or increasingly to reduce Western control to mere vestiges of its former self, as Egypt did up to 1956 and China did in the 1920s. At the same time these reformed Eastern states set a very convincing and attractive example to other non-European countries still under Western control or under Western imperial jurisdiction.

This brings us finally to the current world-wide debate on imperialism; it is one of the major themes of international controversy. One of its main features has been the tendency of the two great power groupings of the Cold War to accuse each other of imperialist practices and policies, while denying or attempting to minimize the existence of any imperialistic features of their own régimes. In the process, the meaning of the word 'imperialism' has become so degraded and debased that it has come to stand for almost any kind of exploitation by a state of its own power to which another state raises objection. The Soviet Union has been accused of imperialism by the Western Powers on account of the alleged domination of the Soviet federation by the Great Russian Soviet Socialist Republic and the alleged domination of Eastern Europe by the Soviet federation. The Soviet Union, on its side, regards the Western Powers as imperialist by definition since capitalism and imperialism are in the Soviet dictionary practically interchangeable terms, while Soviet policies cannot, again by definition, be anything other than counter-imperialist. The other prominent feature of the current debate on imperialism—or colonialism, as it now seems to be more usually called[18]—is the confrontation between the new Afro-Asian states, formerly colonial dependencies themselves, and the old imperialist Powers of Europe, which, in the Chinese Communist view, now include the Soviet Union. One form taken by this confrontation is the demand of the newer countries at the UN for the elimination of all remaining traces of imperialism in the old juridical or administrative sense.

This contemporary debate about imperialism or colonialism has in a sense nothing to do with the capitalist versus communist controversy (as the Marxists argue), and nothing to do with the 'march of progress towards the independence and equal dignity of all peoples' (as Mr. Nehru and Dr. Soekarno used to say). It is in fact one aspect, or example, of the immemorial conflict in the history of mankind between reality and the ideal, between the world as it is, with some states and peoples having more power than others, and the world as it might be, with all states and peoples equal. It is, in short, the conflict between *Kratos* and *Ethos* which has been with man since at least the beginning of his recorded history. The peculiar thing about this struggle is that it does not seem to have begun on the plane of international relations, but on the plane of individual experience and aspiration. The demand for equality, as de Tocqueville pointed out, is in the last resort irresistible; once people begin to feel that they are equal human beings and have a right to be treated as such, it takes immense power, or force, to compel them to be satisfied with their inequality. From that point on, imperialism—the international form of inequality—becomes intolerable, not only to the subject peoples, but to people within the imperialist state itself.

On the other hand, the fiction of the equality of states, to which the fiction of the equality of individuals insensibly leads, is a defiance of the conspicuous facts of life: states are not equal and, what is more, the stronger states are bound to want to demonstrate and exploit their strength. The idea of the equality of individuals is a fiction, too, but within the state there is a system of law binding upon all, and this, if it is backed by a suitable popular consensus, can serve to bring the fiction of the equality of individuals closer to the facts of life. It is true that, even in the most perfect welfare state, there cannot be complete equality, or equality of opportunity, for all, but nevertheless there can be a considerable approximation to it, and, what is more, the hope can remain that some day there will be a complete approximation. Internationally, however, the factual inequality between the strong and the weak is hardly tempered at all by a system of law inspired by distributive justice. All that schemes of foreign aid and revisions in the terms of trade in the world between the strong and the weak can do is to moderate to a slight degree the immense factual gap between the two.

What follows from this is that the formal abolition of imperialism, which occurs, for example, when decolonization takes place, cannot abolish the factual inequalities between states; in certain circumstances, as for instance when a formerly dependent territory is excluded from the tariff barrier of the former imperialist state, it might increase those inequalities. Relations of dominance and submission are bound to remain after decolonization, however much they may be overlaid by the polite fictions of legal equality. Outwardly the effect may look more respectable than the old régime, but the inward reality may be harder to detect.

NOTES

1. See above, Chapter Seven.
2. Luigi Villari, *The Expansion of Italy*, Faber and Faber, London, 1930, p. 7.
3. As late as 1947 L. S. Amery was introduced to a Conservative Party conference as 'the greatest imperialist in our midst', and that was intended as a compliment.
4. Nisbet, London.
5. *Imperialism. The Highest Stage of Capitalism*, Foreign Languages Publishing House, Moscow, 1947.
6. Gollancz, London.
7. Translated into English by E. W. Dickes and O. S. Griffiths, London, 1954, from the original *Les guerres en chaîne*, Gallimard, Paris, 1951.
8. Book V, Sections 87–111.
9. Chapter XIII.
10. *The Federalist Papers*, esp. Nos. 15–20, Selected and Edited by Roy P. Fairfield, Anchor Books, New York, 1961.
11. See L. J. Halle, *The Cold War as History*, Chatto and Windus, London, 1967.
12. A. T. Mahan, *The Problems of Asia*, London, 1900, pp. 43–4.
13. Harold Nicolson, *Curzon: the Last Phase*, Constable, London, 1934.
14. See Richard Koebner, *Empire*, Cambridge University Press, 1961, Chapter I.
15. Seeley's work, *The Expansion of England*, which criticized Turgot's idea of colonies 'falling off the tree like ripe fruit', was first published in 1883.
16. Lord Curzon, The Romanes Lecture, *Frontiers*, The Clarendon Press, Oxford, 1907.
17. Curzon, ibid., p. 47.
18. See the interesting article on Colonialism by A. P. Thorton, *The Review of Politics*, April 1963.

Eleven

The Mutual Impact of States

As we have observed in an earlier chapter, the interests of states in the international system are at one and the same time diverse and stable.[1] They are diverse in the sense that they derive from the unique geographical situation of states, their peculiar economic and social composition and structure, their national psychology or character, if there is such a thing, and other such idiosyncratic features of states. But interests are stable too, and often for much the same kind of reasons: the geographical position of a state is relatively unchanging from one generation to the next; economic and social factors are comparatively slow to alter; national psychology is normally inert and persistent, and national attitudes built up over generations change only slowly. There are, too, in all countries the 'sacred cows' of foreign policy, the long revered and established practices, which even the most popular governments are reluctant to challenge.

When we now come to consider the means by which states characteristically defend or advance their interests in the international system, the answer to this is quite simply: international co-operation. After the First World War international co-operation was often considered to be a 'new method of conducting international relations' by supporters of the League of Nations in the different countries. But it is, and was, plainly nothing of the sort. International co-operation has always been the way in which the states of the world have conducted their business. No state, especially in these last decades of the twentieth century, is so remote and detached that it does not require the goodwill and help of other states; none is so powerful that it can impose its will on all other states. Governments quite often complain that other governments 'will not co-operate' or 'will not negotiate'. But that is contrary to commonsense. Every state will co-operate with any state provided that that state co-operates on terms favourable

H

to itself. Winston Churchill said, and quite sensibly, even before the Germans attacked the Soviet Union in June 1941, that if Hitler invaded Hell, he himself would have something favourable to say about the Devil in the House of Commons. Conflict does not arise between two states because one or the other refuses to co-operate on any terms: it arises normally because the two states want to co-operate on different terms. The purpose of conflict in fact is to reduce the terms on which one side or the other, or both, will co-operate on some disputed issue between them.

Broadly speaking, there are four different ways in which co-operation is brought about within any system of social relations, although in the international system these are not related to one another in the same manner as they are within other social systems. First, there is law, that is, the promulgation, by an authoritative and competent body, of rules which the community regards as binding upon itself. Law, as Roscoe Pound once wrote, is a form of social control; in other words, it helps assure the essential minimum co-operation without which there can be no order in society. In the international system, however, law does not serve quite the same function. Public international law does not emanate from an authoritative body for the purpose of co-ordinating wills in the international system. Its aim is rather to register in a solemn form the co-ordination of different wills which results from a previous process of bargaining. International law, as for instance a treaty between two or more states, sets the seal upon agreements previously arrived at. To some extent this is also true of domestic, or municipal, law, too, but in that legal system there needs to be at least the fiction, or the illusion, of the community, the electorate or the people willing certain rules which are later enacted by the legislature, in order that the rules should be accepted as binding. In the international system we are more conscious of separate wills being reconciled by a process of argument and negotiation and then embodied in legal form, rather than the projection of a common will into law.

A second means of achieving social co-operation in any society is the practice of rational argument. The co-operation of others on terms more or less favourable to oneself can be obtained by an appeal to the reason of the case, to the 'common sense of most', or to the enlightened self-interest of the other party. This method does have an important and extensive application in the field of international relations, certainly far more than most people imagine. After all, what is the complex network of diplomatic missions throughout the world for, if not, among other things, for the rational persuasion of other states to the rightfulness of the home government's policies? Nevertheless, the scope of rational persuasion is undoubtedly limited in international affairs, one obvious reason for this being that national decision-makers do not act for themselves in the international system, but for millions of people in the state, who cannot or will not see the reason of a case where their own interests are powerfully engaged. As a rule, a Minister does not object to seeming unreasonable if in doing so he satisfies his own people, who determine how long he will remain a Minister. The dictators of the inter-War period, Hitler and Mussolini, appeared positively to simulate madness on occasion in order to frighten democratic statesmen into giving way to them, and often they were successful. The lunatic, or he who pretends to be a lunatic, can frequently get what he wants by threatening otherwise to cut his throat.

Thirdly, there is and always has been naked force *simpliciter*, that is, the imposition of physical restraints to the body of the other party in order to compel him to co-operate, either by desisting from actions unfavourable to the applicant state or by conforming with the applicant state's wish to co-operate. Force, coercion, violence—each of which has slightly different meanings —clearly have their role to play in securing international co-operation on terms favourable to the applicant, but in most of international life that role is probably much smaller than many people suppose. Brute strength, especially in the present nuclear age, has to face many obvious inhibitions and disabilities. It has to be used, as George Canning once said, 'only in emergencies, and then with commanding force'. The days when Theodore Roosevelt uttered that famous axiom of diplomacy—'walk softly and carry a big stick'—are long receded into the past. As a rule, most states, and even the greatest Powers, normally wait a long time for the apparatus of peaceful diplomacy to work its way, if it possibly can, before they begin to talk of force, appropriately named the 'last resort of kings'.

Somewhere intermediate between rational argument (the eliciting of consent to co-operate) and naked force (the imposition of physical compulsion to co-operate) there lies a broad spectrum of inducements and deprivations ('carrots and sticks') which are normally called pressures, the fourth of our established methods of ensuring international co-operation on terms favourable to the applicant state. It is in fact generally on the basis of the use of pressures that the quest for international co-operation proceeds. As a general rule, states are unable to issue binding rules to each other; they cannot always ensure conformity with their own will by reasonable argument; they normally find the resort to force cumbrous and unpredictable. For these reasons there is throughout the international system a continuous resort to pressures since these constitute a convenient half-way house between the hazardous resort to force and the frequently unavailing appeal to rational argument and the common good of all. In effect, a government applying pressure to another government is asking it whether it is not preferable to give way rather than face the prospect of continuing disagreement with the risk of force having to be used at a later stage and to the disadvantage of both sides.

Pressures applied by states on one another in the international system may be defined as systematic efforts to narrow the field of choice before the other state (the target state) by acting so as to increase the attractions of policy options favourable to the state applying the pressures (the applicant state). Pressures may be either positive or negative or a combination of both. Positive pressures are intended to enhance the attractions of options preferred by the applicant state, while negative pressures heighten the unattractiveness of options unfavourable to that state. Hence the pressures that are available to states in the international system may be arranged along an imaginary graduated scale running from the positive, or non-compulsive pole at one extreme, where the emphasis is on persuasion and the positive attractions of the preferred option, to the negative, or compulsive pole at the other extreme, where the emphasis is on coercion and the drawbacks of the less preferred option. One general rule which can be formulated is that the costs to the applicant state, and the unpredictability of pressures, tend to rise towards the compulsive end of the scale, so that there is invariably a strong inducement to keep the emphasis on the recruitment of consent rather than on the imposition of force. While the subject of pressures in the international system is extensive and complicated, five types of normal pressures may be discerned, ranging from the non-compulsive to the compulsive poles: the diplomatic, the judicial, the moral, the economic, and the physical. The spectrum is shown in the following diagram, in which the curve *a–b* stands for rising costs and the curve *c–d* represents declining predicability.

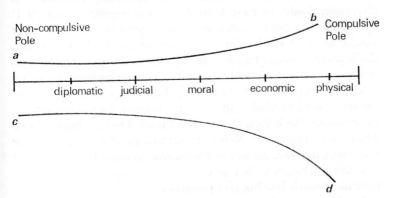

Diplomatic pressures in international politics are perhaps the most normal, continuous and regular. Certainly they are the most unspectacular and possibly the most effective in the long run of all the repertoire of pressures. Included in this category are what may be called unilateral representations, or reasoned arguments in favour of a certain policy choice by the target state, which may be a change in policy desired by the applicant state or the continuation of a desired policy, if a change is in contemplation, mediated through the normal and established diplomatic channels. Sometimes, and increasingly since the First World War, such representations are publicized, possibly on a world-wide scale, in order to win over public opinion in the target state and perhaps elsewhere, too. In the years since the end of the Second World War ambassadors have been considered not to be acting improperly if they make public defences of their country's policy in the state to which they are accredited, though such behaviour would have been considered a breach of diplomatic propriety in many countries as late as 1939.

Then come third-party representations, or the appeal to the good offices of a third country in the expectation that it will use its friendly influence where there is a deadlock between two or more disputing states, or where the states in dispute do not happen to be in diplomatic contact with each other. In 1940, for example, after the military collapse of France, the British Prime Minister, Winston Churchill, appealed to Franklin Roosevelt, the President of a great neutral state, to intercede with the French Vichy régime so that they would not surrender the battleship *Dunkerque* to Germany. Again, in 1965 United Nations Secretary-General U Thant tried to use his influence with Algeria in the hope that it would act as a moderating influence on North Vietnam. But third-party representations are in fact a daily occurrence in diplomacy. The decline of neutrality and its contemporary form, neutralism, in the twentieth century, however, has much reduced the scope for this kind of diplomatic pressure. In the mid-1950s, for example, the British Government tended to look to the Prime Minister of India, Mr. Nehru, to act as a third-party intercessor with the Chinese Communist Government. With the outbreak of hostilities between China and India in the 1960s this obviously became a much less hopeful possibility.

In the event of failure, diplomatic representations may be followed by the withdrawal of ambassadors or other diplomatic representatives, either permanently or on leave. This is the 'diplomatic rupture' or 'breach of diplomatic relations'. It is generally regarded, especially by European states, as a serious measure, not to be embarked upon lightly, largely because of the inconvenience which it causes for both sides. Moreover, the restoration of diplomatic relations after the breach has to be carefully handled by the applicant state lest it give rise to loss of face and suggestion of a moral defeat; for example, the Federal German Republic's famous 'Hallstein doctrine', which seemed to oblige it to break off diplomatic relations with all states, except for the Soviet Union, which recognized East Germany as a separate state, caused the Bonn Republic a certain amount of embarrassment when it embarked on its *Ostpolitik*, which compelled it virtually to eat its words as far as East Germany was concerned. Nevertheless, diplomatic rupture has been not infrequently resorted to by some of the newer African states to indicate displeasure with the target state's policies when the dispute was on a much less serious plane than the issues which a diplomat of the old school would consider to justify a rupture. The United Kingdom, for example, has suffered diplomatic rupture at the hands of several African states when her efforts to solve the

Rhodesia crisis since 1965 vexed them for one reason or another. In the old (pre-1939) days of the European international system an ambassador might indicate distaste for the policies of the country he was accredited to by refusing to drink its wines. Today, with the general depreciation of the currency of diplomacy, much stronger measures are thought necessary to express much less dissent from another state's policies.

A novel form of diplomatic rupture is the concerted or multi-lateral breach of diplomatic relations: a kind of general diplomatic boycott or ostracism. This was for a time practised by the United Nations, in the early years of the Organization, against Spain as a way of expressing distaste for General Franco's régime as a survivor of European Fascism before the War. This particular boycott was of doubtful value; it had no discernible influence on the Franco régime and that régime achieved something of a moral victory when it became apparent that the disabilities created for the applicant state through not having formal relations with Spain became too inconvenient. It was a case of UN member-states biting off their noses for the doubtful pleasure of expressing their contempt for Franco and his works. A modified form of the multi-lateral diplomatic boycott, which is far less costly to the applicants, is the concerted walk-out of several delegations from a conference or other international meeting when the representatives of an un-popular state begin to speak. The independent African states have practised this pressure more than once against British delegates at the United Nations, especially during some of the most tense stages of the Rhodesia dispute in the late 1960s. A good deal of this kind of behaviour is no doubt intended more to satisfy public opinion at home, or to preserve the solidarity of a regional group of states, than to change the policies of the target state.

Another type of diplomatic pressure, though this tends in any longish term to be equally inconclusive, is the refusal to take note of a situation which has been brought about illegally or against the will of the state or states applying this pressure. The United States, having made much use of this practice of non-recognition as a form of pressure in its dealings with Latin American countries, applied it against the Soviet régime in Russia until 1933 and then again against Communist China for many years after the Communist Chinese revolution in 1949. The American Secretary of State, Henry Stimson, proposed the general non-recognition of the Japanese puppet state of Manchukuo which resulted from the Japanese attack on Manchuria on 18th September 1931, which Mr. Stimson alleged was a breach of the Nine-Power treaty on the integrity and sovereignty of China, which Japan, along with others, signed at Washington in 1922. The Stimson proposal, though adopted by the League of Nations, is not known to have had any effect on the Japanese authorities; nor, it seems, did the American non-recognition of Bolshevik Russia until 1933, and of Communist China after 1949, have much effect on those two states, except perhaps to increase their hostility towards the United States. On the other hand, it has clearly been a distinct disadvantage for the illegal Smith régime in Rhodesia since 1965 not to be recognized by any state up to the time of writing (May 1975). By the same token, a promise to extend recognition to another state can sometimes be used to extract concessions from it, and this in itself could be regarded as one of the gains of non-recognition. The Federal German agreement to accept the Oder-Neisse line as the boundary between the German Democratic Republic and Poland seemed to smooth the way to the Federal German-Polish treaty of 1970, which the Bonn Government was seeking as a step in its *Ostpolitik*.

Finally, we may include among diplomatic pressures—the most lenient and least compulsive in our imagined spectrum of pressures —the use of international organizations for moving a resolution, hopefully intended to produce a change of mind in another state or government; or as a face-saving device when every other expedient has been tried and failed; or to put oneself right with world opinion, and perhaps also with public opinion in the target state, while more forceful measures are in preparation. One cannot always expect that the people or government of another country will necessarily be much impressed by such measures when they have vital interests of their own to secure: one thinks in this connection of the evident deafness of Israel to condemnatory UN resolutions since the Six-Day War in 1967. The Israeli Government apparently thought that, since the United Nations did nothing to help Israel when President Nasser closed the Gulf of Aqaba at the start of the Six-Day War in 1967, there was no strong reason why they should heed UN resolutions, when Israel had won its security by its own efforts and military victories. None the less, if a UN resolution is backed by a powerful state or states

in the Organization, this might be a signal to the government of
the target state of the kind of diplomatic reception it is likely to
get outside the Organization and in the diplomatic world as a
whole. The UN, it has been said, is like a fuse-box in an electric
light system. A 'blow-out' there may cause less damage than an
explosion somewhere else in the system.

The second of our major categories of pressures normally
practised in the international system may be sited on our scale of
pressures at about the same distance from the non-compulsive
end of the scale as the diplomatic pressures with which we have
just been dealing. This is the group of judicial pressures, which
can be dealt with quite summarily. The exercise of judicial
pressures in international relations can be described as the resort
to the international courts and tribunals which now exist in
abundance, not so much for the *bona fide* purpose of settling a legal
controversy between two or more states, but to obtain an authoritative judicial ruling, which can then be used as part of a political
campaign intended to discredit the other state or government. A
classic example is the successful effort made by France in the
1930s to obtain an Advisory Opinion from the then Permanent
Court of International Justice at The Hague to the effect that the
proposed Austria-Germany customs union was inconsistent with
Austria's independent status as confirmed by the Treaty of St
Germain signed in 1919 and with the conditions under which
Austria was granted certain loans by the League of Nations for the
purposes of post-War reconstruction. As a matter of fact, this
move was only part of the apparatus of pressures organized by
France against the customs union proposed; France had to all
intents secured the withdrawal of the proposal simply by refusing
financial assistance to Austria, if the customs union proposal were
to go through. The Court's Advisory Opinion in the case therefore did little more than complement the older forms of pressure
which the French Government had already set in motion.

Obviously, judicial pressures may have only limited effectiveness. A number of difficulties exist. The Court's judgment in any
intensely contested issue is bound to be highly controversial. No
one can be sure how its judges will vote, or even whether the Court
will accept the legality of its own competence in the case. The
world court at The Hague, or any subordinate court, may give a
verdict opposite in its political implications from that desired by

the applicant state, or perhaps one so reserved and qualified that the target state may feel that it has secured a moral victory. Perhaps this was the case when the world court gave a negative verdict when Liberia and Ethiopia in the 1960s raised before it the issue of their rights in the administration by South Africa of Namibia, or South-West Africa. The negative verdict may have done more to raise spirits in South Africa than it did to depress them amongst the independent African states. Another difficulty is the long delays which normally ensue during the consideration of cases before the world court, which often makes the impact of judicial pressures, even when a favourable verdict is returned, protracted and ineffective. This may have been the reason why the British and French Governments decided in 1956 not to submit the issue of President Nasser's nationalization of the Suez Canal Company to the International Court, though they had consistently argued the illegality of Nasser's action. They surely recognized, first, that waiting for the Court's verdict must rule out the taking of other, and more forceful, measures against Nasser which they had in mind, and, secondly, that by the time the Court had made up its mind about the case the Egyptians would be securely based in the canal and it would be virtually impossible to expel them.

Two other difficulties arise in the attempt to use courts of law as a means of international pressure. One is that there is no compulsory jurisdiction in present-day international courts and tribunals. No state is legally obliged to appear before a court, unless it has signed the so-called Optional Clause of the Statute of the International Court at The Hague.[2] Most of the thirty-odd states which have made declarations under this Article accepting the Court's compulsory jurisdiction have made very substantial reservations in their declarations, and these may be recalled and altered at any time. It is true that the International Court can be asked to give an Advisory Opinion, and this does not require the consent of any state, but by the Court's Statute only international organs, as distinct from individual states, can solicit the Court for an Advisory Opinion.[3] The second difficulty is that the attitude of the target state towards international courts and tribunals may preclude it or its people from being influenced by adverse judgments against them. When in 1947 the ICJ pronounced in Britain's favour when one of her naval vessels was mined in the

Corfu Channel and awarded her damages against the littoral state, Albania, the latter state ignored the verdict and has never paid one penny of the damages since. Similarly, when the United States in 1964 secured from the world court an Advisory Opinion that United Nations peacekeeping forces were a legitimate call on the Organization's budget and therefore that states like France and the Soviet Union, which refused to contribute towards the upkeep of these forces, were in default of their obligations under the UN Charter, those two Powers paid no heed to this Opinion and other states felt that it would seriously damage the world organization to invoke the sanctions provided for in Article 19 of the Charter for non-payment of members' financial contributions.

Moving now along our spectrum of pressures habitually used in the international system we come to the third category, which may be called 'moral' pressures or the pressures of 'mass persuasion'. These represent systematic and direct attempts to appeal to the public opinion of the opposing, or target, state or of the world at large. These are naturally different from diplomatic pressures in that the target of mass-persuasion pressures is the ordinary people of the opposing state and not necessarily the official elements on the other side. For this reason, mass persuasion can only hope to be effective where the people in the target state are able to exert some influence on the direction taken by their government's policies, or at least to prevent a policy unfavourable to the applicant's state from being effectively implemented. Thus, governments of liberal democratic states are usually at a distinct disadvantage, as compared with totalitarian régimes, in attempting to use direct influence on the people of a target state. This is not normally offset by the suspicions aroused in the mind of the people in a totalitarian state that their government must have something disreputable to hide if they are not free to expose themselves to world opinion. And even if they do harbour such suspicions, the probability is that they can do nothing about them.

Almost all the actions of governments, Ministers and diplomats in the field of external affairs have some 'mass-persuasive' elements in them. They are intended, among other things, to affect the opinions and emotions of people in other countries in a manner which suits the purpose of the state doing the 'mass persuading'. But mass persuasion can also be, and in most parts of the world is in fact today, a specialized activity carried on by specialized agencies, staffed by skilled manipulators of opinion under general government direction. In this case it is more usually known as propaganda, that is, the professional dissemination abroad of biased images, using suggestion for the most part, rather than rational persuasion, in order to influence attitudes abroad and also, hopefully, the policies of relevant governments. Propaganda may be purely verbal, in the form, for example, of the Voice of America, Radio Free Europe, the external services of the BBC and those of Moscow and Cairo, or American leaflet raids on North Vietnam, but it may also take the form of 'propaganda of the deed', that is, the taking of overt and visible action from which it is hoped that appropriate inferences will be drawn abroad. It could be said as a general rule that propaganda is probably most effective, not when it is self-consciously arguing an arguable case, but when it is presenting incontrovertible facts and pointing out certain implications which follow (or are supposed to follow) from them. Once, when rumours were circulating that President Roosevelt in one of his election campaigns was seriously ill and hence a doubtful runner for the next Presidential term, he chose to be driven about in an open car in the drenching rain. That Roosevelt was allowing himself to be soaked to the skin was a fact which could not be disputed; that this meant, as it was supposed to imply, that he was a thoroughly fit man was highly controversial.

Propaganda of the deed merges, as one moves along the scale to the compulsive pole, into the 'war of nerves', in which threatening communications pass from the applicant to the target state to the accompaniment of threatening, but nevertheless easily reversible, actions, to which the widest publicity is given. The range of threatening actions available to states for this purpose is of course immense, ranging from the mobilization of troops, to the holding of nuclear-weapon tests and the putting of one's military forces on the alert, and is intended to rub home the point that the applicant state is in no mood to be trifled with, and that, if it is provoked to action, its power to inflict damage is awesome. In the 1930s Adolf Hitler showed himself to be a consummate master of the 'war of nerves'. During the Czech crisis in 1938 he was able to give the impression of a responsible statesman, conscious of the horrors of war, but barely able to keep in check a nation boiling with indignation at the treatment meted out to their kinsmen in a neighbour state. Mussolini, the Italian dictator of the period, succeeded, too, in convincing many democratic politicians that he was a 'mad dog', as many of them called him, capable of tearing an arm or leg off the world unless his merest whim was satisfied. In the years since 1945 new refinements of the 'war of nerves' have appeared: the organization of students to pelt with inkpots and rotten eggs the embassies of unpopular states; the stirring up of public indignation by inflammatory speech-making; the mobilization of hatred of one nation by another; the giving of encouragement to bomb-throwers and skyjackers to draw attention to the cause and to communicate the warning that more trouble lies ahead, and that more innocent people will suffer, unless the opposing side gives way. It is not implied that every murder of a diplomat, every bomb thrown at an embassy, is necessarily a calculated act by some government in the furthering of its foreign policy. But it is clearly expedient for certain states, especially when they have exhausted the resources of their ordinary diplomacy, to stimulate fears that all Hell will be let loose unless they are allowed to have their way. Such states are inclined to echo the famous words of Mark Antony in Shakespeare's play *Julius Caesar*:

> *Now let it work. Mischief, thou art afoot,*
> *Take thou what course thou wilt.*

The use of propaganda in international politics is hedged about with difficulties; and it may, like many other of the types of pressures considered in this chapter, have adverse 'boomerang' effects on the applicant state. It is certainly not true, as Hitler claimed in *Mein Kampf*, that 'by clever and persistent propaganda Heaven can be made to look like Hell and Hell like Heaven'. In the first place, the population of a totalitarian state may be effectively insulated by the criminal law of the country against the receipt of information or propaganda from abroad. It may be a serious criminal offence to listen to, or read foreign news or foreign opinions. Moreover, even if there are no legal restrictions on the receipt of ideas from abroad, the people of a country may be psychologically insulated against those ideas. This may be due to inborn or cultivated suspicion of everything or anything that the foreigner says on the principle *timeo Danaos et dona ferentes* ('I fear the Greeks, especially when they are bringing gifts') or to purposeful indoctrination of the people of a target state in a political direction contrary to that which the applicant state intends. So much is this so, that under certain conditions propaganda offensives levelled against a country may have counterproductive effects in so far as the people of that country may feel that there is an even greater need to rally round their country and its leaders if they are under attack from outside. Or the target government may conclude that they must do even more to isolate their people from external influences if they are already being 'got at' from the outside.

Because of these difficulties which face the practice of mass persuasion in the international system in the twentieth century, there has developed the Trojan Horse or Fifth Column technique of attacking the target state from the inside.[4] The attempt here is to penetrate what is sometimes called the 'hard shell' of the target state by arranging for a friendly faction to be organized within it, which can agitate on behalf of the applicant state, spread alarm or pessimism, cut communications, seize key points such as radio and television stations, printing presses and telephone exchanges, possibly timed to coincide with an armed attack by the applicant state from outside. The use, by Hitler, of armed bands of Sudeten Germans in Czechoslovakia in the late 1930s is one well-remembered example; the use, by the Communist authorities in China, of guerrillas or 'volunteers' in neighbouring countries is an example from the period after the Second World War. Obviously, the success of these penetrative techniques will depend on the morale and public spirit of the people of the state under attack, their loyalty to the basic symbols representing the state, and the presence or absence among them of groups alienated, for one reason or another, against the existing order in the target state.[5]

Fourthly, as we proceed along the scale of pressures towards the compulsive end, there is a long and complicated repertoire of economic, financial and commercial pressures. These are not always easy to classify in a logical order, but it is possible to arrange them in a sequence representing increasing gravity and also formality of organization. This is in accordance with the general design of the present chapter, which is to review these pressures along a graduated scale ranging from the less coercive at one end, to the more coercive at the other.

First, then, under this heading come mild retaliatory trading measures intended to inflict a moderate degree of inconvenience on the target state, with intimations of more serious penalties to follow if these initial measures are ineffective. Included in this category are the imposition of discriminatory tariffs and quotas on goods exported from the target state, the interruption of financial payments, as for instance by 'freezing' the target state's bank balances in the applicant state's territory, or that of its friends and allies, and, before 1939, competitive exchange depreciation, that is, the lowering of the value in the world's money markets of the applicant state's currency, thus injuring the target state's export trade and 'exporting unemployment' to that state. It was to try to prevent competitive exchange depreciation that the International Monetary Fund (IMF) was founded at the Bretton Woods conference in 1944. The idea was to provide member-states with additional sources of foreign currency when in temporary balance-of-payments difficulties. A certain parallel to the competitive exchange depreciation of the 1930s exists today in the practice of compelling another country to devalue its currency by stimulating the sale of it in the markets of the world. It was alleged by some people in Britain that the French authorities had done this to the pound sterling before the official British devaluation of the pound in November 1967; it thus became easier for President de Gaulle to argue in the same month that Britain was in no fit condition economically to stand the strain of joining the European Common Market. Alternatively, it is possible to force another country to revalue its currency by stimulating the purchase of that currency in world markets. But here, it must be said, we are in the undisclosed marginalia of world politics in which a nod or a wink in the relevant financial circles can convey as much, and often as damagingly, as a diplomatic note. In this periphery of international affairs one country can harm another through the machinery of the banking system as much as it can by weapons in the field of battle.

These relatively mild forms of economic or commercial pressure must always be decided upon only after the most careful scrutiny of the possible gains and losses to the applicant state. There must always be some losses, however slight, and the gains on the other side of the balance sheet may be quite hypothetical. Trade may be diverted, perhaps permanently, to the advantage of some third state; it seems as though, for instance, after the British Labour Government's decision to continue the embargo on the sale of arms to South Africa in January 1968, despite the severe economic crisis in Britain, that country began to look for other sources of supply, which was not difficult in the prevailing world buyer's market. Hence when the Conservatives returned to office in June 1970, with less enthusiasm about the embargo than Labour, they found that South African orders for British weapons were not nearly as profitable as they had supposed them to be. In addition, a legacy of mutual suspicion may be left behind in the minds of the business communities and relevant government departments on both sides, so that trade between the two countries fails to return to its former levels even when the diplomatic *contretemps* is at an end.

Next in order comes economic and technical assistance, either practised in a positive sense, with the applicant state giving or lending such assistance to the target state, or practised negatively, in the form of the applicant or donor state withholding or withdrawing aid or threatening to do so. In the inter-War period Britain, with little in the way of co-operation from France, tried to negotiate loans to the new Soviet Russia in the early and middle 1920s as a way of incorporating it into the reviving European economic system. Mr. Lloyd George was one of the most active partisans on behalf of this cause. Again, United States loans to the Weimar Republic in Germany under the Dawes and Young plans of 1924 and 1930 respectively were intended, on the political side, to keep Germany well-disposed towards the Western Powers and to encourage it, if possible, to reduce its ties with Soviet Russia under the Rapallo treaty of April 1922. After the fall of the Weimar régime in Germany in 1933, the Nazi authorities in Berlin made the most adroit use of bulk contracts to buy raw materials from the states of South East Europe and hence to induce them to remain within the German political orbit.

Since 1945 it has become common form for the richer and more powerful states to extend economic aid of various types to weaker states, as a means of acquiring political influence over them. The most striking examples are the massive injections of American dollar aid to Western Europe under the Marshall Plan of 1948–1952, without which the economic recovery of Europe after the War would have been far more difficult; American and Soviet economic assistance to client states (and allies, like Communist China during the brief period of Sino-Soviet friendship after the

Chinese Communist revolution in 1949) during the Cold War; and American, Soviet and, most notably, French aid to the less developed countries. The European Economic Community (EEC) has incorporated within its structure the most elaborate provisions for levying taxes on member-states to supply a Development Fund intended for the assistance of poorer countries. This is the first example of an international organization not primarily designed for foreign aid, yet which has provision for such aid, built into its actual constitutional structure.

Assessments of the effectiveness of economic aid and economic penalties as means of persuasion in the international system must be cautious.[6] Some of the pitfalls to be encountered by applicant states using such methods are fairly obvious. Economic assistance, perhaps intended to stimulate social and other types of reform in another country and hence, hopefully, make it more sympathetic towards the donor country, may have the effect of lining the pockets of a reactionary régime. When a *coup* takes place against that régime and revolutionaries come to power, they may be hostile towards the giver of aid for having kept the previous régime in office. Again, economic or other kinds of aid given to one country, say, Pakistan, may have the effect of alienating its rival—in this instance, India—against the donor. Or the withdrawal of, or any interruption in, the flow of foreign aid may drive the target state into the arms of the rival of the applicant state; a notable example of this was the British and American decision in 1956 to withdraw their promises to help Egypt with the building of the Aswan Dam, resulting in the Soviet Union stepping into the West's shoes and cementing an alliance with Egypt which lasted until President Sadat asked Russian military advisers to leave his country in 1972. Above all, aid from a rich state to a poorer state does not always produce a feeling of gratitude in the latter; often it results in resentment and envy. Similarly, the cutting off of aid from a country does not always affect the recipient's policy in a manner favourable to the donor; as the example of the cessation of Soviet aid to Communist China in the 1950s shows, it can make the target state even more hostile towards the donor country. On the other hand, it seems to be true that where relations between the applicant and the target state are otherwise good and opinion in the target state is sharply divided over a policy which offends the applicant state, economic restraints imposed by the latter can be

the 'straw that breaks the camel's back' for that policy. Thus, in
1956–1957 the refusal of the United States to support the pound
sterling during the Anglo-French action in the Suez crisis seems
to have had a finally decisive effect on the British effort to subdue
President Nasser by force.

We may now look rather more closely at the conditions necessary for the effective application of economic pressures, whether
positive or negative, by one state against another. If the applicant
state is hoping for a change of policy in the target state, or the
reaffirmation of a policy when a change is under consideration,
much will depend upon whether the end-product desired is
genuinely felt to be in its national interest by the target state. In
the case, for example, of Marshall Aid to Europe after the Second
World War, perhaps the most successful example of foreign aid in
peacetime in history, or of American Lend-Lease aid to Britain
and the Soviet Union during that War, in each instance the United
States was helping her friends to do things which they had no
doubt was in their national interest. The will to do those things
was certainly there and, as a British Minister said to the American
Government in the Second World War, 'give us the tools and we
will finish the job'. In the case, however, of great-Power assistance
to the developing countries of Africa and Asia during the decolonization period, hardly anyone has been able to forecast what
they would think to be in their national interest after the aid had
been assimilated. Perhaps this is the reason why such stalwart
erstwhile supporters of foreign aid as Senator William Fulbright,
chairman in his day of the Foreign Relations Committee of the
United States Senate, himself eventually became disenchanted
with it.

Moving now further along the scale of gravity of economic
measures, there may be a boycott, or refusal to buy the goods of
another country—this was practised unofficially before the Second
World War by the Chinese against Japan and by world-wide
Jewry against Nazi Germany—and the embargo, or refusal to sell
goods to another country, illustrated by the NATO embargo on
the sale of strategic goods to the Communist world, and the
embargo imposed unilaterally by the United States on its trade
with Castroite Cuba. The NATO strategic embargo against the
Communist bloc illustrates many of the shortcomings and drawbacks of economic pressures; it is still questionable today whether

these strategic embargoes have inflicted as much harm on the Communist states as they have on the Western Powers themselves.[7] On the negative side of the balance sheet are to be set the frictions inevitably arising between the states practising the embargo—where there are more than one—the accusations on all sides of sharp practices by way of evasion of the common agreement to embargo, and suspicions of unfair burdens being laid upon one or other of the important trading states involved in the operation. The embargo of the Western Powers on trade with Communist China, Cuba and the Soviet Union has been a constant source of mutual complaint and backbiting between Britain, Federal Germany, France and the United States. Again, embargoes tend to create strong compulsions in the target state or states to manufacture the embargoed goods for themselves, and hence to be less dependent upon foreign imports. The Communist states today are probably much less vulnerable to concerted economic sanctions imposed from outside than they were when the Western strategic embargoes were first imposed. Lastly, there is the distinct possibility that embargoes imposed on two or more target states at the same time may have the effect of driving them together for mutual support. Whereas the traditional, and still wise, rule of diplomacy has been to divide opposing states if possible, the practice of the embargo tends to unite them. The probability is that Communist China and the Soviet Union remained friends as long as they did because they were both targets of Western economic pressures. The Sino-Soviet dispute, perhaps the most dramatic schism in the whole history of the Communist camp, took place, it seems, not because of Western diplomacy but in spite of it. Perhaps embargoes have some useful effects in allowing the applicant state or states to let off some psychological steam. This is no doubt why the Western strategic embargoes against the Communist world tended to be more stringent against Communist China than against the Soviet Union. In this way the United States discovered some emollient for its feeling of outrage that its old *protégé*, China, should have bolted into the Communist camp. But even this relief of psychological tension, if that was in fact a principal factor, could not be of long duration.

A more rigorous form of the boycott and the embargo combined is the pacific blockade or 'quarantine', that is, the interdiction of trade between the target state and the rest of the world, and not merely with the applicant state or states. Older examples of this form of pressure are the pacific blockade by the European great Powers of certain portions of the Greek coast held by Turkey in 1827 during the Greek War of Independence; the British blockade of the Greek coast in 1850 during the so-called Don Pacifico crisis, when the British authorities were protecting one of their nationals against mob violence; in 1902 when Britain and Germany blockaded Venezuela when that country defaulted in the payment of interest on debts owing to European bankers and investors; in October 1937, when President Roosevelt unsuccessfully appealed for a 'quarantine' of the European Axis Powers by all countries interested in the maintenance of peace; the blockade of Israel by the Arab states since 1948, when Israel was officially born, though the Arabs claim that a state of war still exists between themselves and Israel and hence that this is not a case of pacific blockade; and in 1962, when President Kennedy interdicted Cuba from certain kinds of trade while the Soviet Union was still trying to place missiles in Cuba levelled against the United States, which was not much more than 90 miles away.

In time of war the blockade of an enemy state is said to be legal provided it is effective, which means that it should be operated impartially and without discrimination between all the various countries which habitually trade with the target state. Such blockades are also legal in peacetime if they are instituted by the Security Council of the United Nations acting under Chapter VII, Article 42, of the UN Charter. But they are recognized to be of doubtful legality if practised by a state unilaterally and outside the UN framework in time of peace. Thus it might be hard to draw up a clean legal sheet for President Kennedy when he imposed a total blockade on Cuba at the height of the Cuba missiles crisis in October 1962. The then British Prime Minister, Mr. Harold Macmillan, said that no great state could preoccupy itself with 'legal niceties' when its security was at stake, and that may be taken as being in line with the common rule in international politics: *salus populi suprema lex* ('the security of the people is the supreme law').

This leads finally to a consideration of that most intricate subject, international economic sanctions, or the concerted, multilateral interruption of economic and financial relations with a state which, as in the Covenant of the now defunct League of Nations, has resorted to war in violation of its obligations to pursue the pacific settlement of its disputes with other states, or, as in the case of the United Nations Charter, the Security Council, by virtue of its authority under Article 39 of the Charter, has been declared subject to sanctions in view of the existence of a threat to peace, breach of the peace or act of aggression. Sanctions, it is most important to emphasize, differ from the kind of multilateral pressures, such as strategic embargoes, with which we have just dealt, in that there must be some infringement of the public law of the international system, as declared by some official institution of that system. States applying economic or other restraints on other states are inclined to call what they are doing the application of sanctions, just as they often call their military alliances examples of 'collective security', whereas it would be more proper, and in accordance with the language of the UN Charter, to call them 'collective defence'. But this is only a matter of public relations, though it can be misleading if read as anything other than a diplomatic euphemism.

International economic sanctions, which were popular with the peacemakers in 1919, owing to the alleged success of the wartime Allied blockade of Germany, have encountered the greatest difficulties when attempts have been made to institute them since that time. This is reflected in the fact that they have only been operated twice since 1919, once by the League of Nations against Italy after she invaded Ethiopia in 1935, and again in December 1966, when the United Nations Security Council, on the initiative of Britain, was seeking to discipline the Smith régime in Rhodesia which had unlawfully declared its independence of Britain some thirteen months before.

First, there is the problem of how to get agreement among many different states with different outlooks and interests on a sanctions resolution. Such questions have to be resolved as: is there a case for sanctions? Which is the 'guilty' country against which sanctions should be directed? What should be included, if not everything, in the list of sanctioned articles of trade? What are the objects of the sanctions to be exercised, under what conditions should sanctions be terminated and what penalties, if any, should be imposed on states violating the sanctions agreement and trading illegally with the 'guilty' state, and who should impose them?

Connected with the last of these questions—the problem of penalties for infringement of the sanctions system—is the fact that once the sanctions system is violated by one state illegally trading with the target state, the temptations on the other states to follow suit become virtually irresistible, especially in periods when international trade is slack or in a state of extreme competitiveness. In effect, this means that a second sanctions system has to be created, directed against the state or states which infringe the primary system. Secondly, it is an undoubted fact that states contemplating the performance of some act which is likely to incur the risk of sanctions being imposed against them will probably take good care to see that they have laid in adequate stocks of provisions, raw materials, weapons, munitions of war and so on in advance. Since normally only they know for sure when and where their infringement of the law is going to take place, they tend to have a marked advantage in this respect over sanctionist states.

Thirdly among these problems of sanctions, there is the fact that the burden tends to fall unevenly on the different states joining together in a multilateral system of sanctions, and those with the greatest interest in international trade, or with the greatest share of trade with the target state, tend to suffer most. Thus it was easy enough for the Afro-Asian and Communist states to applaud the application of sanctions against Rhodesia in and after 1966, but it was Britain and such adjacent African states as Zambia which had to foot most of the bill. Provision was made under the League of Nations system for states which suffered unduly through sharing in the imposition of economic sanctions to be compensated by those who suffered less, but the mere problems of measurement of loss are formidable. Fourthly and finally, it is conceivable that an advanced and highly specialized national economy which is an active participant in the world trading system could be brought to its knees by rigorous international sanctions—though the example of Italy in the 1930s is by no means encouraging. On the other hand, when the target state happens to have a subsistence, or semi-rural economic system, shutting off its access to world trade can also be effective, though here again the example of Rhodesia since 1966 seems to show that even such an economy has a reasonably good chance of defying the world, if its national will is strong, and if it has the friendship of powerful states outside. Rhodesia seemed to have the support of South Africa, at least until independence became a reality for the former Portuguese colonies of Angola and Mozambique in 1974–1975.

To bring to an end this catalogue of pressures available to states to use against one another in the international system, we finally approach the compulsive pole of our imaginary scale of pressures. Here we have to distinguish between two types of compulsive restraints. First, come the legal categories of retorsions and reprisals.[8] 'Retorsions' are generally recognized as compulsive measures taken against unfair and unfriendly, but nevertheless, legal acts. They are defined as 'retaliation for a noxious act by a similarly noxious (though nevertheless similarly legal act)'. 'Reprisals', on the other hand, are otherwise illegal acts performed in order to secure redress for some international delinquency and hence legally justified. An example of reprisals might be (as the United States legal authorities have claimed) the American bombing of ports in North Vietnam during the American involvement in the Vietnam War in retaliation against North Vietnamese forceful intervention in the political life of South Vietnam. Thus, both retorsions and reprisals would seem to be in accordance with customary international law, but only if both are proportionate to the damage suffered by the applicant state and if these measures are applied only after local remedies have been exhausted. In other words, retorsions and reprisals must be no more than an eye for an eye and a tooth for a tooth, and are not legal unless, and until, the applicant fails to achieve justice in a local court of law.

Secondly, there are many other violent acts which may, or may not, fall into the categories described in the previous paragraph, and which may, or may not, be legal. There can be included under this heading such measures as: the forcible sequestration of the property of another state or of its nationals; forceful acts in defiance of treaty obligations and commitments; armed intervention in another state or the dispatching of hostile forces into the territory of another state; putting the applicant state on a war footing and intimating that as a last resort war could ensue unless the other state complies with the applicant's will; invasion and other armed actions levelled against the political independence and territorial integrity of another state; finally, war itself and its modern variants, such as 'war by proxy', that is, giving encouragement to the people of a third state to use armed force against the target state, the will or policy of which it is desired to change. However, when we come to war, which lies at the extreme compulsive end of the spectrum of available pressures in the international system to secure the co-operation of other states on terms acceptable to oneself, we are moving beyond the area of pressures, considered as instruments of policy, into the area of conditions of international relations. Whatever else may be said about full-scale war in the twentieth century, it can no longer be regarded simply, as was the case in the 1920s, as an 'instrument of policy'. Accordingly, we will deal with war, considered as a condition of international relations, in a later chapter in this book.[9]

It need hardly be said that in the last three decades of the twentieth century very important restraints have developed on the use of force as a form of international pressure. It is certainly not the 'big-stick' method of compelling compliance which it used to be in the days of 'gun boat diplomacy'.[10] The United Nations, to which most of the world's states now belong, rules out the use of force in international relations, with the sacred and inevitable exception of cases of individual and collective self-defence in situations in which the Security Council is unable to act (Article 2, paragraph 4, and Article 51). Even those states which are not deterred by such Charter obligations no doubt do not relish debates on their use of force in the General Assembly or the Security Council. A Western great Power, caught in the act of using force against a small and weak Third-World state, is almost bound to be pronounced guilty in any discussions within UN organs. Then again, one or other of the super-Powers can be quite an effective deterrent to hostilities between smaller and weaker states, just as the United States and the Soviet Union joined together to prevent a development of the war between India and Pakistan in September 1965. Or the use of force by one of the super-Powers against a smaller state can be deterred or stopped by the other super-Power entering upon the scene to defend the smaller state, which may be its ally or client. Further, there are the effects of domestic public opinion in the applicant, and in the target, state; the former, especially in a Western-type democratic state may disown its government's use of force—as British public opinion, or substantial sectors of it, did during the Suez crisis in 1956—while the latter may consolidate around its government when under attack from abroad—this seems to have occurred in

North Vietnam after years of concentrated bombing by the United States. It is by no means automatic that a government will be admired by its own people, or by foreigners, once it unsheathes its sword in the campaign of mounting pressures. But, above all, perhaps the most effective deterrent against the use of force as a means of international pressure in the twentieth century is the difficulty, or impossibility, of knowing how much force will have to be used, and how long the struggle may go on until the object of force is achieved, if indeed it ever is. The United States military intervention in Vietnam during the 1960s and 1970s is a dramatic and tragic warning that, under modern conditions, wars are terribly easy to get into, and just as hard to get out of.

NOTES

1. See above, Chapter Nine.
2. Article 36.
3. Article 65 of the statute.
4. It may be explained, for the benefit of younger readers, that during the civil war in Spain (1936–9) General Franco, the Nationalist leader and ultimate victor, spoke of 'my four columns' approaching Republican-held Madrid from the outside and 'my fifth column' already within the city.
5. For a useful discussion of this subject see Andrew Scott, *The Revolution in Statecraft*. Also above, p. 82.
6. See the discussion of this in G. Liska, *The New Statecraft*, University of Chicago, Centre for the Study of American Foreign Policy, 1960.
7. See Susan Strange, 'Strategic Embargoes', *The Yearbook of World Affairs, 1958*, Stevens, London, 1958.
8. L. Oppenheim, *International Law*, 7th edition, edited by H. Lauterpacht, Longmans, London, 1952, Vol. II, Part I, Chapter II.
9. See chapter Thirteen below.
10. See *The Use of Force in International Relations*, edited by the present author, Faber and Faber, London, 1974.

Twelve

States of International Relations

IN the present chapter, and the one which follows, we will be concerned with the various circumstances which go to shape the relations of modern sovereign states with each other, and also with that scale of international relations which runs from harmony, or amity, at one extreme, to competition, rivalry and conflict at the other extreme. Again, as in the whole of this book, our primary emphasis is on the official relations between the state-members of the international system. It may be that in the opinion of some, the mutual relations of other entities in the international system, such as non-governmental groups like trade unions or business organizations, or the relations of these with organized states, are more interesting and ultimately more important, though the present author doubts it. Nevertheless, as far as this book is concerned, it is the doings of states with one another which, as we have emphasized in other places, form the main focus of our subject.

Two important implications follow from this. One is that those who shape and formulate their own state's relations with other states act out, as we have previously pointed out, the roles, dispositions and interests of states, not of private individuals.[1] It is true that Ministers and diplomats may have, and perhaps not infrequently do have, some private axe to grind when they act on behalf of their state in the international system. It would be indeed strange, if they could do their daily work without deriving some private satisfaction from it, other than the pleasure stemming from membership of, and service to, that large, anonymous group, the state. Nevertheless, in his dealings with the representatives of other states the Minister or diplomat must take on the personality of his own state and shed, as far as possible, his own personality. Probably most people would criticize a Minister or diplomat who allowed his personal distaste for his opposite number in a state, with which he was negotiating, to spoil an opportunity for profitable transactions, just as they would criticize a businessman, who allowed his personal feelings about other leaders of trade or industry, to interfere with chances of a beneficial deal. It is said that in the 1920s the British Foreign Secretary, Lord Curzon, was so upset by the personality of the French Ambassador, the Count de Saint Aulaire, that he was known to faint in his company. That was not a service to British diplomacy.

On the other hand, we should not overstate the contribution made by the personalities of the negotiators in diplomatic relations to the success or failure of their mutual dealings as representatives of their own states. As already implied in the previous paragraph, a responsible spokesman for a state should be sufficiently disciplined and self-controlled to be able to distinguish between what in the diplomatic situation is personally agreeable to himself, and what is profitable to his own state, if in fact there be such a difference. At the same time, he should not be distracted by personal feelings between himself and his partner in negotiation as to be blind to the actual potentialities inherent in the situation for co-operation or conflict between the states concerned. It is true that there is a strong temptation for people to ascribe success or failure in diplomacy to personal likes and dislikes between the representatives who negotiate. Personality in this sense may have some marginal influence on the outcome of diplomatic negotiations, certainly the impression that it has finds some confirmation in the good personal relations between Briand and Stresemann in the 1920s, Prime Minister Heath and President Pompidou of France in the early 1970s, and between President Nixon and Leonid Brezhnev of the Soviet Union in the same years. But the general truth remains, nevertheless, that if there is a distinct congruence of convenience between states, bad personal relations between their representatives cannot in any long run destroy it, though they may prevent it being recognized and acknowledged for some time. On the other hand, the most excellent personal relations between representatives of different states cannot bring about a genuine congruence of interest between states at the level of reason of state where none exists, though for some time they may give the appearance of doing so.

The other important implication which derives from the fact of inter-state relations being those of organized political groups and not those of individual persons is that an improvement, or the reverse, in the relations between the peoples of different states at the personal level cannot usually affect, in any important way, the official relations between the states concerned. One of the strongest beliefs of the so-called liberal democratic peoples of the world is that more 'mixing up' of people of different nationalities is a powerful factor in promoting international 'understanding' in the diplomatic sense of that term. It is linked with the common liberal assumption *'tout comprendre, c'est tout pardonner'*. Hence the strong Western incentive to accelerate international contacts at the non-political level as a means of initiating, strengthening or consolidating political *détentes* between nation-states: more visits by people of one country to other countries, more exchange visits of teachers and students across national frontiers, and so on.

No one would wish to deprecate the intrinsic value of international exchanges of this kind, whether as forms of entertainment or as professionally useful contacts. It is also better that people should see more of other countries and *their* people than that they should sit at home harbouring illusions, whether favourable or unfavourable, about foreigners, provided of course that the visitor abroad, as is often the case, does not allow a two-week trip to another country to strengthen long-entrenched prejudices about that country. But it is vital to recognize that the tourist abroad is not often conscious of the common interests which bind him together with his own countrymen in opposition to, or it may be in league with, the national interests of the country which he happens to be visiting. Lying on holiday on an Italian beach, or drinking wine in a *bistro* in Paris, induces a different frame of mind from being represented at an international trade union conference by delegates defending British working-class interests against Italian or French working-class interests. The same is true of relations between men and women: the individual man and woman might find that their mutual relations are delightful in every possible sense, yet each may be involved, in quite another capacity, in the 'sex war' which ranges men and women in opposition to each other over such matters as wages, discrimination against women in jobs, legal matters, marriage, and so on. It used to be said by men who fought in, and survived, the First World War that British soldiers in that holocaust had far more personal liking for the Germans, and especially for the Turks, than for the French and Italians with whom they were fighting as allies against the Germans and the Turks. And who is surprised that Government Ministers and Opposition leaders in the House of Commons in Britain can be the best of friends in the bar after they have bitterly attacked each other in the Chamber? Is this hypocrisy? Does it mean that either or both the comradeship at the bar, and their hostility in the Chamber, are false? The more likely explanation is surely that each of the two situations is a unique social context: in one situation the M.P. is defending the interests of thousands of people whom he represents, interests opposed to the interests of the thousands represented by the other Member; in the other situation he has for the time being stepped out of that role and shed his *persona* as a representative.

Returning now to the subject of the state of relationships between states, one image of those relationships which we must discard at the outset is the Hobbesian conception of the state of man without a common power above all men: that is, the image of a *bellum omnium contra omnes*, a war of all against all, the word 'war' being used, as Hobbes explains in the *Leviathan* (Chapter XIII), to refer, not to fighting, but to a 'disposition thereto during all the time that there is no assurance to the contrary'.[2] Our modern knowledge of the behaviour of wild animals, which was not available to Hobbes, teaches us that they do not normally prey on other animals of the same species as themselves. Fighting between animals of the same species only occurs in the form of play between young animals, or between adults for the possession of the female, or for territory for breeding and for rearing the young. Even so, the fighting is generally on an individual basis, without the massed battalions of human warfare. Organized war between wild animals of the same species would be contrary to nature, since it would threaten the survival of the species. Even fighting between animals of different species is normally infrequent and only occurs when there is some quite compelling immediate motivation, such as the need for food or the protection of territory.

It is a normal rule of human society, however, especially in the historically recorded period, for organized warfare to take place in the absence of any superior power to prevent it, the object normally being to distribute the objects at stake in the conflict, which may be abstract, such as honour or prestige, if for one reason or another the peaceful settlement of this question cannot be achieved. It is also a logical result of the situation of human conflict that the struggle between two individuals, tribes, gangs or nations, necessarily involves a state of neutrality between the contestants and third parties; or if not neutrality, a more intimate form of relationship between the contestants severally and third parties, as for instance an alliance. No organized human group, unless it is strong enough to establish a hegemony over all the rest of the human race, can take on the rest of humanity in a winner-take-all contest. Normally, the closer a group moves towards forceful conflict with another group, the more it must try to remain at peace with on-lookers who are not yet involved. Either it will wish to have the on-lookers on its own side as allies, or to have them remain neutral.

From this follows the simple, yet all-important conclusion, that in the international system, hostility is not, and cannot be, uniform between all possible pairs of states. Assuming that the member-states of the international system have some minimum degree of contact with each other, a map of the world showing 'psychological frontiers' between the different states, that is, the affinities and discords between any particular state and its neighbours, would not be identical for all states, This is, of course, reflected in the basic nature of defence policy in international relations. There may be some rare occasions on which a state is so diplomatically isolated and bereft of friends, that it has reason to fear attack from every quarter of the compass at the same time. This condition is sometimes known, though not quite accurately, as azimuthal defence; for some time during General de Gaulle's Presidency of France (1958–1969) French defence policy was represented as being based on this principle. But no General Staff could possibly make its military dispositions and preparations for any long period on that basis. Most countries of the world have 'traditional' enemies and friends over a longish period and, if changes have to be made in that fairly stable pattern, the balance is normally made up by adjustments elsewhere: that is, if enemies, or likely aggressors, increase, more friendships are sought; if friends increase in numbers or strength, the generals believe they can take on more enemies.

It is relevant here to return once more to the idea of 'security community', referring to a degree of more or less established harmony between two or more states. K. W. Deutsch, who seems to have invented the term, writes that 'the concept of security community implies stability of expectations of continuing peaceful adjustment'.[3] He distinguishes between three different kinds of security community: (1) where the volume of intercourse between the two states is such that for all practical purposes they hardly seem to belong to the same international system: the examples which Deutsch gives of this state of affairs are Thailand and Ecuador; (2) states in which there are 'amalgamated political institutions', such as states belonging to a federal system in which the power of ultimate decision has passed, within the framework of a formal constitution, to a federal body, as in the United States; (3) states which are not yet politically amalgamated and yet are without the expectation of mutual violence. To return to our reference to the planning of defence in a national state, in the case of security communities of this third type, war is such an uncommon experience that no special defence provision has to be made against it; it is almost unthinkable. Relations between Canada and the United States, between Britain and the older members of the Commonwealth, and between Britain and the United States may be said to conform to this kind of security community. It is not only difficult to conceive of war occurring between the members of these pairs of states, it is hard even to think of them ranged on opposite sides of a military line and facing each other as members of opposing alliances.

Obviously, type (3) of Deutsch's security communities is the one most relevant for our present purposes. Relations of type (1) above, if relations can be said to exist at all, naturally still occur, but it has to be admitted that, with intercourse between the different countries growing as a result of the increasing speed of travel and ease of communications, insubstantial international relations of this kind are undoubtedly becoming fewer and less typical. As for type (2), this would not be considered normal in the international system as we understand it in this book. As soon as political authorities assume the final right to make law which is binding on states, the latter can no longer be considered as sovereign, the basic conditions of international relations no longer exist and, we are left with relations between individual persons and non-sovereign organizations under a common source of ultimate legal authority. Type (2), that is, is the kind of security community which cannot be said to exist between the sovereign states in the present international system.

We are left, then, with the security community of the third type, that is, a state of relations between two or more sovereign states between which war is considered to be so unlikely that no special provision has to be made for it; neither side, in other words, normally plans for the possibility of hostilities with the other. It is difficult, however, to agree with Deutsch that the degree of intimacy between states in this third kind of security community can be either accounted for, or even established, by the volume of 'transactions'—that is, letters, parcels, telegrams, business communications and so on—going on between the inhabitants of the states concerned. For it is quite clear that, on the one hand, a *détente* in relations between two or more states which were previously hostile can lead to, and perhaps more often than result from, an increase in the kind of inter-state transactions which Deutsch refers to. In relations, for instance, between the Western states and the states of the Soviet bloc in the years after 1962 *détente* was expressed in contacts between the peoples of the two worlds rather more so than it was a consequence of these contacts. The same would seem to be true of security communities of this third type which are formed from states of the same ideological faith. In the second place, it is quite evident that the great international wars of the twentieth century, which have given it the name of the 'age of conflict', have taken place more especially between the highly urbanized, industrialized, comparatively wealthy states of Europe, as between which commerce and all the other forms of international transaction in Deutsch's sense of the term are at their maximum. It is hard, then, to avoid the conclusions, first, that conflicts, such as have rocked the international system to its foundations in recent times, seem to have sprung up between states which already formed a fairly closely-knit international community, rather than between states with fewer mutual contacts; and, secondly, that in the present age governments tend to foster contacts of all kinds and at all levels between their respective peoples when they wish to consolidate and entrench essentially politically motivated accords between them.

We can therefore assume that all the state-members of the international system can be ranged along a graduated scale of relationship with every other member of the system, and that the scale represents all the different degrees of friendship and hostility, extending from the ideal security community, as we have defined it, at one end of the scale, to the extreme pole of continuous tension and outright war at the other. We can assume, further, that, in the interests of the best economic use of their national resources, governments will, on the whole, try to balance friendships with hostilities; that is to say, if friendships with other states are marked with a positive sign (+) and hostilities with a negative sign (−), policy, perhaps unconsciously, will tend towards a total of friendships and enmities which is either positive or at least zero. This, it is true, is not invariably the case. Some states do not, outwardly at least, seem to fear relative isolation, which can be described, in the language we have been using, as a balance of negative over positive signs. This may be true for some periods in the history of the foreign policy of the Soviet Union, Communist China, South Africa, and perhaps France in some phases of its relations with other Western Powers. On the other hand, however, states which are compelled, through force of circumstances, to have many 'minuses' in their international account tend to straighten out the imbalance by increasing, if they can, the intensity of their friendships with the few friends that they have: this could be true of Communist China's friendship with Albania in recent years, and France's relations with the Federal German Republic during the presidency of General de Gaulle.

This raises the question as to which is the 'normal' state of international relationships, friendship or enmity, though we should remember at all times that these are metaphorical terms drawn from the vocabulary of inter-personal relations and applied with some artificiality to states. Which of the two conditions, friendship or hostility, is the equilibrium state towards which international relations tend to move, unless extraneous factors force a movement in the opposite direction towards the 'abnormal' or 'pathological' end of the scale?

The conventional language of diplomacy, which is in its origins still the language of eighteenth- and nineteenth-century European international politics, tended to conceive of an original Eden, from which current international relations are conceived as having been driven by 'misunderstanding' or faults of diplomacy on one side or the other. It was felt that the prime object of diplomacy, at least in the polite language in which governments before, say,

I

1914 tended to talk to each other, should aim at the 'restoration of good relations'. The same idea was reflected in such language as the *reduction* of international tension and the *outbreak* of war, echoing the notion of the outbreak of an epidemic or some other abnormal evil. These technical diplomatic assumptions had their counterpart in the somewhat optimistic liberal philosophy of nineteenth-century Britain, with its vast influence on the theory and practice of international affairs. Britain, then in the high noon of her commercial and imperial dominance, could not fail to impress on international affairs the idea that ever-widening contacts in trade and business between the different nations must somehow restore them to an earlier composure, in which the well-being of every man and every nation would be merely part of the well-being and happiness of them all. This elevated doctrine cast its spell over the League of Nations after the First World War. It still survives, and with some vigour, in the commonplace Western assumption that ever-increasing trade and human contacts between the Communist East and the liberal West can tame the conflicting demons of ideology and national pride and power, and cause the lions of world politics to lie down with the lambs.

This easy-going, essentially liberal conception of international relations is echoed even in the standard Marxist prognosis of the future development of world affairs. While in the Marxist theory of history there is assumed to exist a conflict of opposites which results in the ultimate victory of one of the embattled social forces, and in the victorious force there lives the embryo of a new social power destined to fight against and overcome, in its turn, the old order which rears and nourishes it, it is also assumed that this process of perpetual conflict and renewal will finally cease in history when at length the proletarian class comes into its own all over the world. The struggle of the working class under the leadership of the Communist party against the capitalist system will finally mark the termination of the entire historical process. Then will ensue the perfect, tension-less peace which has no ending. Indeed the Marxist is so confident of the future proletarian world society being perpetually peaceful that he forecasts the disappearance of the state and all its apparatus of defence against other states. To this extent the political and historical feet of Marxism are firmly planted in the soil of mid-nineteenth-century liberalism, and both are confronted by the really revolutionary creed of Fascist and Nazi totalitarianism, which does indeed contend that strife in the international, as well as in other social fields, is not only unavoidable but works towards the physical and mental perfection of the human organism. Here we have a fundamental philosophical conflict, which goes back at least to Heraclitus, between the apostles of perpetual peace and the apostles of perpetual strife. This is not the place, however, to follow this confrontation further. It is more to the point to underline the factors in the modern development of the international system which have loaded the dice, so to speak, against the apostles of an ultimate and perpetual peace, though it is worth remembering that, as the occasions and opportunities for conflict as the 'normal' condition of international relations have grown, so has man's determination, in the interest of his own survival, to bring these occasions of conflict under control. Conflict, we may say, has also bequeathed its bias.

The first, and most obvious point, is that as contacts, or, to use Deutsch's term, transactions, between the different states have grown in number and complexity, along with the progress of human technology and man's general mastery over nature, so have the occasions of friction between states. Points of contact in the international system, it must always be recalled, are at the same time points of conflict. The recent exploitation of the resources of the sea and the sea bed is an obvious example of this. During the greater part of man's history, when the sea has never been much more than a means of communication and transport, and a source of food, international struggles to control the sea or critical parts of it have focused, appropriately, on domination of the oceans as maritime and naval highways, and on territorial waters as fishing grounds. Now that, in the last quarter of a century, the seas have gripped the imagination of men, as the source of infinite and varied national wealth, international conflict to control the seas has broadened its character. The focus of conflict, once the three-mile breadth of territorial waters, has in the 1970s extended to commonplace claims to 200-mile territorial belts. Countries, such as those in Latin America, which have played no great part in the general competition between the nations, have now been thrust, through the economic importance of the seas, into the midst of it. It is true that today, in contradistinction to the times of Sir Francis Drake, when nations contend with each other for control of the sea, they are more inclined to do so at the conference table rather than from the decks of warships, but the conflict is there none-the-less, and the issues at stake may be much the same. Contacts between nation-states do indeed multiply the common interests of states, but they also multiply the occasions of conflict between them.

And, of course, in addition to the swelling number of inter-national transactions, there has been, especially since the Second World War, the swelling number of state-members of the inter-national system between which conflicts are liable to occur. Shortly before his assassination in 1963 President J. F. Kennedy told the United Nations General Assembly that conflicts outside the major axis of tension between Communist and non-Communist nations could be as destructive of peace as that major tension.[4] The relation between the number of states in the inter-national system and the number of potential conflicts in that sys-tem has been represented algebraically as x (the number of potential conflicts) =

$$\frac{n \text{ (the number of states) } (n-1)}{2}$$

In other words, as the number of states in the international system increases arithmetically, the number of potential conflicts or quarrels increases geometrically.[5] We do not have to take this mathematical formula with strict seriousness to appreciate the point, that as states increase in number (assuming that the new states have roughly the same kind of international contacts as the old states), the occasions of international conflict increase at an even greater proportion.

Moreover, many of the new entrants into the international system since 1945 have been characterized, not surprisingly, by sharp internal, racial, tribal, ideological and regional conflicts themselves. The general problems of internal social cohesion for the new Afro-Asian members of the world system are apt to be greater and more strenuous than they are for the older established states. Problems of internal cohesion may mean greater instability of governments, the susceptibility of existing régimes to sudden coups d'état, often by army officers, and hence the concentration of governments on the strictly domestic problems of holding on to

power. At the same time, it is almost a rule of history that governments which are insecure in power sometimes endeavour to retain
it by adopting a belligerent posture towards neighbouring states
and their political régimes. Dr. Soekarno's attitude towards
Malaysia during his Presidency in Indonesia in the 1960s and no
doubt, too, President Idi Amin's hostility towards Israeli and
Asian residents in Uganda and Tanzania, were partly understandable in terms of their efforts to retain the loyalty of their people at
home, both to the political régime and to the idea of the nation
itself, and this, both in Indonesia and in Uganda, has never been
an easy undertaking. Moreover, in many of the new states, and in
some of the less developed old states, the population problem
itself is, and increasingly will be as time goes on, a serious factor
in government instability and also in pressure on the state's
immediate neighbours. While almost all states in the world have
experienced problems of population growth, especially during
periods of industrialization, the problem is even greater for the
newly decolonized states of today. The new states have benefited,
if that is the right word, from the medical knowledge, and other
techniques for saving and prolonging life which the old states
had to acquire through long periods of research and experimenta-
tion. The new states, one might say, have the scientific means of
vastly increasing the population before they have the social skills
in limiting it, or the economic power to maintain it. It was
generally the other way about in the older established states.

Lastly, among the factors which tend to raise the potential for
hostility between states in the international system as a whole,
there are certain effects of industrialism and its spread throughout
the system. Industrialism, as we have experienced it in the past,
both depends upon, and enhances, the acquisitive tendency in
men and women, whether that tendency is original or derivative in
human psychology. The general desire for better living standards,
intensified no doubt in an age of commercial advertisement,
forces on the government the need continuously to raise the
economic levels of the state. This may encourage policies of
peaceful co-operation between states, designed to heighten the
common benefit of all; but it can also have contrary results. At the
same time, the growing industrial power which feeds and is fed
by man's acquisitive propensities also puts in his hands means and
resources which he, or rather his state, can use either for good or

for evil, for co-operative or destructive purposes. Of course, this is, and must be, too slight a sketch of the effects of industrialization on the international system to be adequate by any test; it would require at least another book to examine and explain fully those effects. But it is enough for the present if we do no more than take note of them.

Turning now to the distribution of hostility throughout the international system—the constellation of international discord, as we may call it—this is normally explained by reference to two or three common basic factors, each of which deserves some words of explanation. There may, in the first place, be a conflict of interest: the conflict may not 'really' exist—it may simply be perceived as though it existed, or in other words it may be imagined to exist. But it is surely foolish to argue that, in the last resort, *all* conflicts of interests between states, as between other social groups, are 'all in the mind', and do not objectively exist in the 'real' world. This becomes clear, if we think, as before, not so much of interests as though they were the communal *wants* of the state, but as collective *requirements*, or needs which the state, or its agents, must satisfy if it is to remain an independent and self-contained member of the international system. It is no good saying that it is only 'imagining things' for Britain to have a national interest in the importation of abundant and cheap oil; only by undergoing a serious fall in the British standard of living can the country afford to buy scarce and expensive oil. Equally, it is foolish to say that Kuwait and Saudi Arabia do not 'really' benefit from high oil prices; their present social services, hospitals and schools are 'real' enough rewards which they have won for themselves by compelling Europeans and Japanese to pay more for their oil. No doubt the oil-producing countries might (though this is entirely speculative) be even better off if they could form a more co-operative relationship with the oil-consuming countries. But in the state of the world as it exists at present, who is to blame them for thinking that if the other fellow gets more from a certain deal, they themselves are bound to get less? 'In the long run' conflicts of interest between states, and within states, may fade away, but people do not generally think or act in terms of the 'long run'; they are quite satisfied, as a rule, if they can make profits in the short run.

Secondly, there may be, as a source of hostility between states, what may be called a *credal* incompatibility, a conflict of moral values, belief-systems or ideologies. The eminent Yale philosopher, F. S. C. Northrop, was one of those who attribute conflict between groups to discontinuities or incompatibilities of what he called 'basic norms', the inarticulate major moral premises of action.[6] Perhaps this kind of conflict is more likely where one or other or both of the two competing groups are actuated by creeds of a dynamic, chiliastic or messianic kind, as many states have been in the twentieth century, creeds which forecast their own eventual triumph on a world-wide scale and the total destruction of their rivals. Perhaps, too, we have to think of the credal conflict as one in which the two rival political creeds, which unite the two states, happen to have each other, so to speak, as their 'anti-propositions'. Every ideology in the modern world seems to impose on its adherents the duty to believe something, and the duty to disbelieve or renounce something else, and it may happen that the articles of faith renounced by one of the two creeds are the very same articles of faith upheld by the other creed. The two states committed each to one or other of these belief systems are not perhaps predetermined to feel and act with hostility towards each other. But the credal dissonance must make the more intimate kind of co-operation difficult to achieve, especially when we remember that it is often easier for men to reject things, including ideas, than to accept them.

Thirdly, there can be differences between groups of a much less articulate kind, than incompatibilities of creeds. This occurs, for example, where human groups temperamentally 'jar upon' one another, or where racial, physical, cultural or other differences are sufficient to create antagonisms which have more of a subjective than objective basis, and which arouse fears or feelings of guilt or estrangement that lie more on the unconscious, than on the conscious plane of the mind. These are the kind of hostile attitudes which Gentiles have shown towards Jews, or Catholics towards Protestants and *vice versa*, or whites and blacks towards each other. We can call these simply psychological incompatibilities. Certainly there may, in fact, be a historical record of ill-treatment, persecution or injustice inflicted by one party on the other, perhaps very long ago; but it is quite clear that whole patterns of sentiment and emotional associations tend to cling to discordances of this kind, so that, what are in reality historically or culturally acquired aversions, begin to be looked upon as though they were primary and underived instincts.

We have, then, these three principal groups of factors responsible for the 'emotional distance' which often lies between organized entities, such as sovereign states: incompatibilities of interest, of implicit value structures, and of communal psychology and collective sentiments. Naturally, there must at all times be a considerable extent of overlap between these groups of influence, and equally it cannot be ruled out that one or the other, or all three, may be playing a part together in the manifold tensions and confrontations which spring up between states as they deal with each other in the practical world of politics. This is merely another way of making the obvious point that in human relations nothing is quite so simple and straightforward as it might seem at first sight. As we listen to quarrels between groups, as they are portrayed and explained by their individual members or spokesmen on both sides, we realize that, not only are men disposed to deal in monocausal analysis, and one which as a general rule places the blame for the conflict squarely on the shoulders of the other side, but the disposition towards monocausal explanations can be, and quite often is, a factor in the very inter-group conflicts which those explanations are supposed to account for. As a familiar instance of monocausal explanation, there is the common view that states and other groups make friends with others from a basis of common interest, and make enemies from a basis of conflict of interest. It is clear, however, that conflicts of interest may well exist within security communities as we have defined them earlier in this chapter. It is a common experience that quarrels can arise, often from clear incompatibilities of interest, within an otherwise closely-knit alliance. The point is, of course, that incompatibilities of interest such as these are for the time being overshadowed by much greater conflicts, based on even deeper incompatibilities of interest, between all the members of the alliance taken together and third states, or perhaps even one third state. Or it may be that the two or more states at loggerheads are fully aware of the incompatibilities of interest between them, but are also conscious of their even greater common interest in the avoidance of an open breach between them, which may have some quite drastic outcome for them or for third parties. Or the conflict of interest may be carried on within a common or shared ideological framework which allows it to be handled without the peace between them being broken.

The factors, which we have singled out as affecting the general distribution of friendship and hostility throughout the international system, do not in themselves help to explain variations in that distribution over time. We may assume that some degree of tension, conceived of as a sense of strain and mental dissonance, is present in all social systems. It may be, that tension is inherent in the mutual relations of all social groups, in so far as the cohesion achieved internally by those groups seems to be built upon an external refocusing of the 'negative' or anti-social tendencies of the individual members of the groups in question. Life, for the individual, even in the most ideal circumstances, can never be completely free from a certain amount of discontent with one's position. In so far as this generates hostility towards others, the external system, the system which lies outside the narrower social circle of the discontented person, is always available to take the shock of the hostility thus aroused. Until life and the whole world are perfect, and men are like gods, we are justified in finding some place for resentment, irritation, dissatisfaction, frustration, in all social relations. To this may be added all the more objective factors in social discord to which we have already referred. Beyond that, we have given in this chapter some reasons for thinking that tensions, and certainly political tensions, between states have developed with the development and maturation of the international system. But we must also remember, that the diplomatic alignments between states in which tension is canalized and expressed, are in a continuous process of change. As tension declines in one geographical area of the system, it is likely to spring up in another. As tensions rise between states, friendships also tend to increase between those states and third states. Tensions and friendships are in fact interlocking processes.

This leads to the question whether there is not a law (or tendency, or quasi-uniformity) of conservation of tension in the international system, in much the same way as there is a law of conservation of energy in the physical world as known to the natural scientist. This would mean that the 'pluses' and 'minuses' of international relations (as we have previously defined them), or the loves and hates of states for others of their kind, would always tend to add up to the same figure, perhaps zero in a perfect state of international equilibrium, if such a state be attainable. One thinks of a blob of mercury resting on a surface and how, if pressed from above, it will flow to another place; in much the same way, hostility between two states, if settled and converted into *détente*, tends to spring up in other areas of the international system, perhaps between each of the two states and third parties.

It could be—as an explanation of such a 'law', if that is not too rigid and formal an expression—that psychologically most people, whether as individuals or organized collectivities, are capable only of a given amount of love or hatred. All collectivities such as states, for example, tend to generate hostility towards 'out-groups', if only as a means of achieving inner solidarity. But there may be an upper limit to this; if 'enough' hostility has been generated to serve the purposes of internal cohesion, there may be no need, and perhaps no incentive, to produce more. Also, if we are preoccupied with the sins and shortcomings of a certain state, those of yet another state may come to seem trivial and harmless in comparison. It may be, too, that human beings have limited power to concentrate on a certain object, and hence limited capacity for loving and hating. This may explain why hostility, and no doubt friendship, too, are never quite so intense on both sides of a human relationship. It was once said by a Cypriot in the days when Cypriots were fighting for self-determination and independence from Britain, that relations between Britain and Cyprus were somewhat like relations between a large cat and a small mouse which the cat holds captive between its paws. All the mouse can think about is the state of its captivity and when and how it will end, whereas the cat, like Britain in the days of its world power, has many more things to think about than merely its captive; often it will, after a period of gazing around absent-mindedly, bring the captive mouse under its control again, if it has tried to escape while the cat's attention was diverted to other things.

On a somewhat more practical level, it is pragmatically necessary for states to improve their relations with former enemies and rivals if strains are developing between themselves and third states. One thinks of the Soviet Union and Communist China both seeking the friendship of the United States in the early 1970s as relations between the two Communist states deteriorated. On the other hand, a state which finds that hostility between itself and another state is beginning to diminish, or that problems between them are being resolved, is now in a position to take up and perhaps develop an incipient conflict with a third state; it now has more time and other resources to commit to that conflict. This phenomenon perhaps helps to explain why this 'law of conservation of tension' seems possibly more valid for collectivities such as states than it is for individual persons. An individual, especially if he has some form of private income which enables him to satisfy all his bodily needs from his own pocket, can afford to be misanthropic, to hate the whole world. States, like needy individuals, can hardly ever afford to be diplomatically misanthropic; they must contrive, at least outwardly, to 'grin and bear' it when they hold out a sympathetic hand to other states for political reasons, though they may entertain no genuine sympathy for those other states. As on other occasions, the statesmen and diplomats must be sufficiently self-controlled to act, or seem to act, cordially towards other states, when it is in the interests of *raison d'état* to do so, even though they may be filled with loathing at the whole idea. Marshal Stalin and Ambassador Ribbentrop did not forget how to smile when they signed the Nazi-Soviet pact in Moscow on 23rd August 1939.

But we must now move on to consider in somewhat more detail the uneven distribution of hostility and friendship throughout the international system. In the interests of convenience we will confine ourselves in the first instance to hostilities; it should be remembered that the same observations apply *mutatis mutandis* to the mutual friendships of states. First, then, we must consider the effects of changes in the composition of the international élite of states, or what may be called the circulation of élites in the international system, the changing composition of the greatest Powers of the day. The major tensions of the international system —meaning not merely those tensions in which incompatibility of interest, creed and psychology are exceptionally intense, but those of which the consequences, if an armed conflict should ensue, are the greatest—lie between the major Powers, just as the direction of major conflict within a Parliamentary democracy lies between the two largest political parties. Hence the distribution of political and military power within the international system will tend to determine where the major rifts in that system will appear, and these in their turn will affect the distribution of the minor stresses and strains. Thus, during the East-West Cold War from 1945 until about 1963 all international relations in every part of the world tended to be overshadowed by the momentous divide between the two super-Powers, the United States and the Soviet Union. Any full-scale armed conflict between these two giants would have raised a question mark, not only over all the activities of all lesser states, but even over their continued existence. However, as soon as the mutual relations of the super-Powers began to take a turn for the better in the early 1960s, all the mutual friendships and hostilities of lesser states began to change. Dangers to national security which once existed under the shadow of the Cold War now began to be replaced by dangers of another kind. Possibilities of better relations with other states now began to open, or perhaps in some instances to close. The world pattern of tensions and alliances was altered as the supreme states of the system moved from the confrontation of the Cold War to the limited co-operation of *détente*, just as movements in the major faults in the earth's surface shift the pattern of the world's minor cleavages.

We may follow this up by saying that changes, especially those of a long-term character, in the levels of tension between any two members of the international system will tend to result in re-assessments of their relations with other states throughout the international system, depending upon the power, status and extent of diplomatic contacts of the two states originally concerned. Or, to put the point another way, the rise and decline of friendship or discord between a given state and any of its partners within the international system will tend to encourage that state to reconsider and perhaps revise its relations with all the other members of the system with which it has diplomatic contact. A dramatic illustration of this is the effect of the changed relations between Britain and Germany, on one side, and France and Germany, on the other side, since 1939 on the relations between Britain and France, or, to be more precise, on the Anglo-French Entente, first signed in 1904. As long as Britain and France were both opposed to Germany, as in the First World War and in the 1930s, the Entente held firm through many tests. It weakened only for those Frenchmen who collaborated with the Nazis after the military collapse of France in 1940. Then came the reconciliation between defeated Germany (or what became later the Federal German Republic) and all the other Western Powers after the Second World War, and with this came a decisive weakening, if not the final demise, of the Entente Cordiale. During the period of General de Gaulle's Presidency of France (1958–1969), in which he based his foreign policy on a French alliance with Federal Germany, relations between Britain and France, and between France and the United States, were almost as hostile as if these pairs of states were actually at war with each other. Hence we can formulate the basic proposition that relations between two states, whether of friendship or hostility, are never only the product of the policies and attitudes of the two states involved. On the contrary, they reflect the state of all the other relations between the two states and the rest of the world, and may even indeed reflect the state of international relations in the international system as a whole. Possibly this is another way of saying that international, as distinct from interpersonal, relations are rarely matters of temperamental likes and dislikes between two or more parties, and hence our category of psychological incongruities between states to which we referred earlier in this chapter must never be overstated. Inter-state relations are almost always more carefully considered, more self-conscious, more ruminated about, and reflected on, than the loves and hates of individual men and women.

We may conclude this examination of factors which affect the uneven distribution of friendships and hostilities throughout the international system by adding two more to our list: one is the process of obsolescence of old interests and commitments of states and the acquisition of new ones, and the other consists of internal changes in the parallelogram of social forces within the frontiers of states. As to the former, we must conceive the international system as being highly responsive to environmental changes such as alterations in the distribution, composition and size of world population, the process of economic growth or decline of different states, improvements in technology, communications and other man-made controls of this world. It is easy to see that such changes are capable of affecting the pattern of a state's interests and hence the state of its relationships with other states. History is full of examples of this. When in February 1947 Britain found herself no longer able, on economic grounds, to give further assistance to Greece and Turkey, which were at that time seemingly threatened by Communist pressure from within and from without, that responsibility was taken over by the

United States Government in the so-called Truman Doctrine.
The United States now found that it had acquired a new interest
in political stability in the Eastern Mediterranean: this strengthened its friendly relations with Greece and Turkey and for that
reason tended to increase somewhat the strains between the
United States and the Soviet Union. Or, again, when in 1953–
1954 Britain found that its great historic military base in the Suez
Canal zone was no longer defensible against nuclear attack, its
incentive to build up a new and different kind of foothold in
Cyprus in order to influence events in the Middle East tended to
increase; this, in its turn, meant that relations improved between
Britain and Egypt, then governed by the new Revolutionary
Command Council headed by Abdul Nasser, while at the same
time British relations with Cyprus, still a British-ruled dependent
territory, took a decided turn for the worse. But the most dramatic
example of changing interests affecting the friendships and
hostilities of states towards each other is that of the Soviet Union
under the leadership of Nikita Khrushchev and Leonid Brezhnev.
The years of the advent of the hydrogen bomb in international
relations—1952–1954—were years in which the super-Powers,
and indeed everybody, had to consider the impact of this new
leap forward in the technology of war on the whole position of the
use of force in relations between state-members of the international system. As Russia acquired a new and lively interest in
the avoidance of nuclear war, her entire picture of the conduct of
international affairs, at the instance of Mr. Khrushchev in the first
place, underwent a striking change. This was reflected in the
desire, which Mr. Brezhnev later inherited, for improved relations with the Western Powers. At the same time, a new acerbity
developed in the relations between Moscow and Communist
China, which felt that Soviet fears about nuclear weapons were
causing the Russians gradually to abandon their interest in world
revolution and to take more seriously their own survival as an
organized state. In all these instances, and many hundreds more
could easily be cited, the state is presented to us as a mass of
constantly changing needs, wants, requirements, which relations
with other states can either help satisfy or help frustrate. The
effects of these changes of wants and interests on the state's friends
and enemies in the international system are sufficiently clear.

Then there is the impact on a state's alignments with other

states in the international system of social changes which occur within its borders. Perhaps the easiest of these changes to deal with are those in the relative influence on government of the different social and economic groups within a particular country. One dominant social group in a country, such as the army, the commercial and business classes, the Left or Right, the churches, and so on, will tend to have external interests of their own, which are not always the same in character, strength or geographical location, as those of a less dominant social sector. We have in an earlier chapter defined the national interests of a state as a certain formula stating its external wants which is backed by sufficient of the effective social forces within the state to keep the prevailing government in office.[7] Hence a change in the balance of forces will tend to produce some change in the definition of the national interests of the state which is offered by the government of the day. The change in the latter may be relatively trivial: the rise and fall of the campaign for unilateral nuclear disarmament in Britain since the early 1950s, for example, may have had some slight effect on the way in which British governments have defined and defended their defence policies, as distinct from the substantive content of those policies. But where, as in the French Revolution of 1789 and the Russian Revolution of 1917, there is a complete change in the predominating social order in the state, the impact on the distribution of friends and enemies of the state is likely to be very far-reaching.

For all the reasons given above, then, we must expect the pattern of international alignment, states with states and states against states, to be in a continuous condition of flux and change. From day to day, perhaps from hour to hour, the attitude of the political authorities of a state towards its neighbours in the outside world is perpetually facing reassessment and revision, and the resulting changes in attitude, if any are effected, will have some influence on the attitudes of other states towards the state in question, and this in its turn will to some extent affect its future attitudes towards them. But now we must consider finally, and briefly, how the international system handles friendship and hostility between the different states of the system. What are its means and methods for dealing with such conditions of international affairs?

We tend to assume all too easily that everyone concerned with the operation of the international system, the politicians, diplomats, military men and so on, are all actively striving to reduce international tension, just as doctors are assumed to be concerned with the reduction of ill-health and disease, that their aim is, if it is humanly possible, to transform relations of tension into relations of 'good understanding' between states. The success of a Foreign Minister or Foreign Office official often tends to be judged in terms of how successful he is in achieving that object. That this is publicly professed by every practising Minister, diplomat or military man is obvious from the kind of public posture and tone of speech adopted by these professionals: 'our vocation is peace' is the normal slogan. But we should remember that this has not always been so, and that even today the reduction or elimination of tensions in international relations cannot be desirable always and in all circumstances. In the past certainly, some states and some leaders of states have openly idolized international struggle and conflict, regarding them both as virtually a law of life and as capable of bringing states and nations up to the highest pinnacle of their achievement. Much of the late nineteenth-century European expansion into Africa and Asia, for example, appears to have been sustained by the idea that nations improved themselves by struggle and conflict, and, as a consequence of the spread of the ideas of Charles Darwin, all animals, man included, were considered to have raised themselves on to higher and higher planes of attainment through struggle, ending in mastery over breeds less well equipped to survive.

At the same time, there is quite a respectable belief among many people today that conflict is inherent in life in general and in international relations in particular, and that hopes of eliminating it are not only unrealistic, but also run the risk of 'hybris', or the transformation of conflict, which should be considered normal, into a life-and-death struggle between the Forces of Darkness and the Forces of Light. People who believe that they have a special mission or duty to extirpate conflict once and for all from human affairs may find themselves eventually locked in a war without end with those whom they hold responsible for the confict. It may be a more modest, possibly more humane, undertaking to assume that conflict and competition are inherent in the human situation, to learn somehow to live with it and to do one's best to minimize its harmful consequences, rather than to hold the 'other side' responsible for all the conflict that exists or has existed. 'Who caused the war?' may be the kind of question which helps perpetuate war in international relations.

The assumption, too, that situations of discord can be transformed by persistent diplomacy into situations of amity and co-operation begs the great moral question whether, for the sake of peace and quiet, we are right to abandon the struggle against that which we genuinely recognize to be a great evil. Here, of course, is one of the central dilemmas of foreign policy which has confronted states from age to age, and which does so now in an even more agonizing form owing to the destructive potential of modern armed conflict. That is, how far should states prepare themselves for open battle with the kind of forces in the international system which, if allowed to triumph, may make much more difficult the resolution of international conflict in the future? This dilemma is inherent in Western attitudes towards Communism, namely, how big a price in terms of the human beings who suffer under Communism should we be prepared to pay in return for peaceful co-existence with Communism? Possibly the Communist world on its side has the same dilemma of conscience in regard to its dealings with the West. In peacefully co-existing with Western capitalism is it delaying, rather than plucking out the causes of, a future war of infinite destruction?

Looking now at the methods of resolving conditions of discord in the international system, a number of well-known techniques need to be recalled. Obviously, one must begin with the most commonplace of these techniques, diplomatic negotiation, that is, a process of bargaining between states hopefully aimed at the co-ordination of the divergent interests of the states concerned. Professor H. J. Morgenthau, in an essay entitled 'The Permanent Values in the Old Diplomacy', has argued that the composition of differences between states and the restoration of an original state of equilibrium in the international system have been the eternal objectives of diplomacy.[8] But that is open to question. Carl von Clausewitz's famous phrase about war being a continuation of diplomacy by other (or with an admixture of other) means can be read in the reverse sense of diplomacy being a continuation of war by other means, which surely implies the continued use of diplomacy in conditions of competition and rivalry between states. The difficulty about diplomacy, when considered

K

as a panacea for the elimination of conflict between states, is that diplomacy works on specific conflicts of interests and outlooks between states, and our 'law of conservation of tension' in international relations teaches us that the reduction of tension in one area of the international system not only fails to prevent tension arising in another area, but may quite positively aggravate and encourage it.

The same may be said of another well-recommended route to the general demise of international tension and conflict, that is, the formation of units larger than the nation-state, which might be supranational bodies, like the communities of the nine states of Western Europe, or, at a less radical level, the formation between states of wider agreements in which local tensions could be resolved. Many people in the non-Communist West, for example, have looked wishfully at the possibility of a peaceful reunification of Germany within a scheme of great-Power agreements for the achievement of greater security in Europe. But the outcome of such devices is likely to be similar to that of specific diplomatic accommodations, as referred to in the previous paragraph, that is, the deepening of conflicts between the newly integrated group of states, on one side, and other states, on the other side, *pari passu* with progress towards the elimination of differences within the integrated area. It is surely no accident that integration between the nine states of the European Community was accompanied, at least for a certain period, by increased tensions between the nine and the Soviet Union, and also, though this is far less important, between the nine Community states and the United States.

Perhaps one of the most efficient means for the lessening of inter-state hostilities, though it is hard to see how it could be deliberately developed and practised, is the natural efflux of time. In the passage of time the sting may be taken out of international differences, as the two states learn to live with these differences and make efforts to see that their differences do not get out of hand. The key question in this kind of situation is often this: to what extent is the issue, or are the issues, in dispute, tied up with the whole integrity and continued existence of one or other or both of the states concerned? It seems that the more intensely public opinion within a state tends to regard the frustrations of its own hopes and expectations as being tantamount to its total extinction as an organized force, the less probable no doubt is it that the efflux of time will have a healing effect on the disputes which exist between that state and its neighbours.

One conclusion which may be drawn from this consideration of the range of factors affecting the growth of hostility and friendships between state-members of the international system is somewhat of a paradox. It is, that calculated efforts to eliminate tension between states often have the effect only of creating new sources of conflict. Perhaps the safest rule in international relations is quietly to accept and proceed upon the assumption that a certain degree of tension is inevitable in inter-state relations for reasons already stated in this book. That it may be reduced and made more manageable, is at all times possible, but that it can be eliminated is not within the reach of human action.

NOTES

1. See above, Chapter Nine, p. 183.
2. See above, p. 129, footnote 19.
3. See Deutsch's article on this subject in James N. Rosenau (ed.), *International Politics and Foreign Policy*, Free Press, New York, 1969.
4. On 20th September 1963.
5. See Felix Morley, *The Society of Nations*, Brookings Institute, Washington, 1932.
6. Northrop, *The Meeting of East and West*, Macmillan, New York, 1946.
7. See above, Chapter Nine, pp. 191-9.
8. In Stephen D. Kertesz and M. A. Fitzsimmons, *Diplomacy in a Changing World*, University of Notre Dame Press, 1959.

Thirteen

War in the International System

IN an earlier chapter we mentioned war as the most extreme form of the compulsive pressures available to states for the purpose of inducing a more co-operative frame of mind in other states.[1] It may be correct to regard this as a pre-nuclear definition of war. Since 1945, and perhaps even earlier, it is more accurate to conceive of war between state-members of the international system as an experience, or condition, or recurrent phenomenon, in that system. It is a state of affairs which overtakes the system and could occur even in the absence of any desire among the belligerents to employ war, as it has been employed in the past, in order to implement certain, essentially political ends.

What is war then? In the most general sense it has been defined as 'any violent contact between distinct but similar entities'. Thus we can speak of civil war, racial war, tribal war, jungle war, industrial war, war even of the planets or of the elements. The kind of war which we are considering as a condition of international relations is a type of that 'violent contact between distinct but similar entities', the entities being, of course, the state-members of the international system. But the nature of international war is wholly governed by the nature of the international system in which it occurs. If the rest of the international system apart from our own country did not exist, our country could not be at war except internally, and if the system were to undergo a kind of amalgamation which would consist in its conversion into a single state, wars, if they still occurred within it, would be civil, not international, wars.

The connection between the nature of international war and the international system in which it occurs can be illustrated in at least three ways. First of all, war is historically associated with the law of the international system, that is, public international law. War of the kind we have in mind in this chapter is a violent conflict between the legally equal members of the system, that is, the states. It is a type of intercourse between states which is defined and permitted by the law between the states; in fact, international law is the only known human legal system which acknowledges and regulates violence between its subjects, whose conduct it binds. 'War', it has been said, 'is seen to be a state of law . . . or, more simply, the legal condition which equally permits two or more hostile groups to carry on a conflict by armed force'.[2] Those words were first published in 1942, but there may be some question today whether total international war, were it ever to occur again, could be described as a legal condition. A nuclear war, for instance, if the world were ever so unfortunate as to suffer one, might be described as a *de facto* state of affairs which could be over and done with long before its legal implications and standing could be worked out. And even conventional or non-nuclear wars and other forms of armed action, such as 'wars of national liberation', are often, and even more often than not, waged today without anything being said by either side about the legal status of the conflict. A declaration of war, the traditional way of bringing a legal state of war into existence, seems now to be an anachronism. Nevertheless, up to the Second World War, at least, the question has been when states go to fight each other: does a legal state of war exist? And are the belligerent states in the kind of legal relationship towards each other which permits and regulates the use of armed force between them?

International war is also a function of the international system in that a common object of war, though by no means the only object, has been to preserve the system of independent states against efforts to destroy it and establish in its place the hegemony of a single state over the system as a whole. Once a system of relationships exist in which the principal values and interests of the member-states are protected by and through the system, it follows that threats to the system by one or more of its member-states will be met by resistance, and in the last resort by acts of force on the part of the other member-states of the system. In addition, efforts to change by force the existing state of relations and the balance of power within the system are likely to be confronted by the armed determination of other states to preserve the *status quo*. The three great European wars of 1792 to 1815, 1914 to 1918, and of 1939 to 1945, were fought to a large extent to maintain the *status quo* within the international system against efforts to subvert it.

Finally, wars may be described as a function of the international system in so far as the object of the fighting may be to preserve the independence, prestige and cohesion of states against forcible attempts to overthrow them. States, as we have had much occasion to point out in this book, are solidarity groups united in the collective defence of certain values shared by their individual members. When a state of war occurs, what binds together the peoples of the states involved is the will to preserve the framework of the state, since this is what provides the people with the means of achieving their self-fulfilment.

Now, reverting to our original definition of war as the extreme type of forcible pressure, applied for the purpose of bringing the opponent's will into harmony with one's own, this was the conception of war expounded in Carl von Clausewitz's treatise *Vom Kriege* (*On War*), published after his death in November 1831. In that book Clausewitz defined war essentially as a form of international pressure, what he calls 'an act of violence intended to compel our opponent to fulfil our will'.[3] This may still be true of the *threat* of war today: when, for instance, the Soviet government declares that, despite their policy of peaceful co-existence, they will meet any aggression against the territory of the Soviet Union or its allies with force, they are using the threat of war to dissuade other states from certain kinds of action, and in this respect they are acting no differently from the official authorities of almost every other state. Nevertheless, it is doubtful today, and it is becoming more doubtful with the lapse of time, whether modern war can be properly considered as a form of pressure. This is not only because nuclear warfare now means the destruction of both sides, the state applying the pressure and the state receiving it; for at least sixty years war has been questionable as a means of bringing pressure to bear on another state for the simple reason that its course, and ultimate outcome, are generally unpredictable.

The vast increase in the technical destructiveness of modern war since, say, 1914 has made war a highly inefficient means of changing the opponent's will. More importantly, the social and political changes effected by modern war within the territory of the belligerents, and the tendency since 1914 for war to spread throughout the whole international system and to obliterate areas of neutrality within the system means that predictions cannot be made, at the outbreak of an armed conflict, as to what the ultimate outcome is likely to be. The First World War quite unexpectedly destroyed four great empires and gravely weakened two of the victors who had fought from the beginning, Britain and France. That War unleashed the Russian Revolution, with its enormous consequences for the international system and the course of human history. Both the First and the Second World Wars were fought by different coalitions of nations from those which took the first shock of war. Hence Maxim Litvinov's famous principle of the indivisibility of peace and Neville Chamberlain's famous statement in 1939 that at the end of a modern war no one can foretell who one's enemies and who one's friends are going to be. This tendency of modern war to achieve quite different objects from those, which were intended by both sides at the beginning, is well illustrated by the fact that Britain and France went to war in September 1939 partly to defend Polish independence, yet when the War ended in 1945 Poland was as effectively under Soviet control as it had been under great-Power control throughout the nineteenth century until its liberation by the Allied Powers in 1919. Czechoslovakia, on the other hand, which Britain and France were afterwards criticized for failing to defend, even at the cost of war, in 1938, remained on the whole untouched by the Second World War, though under Nazi German control. War has accordingly been compared with the floods of water conjured up by the sorcerer's apprentice while his master is away, or to an uncontrollable forest fire in a high wind. And from this springs a familiar attitude of the great Powers to war since 1918: not so much a desire to go to war and win in order to impose their will on other states, more a strong inclination to remain outside of wars which exhaust other Powers and then to step in when the war is moving towards its close in order to emerge as the *tertius gaudens* and with little loss of blood and treasure. Marshal Stalin's famous refusal in May 1939 to take the brunt of a German attack in order, as he put it, 'to pick chestnuts out of the fire for other states' and his agreement at the Yalta conference in February 1945 to enter the war against Japan in the Far East in its final concluding stages are more typical of the contemporary state's attitude towards involvement in war than is that of the Clausewitzian state, resorting to war as a means of changing the opponent's will.

If war in the present age is therefore not accurately described as a form of international pressure, a means of achieving certain premeditated international effects, another way of conceiving it is as an experience of the international system, a contingency or liability of the system, in much the same way as unemployment is a contingent liability of the market economy, divorce a contingency of married life, and failure a contingency of a system of academic examinations. Given that the international system is such and such, and that people all over the world seem to prefer to make do with this system, with all its dangers, in return for the benefits it confers, including national independence, events such as wars are likely to occur within it; how likely depends on the skill and wisdom with which the system is managed. Because war is an experience of the international system, it cannot be fully accounted for by reference to the motivations of the individual states which participate in it. We are unable to say that wars occur because men seek certain ends which they hope to achieve by war and which cannot be achieved except by going to war. The fact is, that they have much the same kind of ends within the system of domestic politics, yet that does not as a rule terminate in civil war unless the state of the domestic system approximates to the normal state of the international system, which it sometimes does. All the motives usually considered to account for war—greed, ambition, fear, pride and so on—must be assumed to be sufficiently strong to overcome both the fear of war and the moral inhibitions against fighting, and to combine together within the different states when they resort to war. The most we can say is that in the international system there is nothing to prevent such motivations resulting in the resort to armed force, if the will is there. Assurances are lacking in the international system that if the states abandon their capability of making war, they will be able peacefully to defend their most important interests, and indeed their very existence, against the war-making propensities of other states.

Since therefore there is a strong case for considering war as an experience or contingent liability of the international system, the question arises as to the incidence and periodicity of this experience. Is there anything, for instance, which statistical study can tell us about this incidence and periodicity? Some of the most complete and revealing information about the statistics of war were compiled by Quincy Wright and published in the two volumes entitled *A Study of War* almost a generation ago. These statistics disclose the obvious enough fact that war is a *regular* experience of the international system, which in itself may lead us to suppose that more is to be gained by the international community in a practical way by attempting to mitigate the dispositions to war inherent in the system, rather than by seeking, as many have imagined, to pluck it out of the international system root and branch. A war deferred, one might almost say, is a war averted. Quincy Wright also shows that, although there has been a decline in the number of wars per century since the sixteenth century— war being defined as a formal legal condition of the relations between sovereign states—the intensity and geographical extent of those wars have been increasing in the past three hundred years. In the sixteenth and seventeenth centuries, according to Quincy Wright, the European states (at that time the only members of the international system as we have defined it) were at war about 65 per cent of the time; the figure dropped to 38 per cent in the eighteenth century, 28 per cent in the nineteenth century, but only 18 per cent in the twentieth century so far.[4] But Quincy Wright adds that if 'colonial-type' expeditions and interventions in America, Africa and Asia are included, 'most of the great Powers have been at war for a large proportion of the time even in the past century'.

The Harvard, Russian-born sociologist, P. A. Sorokin, has also compared by centuries the number of wars which the international system has encountered, but has done so by weighting them, perhaps in a rather arbitrary manner, in order to take account of the duration of the war, the size of the fighting forces involved, the number of casualties, the number of states affected and the proportion of combatants in each case to the total size of the population. His resulting scale of the incidence of war, drawn up over nine centuries, brings out very forcibly the point already made about the escalation in the intensity of wars, century by century up to the present. His indices are as follows:

12th century	*13th*	*14th*	*15th*	*16th*	*17th*
18	24	60	100	180	500

	18th	*19th*	*20th*	
	370	120	3,080	

The remarkable fall in the impact of war in the nineteenth century is to be especially noted, together with the steady and depressing rise in the toll taken by war of human life and wealth.[5]

As to the steady increase in the number of belligerent states involved in war, and the rapidity with which wars have tended over the centuries to spread in a geographical sense, Professor Wright examined 126 wars between 1475 and 1940 and found that the 42 which began in the late fifteenth and in the sixteenth centuries averaged 2·4 participating states. The 22 which began in the seventeenth century averaged 3·5 states each; the 19 which began in the eighteenth century averaged 4·8 each; the 32 which began in the nineteenth century involved 3·1 states each, and the twentieth century, the era of world wars, had so far, according to Quincy Wright, experienced up to 1942, the date of publication of his *Study*, 11 wars which averaged the greatest number of belligerents each, that is, 5·6.

But the most interesting of these statistics gathered together by Professor Wright and his collaborators to show the general prevalence of war in the international system, are those which seem to indicate that it is not so much the martial or aggressive qualities, or other moral or cultural attributes of a state which dispose it towards war with other states, but simply its position in the world scale of power. States, it seems, if the evidence of history is to be believed, become great Powers by overcoming some existing great Power, as Japan did to Russia in 1905. They defend their position at the head of the table by successful wars and eventually they fall from primacy through defeat, or a series of defeats, in war, or, as in the case of Britain in the twentieth century, by national exhaustion brought about by war. 'Clearly the great Powers', Quincy Wright concludes, 'have been the most frequent fighters'. Of all the wars involving European states between 1480 and 1940, he writes, Britain participated in 28 per cent, France in 26 per cent, Spain in 23 per cent, Russia in 22 per cent, Austria in 17 per cent, Turkey in 15 per cent, Poland in 11 per cent, Sweden in 9 per cent, the Netherlands in 8 per cent, Germany (or Prussia, before 1871) in 8 per cent—so much for the so-called 'Black Record' of Germany in international affairs!— Italy (formerly Savoy and Sardinia) in 9 per cent and Denmark in 7 per cent. During most of this period, Wright explains, Prussia and Sardinia ranked as small states, but the degree of their participation in war grew along with their power in the international community; the proportion of participation in war of the Scandinavian states and the Netherlands diminished as their status in the international community dwindled. Both these facts indicate, again, the close relationship between the incidence of war in the international system and changes in the nature and structure of that system. Moving away from Europe, Quincy Wright adds, somewhat drily, that the United States 'has, somewhat unjustifiably, prided itself on its peacefulness' but 'has only had twenty years during its entire history (since 1783) when its army or navy has not been in active operation some day, somewhere'.[6] The United States' record in war-making since Professor Wright wrote those words is fully in accordance with them. What all this may be interpreted as meaning is that, at least within the traditional international system, wars have hitherto been fought by those most physically capable of fighting them. Or, to put it another way, it is, it seems, the order of power in the international system, rather than the character of particular states, which determines the frequency and intensity of their involvement in war.

But no doubt these generalizations require some qualification in the light of international experience since the Second World War. In this period, and especially since the early 1960s, we have seen the two greatest Powers, the United States and the Soviet Union, successfully avoiding war between themselves and the lesser Powers—Britain, France, Federal Germany, Italy and Japan —inhibited by a variety of factors, which include the disapproval of the two greatest Powers and their own desire to re-establish themselves peacefully in the international system, from resorting to armed force in almost any form. The shape which serious fighting has tended to take in the thirty years or so since the Second World War has been the use of force by the United States within countries divided by the East-West Cold War, such as Korea and Vietnam, while the Soviet Union and Communist China did as much as they could to give aid and comfort to the anti-American sides in these conflicts. Then, after the final disengagement of the United States from Indo-China in the early and mid-1970s, both Washington and Moscow were active in their own renunciation of force, and at the same time some of the smaller states, such as India and Pakistan in 1965 and 1971,

Israel and her Arab neighbours in 1967 and 1973, and Greece and Turkey over the Cyprus situation in the summer of 1974, felt emboldened enough to try conclusions with one another through the use of armed force. It was a case of the mice coming out to play while the cats, for one reason or another, were reluctant to intervene.

However, the statistics we have quoted lead on to a question asked since ancient times about relations between organized groups of people, namely, is war inevitable? Is it endemic in the international system? We must, of course, at this point resort to the distinction commonly made between particular wars and the disposition, if we are correct in speaking of one, towards war in the international system. The particular war may perhaps be circumvented, by persistent and vigilant diplomacy, by patience and restraint on both sides, by the organization of deterrent forces in defence of the *status quo*, or by some other means; but the disposition towards war may be described as inherent owing to the expectation, in a society without the agencies for the effective enforcement of the peace, that war might occur. We must remember here the famous formulation by Thomas Hobbes to the effect that, war is not to be determined in terms of actual fighting but of the 'known disposition thereto during all the time that there is no assurance to the contrary'.[7] Perhaps this Hobbesian formula may give us a clue to the permanent avoidance of war, assuming that the people of the world are still unwilling to combine their national states into an 'amalgamated security community'. That clue lies in the word 'expectation', and here too is the all-important link between particular wars and the general disposition of the international system towards war, which we have discussed earlier. If the particular war can be avoided by the kind of remedial methods referred to earlier in this paragraph, the expectation that all international crises run the risk of escalation into all-out war would in the course of time diminish. If on each occasion that states confront a political conflict between two of their number with the increasing confidence that the danger of war can be outflanked and there is no inevitability of all-out war, mutual fear and mistrust might gradually recede from the international system.

It is clear, however, that there are forces in the international system which make the expectation of war exceedingly difficult to root out, or even to mitigate. One is the basic instability in the balance of power. There well may be the appearance of equilibrium in the international balance of forces; a system for the deterrence of attempts to change the state of international relations by armed force may have been effectively established. But we have to be aware at all times of the forces which are ceaselessly at work undermining that system: the weakening of the will of the Powers which stand for the *status quo* to defend it by armed force if need be, the hidden growth in the strength and self-confidence of those with deep-seated grievances against the existing order. Vigilance, it cannot be affirmed too often, is the permanent price of stability in the international system. There is also the factor of discontinuity between the developments taking place within the different states: it is not merely that the rate of economic growth and expansion of material power is greater in one state than in another, but that the tone and mood of public feelings in different countries are at all times changing, though not necessarily at the same speed, or in the same direction. Public opinion in one state may be becoming more suspicious and aggressive, while in its neighbour there is a growing lethargy and reluctance both to defend established positions and to work with opponents of the existing order to the greater good of both. We should remember, too, that every generation, especially in its memories of the past, is different from the preceding generation and its experience of international relations. The horror of war and social revolution which, after Napoleon I's campaigns, helped to keep Europe at peace during the long nineteenth century eventually faded towards its end. British jingoism in the 1870s, the waves of nationalism which swept Germany after the fall of Bismarck in 1890 and the chauvinism of the Italian Risorgimento were signs that new generations in Europe were facing the war situation all over again, uninhibited by the experience of the French Revolutionary and Napoleonic Wars. Similarly, in the 1930s the young Germans and Italians who professedly yearned to revitalize a world abandoned by their fathers, had none of their fathers' acute and personal experience of modern war. To some extent, no doubt, the unforgettable *cameraderie* of the trenches in the First World War lived on in the masculine herdmindedness of the Right-wing European nationalism of the 1930s, but it was youth that the Fascists and Nazis in Italy and Germany glorified, and the international Communist movement, though to a lesser extent, did so, too. The Dictators' summons to youth to emancipate themselves from their fathers was possibly based on Hitler's and Mussolini's wishes to be themselves the new fathers of the new youth: but it was also a summons to youth to gird itself to face nationalist military struggles for which the men of the 1914–1918 war no longer had any stomach.

We should remember, too, that the horror of and revulsion against war which the two World Wars of the twentieth century implanted in liberal minds are essentially new phenomena in human history. For the greater part of man's history, at least until the late nineteenth century, war was looked upon, if not quite with the excitement attending modern sporting competitions, at least with a feeling of normality or inevitability. It was as natural for the young man to serve in the country's defence as it was for the worker in the fields or in the towns to see the product of his efforts either destroyed or appropriated by plundering armies, whether of his own country or its enemies. It required immense courage for a British poet of the First World War to describe the old profession, *dulce et decorum est pro patria mori*, as a 'lie', and even after the First World War, and certainly after the Second, the idea of war as an adventure, or the subject of nostalgic sentiment, was expressed in countless novels and reminiscences.[8] It takes courage, even today, even in Europe which, more than any other continent, has drunk the cup of war to its dregs, to renounce war under all conditions and without any reservation.

But one can put the question of the inevitability of war in the international system in a more particular and direct way by asking the question: were the two World Wars in the twentieth century inevitable? Could the conflict, or the complex of conflicts, represented by the two World Wars have been resolved in some other way? Most people would probably say that the war which broke out in Europe in September 1939 was less inevitable than the war which was concluded twenty years earlier. Germany's grievances in the 1930s, it is felt, could have been remedied without war, were in fact remedied in the main by the time Hitler became Chancellor of the Reich in January 1933. Britain from 1919, and even France after 1930, were only too willing to modify the Treaty of Versailles in Germany's favour. But it was inevitable, the consensus of opinion in Britain now has it, that Britain and France should have declared war on Germany in September 1939 since their whole national independence was threatened by Hitler. If the British and French governments had not gone to war in September 1939, it seems that public opinion, certainly in Britain, would have found Ministers who *were* willing to go to war. Was it inevitable, then, that Hitler should seek the hegemony of Europe, which caused Britain and France to feel that they must fight? We may take the view that a national revolution, like the Nazi revolution in Germany in the 1930s, cannot stop in its tracks; short of being violently thrust out of power, it cannot become conservative and respectable, all the force and passion which generated it could not be transformed into a moderate acceptance of peaceful change. But was it then inevitable that Hitler, as the head and moving spirit of the Nazi revolution, should have come to power in 1933? We know that the Weimar Republic, quite apart from its failure to capture the loyalty of the round bulk of the German people in the 1920s, was unable to deal with the economic crisis of the early 1930s, did not know how to cope with six million unemployed, could not reconcile the conflict over the social services between the East Prussian landlords and the government intervention policies of Chancellor Brüning. We cannot, strictly speaking, perhaps in all this, talk of inevitability, in the sense of a chain of events, which no man or body of men could break. But what we do seem to see is a succession of piecemeal adjustments on the part of many millions of people, adjustments which no doubt appeared to be rational and sensible at the time, but which nevertheless insensibly added up to the confrontation of the states involved in war against each other.

As far as the First World War is concerned, this is often regarded as having had its origins in Austria's fear that Serbia was bent on the breaking up of the multinational Austro-Hungarian Empire and the resulting determination in Vienna 'to teach Serbia a lesson'. Russia, as a sister Slav state, viewed herself as a protector of Serbia and in addition was at odds with Austria-Hungary over influence and control in the Balkans. Germany backed Austria-Hungary because she felt that Bismarck's Dual Alliance with Austria-Hungary of 1879 was an essential counterpoise to the Franco-Russian alliance of 1891. Russia, then, had adopted the cause of the Slavs in the Balkans which automatically ranged her against Austria-Hungary, and France, after

1871, had her own fears of, and grievances against, Germany. Britain, though involved in naval and commercial rivalry with Germany, had no wish to fight Germany on that account: but, given that the Dual Alliance and the Franco-Russian alliance of the 1890s appeared to be bent on mutual conflict, Britain was hardly in any position to stand aside, since that would mean that she would have no influence on the distribution of power at the ultimate peace conference, whichever side won the war. As for the United States, that country ostensibly entered the war in April 1917 on account of Germany's unrestricted submarine war in the Atlantic; but, at a more significant level, it was clear, as it was in 1939–1941, that the United States could never allow Britain, a guarantor of the freedom of the seas, as Americans then understood it, to be overwhelmed by a continental European great Power.

The impression one therefore receives of the First World War is of a grip of interlocking conflicts. This was not, in truth, a war: it was rather a number of wars in each of which one great Power attempted to settle its differences with another. None of the Powers, and hardly any of the statesmen, knew the kind of war on which they were embarking. The catastrophe of the war itself may not have been exactly inevitable; for none of the belligerents could the gains of the war have possibly been worth the price. But there was a certain inevitability, as in the approach to the Second World War, in the reaction of each of the states to the determinate situation facing it at each step of the road to 1914. From this there is one important conclusion which seems to emerge: namely, that it is possible for a state, or a government acting on behalf of a state, to react with perfect rationality to the situation confronting it at a particular time, or with no less rationality than that with which it confronts domestic situations, and yet for all these separate reactions to add up to a total catastrophe which no one can be said to have willed or foreseen.

The catastrophe occurs, or war becomes catastrophe, because the twentieth century is an age of 'total' or 'hyperbolic' war.[9] Total war means in our own day the mobilization of the total resources of the state for the purpose of achieving victory in war against another state. It is the consequence for modern war of the industrial revolution which began in Europe in the eighteenth century and has since then spread to the rest of the world, and of the advent of popular democracy and the modern bureaucratic state. Once the French revolutionaries after 1789 had identified the whole nation with the French war effort and had introduced conscription without exception, once the productive capacity of modern machine industry had been yoked to war production, once the resources, output, operations of the modern state could be monitored and controlled by a professionalized civil service, the foundations of the twentieth-century nation-in-arms were well and truly laid. When the effects of these three combined revolutions were seen in the First World War, after the long peace of the nineteenth century, the event happened to coincide with a temporary victory on the battlefield of defence over offence. The fact that in the 1914–1918 war the concrete strongpoint, barbed wire, the machine gun, held up the invading armies meant that on the decisive Western Front of the War the conflict had to be fought out in a confined space with massive casualties as the able-bodied male population of all belligerent nations was sucked into the narrow vortex. Raymond Aron argues that if the Schlieffen plan on the Western Front had been successful, or if Tzarist Russia had collapsed sooner or had fought better and defeated Germany earlier, the world might not have had the experience which it did in 1914–1918 of total war. There might have been a quick victory for one side or the other, followed by a swift and lenient peace on the ninteenth-century model. The implications of total war would in that case have remained hidden.

But the War went on, drawing into itself ever increasing proportions of the belligerents' manhood and using masses of explosive hitherto unconceived. The effect was, according to Aron, to confuse in people's minds the technical destruction effected by the war machines and the morality of the opponent: it was felt, illogically, that the enemy must be very wicked indeed to inflict casualties on the other side so unprecedented in recorded history, whereas it was in fact machine industry which was doing the killing and wounding. Moreover, the rising cost in life and treasure of the First World War soon made the limited war aims of 1914 on both sides look exceedingly moderate, even old-fashioned. Also, as the geographical spread of hostilities grew and both sides rivalled each other in their bids for neutral support, their programmes for peace had to become more total and all-embracing. This is what Aron calls 'hyperbolic' war, that is, the growth in the scale and intensity of war as its technical basis in machine industry grows.

Thus are created the conditions of total war: that is to say that, besides the total mobilization for war of the belligerent states, there is an increasing interpretation of the conflict on both sides as the eternal struggle between good and evil, light and darkness, civilization and barbarism, the issues being no longer conceived as limited ones of territory or the revision of treaties, but as though the thing at stake was the total triumph of the 'way of life' of one side or the other. There comes, too, the refusal to abandon the conflict, short of the total fulfilment of increasingly escalated war aims, and the attempt, once final victory is won and the enemy surrenders, to disarm and demobilize him, and, as far as possible, to hold him down under constraint for ever. With 'hyperbolic' war, in other words, war ceases to be an element in international bargaining; it becomes a condition of international relations in its own right.

This form of total war, which entered the present international system with the First World War, has had a profound influence, not only on the national and international politics of the period between the two World Wars, but even in the military strategy of the Second World War and the way in which it was fought. As far as national politics in Europe and the United States were concerned, it made the question of responsibility for the War in 1914 and, in the case of Germany, for defeat in that War central subjects of debate. It is difficult to think of any national leader or party in Europe or America during the inter-War years with a foreign policy which did not in some way take as its starting point the question of responsibility for 1914 and 1918. The Treaty of Versailles in itself, in its allocation of responsibility for the war, made this inevitable. As far as the international diplomacy of the inter-War period is concerned, one of the main themes in that period was to try to remain uninvolved in international conflicts which might lead to war until the last possible moment in order, if it could be done, to share in the spoils of victory without having to pass again through the tragic bloodbaths of the First World War.

If we turn to the effect of the total war of 1914–1918 on the military strategy used, at least by the originally successful belligerent, Germany, in the first two or three years of the Second World War, we can see that that conflict was in many ways not total war on an even more frightful scale than the First World War. It was rather the opposite of total war; it was an attempt to avoid the appalling cost of the earlier war while achieving, this time, total success for Germany. Hitler's military strategy, known as *Blitzkrieg*, was assuredly not an invitation to the democracies to meet him once again in the mud of Flanders and to see whether, this time, better preparations would assure for Germany its just and final victory. It was rather an attempt, more by psychological than physical means, to stun and bludgeon the enemy into surrender before any real battle actually began. It was a strategy which succeeded brilliantly and without big battles in western Europe, which still had all its memories of the War twenty years earlier, in 1940; it was not so successful against Yugoslavia and Greece, perhaps because those countries had not passed through the holocaust of trench warfare on the Western Front in the 1914–1918 war and hence could not be stampeded into surrender. Hitler seemed to believe that stunning the enemy into submission, as with France in 1940, could be done with Soviet Russia in 1941 and 1942. In this he failed, and at Stalingrad in 1942 the German army found itself in the same kind of attrition fighting as in the First World War, which it was the whole object of Hitler's military strategy to avoid. Russia's failure to conform to the expected enemy response of submission through psychological defeat was the most serious undoing of the Third Reich.

So far, we have said nothing about the impact of nuclear weapons on the condition of modern warfare, and now is the time to rectify this omission. At first sight, the nuclear or thermo-nuclear bomb and its methods of conveyance to enemy territory, the long-range and now multiple warheaded ballistic missile, seem merely a further refinement in the appalling history of mechanized warfare, another, though this time wholly devastating, chapter in the technical evolution of destructive weapons of which the machine gun, the tank, the long-range gun and the bombing aircraft were previous examples. But there are some ways in which nuclear weapons, even as so far developed, represent a departure from the strategical and social conditions of total war as we have known them in the twentieth century. In the first place, an all-out nuclear war, of devastating effect such as wholly defeats the imagination, could conceivably be fought with inter-continental ballistic missles (ICBMs) without there being any need for the mobilization of the nation, or rather its population of military age, in arms. In fact, in the case of at least one nuclear Power, Britain, nuclear weapons, since at least 1957, have been regarded by the politicians as a means of *avoiding* the total mobilization of the civil population: a popular political measure, the abandonment of conscription, or 'National Service', was paid for at the cost of acquiring and rendering permanent the British independent nuclear deterrent.

Again, a nuclear war need not be fought and, if such a war were ever to occur, would probably not be fought, with the national moral fervour that has traditionally accompanied total war, or indeed any great national war. The nuclear war is coldly planned by the existing nuclear Powers as a means of defending peace and national independence when every other deterrent resource has failed; only a few totally unrepresentative psychopaths, if such there be in any country, really think today of nuclear war as a means of wiping out what they consider to be an immoral régime in another state. In any case, should nuclear war ever be the world's misfortune, the actual time of conflict would in all likelihood be too short for the working up of moral feelings against the other side: no doubt most people in most parts of the world would regard themselves as the innumerable victims of a malign fate, rather than of an opposing wicked state. Finally, total war, as we have known it in twentieth-century international relations, has generally aimed at the wholesale overthrow and disarmament of the defeated state, the terms of peace normally being dictated by a coalition of victorious nations. But it is commonly recognized by all the active great Powers today, with the possible exception of Communist China, that such a form of settlement, at the end of any future world war, as the Versailles treaty of 1919 and the Yalta and Potsdam conferences of 1945 at the end of the Second World War, could never be staged after an all-out nuclear conflict between the greatest military Powers. Total war in the twentieth century has sought the total subordination of the defeated state. Nuclear war, on the other hand, is today sadly recognized, at least by all the older nuclear Powers, as effecting the total and final prostration of both sides.

Perhaps the most important effect of nuclear weapons, however, is finally to break the link, which once seemed so clear, between the actual use of force and the political object which force (at least according to Clausewitz) is supposed to achieve within the international system, that is, to change the opponent's will so as to bring it into line with the initiating state's will. Force, which now includes nuclear weapons, is no longer available for changing the opponent's will, since force with the most up-to-date weapons available to states today, will undoubtedly destroy the user along with his adversary. The emphasis has therefore to fall back on the threat, rather than the actual use, of force. War can no longer, in nuclear times, be conceived as a duel: it is a catastrophe which all potential belligerents, having informed themselves of its potential effects, will henceforward use their best efforts to avoid. Clausewitz conceived war as a duel, or rather as a series of duels: it has a determinate aim—to change the adversary's mind. Clausewitz could talk of the 'suspension of the conflict' by one or other of the belligerents if he felt that a later time would be a more suitable occasion for achieving the political objects of the war.[10]

The conception of 'suspension of the conflict' was adhered to as late as the Second World War. It was implicit in the suspicions of the Western Powers that Russia, and of Russia that the Western Powers, contemplated a separate peace with Nazi Germany in order to secure concessions from Berlin in consideration for a withdrawal from the war. It was also implicit in the idea of the unconditional surrender of the Axis Powers, to which Britain, Russia and the United States committed themselves on the assumption that it would be possible, though entirely undesirable, to suspend or break off the conflict with the Axis states if they came forward with some suitably attractive terms of peace. On the other hand, it is unthinkable that in a nuclear war, if ever one was embarked upon, the belligerents should think of 'suspending the conflict', in order to settle for suitable terms from the other side. The momentum and escalation of all-out nuclear war would almost certainly prove too swift to allow time, once the first weapons had been discharged, for the calm consideration of what benefits, at what kind of price, were likely to be achieved by interrupting the conflict.

This obsolescence of the conception of war as a duel, as Clausewitz seems to have pictured it, has had certain consequences in the attitudes of nuclear states to nuclear war. In the first place, it has stimulated certain efforts to bring nuclear warfare under some kind of control, or, in other words, to try to restore to nuclear war the character of a duel, which may be broken off once its objects, for one side or the other, have been attained. These efforts are implicit in the endless, sometimes barely intelligible, discussions which have taken place in the last ten or twenty years between experts and governments about the controlled use of nuclear weapons, that is, the maintenance of the highest possible levels of conventional warfare and the deferment until the last possible moment of the introduction of nuclear weapons into the conflict; the use of tactical nuclear weapons as long as possible in preference to strategic nuclear arms; the idea of graduated deterrence, or threatening to use as much deterrent nuclear power as seems to be strictly necessary, but not more; the resort to counter-force or counter-city strategies; and so on. The idea behind all this discussion and debate, it seems, is to establish, or re-establish, some kind of rational relationship between force, used or threatened, on one side, and the degree of influence over the will of the other side to be desired, on the other. But of course, there is, and must be, much unsettled debate, both between defence experts and the representatives of the different states, as to what this kind of deterrence can mean in practice.

In the second place, there is bound to be a shift of emphasis in the strategic debate in both the Communist and non-Communist worlds from the actual use of force against another state or states with the kind of political objectives which Clausewitz had in mind, to the threat of force as a means and method of deterrence or dissuasion. If the truth be told and the strategic experts are frank with themselves, no one can forecast the form that nuclear war would take if the elaborate paraphernalia of deterrence on either side were to fail. Hence strategic debate in the West, possibly in the Communist world as well, tends to fall back on 'game theory', that is, the attempt to imagine the reactions of the other side to one's own actions, and one's reactions to those reactions, and so on indefinitely, rather than, as in the pre-nuclear age, to plan the actual movements of forces and weapons when war has actually broken out. For some years now there has existed an established branch of international studies which is called Strategic Studies. But that is really a misnomer: Strategic Studies today are not for the most part concerned with the actual use of force, as understood in the traditional staff college, but with the threat of force as a form of pressure, as much psychological as it is military, applied against the other side. The subject Strategic Studies is in reality a study of politics and diplomacy, with special reference to threats of force, used as though in a duel-like situation.

Thirdly, the attempts of the chief nuclear Powers to restore the character of a duel to war, or rather war as imagined in the nuclear and ballistic-missile age, is reflected in the vigorous efforts of the two undisputed super-Powers, the United States and the Soviet Union, first to reach a definite set of understandings or guide-lines between themselves which will enable them to deal with and smother any potentially dangerous situation anywhere in the world, a practice which has come to be known as crisis management; and, secondly, to keep all nuclear power for military purposes well in their own hands as far as may be. Efforts to achieve the second of these objects include attempting to restrict and halt the testing of nuclear devices by all nuclear Powers, including themselves; doing their utmost to prevent the spread of nuclear weapons to non-nuclear states; and discouraging, and if possible preventing, the acquisition of nuclear capability by their respective friends and allies. All these may be conceived as devices, some of them quite desperate ones, to restrict occasions for the spread of nuclear capabilities and for armed hostilities of any kind in the world, and to narrow the risks of nuclear conflict to themselves alone, while hoping, naturally, never to have to use these frightful weapons against each other, and hoping also to settle differences between themselves by an implicit threat of the nuclear consequences of not reaching such a settlement. The two super-Powers, in other words, are attempting to keep war between themselves to the level of a duel, rather than the level of a catastrophe. But it is a duel without weapons, the weapons now available being too destructive to both sides to use, except in the final emergency. The object of the duel without weapons is to persuade both sides to refrain from resorting to weapons.

Wars fought by non-nuclear states with non-nuclear weapons and limited in geographical extent will no doubt long continue as incidents of international relations, though perhaps there never was a time when the supreme Powers of the international system were so concerned to dampen down such local uses of force by their combined efforts. The success of the giant Powers in doing so will almost certainly be diminished as nuclear weapons spread to the lesser states, as now seems inevitable. As between the super-Powers themselves, however, many people now believe that nuclear weapons have all but succeeded in eliminating war; it should nevertheless be remembered that in 1939, before the horrors of atomic warfare were known, war had already been established in the minds of most people as a catastrophe of such dimensions that it seemed inconceivable that it could ever be un-leashed again. As we have tried to show in examining the genesis of the two World Wars of the twentieth century, the movement towards international war in modern times seems rather like a succession of apparently inevitable decisions, the ultimate out-come of which is nevertheless disastrous to all. We may today conceive war between the super-Powers as a fatal accident which can never be altogether ruled out, though the factors which tend in that direction, the circumstances leading to the clash, can be identified and checked. But the responsibility for taking the measures necessary to lessen the risk of the fatal accident have to be taken by the supreme Powers themselves rather than through some vague consensus of the international community as a whole.

The diplomacy resorted to by the super-Powers in their search for a joint strategy to reduce the risks of war between themselves is called 'peaceful co-existence', or the '*détente*'. As compared with the state of relations between the supreme Powers at the time of the Berlin crisis of 1958–1961 or the Cuba crisis of 1962, the *détente* has assuredly been a vast stride forward in international relations, one which would have seemed inconceivable during the grimmest days of the East-West Cold War. There are nevertheless certain inner self-contradictions in the concept of *détente* as a condition of international relations which makes its future, in the context of East-West or any other relations, still precarious. One of these is the obvious fact that the policies of collective defence and united strength through the alliance systems on both sides of the East-West divide have clearly paid off, in the sense that these collective defence systems have brought home to each side the hideous risks of either side attempting to challenge the other to a test of force. Yet, as the *détente* has continued and the risk of war in Europe at least have declined, the incentive to maintain the alliance systems in a permanent state of war preparedness has diminished. We have the spectacle in the West of the United States attempting to control the centrifugal forces in the NATO alliance while being well enough aware that in the last resort it is her own weapons, situated at sea or in her own territory, or perhaps in outer space, which ensure her security *vis-à-vis* the Soviet Union. And the Soviet Union is evidently in the same position. To use an idea of Schelling's, the aim of both super-Powers is to reduce for each other the commitment to use its nuclear weapons when its vital interests are in danger: in other words, the Soviet Union tries to disestablish the NATO alliance in the hope that the United States will no longer feel committed to defend its West European allies, while the United States tries to make its vital interests as clear as possible to the Soviet Union in order that the Soviet Union will not feel committed to attack them or whittle them away. Yet it is these very commitments on both sides which have created the structure of confronting alliances from which the *détente* has sprung.

The other formidable self-contradiction in the present super-Power *détente* is how the two super-Powers envisage the next international developments. Leaders on both sides of the East-West ideological fence no doubt recognize that *détente* is better than Cold War, which in its turn was better than hot war; but both seem to believe that *détente* is but a means to a still more consolidated peace, a step on the road to some more stable condition of the international system which will finally bar and bolt the door against reversion to international tension. But, so far from there being agreement between East and West as to what that further state of international affairs will be, there is the most profound discord, which, as it so happens, is almost totally disregarded in the West. For the West, the *détente* represents a movement towards some imagined state of freedom and harmony in the relations between nations, and this is conceived as the likely consequence of the spread of Western liberalism to all peoples of the world; in short, the state of affairs envisaged in the Atlantic Charter signed by President Roosevelt and Winston Churchill in August 1941. Soviet leaders, now seemingly deeply conservative, may have the same conception of the world beyond *détente*, but it would be a massive repudiation of their political philosophy and their public utterances if they had. Soviet leaders, in their heart of hearts, may be unwilling to pay a high price in terms of national interest, if any price at all, for the realization of their cherished dream of a Communist world, but that they are mentally and emotionally committed to such a world seems beyond reasonable doubt. Events since 1945 may not have provided much substantial basis for their dreams, but they have provided some.

It may be, as Mr. Khrushchev seemed to indicate in the early 1960s, that Communist and Western states can peacefully co-exist side by side indefinitely, vying with each other to promote, though through entirely peaceful means, their own conceptions of the ideal human society. But it would be shortsighted not to be aware of the stresses and strains in the international system which this basic conflict of faiths may yet bring. The hope perhaps must lie, once again, in that phrase of Thomas Hobbes about the ex-pectation of war being as good, or as bad, as war itself. How can the expectation of war be changed into the continued expectation of peace? Certainly not by wishful thinking on one side or the other. The price of continued peace is continued vigilance, no less. But the passage of time, so long as each crisis in international relations is successively overcome by steadiness and restraint, can perhaps breed an idea that the long expected Armageddon may never come. And, with the waning of that expectation, the preparation of minds and weapons for the day of Armageddon may fade away.

Notes

1. Chapter Eleven, above.
2. Quincy Wright, *A Study of War*, University of Chicago Press, 1942, Vol. II, p. 13.
3. *On War*, translated into English by J. J. Graham, Kegan Paul, Trench, Trubner, London, 1940, Vol. I, p. 2.
4. *A Study of War*, University of Chicago Press, Chicago, Vol. I, p. 235.
5. *Social and Cultural Dynamics*, American Book Company, New York, Vol. III, 1937, pp. 348–51, quoted in Wright, op. cit., University of Chicago, 2nd edition, 1965, p. 237.
6. Wright, op. cit., Vol. I, p. 271, n. 1.
7. *Leviathan*, Chapter XIII; see above, p. 129, note 19.
8. *The Collected Poems of Wilfred Owen*, Chatto and Windus, London, 1971, p. 55.
9. The expression 'hyperbolic' to be discussed later (below, pp. 289–90) is borrowed from Raymond Aron's *The Century of Total War*, previously referred to above, Chapter Ten, p. 205 and n. 7.
10. Clausewitz, op. cit., Vol. I, pp. 13–15.

Fourteen

Conflict and Conflict Resolution

WAR, which we discussed in the previous chapter, is an extreme and violent form of conflict between states in an international system in which there is no automatic machinery to prevent it. But, even in the twentieth century, war between established states is a relatively rare occurrence, perhaps inexplicably rare in view of the predispositions towards war inherent in the system of international politics and the nature of man. Conflict, however, in the sense of the visible incompatibility of the policies and interests of the different states, is a permanent and continuous feature of international relations, as it is of all human relations. Strife is all pervasive, and the briefest of glances at world events as recorded in any newspaper is sufficient to convince one of it.

People, or, perhaps more accurately, the kind of people who are drawn into the study of human relations, are disturbed by the fact of conflict, and those charged with the management of human relations profess to be uncommonly disturbed by it. Indeed, so far from taking conflict for granted, as though it were normal in human affairs, many professional practitioners in the management of human affairs sometimes speak as though it were the object of their policy somehow to eliminate conflict from the field of human affairs with which they are concerned. The obvious reasons for this are partly that conflict, especially in the international system, may quite clearly have a warlike outcome, and this has proved quite monstrously destructive in the twentieth century with its most refined means of waging war. But there is also the argument that conflict is 'dysfunctional' in the international system in a more general sense, in other words, that it prevents the efficient working of that system: it makes for the diversion of the world's resources to non-productive uses and it wastes human energies and abilities on comparatively worthless objects.

It is open to question to what extent war and conflict can be said to have a positive function to fulfil in international relations; we have touched upon this question briefly in the previous chapter. But there seems little doubt that conflict, if not actually violence and war, has been such an endemic feature of human history that the idea of its abolition seems to be, not only excessively optimistic, but positively unreal. This is not merely a matter of any ingrained pugnacity, aggressiveness, or inborn impulses towards violence in human nature. It is true that there is enough evidence in academic psychology proving that man is so constituted that acts of violence may have a positive appeal to him, if only vicariously; and, quite apart from this, everyday observation reveals that violence, together with sex, seems to have enough attraction to men and women to diminish seriously whatever restraints and inhibitions there may be on the other side. But we do not, strictly speaking, need evidence from any psychological school of thought to confirm for us that conflict is built into the system, indeed into all systems, of human relations. There are at least three fairly self-evident factors in social relations which are sufficient to account for conflict, whether or not involving overt violence, without any need to accept the (in any case controversial) argument that conflict is somehow rooted in the genes, only waiting for a suitable moment to break out.

One of these factors is that the values or moral preferences of human groups differ from one another: in the most dangerous international conflict since the Second World War, namely the so-called Cold War between Communism and the West, there was, without question, the deepest moral conflict between the Communist thesis that human personality most nearly reached perfection when it embodied the collective cause of the oppressed masses, and the Western thesis that freedom, the highest good, was only attainable when the individual was detached from and independent of the collective cause. No doubt such essentially moral theses were exploited by the politicians on both sides for the promotion of their own ends, especially their retention of power. Possibly, too, these moral convictions on both sides of the 'Iron Curtain' represented merely culturally acquired beliefs which were in no sense primary in the persons concerned. Nevertheless, the sense that a moral void genuinely existed between these two positions was a real element in the estrangement felt by each side towards the other.

But there are also, in the second place, the inherited cultural values and practices of states, which may differ so much between one state and another as to make a common mind on their mutual affairs difficult, if not impossible, to achieve. It is possible that at some remote time in the future new generations of men and women may be brought under common world-wide cultural patterns which could establish a single frame of mind on basic issues between them. But, quite apart from the immense question of whether such a *Gleichschaltung* of the world's cultural standards and practices could ever be desirable, this is not, quite clearly, an eventuality to which we have to look forward in the time scale foreseen in practical politics. For as far ahead as we can hope to see, the established, usually unquestioned and uncritisized basic attitudes towards human relations taken for granted by most people throughout the world are likely to remain so different from one another that the prospect of one state feeling in exact accord with another on such basic questions seems most improbable. We must remember here, too, that the more unconscious people are of their basic values—and their being unconscious at all is a measure of the success of the acculturation process to which all are subjected in the state—the less likely they are to see the conflict as a matter of acquired culture, and the more they will tend to see it as a struggle between the normal and the abnormal, the human—that is, their own—and the inhuman— that is, the other man's standpoint. Language, for instance, has long been recognized as a barrier between the peoples of the world and this, not only because different languages make communications difficult between people, but because the mere sound of a language one does not understand suggests remoteness and even hostility. It is a well-known, but much forgotten fact, that in many pre-literate peoples the words 'stranger' and 'enemy' are synonymous.

But then there is the third element in human conflict which makes us less hesitant about describing it as inevitable in human affairs. This is the obvious point that the goals, intentions, wants, plans, desires, fears, of individual human beings differ; they differ within the same nations, within the same towns, the same families. No doubt there are ways, as we will see later in this chapter, by which the differences and hence the conflicts in human enterprises can be reduced, both in frequency and intensity, to a more manageable scale. But that individuals and human groups should want to do different things, pursue different objectives, enjoy different activities, is surely a fact which we cannot hope to eradicate from the human situation, quite apart from whether it is really desirable that the whole human race should be pulling on the same rope, in the same direction, as the people of a Communist nation are often depicted by the propaganda agencies as working with one will and mind towards a common end. It would not be difficult to cite peaks of human achievement throughout history, and in the arts and sciences and practical politics, which have been scaled because a few differed from, and accordingly quarrelled with, the views of the contemporary majority. Human conflict has most certainly brought its tragedies with it; but it has also made possible some of men's finest achievements.

What we have been saying in the three previous paragraphs about the disposition towards conflict in human affairs may seem sufficiently obvious that it does not need to be spelled out. We could rest content with that statement were it not for the fact that a great deal of recent writing about international relations, especially by academic students and especially since, say, the late 1950s, seems to have set as the object for research the ways and means of eliminating all conflict from human affairs. The ironical situation is that, although these more recent writers are self-evidently liberals or perhaps social democrats in their political convictions, they seem to be deeply affected by the Communist and Fascist myth that, after the appropriate social revolution favoured by each of these belief-systems, a conflictless, or substantially conflictless, world will emerge. The Communist and Fascist argument is that the path to the conflict-free millennium lies through the elimination of certain social classes, the capitalists or the Jews, radicals or Marxists, as the case may be. It is true that the modern Western specialist in conflict or conflict-resolution does not usually have such a clear picture in mind of which social groups are to be eliminated, if a world without conflict is ever to be achieved, but he concentrates on such mental factors as irrationality, prejudice, stereotyping and other forms of misperception, as the basic factors in human differences; and these, he contends, can be reduced by certain novel techniques even if not totally removed.

The objection to this postulate of a conflict-free world, which most modern writing on conflict in the international system seems to uphold, is not so much that it is not in accord with the observable facts of human life and the structure of human relations, but that, if followed to its logical conclusion, it tends to make human conflict still more widespread and intransigent. The would-be abolitionist of conflict tends to focus upon some fact or institution in the world which he regards as bearing the blame for the existence of human conflict. When this 'last enemy' is overcome, the path to final peace and harmony will be cleared. The fact is, however, that after this allegedly final battle is won, conflict, for one or other of the reasons we have already given, tends to recur, stubbornly enough, and the why and wherefore of this the conflict-abolitionist is unable to explain. His natural conclusion tends to be that since he himself, with all his good intentions, cannot logically be responsible for the persisting fact of conflict, it must be the other fellow who is causing the trouble. Hence, once more, there springs up the idea that after that other fellow, now visualized as the 'last enemy', has either left or been removed from the scene, final peace, untroubled by strife, will remain. Owing perhaps to the two vicious and costly Wars in the twentieth century the 'abolition of conflict' school has generated a growing following behind it. Their views combine the satisfactions of self-righteousness with the comforting feeling of being on the side of modern science, with all its esoteric language, alleged certainty, and its computers. We must therefore appreciate that the object in any rational form of 'conflict analysis' or 'conflict resolution' is not, and cannot be, the wholesale elimination of conflict from human affairs. It is rather to improve somewhat the established means of resolving international conflicts, to consider new means of conflict resolution, and, if possible, to reduce somewhat the incidence of conflict between nation-states so as to divert the time and energy now spent on the settlement of international differences to more productive uses.

'Conflict resolution' today can be said almost to represent a new branch of international study: the quarterly journal, *The Journal of Conflict Resolution*, was established at the University of Michigan in 1957. As understood today, 'conflict resolution' involves a collection of proposed techniques ranging from the reduction of psychological abnormalities among the leaders of states, to playing out international conflicts in the form of games so as to release and hopefully eliminate tensions inherent in them. In fact, of course, conflict resolution is a new name for what used to be called before the Second World War the 'pacific settlement of international disputes'. The pacific settlement of international disputes is a term of narrower scope than conflict resolution, in that what it seemed to refer to forty or fifty years ago was the use of some legal or political machinery established as a rule by inter-governmental agreement for the settlement of disputes; conflict resolution today purports to make use of a much wider range of instruments of settlement, many of which may not even be inter-governmental. The pacific settlement of disputes was also directed, or seemed to be directed, to the resolution of international *dis-putes*, in the sense of express or formulated differences between states, whereas since 1945 the world has become accustomed to the notion of 'situations of international tension', in which a for-mulated or specific dispute is not necessarily conceived as existing. On the other hand, the idea of the pacific settlement of inter-national disputes does lay emphasis on the attempts to settle such disputes by *peaceful* procedures. It is always possible to resolve a conflict by forceful means, that is, by the forceful imposition of a solution by one side of the conflict or the other, or by a third party.

We should bear in mind at this point that by far the greatest number of conflicts which crop up from day to day in the relations between states are resolved in the ordinary and routine function-ing of diplomacy. Naturally, most of these quietly resolved ques-tions do not find their way into the mass media, which tend to thrive on the intransigent and dramatic confrontations between the different governments: happy families, Tolstoy once wrote, have no histories, and certainly not in the Fleet Street sense of the term, we may add. We should remember, too, that in the inter-national system many international conflicts may pass away from the active agenda of diplomacy without a specific resolution of the conflict, in the sense of a determinate settlement agreed to by the parties, having been arrived at.

This may come about in a number of ways. First, the conflicting states, having tried and failed to reach a settlement satisfactory to the two sides, or even to one, may simply decide to 'live with the situation', rather than run the risk of pressing ahead with the conflict to the point at which actual peace between the parties is threatened. No solution is arrived at which is wholly satisfactory to either side and even the state which initiated the conflict, if either side can in fact be said to have done, realizes that it is more expedient on balance to reach an unsatisfactory settlement than to incur the risk of continuing conflict, the outcome of which cannot be foreseen. We may conclude that this was the attitude assumed by the Soviet leader, Mr. Khrushchev, in the closing stages of the Berlin crisis of 1958–1961. The crisis had begun, in so far as such crises can be said to have had their beginnings anywhere, with Mr. Khrushchev's famous note of 27th November 1958 in which he had proposed, or rather threatened, the demilitarization of West Berlin on the ground that the presence of Western forces in Berlin long after the formation of the two German states was 'anomalous'. There can be no doubt that, before the building of the Berlin Wall on 13th August 1961, the existence of a West Berlin garrisoned by American, British and French forces was highly inconvenient for the Soviet Union and the Warsaw alliance states as a whole. In fact, however, they had no alternative but to accept the position of divided Berlin, as they accepted the idea of a divided Germany, since they were quite unable to do anything about it other than by initiating a war which the Soviet Union no more wanted than did the Western Powers.

In the second place, one may conceive an international conflict, which may once have been conceived by the parties or one of them as a matter of life and death, at length coming to 'die a natural death', or fading away either as a result of the contestants being unable to determine any specific outcome to it or becoming ultimately bored and mentally exhausted by it. Thus the treaty of Lausanne, concluded by the Allies and Turkey in July 1923, almost five years after the ending of the First World War, in which the opposing parties were belligerents, was called by some newspapers in Britain the 'peace of lassitude', and that was a suitable name to describe the frame of mind of both parties to a conflict which had passed through many phases of intense feeling and many fears of a renewal of all-out war, until in the end both sides agreed to let it die a natural death. Similar, too, was the celebrated quarrel between Britain and France, on one side, and President Nasser's Egypt, on the other, which reached a pitch of intensity over Nasser's nationalization of the Suez Canal Company

L

in July 1956, and which then quietly faded away after the Anglo-French attempt to seize the Suez Canal by force.

Finally, a conflict between two or more states may have a peaceful conclusion even when there is no specific settlement reached by diplomacy or any other means, and this occurs when new sources of conflict appear either between the states concerned and more especially between them and third parties. Without there being adequate statistical material to offer on this, it might not be too reckless to say that this is perhaps the way in which the great majority of international conflicts are resolved or resolve themselves in the course of time. Just as, between individual members of a social club, for example, we can easily conceive of situations in which friendship and hostility develop, not only because of the mutual likes and dislikes of the people themselves, but also because of the state of relations between themselves and third parties. Similarly, and perhaps even more so, the attitude of a state towards a conflict, which it has with another state, will depend to a very large extent on the condition of relations between itself and third states: if the latter relations are good, the state in question will feel freer to develop its conflicts with other states in order to derive what benefit it can from those conflicts; if, however, those relations are bad, the state must be more cautious in handling its quarrels with third states lest it become diplomatically isolated. The classic case of this in recent years has been the triangular relations between Communist China, the Soviet Union and the United States. So long as Sino-Soviet relations were friendly, between, say, 1949 and 1955, tensions between the Western bloc and the Communist world were at their height: each side's attitude to external affairs was wholly dominated by the global East-West conflict. Then, about 1956 or thereabouts, tensions in Sino-Soviet relations began to develop and before very long these two Communist Powers, China and Russia, were little more than thinly disguised enemies, if disguised at all. Almost at once the Soviet authorities began to see the advantages of resolving their various conflicts with the Western Powers, and especially with the United States. Once embarked upon, the process of Soviet-American *détente* continued to a point, and at a pace, scarcely conceivable in the harsh days of the Cold War. At the same time, the Western Powers, and more particularly the United States, while reaching out to grasp the now extended hand of the

Soviet Union, also began to ponder upon the possibilities of better relations with China now that it was evidently estranged from Moscow. For all these reasons, we must not take the over-pessimistic view that if international conflicts are not resolved by peaceful and deliberate means, they are not resolved at all. We certainly need all the devices for the peaceful resolution of international conflict which ingenuity can invent and nations and governments can repose their confidence in. But 'nature', too, or perhaps we should say history and the ever-changing pattern of international relations, often have their way of resolving disputes for us, no matter how tense the conflict between the states may seem at one particular time.

Let us assume, however, that states in conflict find that they are not able to resolve their differences by ordinary diplomacy even when, as is evidently the situation today, there is pressure either from the super-Powers or from the international community as a whole, or from both, that the contesting states should find a peaceful solution to the issues in conflict between them. In such a case, they may have recourse to the many means now established for the resolution of international disputes without violence. Indeed, if they are members of the United Nations, as most states are today, they are obliged by Article 33 (1) of the UN Charter 'to seek a solution by negotiation, inquiry, mediation, conciliation, arbitration, judicial settlement, resort to regional agencies or arrangements, or other peaceful means of their own choice'. The UN Security Council is further charged 'when it deems necessary' to *call upon* the parties 'to settle their disputes by such means'; the verb 'call upon', as used here, is generally assumed to have a mandatory character when introduced into the UN Charter. Independently of such processes of peaceful settlement taken in hand by the parties themselves, the Security Council is authorized in Article 34 of the Charter to investigate any situation which might lead to international friction or give rise to a dispute 'in order to determine whether the continuance of the dispute or situation is likely to endanger the maintenance of international peace and security'.

Now the international community, in all its attempts to co-ordinate and regulate the agencies for the peaceful resolution of international conflicts since 1919, has maintained its classic distinction between legal and political institutions for the speedy and effective settlement of conflicts: on the one side, legal institutions, manned on a permanent or *ad hoc* basis by professional lawyers competent to pronounce on issues arising, if such there be between states, within the framework of public international law, and, on the other side, bodies consisting of political representatives of the various states authorized to pronounce upon the political wisdom or viability of certain proposals for the solution of the conflict. Many scholarly authorities, especially in the field of international law, have argued that the difference between the legal and the political conflicts between states, as implied in the duality of the institutions for their peaceful settlement, is wholly a matter of the subjective attitudes of the conflicting states. If the states so will, neither legal nor political agencies for peaceful settlement can be declared to be incompetent to discover an appropriate settlement.[1]

This may well be so, in a narrowly technical sense; if the states are content with judgments, political or legal, emanating from third parties, no matter how constituted, that could be said to be the end of the story. The reverse is certainly true, namely that if the states are *unwilling* to accept a given form of settlement in a given dispute, it hardly matters whether the forum which it rejects is either legal or political. But the larger point is that it is surely a misdirection to submit to lawyers questions which require political understanding and moral insight, which they are not particularly qualified by their experience or training to possess; and the same applies, *mutatus mutandis*, to political tribunals, made up of men and women whose training and experience are essentially political, when called upon to express an opinion about unquestionably legal matters. The distinction between legal and political conflicts may thus be said to have an objective basis in the existence of essentially distinct bodies of rules with which the court of law and the political tribunal or council respectively are equipped to deal. In fact, the International Court of Justice at The Hague, like its predecessor, the Permanent Court of International Justice, which sat in the same city during the inter-War period, has always been extremely reluctant to stray from the consideration of strictly legal questions, even when expressly called upon by the parties under Article 38 of the Court's Statute to do so.

It is sometimes argued that judges in municipal courts quite frequently make awards and decisions in accordance with what seems to them to be current social need, rather than with respect to existing law, especially when the latter is vague or ambiguous, and that therefore there is no reason why international courts should not on occasion perform a similarly political function, assuming that the states which are parties to the action are agreeable. The practice of municipal courts referred to here is certainly much more familiar in the United States than it is in the United Kingdom; a British judge might concede that law does sometimes 'grow in the hands of the bench' but he would probably say that, if it does, it surely does so slowly and certainly not in such a way as to infringe in any possible respect on the sole right of Parliament to make the law of the land. It is also true that all judges in all countries have what Professor H. J. Laski used to call 'inarticulate major premises'—meaning prejudices—about social justice and social rights and that these may on occasion, as Laski alleged, affect unconsciously the judge's view of the law in a given case. But we would all recognize, including the judge in question, that if this does happen it constitutes a grave aberration from judicial responsibility. The judge, municipal or international, is there to apply the law as he understands it; for any other function, including the political function of determining what the law ought to be, he has no particular qualifications.

It might be stressed that this is even more truly the situation in judicial settlement in the field of international relations. The ordinary citizen assumes in his day-to-day life that the judge will apply the law, and perhaps draw Parliament's attention to the fact, if he thinks that the law is unsatisfactory and that it should be clarified, reformed or repealed. But the citizen has no option but to go to court if an action is brought against him in civil or criminal law. The state within the international system, on the other hand, normally has the option whether or not to comply with another state's call to go to court over some legal issue in dispute between them: even if it is bound under the so-called Optional Clause of the world court's Statute (Article 36) to go before the court as a defendant in a certain action, it can, in any similar later case, withdraw its declaration accepting the compulsory jurisdiction of the court under the Optional Clause, or introduce into its declaration such reservations as to make its adherence to that Clause virtually meaningless. There is no doubt that sovereign states in their international relations cling tenaciously to all the

rights to act in their own interests to which they are, or believe
themselves to be, entitled, and any attempt by international courts
to invade the sacrosanct zones of sovereignty, as for instance by
attempting to take out of the hands of states the right to determine
what the law should be, is bound to lead to even more disrespect
for international courts and tribunals than the states have at the
present time. It cannot be repeated too often that the standing of
the International Court at The Hague, and that of its predecessor,
the Permanent Court, has never been one of steady increase;
rather the reverse. Only about the same number of states have
accepted the Optional Clause agreeing to the court's compulsory
jurisdiction under the ICJ régime as did so under the pre-1939
PCIJ system, even though the number of states in the world
during that period has trebled; the new Afro-Asian states created
since 1945 have been particularly slow in acceding to the Optional
Clause. This is not, most assuredly, because the world court has
not been bold enough in straying into the political realm of
deciding what the law ought to be. The opposite is in fact the
case.

It must remain a cardinal principle, then, in the settlement or
resolution of international conflicts that legal issues in the conflict
—that is, questions as to what the legal position is under international law—should be referred to legal tribunals, and that
political issues—which concern questions of what the legal
position ought to be—should be referred to political councils or
conferences, which range from diplomatic meetings between
representatives of the conflicting parties, to sessions of the UN
Security Council and General Assembly. It is, of course, well-
known that international law tends to lack the crispness and
clarity normally expected in the drafting of municipal law and
the argument is made that for this reason the international court
must try to clarify the law and give fuller expression to it in the
light of the social requirements inherent in the specific case before
it, another argument, in fact, for the court to take up the role of
social engineering. But it should be remembered that if a rule of
international law is vague or ambiguous, this may be because the
states which made it intended that it should be so: they may not
have been able to agree on a more precise formulation of the rule
in question. But this certainly gives the international court or
tribunal no right to step in and try to do what the states failed to

do. To argue that there should be such a right is only to increase the opposition of most states to intervention by outsiders into their sacred right to do as they please, within the limits of an international law which they themselves have deliberately allowed to remain 'vague'.

We must assume, then, not so much that conflicts between states can be neatly divided into legal and political types, which require different forms of, or institutions for, peaceful resolution: but rather that all, or almost all, international conflicts which fill the daily newspaper are divisible into legal and political *issues*, many of each of which are contained within the same conflict; and that the first task of diplomacy between the state parties to the conflict—if they are genuinely bent upon a settlement—is to disentangle one kind of issue from the other, and to refer each kind to an appropriate forum of settlement, whether it be legal or political, as the case may be. The theory of peaceful resolution of inter-state differences hence should be that no tribunal, whether legal or political, can begin to resolve an international conflict without ascertaining, and making clear after having ascertained, what are the *issues* involved in the conflict and how the legal issues are being referred to courts with qualified judges and the political issues to essentially political agencies.

The existing procedures and institutions in the international system for the peaceful resolution of international conflict by third-party intervention—that is, when the parties have failed in their own bilateral efforts to reach a compromise solution which both will accept—are, like all social procedures and institutions, always in constant need of reform, repair and revision. The more is this so in the resolution of international conflict because the procedures and institutions for such resolution are relatively conservative and slow to change, for which the states' jealous protection of their own sovereignty is no doubt largely responsible. In the twentieth century there have been, it is true, across-the-board re-establishments of these procedures and institutions after each of the two World Wars; but, even so, the extent of actual change in all such cases has in fact been remarkably small, as may be seen by comparing the Statute of the world court as it was before the Second World War with the constitution of the court as it emerged after that war. Common among the many proposals for reforming the procedures and institutions for conflict resolution in the present international system are such as the following: streamlining the ponderous and long-drawn-out procedures of the ICJ and making it more representative of the new African and Asian states formed since 1945, which now play such a dominating role in the UN General Assembly; widening the powers and increasing the availability of the UN Secretary-General for mediatory and conciliatory work in cases of international conflict; reinforcing and strengthening the work and powers of regional organizations for the settlement of international conflicts.[2] But the reforms in these procedures and institutions which have been proposed from time to time, both by governments and by private organizations and individuals, are numberless, though all the proposers would no doubt agree that it is one thing to sponsor a proposal, as making for greater 'efficiency'—however ambiguously that expression is defined—and quite another to persuade enough states which matter, that the proposal would be politically advantageous to them, or at least that it would do them no positive harm.

But we are all well enough aware that the difficulty about these procedures and institutions for the peaceful resolution of international conflict is not so much that they are in need of reform, and perhaps supplementation, but that states are for a variety of reasons reluctant to use them—this applies more particularly to international legal procedures and institutions—and, if they are used, to make sufficient and timely adjustments of policy, in order that agreement to settle the conflict, can be reached. In other words, the failure of states to have recourse to third-party settlement of their conflicts does not lie in the unreformed character of the existing instruments for such settlements—after all, the states could quite quickly effect such reforms, if they could agree on them—but in their feeling that they have more to gain by resisting such settlements. Ultimately, therefore, any inquiry into the inadequacy of the existing machinery for conflict resolution becomes an inquiry into the generally unenthusiastic attitudes of states towards such settlement and, even more importantly, their extreme reluctance to agree to make these settlements compulsory for all states.

There is, in fact, a wide range of reasons which actuate the states in taking up such attitudes. In the first place, there is, of course, no compulsion to accept third-party settlement, that is to say no legal compulsion, and almost all states, the super-Powers included, seem to wish it to remain that way. A state therefore which has an advantage over another state, for instance by reason of having won territory from it as the result of a successful war, may decide to stand pat on its gains rather than agree to third-party settlement which may result in the whittling away of its gains. It is true that if there is not a legal reason for submitting to third-party judgment, there may be a strong political reason in the form of pressures to submit applied by the international community as a whole, or by substantial forces within it. One of the interests which the United States and the Soviet Union have in the continuance of the *détente* between them, for example, is that it enables them to exercise their joint pressure on states unwilling to submit to third-party settlements of their disputes. On the other hand, recent history has shown how even a small country, like Israel, can successfully defy the organized international community on issues in which it feels that its very survival is at stake, especially, of course, when it has the support of a powerful minority opinion in one or other of the super-Powers.

Secondly, the government of a state may be fully willing to submit an issue in dispute with another state to an international court or political tribunal, but its people may regard such a policy as a 'sell-out', a betrayal of the vital interests of the country, and in this situation the government's hands are virtually tied. On the whole, the general experience of the twentieth century so far seems to show that the present-day nation is hardly conspicuous for its belief in 'fair play', if 'fair play' happens to be, or even seems to be, contrary to the nation's interests as the nation sees those interests. It is certainly no uncommon experience for leaders of states and diplomats to find their people willing to risk the utmost disaster rather than make a concession, especially a concession which they are forced to make by the long-hated 'other side'. This situation is unfortunately more likely to occur in a liberal democratic state, in which public opinion is more free to express itself, and opposition parties may try to use the issue as an instrument for stirring up bad public feeling against the government of the day.

Then, again, we have to admit the unfortunate fact that, as things are, institutions which intervene from the outside in a conflict between two or more states often do not have the physical power to implement their decisions and judgments, or to take the further consequences of those decisions and judgments. In the international system, as we have pointed out from time to time in this book, every state, or almost every state, is in the last resort responsible for its own security; if a state accepts and carries out a decision by an international court of law or political tribunal when it is in conflict with another state, and as a result of its security, its means of defending itself against attack, is reduced, it cannot always depend upon that court or tribunal to make up for the loss of security which it suffers: it would in fact be a rare situation if it could. This is a common position in the relations *inter se* of the greatest Powers and between them and lesser states. In the Suez crisis in 1956, for instance, the British and French governments considered that the continuance of President Nasser in office was a threat to their own political security and economic welfare. They might have submitted the legal issues in their case against Nasser's nationalization of the Suez Canal Company to the world court at The Hague; they did submit what they regarded as the Egyptian threat to their security in the Middle East to the UN Security Council, though not without reserving the right to act against Nasser by and for themselves. But could they depend upon either the International Court or the Security Council ensuring that their vital national interests in the area of the Suez Canal would not be damaged whichever way the verdict went? The British and French Ministers at the time thought not, and their conclusion sums up the whole problem of third-party intervention into the resolution of disputes in the international system.

An even clearer instance of this is the great East-West conflict over Germany and Berlin after 1945, which culminated in the Berlin crisis of 1958–1961, when the Soviet Union and the West stood at times almost on the edge of war with each other. Some of the issues involved in this conflict were referred to political tribunals—the Security Council, for example, was extensively drawn into the 1948–1949 phase of the Berlin problem—though there was no recourse to the world court at any time. The Western Powers argued that they had a perfectly valid legal right to have their forces in Berlin, rights of access to West Berlin from the Western zones of occupied Germany, and the freedom to form a West German state with its capital at Bonn after the four-Power negotiations to form an all-German state had failed. They knew, though they did not talk aloud about this, that any failure of Western Germany to enter the NATO camp would seriously jeopardize Western security. They knew, too, that any failure of the three Western Powers, Britain, France and the United States, to defend the *status quo* in Berlin would probably have deplorable effects on the morale of the West Germans, and this would again have an adverse effect on Western security. All this was at the same time, as the Western Powers saw it, not a matter which they could turn over to the United Nations, or 'world opinion', or the 'world community' to pronounce definitely upon, and this for the very simple reason that neither the United Nations, nor 'world opinion', nor the 'world community', could shield the Western Powers from the consequences in terms of their own security if the final decision were to go against those Powers. It was another dramatic example of the consequences in international politics of the divorce between the power to decide, and the capacity and readiness to tolerate the outcome of those decisions. 'He who protects Israel determines Israel's fate', the Israelis were in effect saying after their great victory in the Six Day War in 1967. But, with a suitable transposition of words, the same has been true for all states, at all times, in the international system.

Perhaps the most important conclusion we can draw from this analysis is that conflict in one kind of social situation is only very superficially similar to conflict in a different kind of social situation. And it is the difference in social situation which gives rise to differences in kinds of social conflict. A trade union in conflict with an employer over wages, for example, may seem at first sight to be in a similar position to that of a national state in conflict with another national state. Means of resolving conflicts between unions and employers may seem to be altogether relevant to, and useful in, the resolution of conflicts between states. But this is very far from the reality.

The truth is, as we have pointed out in this chapter, that a state's points of friction with another state cannot be understood or even considered outside of its points of friction with all other states, or indeed apart from the current conflicts between all other states themselves. We need to examine the whole network of relations between a state and its partners in the international system and between those partners themselves. It is not an exaggeration to say that the whole 'state of play' in the international system needs to be explained before we can explain why any two states or group of states happen to be in conflict with each other, although it goes without saying that the larger and more powerful the states in conflict are, the more is this likely to be true.

In the second place, when we come to the resolution of any international conflict and ask ourselves such questions as: will the passage of time alleviate or aggravate the conflict? what kind of third-party intervention to attempt a settlement are the conflicting parties likely to accept, if any? and so on, we have to review the total position of the states concerned in the international system. One kind of settlement might help in their settlement of similar conflicts with other states which they currently have on their agenda. At the same time, it might reduce the power of the two states to defend themselves, if the settlement finally breaks down and they see no option but to carry on the next stage of the argument by force. Conflicts between states, in other words, are a product of the entire international system in which the states live, and it is in terms of that system that the resolution of conflicts must be sought.

NOTES

1. This view is upheld by G. Schwarzenberger in his *Power Politics*, 3rd edition, pp. 259–60, and by H. Lauterpacht in his *The Function of Law in the International Community*, The Clarendon Press, Oxford, 1932.
2. See F. S. Northedge and N. Donelan, *International Disputes: The Political Aspects*, Europa for the David Davies Memorial Institute of International Studies, London, 1971, Part III.

Fifteen

The Political Kingdom

IN these last few pages it is proposed to do no more than single out some of the principal themes dealt with in this book, and, so to speak, to underline them, as though in the coda of a piece of music. We have throughout these chapters insisted upon the primacy of politics among the states of the world in the global system which they now form. The word 'primacy' is intended to refer to two things: the dependence, in the first place, of so many of our activities and so much of our experience as ordinary men and women on the state of the political relations between the largest political associations in which we live, that is, the nation-states of the world; and, secondly, the supreme intellectual and moral compulsion for the student extended to him by the high politics of states.

As to the first of these senses of primacy, it is not denied here that people deal with one another across national frontiers on many different planes and many different levels. They interact on the economic and commercial planes, as when a business organization in one country sells goods to a business organization in another country. They interact socially, as when a party of British school-children spend their holidays in France or Germany; and professionally, as when American doctors or lawyers meet their foreign colleagues in conferences in Tokyo or Moscow; and athletically, as when an Australian cricket team plays an English team at Lords or the Oval or a Chinese table-tennis group visits Pakistan; and so on indefinitely. The levels of these international relationships are also indefinite in number: a single person from Paris may go on holiday alone to Venice, or in an organized party or business or trade union delegation, or as an official representative from his or her government. The contention of this book, however, is that all this to-ing and fro-ing across the frontier on so many planes and at so many levels is wholly dependent on the

decisions of the world's governments; these may, in one instant,
encourage it, reward it, subsidize it, or, in another, limit it,
attach penalties to it, or stop it altogether. The more government
in all states has penetrated into private life in the twentieth
century, the more is this so. Before 1939 the Fascist states of
Europe did all they could (which was a great deal) to control
private relations between their own people and foreigners: since
1939 the increased number of Communist states have done the
same with equal or greater determination and efficiency. Moreover,
anyone today, who wishes to visit the United States, or any other
liberal democratic country, will soon realize that this control of
private international movement is by no means confined to
totalitarian states. It is certainly not confined, either, to the old,
unregenerate member-states of the international system.

We are not concerned with the question whether this close
political control of all international relations today is desirable
or politically healthy. More than once, since 1945, British politicians have professed to regret the passing away of the old days
before 1914 when the traveller could go to Victoria Station and
buy a ticket to anywhere without bothering about passports and
visas (except for the Ottoman Porte, which was in any case considered in Paris and London to be beyond the civilized pale). The
fact is, that the politicization of international life has proceeded
apace since 1914 and we have to take account of it. On the other
hand, there are surely some reasons for a liberal democrat to
rejoice at it. The politicization of all our lives in the last sixty
years has been partly due to the demand of the liberal democrat,
or perhaps rather the social democrat, for government intervention in the economic life of the nation in the interest of greater
social equality and social justice. If a state is genuinely a democratic state in the Western sense of the word (though that is a
very big 'if') it should welcome the politicization of international
life, as implying that international relations are under the control
of governments which are, hopefully, the mouthpieces and hired
men of their people. However, as we have already said, in laying
stress on the middle and late twentieth century's politicization of
international life we are calling attention to a fact rather than
expressing a preference.

But even if it were not a fact, and if it were the case that, across
frontiers if not behind them, non-governmental links between

people were usurping the functions of governments, as many modern writers now claim, we would still wish to emphasize the intellectual and moral primacy of international politics and recommend the subject for study. It is a truism which needs little or no elaboration, that since the beginning of man's civilized history the life of politics has cast its spell over him, whether as a practitioner in the dusty arena of public affairs, or as an observer and scholar in the library. Politics as a practical and academic vocation needs no apology. The nature and objects of political activity; the means and methods of political work; judgment on the exercise of political skill and all the arts of politics, and on the use of moral scruples and the practice of evil: all these political questions and many, many more have racked men's minds and delighted their imagination from Periclean Athens until today. Man is not only a political animal in finding the non-political life as deadening as dry land to a fish: but in that the full stretch of his intellectual powers is not reached until he contemplates the political kingdom.

Nor should we, as we have stated earlier in this book, be too concerned that the international political world is not the same as the intranational world of politics. We should not worry overmuch, either, about claims that politics without a single overarching structure of command above the political actors cannot be dignified with the name of a 'system'.[1] International politics are indeed politics without a central government, and that very fact makes those politics a distinct and unique form, demanding a unique intellectual effort of comprehension. But, as we have repeatedly stressed in this book, the interactions of the world's governments have all the attributes of political activity as we know it: the pursuit and exercise of power over men and women, the struggle to use power for the distribution among the world's peoples of the basic values of wealth, security, prestige or deference, and the perpetual argument between men and women of power, as to the better ordering of society and the better arrangement of relations between government and the governed.[2] It is sometimes said that what we call international politics is nothing other than the politics of survival, whereas domestic politics is debate about the 'good life'.[3] But that is far from the truth. What was the protracted and hideously dangerous Cold War between East and West about in the years after 1945 except whether Western or Communist conceptions of the *summum bonum* were preferable one to another? People in the West did not say 'better alive than dead', as though the issue was one of survival: they *did* say, or were alleged to say, or were urged to say 'better dead than Red', and similarly, with obvious changes, for the Communist world. In fact, one might go as far as to say, though our argument so far by no means rests on this, that the political life of nation-states within the international system has a stature as a subject of intellectual interest higher even than that of the domestic politics of any state: it is an exhibition of man at his worst, and, sometimes at his best. And, as it goes without saying, the proper study of mankind is man himself.

But this brings us back to our central concern with the inter-national political *system*. We do not need to repeat here what we have already said about the meaning of the word 'system' as used in this context, and about the nature and properties of that system. But it is important to bear in mind one point made earlier in this book about the international system, which requires the most careful thought. We have emphasized that the international system has, since the First World War, provoked in most people intense moral revulsion and a strong wish to see it either radically changed, or perhaps abolished and replaced with a more humane or more efficient system. We have given the United States and the Soviet Union as examples of Powers, which began their encounter with the international system during the First World War with instant, lock-stock-and-barrel rejection of the system and with plans to substitute another in its place.[4] We stressed that in the course of time the two super-Powers had both wended their way back into the international system, so that, at least to judge from their external behaviour and the public utterances of their leaders, neither seems any longer to entertain ambitions to change the system root and branch.

Some people, out of the immense number of those dissatisfied with the international system, may regret this departure from, and then return to, the system by these two Powers and wish that they had not been corrupted by the ways of this world and had persisted with the ideals of Woodrow Wilson, on one side, and of Lenin, on the other, though what kind of collision would have occurred between them, if they had, is hard to say. At any event, since 1945, and more particularly since about 1957, scholars in the field of international politics—or, to give them their current title,

'analysts'—have regarded as their main objective, not so much
understanding the international system and the ways of states,
but devising methods for improving what they consider to be a
most dangerous, out-moded and utterly immoral system for conducting human affairs. What has, since 1957 or thereabouts, been
called Behavioural Science is in fact a study of possible reforms in
a system which the Behaviouralists instinctively feel to be a worse
social system than any other. Those, such as the so-called 'tradi-
tionalist' or 'classical' students of the subject, who limit themselves
to trying to understand the international system as it is, tend to
be written off as incorrigibly conservative or complacent, or just
plain ignorant. One could, of course, point out that on one famous
previous occasion the wish for fundamental change in international relations, involving in that instance, too, the playing
down of the state and political and military power, badly led
Western Liberals astray in their dealings with totalitarian realists
of Left and Right, and that was in the period between the two
World Wars. 'Other people's illusions about power', said Hitler,
'were my great opportunity'. E. H. Carr's classic work, *The
Twenty Years' Crisis*, remains a well-known record of the price
that has been paid by liberal thinking about international relations.[5] But we need not assume that history will necessarily repeat
itself—it never does exactly—and bestow the same penalties on
wishful thinking. The more important question for us is whether
the international system of sovereign states is really as wicked, or
even as much in need of radical reform, as its critics say.

That the system is dangerous, especially in the present nuclear
age, is beyond question, and every ounce of advice or enlighten-
ment the governments can get from academic students of international relations they should make use of in their awesome task
of managing the affairs of touchy, selfish, irascible nations, like
monkeys playing with matches on a petrol dump. In fact, however, the world in the twentieth century, as we have stressed
before, has probably, on balance, muddled through with less war
than it actually deserved to have. Here you have a collection of
independent nation-states, armed to the teeth (and spending
more on arms with every year) with the most devilish weapons,
each considering itself to be the judge and jury in its own cause,
and with scarcely anyone—and, in the case of the super-Powers,
with no one—able and willing to stop them if they decide to fight

it out: and yet it must be said that all-out war between the different states is a relatively infrequent occurrence, in fact rather more infrequent in the 1970s than fighting between political factions *within* the frontiers of states.

But the plain fact, standing above all this, is that the people of the world could put an end to the international system tomorrow if they wanted to. It would be comparatively easy for envoys of the 140-odd states in the world to meet together at some spot, say, at United Nations headquarters in New York, and agree upon a constitution for a single world state. Many model constitutions for such a state have been proposed and are in fact in existence for the states to choose from.[6] Any such constitution would not rule out bloodshed and armed conflict. Crime would no doubt still persist, as would political unrest, and perhaps even civil war. But if the constitution was so framed and genuinely accepted, one assumes that there could hardly be a First or Second World War again.

The ordinary person in Western Europe or North America would no doubt say at this point that the Russians or the Chinese or the new Afro-Asian states would never agree. It is indeed, as likely as not, that they would never agree with our Western conception of a world state: nor perhaps could the British agree with the American conception, or the French with the Italian, much less with the Soviet, Chinese or Afro-Asian. Most people, when they think of a possible world state, think of a state something like their own state, with the same sort of political and social system, the same sort of laws, and so on. It is significant that the kind of reformed United Nations proposed in the Clark and Sohn study, to which we have just referred, is the sort of body most Americans would like to see: it probably would not attract the Chinese or the Russians. Would the Russians or the Chinese support the same sort of government, with the same sort of programme, policy and ideology as we in the West would? Would the Russians support the sort of world government the Chinese want, and *vice versa*? These questions answer themselves. It is not so much that the human race is shortsighted, selfish, blind, indoctrinated by its own governments, and so on: though all this makes the task of creating a single world political system all the more difficult. The fact is, that the human race's vision of the *summum bonum* is not single or coherent: every nation, every state, has its own *summum bonum.* It is easy for any one person to deny that another nation's social and political ideals are valid or even genuinely or freely held. But tell him that the ideals in which *he* has been reared are false gods, the poisonous fruits of ignorance and indoctrination, and his anger will soon rise.

For these reasons we must surely see our present international system, not as a driverless, high-powered vehicle speeding to its destruction, with ourselves, bound and powerless, inside, but rather as a guarantee and guardian of continued national freedom for each of us. When that national freedom, the liberty to lead our national lives as we think best, comes to seem valueless to most of us, most of the time, the road to a world state will be clear, But that day is far from being here yet. As things are, most of us, most of the time, want to have our cake and eat it: we want to remain British, American, French, Chinese, Russian, as the case may be, but at the same time we want these different nations to rub along with each other without friction or conflict, and certainly without war. When this occasionally fails to happen, we, or almost all of us, are quick to see the other fellow, or the other nation, as responsible for the trouble.

The present-day international system described in this book is, like Winston Churchill's democracy, the worst possible way of conducting human affairs—apart from all the others. It is one formula, not without faults, but perhaps with fewer faults than any alternative which the world could agree upon, for satisfying those two wants: local freedom and some minimum of order in the whole. The system does not exist only to keep our own nation secure and unsullied by foreign interference; neither does it exist merely to keep order between the different states. It seeks to combine the maximum of national freedom and the minimum of disorder in the whole. A better system, or a more efficient formula, for achieving these two purposes at the same time, than our present international political kingdom, has not yet been found.

NOTES

1. See above, p. 18.
2. See above, pp. 18–19.
3. See Martin Wight, 'Why there is no International Theory'; see earlier reference, above, p. 123, n. 14.

4. See above, pp. 29–30.
5. First published in 1939, Macmillan, London.
6. See, as one example, Grenville Clark and Louis B. Sohn, *World Peace through World Law*, Harvard University Press, Cambridge, Mass., 1958.

Bibliography

Books and articles on international politics past and present are infinite in number and diverse in quality. The following is intended to be no more than a list of some selected works for further reading.

R. Aron: *Paix et Guerre entre les Nations*, Calmann-Lévy, Paris, 1962; translated as *Peace and War*, Weidenfeld and Nicolson, London, 1966.

G. Barraclough: *Introduction to Contemporary History*, Watts, London, 1964.

A. B. Bozeman: *Culture and Politics in International History*, Princeton University Press, 1960.

A. Buchan: *War in Modern Society*, Watts, London, 1966.

H. Butterfield and M. Wight (eds.): *Diplomatic Investigations*, Allen and Unwin, London, 1966.

P. Calvocoressi: *World Politics since 1945*, Longmans, London, 2nd edition, 1971.

I. L. Claude: *Power and International Relations*, Random House, New York, 1962.

P. Dukes: *The Emergence of the Super-Powers*, Macmillan, London, 1970.

M. G. Forsyth and others (eds.): *The Theory of International Relations. Selected Texts*, Allen and Unwin, London, 1970.

J. Frankel: *International Politics*, Allen Lane, London, 1969.

J. Frankel: *Contemporary International Theory and the Behaviour of States*, O.U.P., London, 1973.

L. J. Halle: *The Nature of Power*, Hart-Davis, London, 1955.

F. H. Hartmann: *The Relations of Nations*, Macmillan, New York, 4th edition, 1973.

J. H. Herz: *International Politics in the Atomic Age*, Columbia University Press, New York, 1959.

F. H. Hinsley: *Power and the Pursuit of Peace*, C.U.P., 1963.

F. H. Hinsley: *Sovereignty*, Watts, London, 1966.

K. J. Holsti: *International Politics*, Prentice-Hall, Englewood Cliffs, N.J., 1967, 2nd edition, 1972.

K. Knorr and J. N. Rosenau (eds.): *Contending Approaches to International Politics*, Princeton University Press, 1969.

W. W. Kulski: *International Politics in a Revolutionary Age*, Lippincott, New York, 2nd edition, 1968.

J. Larus (ed.): *From Collective Security to Preventive Diplomacy*, John Wiley, New York, 1965.

D. W. McLellan, W. Olson and A. Sondermann: *Theory and Practice in International Relations*, Prentice-Hall, Englewood Cliffs, New Jersey, 3rd edition, 1970.

C. A. W. Manning: *The Nature of International Society*, Bell for The London School of Economics, London, 1962.

C. H. Meinecke: *Machiavellism*, tr. by Douglas Scott, Routledge and Kegan Paul, London, 1957.

H. J. Morgenthau: *Politics Among Nations*, Knopf, New York, 6th edition, 1972.

R. Niebuhr: *Nations and Empires*, Faber, London, 1960.

F. S. Northedge and M. J. Grieve: *A Hundred Years of International Relations*, Duckworth, London, 1971.

F. S. Northedge (ed.): *The Use of Force in International Relations*, Faber, London, 1974.

R. L. Pfaltzgraff: *Politics and the International System*, Lippincott, Philadelphia, 2nd edition, 1972.

R. Purnell: *The Society of States*, Weidenfeld and Nicolson, London, 1973.

P. A. Reynolds: *An Introduction to International Relations*, Longman, London, 1971.

C. L. Robertson: *International Politics since World War II*, John Wiley, New York, 2nd edition, 1975.

J. N. Rosenau (ed.) *International Politics and Foreign Policy*, Free Press, New York, 1969.

J. N. Rosenau and others (eds.): *The Analysis of International Politics*, Collier-Macmillan, New York, 1972.

A. M. Scott: *The Revolution in Statecraft*, Random House, New York, 1965.

L. L. Snyder (ed.): *The Imperialism Reader*, Port Washington, New York, 1973.

J. W. Spanier: *World Politics in an Age of Revolution*, Pall Mall Press, London, 1967.
D. Vital: *The Inequality of States*, The Clarendon Press, Oxford, 1967.
K. N. Waltz: *Man, the State and War*, Columbia University Press, New York, 1959.
A. Wolfers: *Discord and Collaboration*, Johns Hopkins Press, Baltimore, 1962.

Index

(Entries for 'international system' and 'state' are not included in this Index since these words appear on almost every page of this book.)

Abyssinia, *see* Ethiopia
Acton, Lord, 68, 69
Adenauer, K., 162
Admiralty, 158
Adowa, 90
Aegean Sea, 160
Africa, 76, 77, 78, 83, 90, 104, 126, 134, 148, 167, 242
Africa, East, 148
Africa, North, 218
Aggression, 43, 56, 70, 98, 122
Albania, 174, 235, 257
Algeçiras conference, 77
Algeria, 230
Amau Declaration, 96
America, Latin, 75, 157, 160, 259
America, North, 155, 213
Amin, I., 261
Anarchy, international, 85
Anatolia, 76
Angell, N., 87
Anglo-Iranian Oil Company, 218
Angola, 247
Apartheid, 72
Arab-Israeli conflict, 128, 195
Arab states, 75, 196, 197, 244
Arbitration, 45, 84
Aristotle, 178, 203
Armageddon, 85, 128, 298
Armaments, 25, 28, 98, 128, 197
Arms control (and disarmament), 104, 171
Arms race, 25
Arnold, M., 87
Aron, R., 205–6, 289, 298
Arthasastra, 43, 44, 49
Ashur, 38, 50
Asia, 76, 77, 78, 83, 90, 103, 104, 126, 161, 162, 242
Asia, Central, 161
Asia, East, 83, 95, 96, 97, 163
Asia, South East, 127, 160, 185
Assyria, 39, 51
Aswan Dam, 241
Athens, 45, 46, 47
Atlantic Charter, 173, 297
Atlantic Ocean, 88, 193
Augustine, St., 37
Augustus Caesar, 48, 212
Austin, J., 118
Austria, 46, 47, 55, 83, 91, 92, 168, 233, 282, 287

Austria-Hungary, 83, 86, 88, 89, 90, 287
Axis Powers, 293

Bagehot, W., 116, 186
Baghdad, 83
Balfour Declaration, 158, 176
Balkans, 88, 90, 287
Baltic Sea, 88
Bandung conference, 104
Belgium, 93, 155, 160, 170, 203
Bentham, J., 14, 32
Bentley, A. F., 113, 117
Berlin, 85, 92, 314
Berlin Congress, 168
Berlin crisis (1958–1961), 296, 305, 314
Berlin Wall, 305
Berlin, West, 193, 305, 314
Bevin, E., 119
Bismarck, O., 28, 76, 83, 88, 285, 287
Black Sea, 88, 160
Blitzkrieg, 291
Blockade, 158, 243–4, 245
Blum, L., 93
Bodin, J., 56
Bolsheviks, 22, 29, 85, 220
Bolshevism, 92
Borkenau, F., 72, 73
Boxer Rebellion, 77
Boycott, 242, 243
Bozeman, A. B., 35, 44, 49, 65
Brest-Litovsk, 30, 85
Brezhnev, L., 251, 270
Brezhnev Doctrine, 217
Briand, A., 251
Brierly, J. L., 113, 132
Bright, J., 204, 209
Britain: in 1939, 189, 287; and Albania, 234; and Berlin, 315; and China, 41, 75; and Commonwealth, 255; and Communist world, 243; and Cyprus, 266, 270; decline in power, 109; and disarmament, 271; and Egypt, 305; and Europe, 138, 193; in First World War, 90, 91, 279; and France, 76, 77, 152, 169, 195, 239, 268, 269; and Germany, 92, 93, 156, 244, 268, 286, 288; government in, 124; as 'have' Power, 170; and Iceland, 121; as integrated state, 161; interests of,

Britain, cont.
166, 262; and Japan, 96, 97, 159,
163; and League of Nations, 101;
Left wing in, 72; as maritime
Power, 155, 158; at Munich conference, 168, 180; and New World,
177; and New Zealand, 127; in
nineteenth century, 83, 86, 87, 88,
258; and nuclear weapons, 292;
political parties in, 185–6; radical
opinion in, 77; and Rhodesia, 245;
and Russia, 30, 94; social cohesion
in, 142; and South Africa, 240;
sovereignty in, 143; as unitary
state, 172; and UN, 73, 165, 246;
and US, 74, 99, 206; and war, 282
Brooke, R., 81, 106
Burke, E., 142, 215
Butterfield, Sir H., 132
Byzantium, 46, 49

Cambodia, 191
Campaign for Nuclear Disarmament,
28, 271
Canada, 214, 255
Canning, G., 75, 227
Capitalism, 97, 204, 205, 206, 222
Caporetto, 83
Caribbean Sea, 160, 211
Carr, E. H., 91, 106, 176, 321
Castlereagh, Lord, 28
Chamberlain, Sir A., 201
Chamberlain, N., 74, 87, 111, 279
Charlemagne, 37, 49
Chauvinism, 285
Chiang Kai-shek, 80
China: ancient, 39, 40; Communism
in, 149, 185; and Europe, 77; and
Japan, 75, 95, 96, 159, 163; and
India, 230; as integrated state, 161;
and international system, 41, 42;
and Nine-Power treaty, 232; recog-
nition of, 157; and Russia, 174, 243;
status as Power, 165, 169; and
UN, 73; and US, 102, 103, 164,
211; 'volunteers', 238; and West,
222, 307; Westernization of, 221
China, Communist, 17, 42, 231, 232,
240, 241, 242, 243, 257, 266, 270, 283,
292, 306
Christian Democrats, 162
Christianity, 58
Churchill, Sir W., 73, 91, 111, 217,
226, 230, 297, 323
Civilization, Western, 13, 57
Clausewitz, C. von, 85, 273, 278, 293,
294
Cobden, R., 204, 209
Collective defence, 180, 245, 296
Collective security, 180, 245

Colony, colonies, 71, 90, 143, 170,
204, 206, 210, 211
Colonialism, 222, 224
Commission of Human Rights,
European, 145
Commonwealth, 79, 255
Communism, 20, 103, 126, 149, 157,
185, 273
Communism, Soviet, 87
Confederation, 208
Conflict, passim, esp. 299–316
Conflict resolution, 299–316
Confucius, 39
Congress system, 85
Conscription, 289, 292
Consensus, 22, 116, 123, 183, 192,
200, 296
Consensus-formation, 201
Conservation, 13
Conservatives, British, 28, 185, 240
Constantinople, 37, 49, 60, 77, 83,
158, 212
Corn Laws, 87
Counter-Reformation, 110
Crisis management, 295
Cuba, 211, 242, 243, 244
Cuba missiles crisis, 160, 244, 296
Curzon, Lord, 213, 216, 218, 219,
221, 224, 251
Cyprus, 266, 270, 284
Czechoslovakia, 70, 74, 155, 180, 238
279

Darwin, C., 272
Dawes Plan, 93, 240
Decolonization, 202, 223
Defence, 255, 271
De Gaulle, C., 64, 104, 138, 155, 167,
188, 239, 254, 257, 269
Degras, J., 65
De Jouvenel, B., 117–22
Delian League, 46
De Missy, J. R., 60
Democracy, 72, 152, 157, 184, 289,
323
Denmark, 83, 282
Détente, 104, 169, 252, 256, 266, 268,
296, 297, 306, 313
Deutsch, K. W., 127, 133, 255–6,
259, 275
Diplomacy: British, 183, 251; of
détente, 296; European, 152; inter-
war, 290; language of, 154, 231,
257; Renaissance, 53; secret, 28;
for settlement of conflicts, 273–4,
304; and state system, 15; and
Strategic Studies, 295; Theodore
Roosevelt's, 227; world-wide, 74
Diplomacy, mediaeval, 50
Diplomatic immunity, 45, 53

Diplomatic rupture, 230–1
Disarmament, *see* arms control
Drang nach Osten, 83
Dual Alliance, 89, 287–8
Dubois, P., 63
Dulles, J. F., 103, 126, 150, 183

Ecuador, 255
Eden, Sir A. (Earl of Avon), 119, 167,
    183
Edward VIII, 130
Egypt, 76, 78, 160, 195, 196, 221, 222,
    241, 270, 305
Eisenhower, D., 78
Eisenstadt, S. N., 36
Embargo, 240, 242–3, 245
Empire, 34, 36, 38, 46, 207, 209, 210,
    211, 213, 214; Assyrian, 35, 37, 38,
    39; Athenian, 46; British, 89, 158,
    202, 213, 214; Byzantine, 47, 49, 51;
    Chinese, 39–42, 49; Egyptian, 38,
    39; German, 86; Habsburg, 69, 86,
    88; Hohenzollern, 69, 202; Holy
    Roman, 37, 49, 50, 212; Japanese,
    202; Mogul, 43; Ottoman, 69, 75,
    220; Persian, 38, 39; Roman, 15,
    36, 37, 47, 48, 49, 51, 95, 124, 131,
    212, 213; Romanov, 69, 86;
    Spanish, 207
England, 28, 55, 81, 86, 87
Entente, 92, 178
Entente Cordiale, 76, 155, 195, 268,
    269
Entente Powers, 91
Environment, 13, 193
Equilibrium, 43, 89, 90, 91, 114, 116,
    257, 266, 273, 285
Espionage, 178
Ethics, 25
Ethiopia, 76, 77, 90, 100, 170, 234, 245
Euro-Asia, 83, 160
Europe: before 1914, 206; and Britain,
    159, 193; as centre of international
    system, 73, 74, 78, 82, 90; Chris-
    tian, 61, 63; cohesion of, 76; Cold
    War in, 104; and Far East, 97; and
    France, 155; and Germany, 162;
    and Hitler, 287; industrial revolu-
    tion in, 86, 87; and Marshall Plan,
    240; mediaeval, 49, 50, 53, 59;
    modern, 64; nationalism in, 68; and
    New World, 177; nineteenth cen-
    tury, 71, 83, 84, 107; peace in, 92;
    and Russia, 161; and total war, 290;
    and Turkey, 60, 158; united, 55,
    169; war in, 256
Europe, Concert of, 76, 84
Europe, Eastern, 70, 83, 92–4, 103,
    111, 157, 159, 160, 162, 168, 173–4,
    212, 215, 217

Europe, South East, 160, 240
Europe, Western, 105, 138, 156, 162
European Community, 74, 163, 200,
    274
European Defence Community, 150
European Economic Community, 28,
    172, 185–6, 241

Far East, 95, 97, 101, 155, 158
Fascism, 97, 205, 231, 259
Fashoda, 76, 90
Federal German Republic, 172, 180,
    230, 243, 257, 268, 269, 283, 315
Federation, 105, 172, 208, 214
Fénelon, F., 60, 68, 152
Fifth Column, 238, 249
Fifth Republic, 64
Filmer, Sir R., 122
Fiume, 85
Florence, 53
Force, 26
Ford, G., 191
Foreign Office, 152, 158, 183, 199
Formosa, 96
Fox, W. T. R., 164
France: in 1918, 174; and Berlin, 315;
    and Communist states, 243; de
    Gaulle in, 104, 138, 188; and
    Egypt, 305; and Europe, 159, 172;
    and force, 283; foreign policy, 32;
    and Germany, 77, 83, 91, 93, 156,
    233, 257, 268, 286; imperialism of,
    170, 203; as integrated state, 161;
    at Munich conference, 168, 180;
    and League of Nations, 100, 101;
    outlook of, 155; revolution in, 185;
    in Roman Empire, 162; and
    Rumania, 19; in Second World
    War, 230, 279, 291; in sixteenth
    century, 55; and UN, 73, 165, 235;
    and US, 150, 269; war record, 282;
    and Washington conference, 24
Franco, F., 231, 249
Franco-Russian alliance, 89, 287–8
Free trade, 87, 101
Frontiers, 23, 25, 70, 90, 100, 134,
    135, 142, 143, 145, 149, 158, 159,
    185, 211, 218
Fulbright, W., 242

Geneva, 101
Geopolitics, 212
George, D. L., 240
Germans, 69, 83, 91
Germany: between wars, 93, 94, 98,
    101, 286; blockade of, 245; and
    Britain, 92, 156, 169, 206, 268, 288;
    colonies, 220; divided, 305, 314;
    and Entente, 155; in Europe, 90; in
    First World War, 91, 289, 290; and

Germany, cont.
  imperialism, 207, 211, 214; and
  Italy, 99; and Japan, 96, 97, 99;
  and League of Nations, 164, 179; as
  marginal state, 161–2; Morgenthau
  plan for, 152; at Munich con-
  ference, 168; nationalism in, 285;
  Nazism in, 287; in nineteenth cen-
  tury, 86, 88; reunification, 274;
  Rhineland, 100; and Russia, 83;
  unconditional surrender of, 125;
  unification, 89; war record, 282;
  Weimar, 205, 240
German Democratic Republic, 232
Germany, East, 230
Germany, Nazi, 17, 30, 94, 96, 111,
  230, 242, 293
Gibraltar, 147
Giscard D'Estaing, V., 138
Gladstone, W. E., 214
Goa, 147
Gold Standard, 87, 97
Government, 22, 24, 51, 53–6, 63,
  114–17, 120, 123–4, 140, 145, 146,
  152, 184, 192, 198, 200, 318
Graduated deterrence, 294
Greater East Asia Co-prosperity
  Sphere, 95, 96, 163
Greaves, H. R. G., 142, 145
Greece, 37, 44–7, 51, 62, 84, 170,
  269–70, 284, 291
Greeks, 45, 47
Grey, Sir E., 82
Grotius, H., 60, 78
Guarantees, 159, 196, 197
Guerrillas, 17, 135, 140, 238
Guinea, 167
Gunboat diplomacy, 137, 248

Hallstein Doctrine, 230
Hamilton, A., 208
Hassall, C., 81
Haushofer, H., 212
Hayes, C. J., 50
Heath, E., 185–6, 251
Heraclitus, 110, 259
Herz, J., 68, 106, 153
Hinsley, F. H., 59, 60, 62, 63, 65, 106
Hiroshima, 146
Hitler, A.: Chancellor of Reich, 286,
  287; and economic recovery, 99;
  and European unity, 37, 64; and
  fifth column, 238; and France, 93;
  and Italy, 83; and Lebensraum, 162;
  Marxist-Leninist view of, 205;
  military strategy of, 291; at Munich
  conference, 179–80; and pro-
  paganda, 237; and rationality, 227;
  and war, 95; and 'war of nerves',
  236

Hobbes, T., 127, 129, 208, 253, 284,
  298
Hobson, J. A., 204
Holsti, K. J., 36
Holy Alliance, 67
Hsü, I. C. Y., 41–2, 52, 80
Hungary, 97
Huns, 40

Iceland, 121, 194
Idealism, 189, 219
Ideology, 101, 173, 189, 199, 258, 263,
  264–5
Imperialism, 63, 95, 161, 202–24
Imperialism, Western, 77
India Office, 158
Indo-China, 283
Indonesia, 104, 179, 203, 261
Industrialism, 261
Informal penetration, 45, 82
Insecurity community, 129
Integration, 105, 109, 138, 140, 172,
  185
Interest, national: in Arab-Israeli
  conflict, 196; of China, 42; classification of, 198–9; in détente, 104;
  and foreign aid, 242; and inter-
  national system, 28, 55; legal pro-
  tection of, 314; H. J. Morgenthau
  on, 188–9; as motive of foreign
  policy, 191–2; and national consensus, 119, 201; and national
  policy, 50, 115; and private interests,
  210, 271; and Third World, 105; in
  trade depression, 98; of UN members, 71; Woodrow Wilson on, 54
Interests, 192–201, 210, 225, 262, 264,
  269, 270
International business, 139, 141
International Chamber of Commerce,
  17
International Confederation of Free
  Trade Unions, 17
International Co-operative Alliance,
  17
International Court of Justice, 199,
  234, 308, 310, 312, 314
International Labour Organization,
  164
International Monetary Fund, 239
Iraq, 17, 38, 203, 218
Iraq Petroleum Company, 218
Ireland, 86
Ireland, Northern, 142
Irish Republican Army, 17
Isolation, 157
Israel, 148, 149, 195, 196, 232, 244,
  284, 313, 315
Italy: in 1930s, 97, 98, 285; and
  Abyssinia, 90; colonialism of, 207;

Italy, cont.
  and Eastern Europe, 93; and empire,
  214; in First World War, 76, 91; and
  Germany, 92; as 'have-not' state,
  170; and League of Nations, 99,
  179, 245, 246; at Munich conference, 168, 180; Renaissance, 36, 37,
  53; in Roman Empire, 15; in
  Triple Alliance, 89; war record,
  282; at Washington conference, 96
Ius gentium, 15, 48
Japan: and Britain, 89, 97; and China,
  159, 242; and economic recovery,
  98; her Greater East Asia Co-
  prosperity Sphere, 95–6; as 'have-
  not' state, 170; imperialism of, 207,
  214; enters international system, 75;
  and League of Nations, 99; as
  marginal state, 161, 163–4; as
  maritime Power, 155; power status
  of, 168–9, 282; and Russia, 83, 90;
  and UN, 165, 179; Westernization
  of, 221
Jingoism, 285
Jordan, 160

Kant, I., 130
Kaplan, M., 18, 19, 31
Kashmir, 203
Kautilya, 43, 44, 49, 150
Kedourie, E., 69, 80
Kennan, G., 137
Kennedy, J. F., 103, 244, 260
Keynes, J. M., 81, 87, 99
Khrushchev, N., 58, 188, 270, 298,
  305
Kissinger, H., 33
Korea, 12, 283
Korea, North, 174, 191
Korea, South, 122
Kurds, 17
Kuwait, 203, 262

Labour Movement, British, 28
Labour party, British, 28, 180, 181,
  185, 186
Laski, H. J., 309
Lasswell, H. D., 19, 33, 115
Latin American Solidarity Organiza-
  tion, 30
Lausanne, Treaty of, 75, 305
Law, 25, 44, 112, 120, 121, 122, 124,
  125, 143, 144, 226, 309
Law, international, 15, 20, 27, 60, 61,
  78, 79, 113, 126, 143, 226, 247,
  276–7, 308, 310–11
Law, municipal, 113, 226
Law, rule of, 221
Lawrence, D. H., 81
League of Arab States, 138

League of Nations: and Austria, 233;
  and British radical opinion, 28;
  Council, 164; idealism of, 181; and
  liberalism, 258; mandates, 220; and
  non-recognition, 232; and rule of
  law, 221; Russia in, 30; sanctions,
  77, 245–6; and UN, 32; weakness
  of, 99–101; withdrawals from, 179;
  Woodrow Wilson's ideas on, 159
League of Nations Covenant, 100,
  101, 159, 220, 245
Lebensraum, 162
Lend-Lease, 242
Lenin, V. I., 22, 29, 30, 83, 85, 204,
  205, 320
Liberalism, 16, 297
Liberia, 148, 234
Lincoln, A., 151, 153, 157
Lindsay, A. D., 80
Linkage politics, 21, 22
Litvinov, M., 279
Livy, 213
Locarno conference, 93, 162
Locke, J., 122
Loewe, M., 40
London, 88, 152, 155
Low Countries, 160

Macartney, Lord, 40
Macchiavelli, N., 25, 43, 56, 146
Mackinder, Sir H., 160
Macmillan, H., 188, 244
Mahan, A. T., 212, 224
Malawi, 155
Malaysia, 203, 261
Manchukuo, 96, 232
Manchuria, 90, 95, 96, 163, 232
Manning, C. A. W., 153
Marshall Plan, 240, 242
Martin, W. A. P., 78–9
Marx, K., 68, 205
Marxism, 29, 258
Mattingly, G., 65
Mazzini, G., 67
Mediterranean Sea, 48, 88, 155, 270
Meinecke, F., 65
Metternich, Prince, 29
Middle Ages, 50, 51, 54, 59, 68
Middle East, 37, 44, 103, 128, 136,
  140, 160, 185, 195, 218, 270
Milan, 53
Militarism, 84, 87
Mill, J. S., 69, 70, 80
Missiles, 291
Mitrany, D., 32
Mongols, 40
Monroe Doctrine, 215, 216
Montague, E., 158
Morgenthau, H. J., 57, 126, 132, 188,
  189, 273

Morocco, 76, 90, 195, 196
Moscow, 37, 55, 78, 270
Mosul, 38
Mozambique, 247
Munich conference (1938), 168, 180
Mussolini, B., 76, 77, 83, 92, 94, 227, 236, 286

Nagas, 17
Namibia, 234
Naples, 53
Napoleon I, 60, 63, 69, 84, 88, 90, 152, 212, 285
Napoleon III, 84, 85
Nasser, G. A., 232, 234, 242, 270, 305, 314
Nation, 14, 15, 67, 68, 70, 72, 73, 152, 209, 214, 221
National Home for Jews, 158
Nationalism, 63, 67, 70, 72, 73, 80, 98, 172, 206, 207, 208
Nationality, 67, 68, 69, 73, 80
National Liberation Front (Vietnamese), 17
National self-determination, 15, 69, 70, 71, 188, 203, 206, 207, 221
Nazis, 93, 205, 268
Nazism, 97, 205, 259
Nazi-Soviet Pact, 94, 96, 173, 267
Near East, 37, 44
Nehru, J., 222, 230
Neo-colonialism, 218
Neo-functionalism, 16
Nepal, 170
Neumann, F., 205
Neutralism, 230
Neutrality, 43, 89, 230, 254, 279
New Deal, 98
New Zealand, 127
Nixon, R. M., 103, 164, 191, 251
Nkrumah, K., 218
Non-alignment, 31-2, 104
Non-governmental organizations, 16
North Atlantic alliance, 185
North Atlantic Treaty, 31
North Atlantic Treaty Organization (NATO), 69, 74, 104, 138, 181, 242, 297, 315
North Pole, 160
Northrop, F. S. C., 263, 275
Nuclear energy, 12
Nuclear weapons, 12, 13, 105, 270, 291-6

Oakeshott, M., 65, 133
Oder-Neisse line, 232
Oil, 262
Optional Clause, 234, 309, 310
Order, 44, 99, 100, 101, 102, 124, 198
Order, international, 26, 27, 34, 196

Organization, international, 82, 84, 99, 100, 101, 135, 139, 141, 145, 164, 179, 232, 241
Orwell, G., 55
Ostpolitik, 162, 230, 232
Overpopulation, 13

Pacific Ocean, 211
Pact of Steel, 83
Padmore, G., 153
Pakistan, 203, 241, 248, 283
Palestine, 148, 158
Panch-Shila, 104
Papacy, 50, 53
Paris, 155
Paris Peace Conference, 85, 96, 163, 168
Peace: British attitudes to, 159; and business class, 87-8; in Kautilya, 43; and League of Nations, 99-100; mobilization for, 82; as motive of policy, 189; in nineteenth century, 81, 84, 86, 90; perpetual, 259, 303; and security communities, 127; between wars, 91-2, 101
Peaceful change, 159
Peaceful co-existence, 58, 102, 273, 296
Peking, 41
Peking, Treaty of, 41
Peloponnesian League, 45, 46
Penn, W., 60
Permanent Court of International Justice, 233, 308, 310
Pershing, General J. J., 91
Perry, Commodore M. C., 75, 163
Persia, 51
Persian Gulf, 160
Persuasion, mass, 82, 235, 238
Peter the Great, 161
Philippines, 203, 211
Philoteus, 212
Poland, 68, 149, 160, 189, 232, 279, 282
Policy, foreign: changes in, 173; continuity in, 186, 225; as conversation, 31; democratization of, 82; dilemmas of, 273; domestic aspects of, 118; environment of, 139; freedom of choice in, 190; issues in, 27; British Labour party's, 28; motives of, 147; and national interest, 119, 192; objects of, 152, 184; and sovereignty, 140; Soviet, 103; in Third World, 104-5, 171-2; US, 150
Polish Corridor, 92
Politics, 18, 19, 21, 56, 59, 101, 113, 115, 127, 135, 295, 317-23
Politics, domestic, 21, 22, 72, 115, 116, 117, 180, 290, 320

Politics, international: altruism in, 219; change in, 109, 111; and domestic politics, 21–2, 117, 118; Europe as centre of, 82; Far Eastern sector of, 96, 97; Indian, 43, 44; issues in, 188; language of, 180; meaning, 16, 18–19; modern, 59, 62; and non-governmental bodies, 139; order in, 26; and political obligation, 124; as 'power politics', 127, 131; pressures in, 229; primacy of, 319; process of, 110, 114, 119; rules of, 25, 112, 116; and sovereignty, 28; stability of, 66; study of, 81; system of, 23, 27; and territory, 150; and types of states, 154

Pollution, 150
Polycentrism, 62, 104
Pompidou, G., 138, 251
Pope, the, 64
Portugal, 215
Potsdam conference, 119, 292
Power, political, 19–21, 43, 59, 62, 88, 89, 115, 120, 121, 124, 126, 164, 166, 167, 169, 191, 319
Power, balance of: and British Labour party, 28, 185; British policy of, 88, 92; in Europe, 96, 100; impact of Germany on, 89–90; instability of, 285; Japan in, 75; and League of Nations, 101; and maritime Powers, 158; modern meaning of, 60; as national interest, 198; revulsion against, 27, 85; Stalin's practice of, 30; and US, 83, 99; as war aim, 277; between two wars, 93–4, 97
Power politics, 27, 44, 126–31
Pressures, 228–49
Propaganda, 85, 100, 219, 236–8, 302
Protectorate, 216, 219
Prussia, 46, 47, 83, 168, 282
Psychology, 187, 209, 225, 264, 300

Quadruple Alliance, 85

Race, 78
Radio Free Europe, 236
Raison d'état, 51, 55–9, 62, 64, 65, 80, 191, 267
Rapallo, 93, 162, 240
Rationality, 24, 25
Rationalization, 181, 182
Raw materials, 160
Rearmament, 98
Recognition, 157, 167, 196, 197, 232
Red Guards, 17
Reformation, 110
Renaissance, 54, 55

Reprisals, 247
Retorsions, 247
Revolution, French, 15, 68, 69, 84, 185, 271
Revolution, industrial, 86, 90
Revolution, Russian, 82, 83, 271, 279
Rhineland, 100
Rhodesia, 142, 231, 232, 245, 246, 247
Ribbentrop, J., 267
Risorgimento, 285
Roman Church, 51
Roman Republic, 48
Rome, 15, 37, 48, 49, 50, 53, 54, 213
Roosevelt Corollary, 217
Roosevelt, F. D., 80, 98, 99, 111, 152, 230, 236, 244, 297
Roosevelt, T., 217, 227
Rostovtsev, M., 37, 38, 39
Rousseau, J. J., 123
Ruhr, 93, 156
Rumania, 19, 75
Russia, Soviet, see Soviet Union
Russia, Tzarist, 75, 83, 86, 88, 89, 90, 91, 158, 161, 163, 168, 205, 212, 221, 282, 287, 289

Sabah, 203
Sadat, A., 241
Sanctions, 112, 120, 125, 126
Sanctions, international, 77, 244–7
San Francisco, 70
Sardinia, 282
Saudi Arabia, 262
Schlieffen plan, 289
Schuman plan, 156, 189, 190
Schwarzenberger, G., 132, 164, 316
Scotland, 142
Scott, A., 52, 106, 249
Scott, J. B., 65
Security, 151, 159, 185, 197, 198, 244, 297, 314, 315
Security community, 127, 128, 254–7, 264, 284
Seeley, Sir J. R., 177
Serbia, 287
Sèvres, Treaty of, 77
Shantung, 96
Shaw, G. B., 81
Sidgwick, H., 131
Silesia, 92
Simmel, G., 32
Singapore, 100
Sino-Soviet dispute, 79, 243
Slavophils, 161
Slavs, 90
Smith, A., 209
Social Democrats, 162
Socialism, 73, 92
Soekarno, Dr., 203, 222, 261
Sorokin, P. A., 281

South Africa, 72, 179, 193, 234, 240, 247, 257
South-West Africa, 234, and see Namibia
Sovereignty, 20, 28, 41, 56, 93, 104, 105, 136, 138, 140, 141–4, 217, 310, 311
Soviet Communist Party, 54
Soviet Union: and Berlin crisis, 314; and Britain, 240; centre of world Communism, 55; Neville Chamberlain on, 74, 111; and China, 306; Communism in, 149; conservatism of, 102–3; and Cuba, 244; and deterrence, 278; and EEC, 274; and Egypt, 241; embargoes on trade with, 243; and Eastern Europe, 157, 163, 174, 217; expansion of, 212; foreign policy of, 185; and Germany, 94, 305; and Hitler, 291; and imperialism, 222; and international system, 28, 29–30, 320; isolation of, 257; and Japan, 96; and Khrushchev, 58; and League of Nations, 99, 164; as marginal state, 161, 162; and Poland, 68; as pseudo-federal state, 172; and Rumania, 19; in Second World War, 293; Stalin on, 54; status as Power, 168; and UN, 73, 165, 235; and US, 12, 136, 160, 169, 231–2, 248, 266, 270, 283, 295, 297, 306, 307, 313
Spain, 55, 109, 147, 168, 206, 207, 215, 231, 282
Spanish civil war, 55
Sparta, 45, 46, 47, 208
Spengler, O., 202
Sphere of Influence, 216, 217, 219
Sphere of Interest, 217–18, 219
Stalin, J., 30, 37, 54, 64, 70, 80, 82, 93, 94, 103, 161, 173, 212, 217, 267, 279
Strachey, J., 97
Straits, Dardanelles, 158, 160
Strategic Studies, 294–5
Stresa conference, 76, 77
Stresemann, G., 251
Submarines, 90
Subversion, 100
Suez, 185
Suez Canal, 158, 166, 306, 314
Suez Canal Company, 234, 305, 314
Suez Canal zone, 270
Suez crisis (1956), 137, 183, 242, 248, 314
Super-Powers, 11, 12, 28, 164, 165, 166, 215, 248, 268, 270, 295, 296, 297
Supranationalism, 138
Sweden, 203, 282

System (not international), 14, 15, 23–31

Tanaka Memorial, 96
Tanzania, 261
Tartars, 40
Technology, 58, 259, 270
Tension, 74, 83, 90, 155, 197, 258, 265, 267, 268, 271, 274, 275, 304
Territory, 23, 41, 143, 144, 147, 148, 149, 152, 157, 165, 198
Thailand, 160, 255
Thant, U, 230
Third International, 55
Third Rome, 37, 212
Third World, 45, 78, 104
Thucydides, 45, 131, 208
Tibet, 185
Tientsin, Treaty of, 41
Tokyo, 96, 97
Touré, S., 167
Toynbee, A. J., 168, 184, 202
Trade, 87, 150, 156, 157, 160, 171, 197, 210, 223, 239, 244, 246, 258
Triple Alliance, 89
Trotsky, L., 30, 85, 161
Truman, D. B., 114, 117
Truman Doctrine, 270
Tuchman, B., 82
Tunisia, 76
Turkey, 75, 77, 88, 158, 170, 221, 244, 269–70, 282, 284, 305
Twenty-One Demands, 95, 96
Two-Power standard, 88
Tyrol, South, 83, 92

Uganda, 261
Unconditional Surrender, 125, 293
Unemployment, 97, 98, 280
United Nations: and African states, 231; and China, 42, 75; and developing states, 170–1; and dispute settlement, 307; and expansion of states, 215; and force, 248; and foreign aid, 220; as fuse-box, 233; and Germany, 125; idealism of, 181; influence of, 137; as international organization, 138; and Israel, 232; and League of Nations, 32; members of, 70, 71, 73; and middle-rank states, 165; as national interest, 196; peacekeeping by, 235; resolutions of, 72; and Rule of Law, 221; and Western Powers, 315; withdrawal from, 179
United Nations Charter, 15, 23–4, 31, 32, 70, 121, 122, 123, 164, 165, 173, 220, 221, 235, 244, 245, 307
United Nations General Assembly, 70, 248, 260, 310

United Nations Secretary-General, 312
United Nations Security Council, 73, 74, 121, 122, 123, 164–5, 244, 245, 248, 307, 310, 314
United States: and Berlin, 315; and Britain, 88, 89, 97, 156–8, 168, 188, 206, 242, 255; and Canada, 255; and Caribbean, 160; and China, 103, 159, 164, 231–2, 243, 266, 306; and Cuba, 211; and Eastern Europe, 173–4; and Eastern Mediterranean, 270; and EEC, 274; and Europe, 83, 93; federation, 124, 172; in First World War, 91, 101, 288; and France, 19, 269; and ICJ, 235; immigration into, 149; and international system, 28, 29, 74, 320; isolationism, 99, 128; and Japan, 96, 163; and Liberia, 148; national interest of, 189; in NATO, 296–7; and North Korea, 191; and North Vietnam, 249; and Philippines, 211; power of, 115, 125; President of, 22; in Second World War, 111, 293; and small states, 20; sovereignty, 136; in South East Asia, 127; and Soviet Union, 12, 169, 231–2, 244, 248, 266, 268, 283, 295, 306, 313; and UN, 73, 165; war record, 283
Utrecht, Treaty of, 62

Vattel, E. de, 61, 65
Venezuela, 244
Venice, 53
Versailles treaty, 93, 156, 286, 290, 292
Victoria, Queen, 214
Vienna, 92
Vienna Congress, 168
Vietcong, 17
Vietnam, 12, 136, 249, 283
Vietnam, North, 174, 230, 236, 247, 249
Vietnam, South, 17, 160, 191, 247
Voice of America, 236

Wales, 142
Walsh, E. A., 65
War: 276–98; after 1918, 84, 101; and business, 87; Clausewitz on, 85; and compensation, 90; in Europe, 82, 86; fear of, 94; Hobbesian, 127, 253; and international organization, 100; and international system, 107, 124, 299; in Kautilya, 43; as pressure, 247–8; problem of, 13; and raison d'état, 58; and security communities, 256; and territory, 147

War, civil, 122, 151, 276
War, Cold, 23, 29, 45, 102, 104, 171, 173, 267, 268, 283, 296, 297, 300, 319
War, Crimean, 73, 83
War, First World: Allies in, 99, 211; causes of, 287–8; effects on balance of power, 94, 279; effects on nationalism, 285; as end of era, 82; Germany in, 89–90, 91; as hyperbolic war, 289; and industry, 86; and revolution, 85; and science, 13
War, Korean, 122
War of nerves, 236–7
War, Peloponnesian, 46, 47
War by proxy, 247
Warsaw Pact, 31, 74, 104, 217, 305
War, Second World: causes of, 286–7; China in, 75; and Czechoslovakia, 279; and European system, 76; international system after, 105–6; Japan in, 163; Mussolini in, 94; and national self-determination, 69; suspension of conflict in, 293; and US, 29, 168
War, Sino-Japanese, 97
War, Third World, 128
War, Total, 81, 82, 152, 288–91
War, Vietnamese, 247
Washington, 96
Waterloo, 60, 86
Webb, S. and B., 81
Weimar Republic, 240, 287
Weizmann, C., 148, 153
Wells, H. G., 81
Westermarck, E., 140
Westernizers, 161
White Man's Burden, 213
Wight, M., 123, 132, 136, 323
Wilson, H., 186, 200
Wilson, W., 28, 29, 36–7, 54, 67, 68, 85, 120, 157, 159, 220, 320
Woolf, L., 81
World Council of Churches, 17
World Federation of Trade Unions, 17
World politics, 16, 26
World society, 16
Wright, Q., 281–3, 298

Xenophobia, 41, 199

Yalta conference, 292
Yellow Sea, 160
Young plan, 240
Yugoslavia, 291

Zambia, 246
Zionist Congress, 148
Zionists, 148